HIGHEST PRAISE FOR
JOVE HOMESPUN ROMANCES:

"In all of the Homespuns I've read and reviewed I've been very taken with the loving renderings of colorful small-town people doing small-town things and bringing 5 STAR and GOLD 5 STAR rankings to readers. This series should be selling off the bookshelves within hours! Never have I given a series an overall review, but I feel this one, thus far, deserves it! Continue the excellent choices in authors and editors! It's working for this reviewer!"

—*Heartland Critiques*

We at Jove Books are thrilled by the enthusiastic critical acclaim that the Homespun Romances are receiving. We would like to thank you, the readers and fans of this wonderful series, for making it the success that it is. It is our pleasure to bring you the highest quality of romance writing in these breathtaking tales of love and family in the heartland of America.

And now, sit back and enjoy this delightful new Homespun Romance . . .

A CHERISHED REWARD

by Rachelle Nelson

A CHERISHED REWARD

RACHELLE NELSON

JOVE BOOKS, NEW YORK

If you purchased this book without a cover, you should be aware that this book is stolen property. It was reported as "unsold and destroyed" to the publisher, and neither the author nor the publisher has received any payment for this "stripped book."

A CHERISHED REWARD

A Jove Book / published by arrangement with
the author

PRINTING HISTORY
Jove edition / July 1996

All rights reserved.
Copyright © 1996 by Rachelle Nelson.
This book may not be reproduced in whole
or in part, by mimeograph or any other means,
without permission. For information address:
The Berkley Publishing Group, 200 Madison Avenue,
New York, New York 10016.

The Putnam Berkley World Wide Web site address is
http://www.berkley.com

ISBN: 0-515-11897-4

A JOVE BOOK®
Jove Books are published by The Berkley Publishing Group,
200 Madison Avenue, New York, New York 10016.
JOVE and the "J" design are trademarks
belonging to Jove Publications, Inc.

PRINTED IN THE UNITED STATES OF AMERICA

10 9 8 7 6 5 4 3 2 1

This book is lovingly dedicated to my kids, who put up with me.

Ry-Guy, you did your darnedest to help me work through the tough scenes, didn't you, honey? Remember to use your powers of imagination for good, okay?

Tabi Too-Bad, see what happens when you don't let yourself say *I can't*?

Travis-Newavis, no, sweetie, God doesn't carry you to bed when you fall asleep on the couch—that's what He created mommies for.

And Dusty-Butt, you always know how to make us laugh. I think we'll keep you.

And always, to David, who deserves a medal for being brave enough to face another year with a crazy writer-wife and loving her anyway.

This book would not be in print but for the dedication of Jean Price and Dee Pace, who read everything I write and still believe in me; and Gail Fortune, who wields a magic wand.

Chapter One

THE MUGGY LATE-June air absorbed the last deep note of an energetic ditty. Tanner slid the thin silver harmonica under his vest, into the pocket of his best cambric shirt. Folding his hands behind his head, he eased back against one of the many crates of squawking hens in the back of the wagon.

A narrow beak pecked at his knuckles. When he rapped lightly on the wooden cage, the hen within scrambled away. As soon as Tanner relaxed again, she resumed her harmless attack. He chuckled. It seemed he'd gained himself an admirer. The scrawny white biddy had been flirting with him ever since he'd climbed aboard.

Hitching a ride with a chicken farmer wasn't his idea of a grand entrance to his new home. He pictured the looks on folks' faces when they saw their new marshal arriving on the tailgate of the smelly, noisy wagon and he chuckled. Oh, well, at least he hadn't wound up walking the last ten miles after the nag he'd been riding had taken her last breath. Old as dirt, she'd been.

'Course, he would have crawled a hundred miles over burning desert sands if he'd had to just to reach Dogwood Springs. This job, the first chance he'd been given to prove himself, was worth losing a bit of skin.

Settled back against the crates, Tanner studied the

frothy clouds drifting across the sky. Now he understood Texas blue. There was no other blue as pale, as pure, as vast as the blue of the skies over Texas. And the clouds . . . light as the foamy cream that clung to his mustache when he drank a glass of fresh milk. One cloud looked like a lamb. Another, a chariot of ancient Rome. And still another took the shape of a star.

A lawman's badge.

Tanner closed his eyes. *Marshal McCay. Marshal Tanner McCay. Marshal Tanner McCay of Dogwood Springs, Texas*. God, he was twenty-nine years old and had dreamed of that title for more than half those years. And that dream was finally being realized.

He didn't know much about the town that had hired him. Thankfully, Dogwood Springs didn't know much about him either. He probably would have been refused the job if they had, just as he'd been refused in every other town west of the Mississippi. Word was bound to leak out, he supposed. He just hoped he could make a good impression before that happened. Maybe then the town council would overlook the blemish on his family's name. Or, at the very least, understand that although he bore the name McCay, he wasn't in the same league with his father and brother.

Yeah, before they made any judgments, he'd show them he was the best danged marshal ever born.

"Dogwood Springs just 'round the bend," the farmer called, saying more in that one sentence than he had the entire trip.

Tanner's eyes snapped open and he sat straight up. His long legs dangled over the tailgate and his feet trailed in the sandy soil. He twisted around, eager for his first glimpse of the town where he would soon be responsible for maintaining peace. He caught sight of a steeple with a big white cross in the distance before a bleached yellow two-story house blocked his view.

The wagon rolled past a peeling white picket fence following a curve in the road and bordering the house on two sides. Tanner's gaze lingered on the structure for a moment, then swerved to the trio of youngsters standing beside a tree in the corner of the yard, craning their necks as they stared skyward. No doubt they were watching a squirrel scamper through the branches. Or maybe a redbird had made a nest up there, he mused, searching for the source of their interest.

He sure didn't expect to see a pair of legs dangling from a limb. A woman's legs, he noticed, grinning at the sight of finely turned ankles encased in black netting. Leaves concealed the rest of her, but legs that long and shapely could belong only to a body of equal proportions.

"Thanks for the ride, mister," he told the farmer. "I'll get off here."

Gripping the carpetbag holding all his worldly possessions, Tanner made to jump off the wagon. The smitten hen stopped pacing her confines to stick her head out between the slats. Her beady eyes shot him an accusing look. Tanner reached through the slats and ruffled her feathers. As an afterthought he asked, "How much for the bird?"

The farmer didn't bother moving. "Layers go for twenty-five cents."

Tanner swallowed his surprise. That was a good quarter day's pay! In truth, he couldn't tell a layer from Sunday's supper but figured these must be golden layers to sell for such a high price. Even so, Tanner rocked onto one hip and dug into his nankeen pockets. He lifted the crate, replacing it with two bits. "Who knows," he told the hen, "maybe you'll bring me luck."

She flapped her wings as though understanding every word.

"What did ya hafta go and break it for, Ruthie?" Lissa Page demanded of her six-year-old sister.

"I didn't break it," Ruthie hotly denied. "I just sat on it and it fell."

Lissa threw down the frayed end of rope she had been studying. Springing to her feet, she jabbed her small fists against her hips. "You did so break it. Pa told you all the time not to do whirlies on the swing 'cuz it weakens the rope."

Dusting sand off the back of her younger daughter's pinafore, Eden Page paused to give her eldest child a reproachful look. "That's enough, Lissa," Eden chided the seven-year-old. "The rope was old, that's all. Constant sawing on the branch just took its toll, not Ruthie's whirlies."

"You're just taking her side again, like you always do!"

Eden shut her eyes long enough to mutter a quick prayer for patience. Then she pulled a plain handkerchief from her apron pocket and wiped away the tears on Ruthie's baby-plump cheeks. "I'm not taking anyone's side. I'm saying that the rope was bound to snap eventually. Ruthie just happened to be the one sitting on it when it did." She returned her hanky to her pocket. "It's not fair to blame her for that."

"See," Ruthie cried. "Even Mama says it wasn't my fault." Driving her point home, she stuck her tongue out at Lissa.

Lissa advanced toward her, grabbing for a long raven braid. Squealing, Ruthie quickly dashed behind Eden's black skirt, nearly upsetting her balance. "Girls"—Eden spread her arms wide to separate the combating pair—"I said that's enough."

"Tell her if she sticks her tongue out at me again, I'll feed it to the buzzards."

"Mama, tell Lissa to stop being so mean to me."

Her palms braced below the scalloped collars of their dress fronts, Eden knelt between the girls. "Both of you stop this instant or I'll make you sit on the hall bench and hug each other for the rest of the afternoon."

They gaped at her in horror, and Eden hid her grin. She always saved this highly effective threat for those occasions when a squabble got out of hand and they were on the verge of scratching each other's eyes out. They would rather eat mothballs than sit on the hard wooden bench, holding each other.

Shaking her head, Eden sighed softly. "Girls, why do

you waste so much time arguing? Don't you understand how lucky you are to have each other?"

Lissa glared at Ruthie. "I understand that I wouldn't have to worry about things getting broken all the time."

The stubborn set of identically rounded chins spoke volumes. Again Eden sighed. If they'd suffered the aching loneliness she had, growing up alone, without a family, maybe they would appreciate each other more.

Then again, her children knew who and where they'd come from. They hadn't been abandoned by their parents and left to live in an overcrowded orphanage where any ties formed were quickly broken.

Rather than engage in another frustrating bout of "count your blessings" that would only fall on deaf ears, Eden sought a diversion. Her eyes lit on the cause of their argument. A slab of wood dangled from a thick rope while the second support lay coiled in the patch of sand beside the oak trunk. Her gaze followed the knotted bark column up to the spread of three thick limbs.

Funny. Trees seem so much bigger from an adult point of view. And more intimidating somehow.

Then again, maybe one's perception just changed the older one got. At Lissa's age, Eden had been all arms and legs and dauntless enough to wrestle any obstacle. Growing up in Chicago, she hadn't left a tree unscaled, an old building unexplored, a gutter unstamped by her footprints.

But times were different, she reflected with a twinge of sadness. That daring child she'd once been no longer existed. The years had tamed her. She was twenty-four now, and had learned to quell the energy of exploration, the recklessness of youth. Life was not kind to those who rebelled against it. That lesson had been learned all too well.

Eyeing the massive live oak shading half the front yard, a fresh pinch of trepidation attacked her. Eden's brow puckered. Maybe she should just set the little scamps to their afternoon chores and ignore the broken swing; they rarely played on it anyway. If someone caught her doing something as outrageous as climbing a tree, the news would be spread all over town by nightfall, and the proper reputation she'd worked all these years to build would be shattered.

But one glance at her daughters, and Eden's resolve weakened. Ruthie looked at her with expectation; Lissa's eyes held an unspoken challenge.

They won. Goose bumps rose down Eden's arm.

She fought the thrilling charge of committing the forbidden and, swallowing the lump in her throat, stretched her hand out. "Please hand me the rope, Lissa."

"What are you fixin' to do?" she asked warily, imitating her father's vocabulary.

Giving a gentle tug to one of Lissa's dark braids, Eden summoned a smile. "I'm *fixin'* to fix your swing."

Lissa grumbled under her breath but fetched the severed rope and brought it back to her. Gripping it in her hand, Eden hitched her heavy cotton skirt above her ankles and moved toward the trunk.

"Are you gonna climb the tree, Mama?"

Eden wrapped her free hand around the lowest limb. "I'm going to try, Ruthie."

"But mamas can't climb trees!"

An indelicate grunt burst from Eden's lips when she heaved herself over the branch. Ruthie, it seemed, hadn't yet grasped the concept that Eden hadn't always been her mother. Once upon a time, she'd been a vibrant young girl herself, before—no, she would not open the door to those memories. They weren't worth dwelling on. "Is there a rule against it?"

Ruthie went quiet for a second. Then she said, "I can't think of one."

"You can't think at all," Lissa goaded. "In fact, if your brains were in a bird's head, the bird would fly backward."

"Ma-maa!"

Clutching the tree, Eden struggled to keep the frustration from her tone. "Lissa, go check on your brother."

"He's under the porch."

"I know. That's why I want you to check on him. Last time he disappeared under there, I found him eating dirt."

Lissa groaned and trudged toward the modest yellow

house they lived in just outside the limits of Dogwood Springs. With a heavy sigh, Eden blew an errant strand of black hair away from her mouth and continued climbing.

Once more it occurred to her that she was failing terribly at helping her children cope with the loss of their father. Ruthie didn't cling as much as she had at first, but she still went into hysterics at loud sounds. And though Little Seth no longer asked about his namesake, he had withdrawn to a place inside himself she couldn't reach, a place far deeper and more private than beneath the house.

And Lissa . . . Eden paused and shook her head. Lissa left her completely baffled.

She'd thought it was a temporary problem. After all, Lissa had always been such a sweet, obedient child—never once talking back or giving in to temper tantrums. But she'd changed, too, after Seth's death. And as time wore on, it became obvious that the girl's unusual behavior wasn't a passing reaction.

But when Lissa began talking about Seth as if he'd been an immortal without faults, Eden grew truly concerned.

It just didn't make sense, Eden thought, suppressing a twinge of bitterness. If Seth had actually spent a little time with the children, maybe she could understand how he'd managed to influence them. But the man had given more consideration to the badge he wore than the children he'd sired.

Of course, she never voiced her negative opinions to the children regarding their father. *Especially* to Lissa. There didn't seem to be any point in destroying the image she carried so close to her heart.

Swinging her leg over the first branch, Eden paused to tuck the rope into her waistband and catch her breath. Yes, all of the children needed to express their grief. She recognized that, just as she realized that in time they would get over their father's death. But meanwhile, Eden had no idea how to console them. They missed him in a way she could not relate to. A tide of guilt rose within her for the ill thoughts, but the plain truth was, she mourned the changes her husband's death had brought to their children's lives more than she mourned the passing of the man himself.

Seth Page was just another mistake, Eden told herself as she stood. She glanced down to judge her footing. Ten feet below, a small replica of herself looked up, pale green eyes filled with trust. And across the untrimmed yard, a five-year-old boy in short pants held up by suspenders over a white cotton shirt, and a telling black band around his arm, emerged from under the porch stairs. Little Seth stretched his grubby hand toward Lissa.

The shell around Eden's hardened heart cracked as brother and sister strolled toward the tree. Both looked so much like their father: auburn-haired, brown-eyed, sullen-mouthed—daily reminders that her eight-year marriage to the lawman had produced a few rewards.

"Mama, whatcha doin' in the tree?" Little Seth cried, sprinting the last few feet to the trunk.

"She's washin' clothes, simpleton. What does it look like she's doing?"

"She's fixin' our swing, L'il Seth."

"Yeah, 'cause Ruthie broke it."

"Mama, tell Lissa again that I didn't break her stupid swing. She didn't hear you the first time."

Eden shook her head, and her lip quirked with amusement. No . . . Seth Page had not been a mistake, she amended. In spite of his faults, he had given her three priceless treasures. She supposed he'd been more like a misjudgment. One she simply knew not to make again.

"Are you done yet?" Lissa shouted.

Taking the first rope from her waistband, she fashioned a doubled half-hitch knot around the branch. "In a minute. I need to retie this other one before it snaps too." If only to save herself another trip, she silently added.

As she reached out to loosen its knot, her balance wavered. "And only if I don't wind up breaking my fool neck," Eden mumbled to herself as she drew back.

Twisting, she hugged the upper trunk and lowered herself carefully onto the branch. The bark scraped against the exposed flesh of her arm below her elbow-length sleeve. Had she known she would be climbing trees, she would have found something much more suitable to wear than the simple black dress. But then, she'd thought her tree-climbing days were long past. It just proved how unpredictable life could be when one had children.

Eden hiked her skirt above her knees and flung her left leg over so that she straddled the branch. With her palms braced between her thighs, she scooted forward. Her stockings snagged, her petticoats bunched, and she desperately hoped that no one would catch her in such an unladylike position. . . .

The crate in one hand, his luggage in the other, and his saddle balanced upon his shoulder, Tanner leapt from the wagon. The chicken regarded him curiously. He winked at her. "I've always had this weakness for women wearing black net stockings," he admitted without shame. 'Course, the way his luck usually ran, she'd turn out as ugly as a two-headed heifer with smallpox.

The front gate made nary a sound as he opened it and walked through. Mockingbirds chattered to one another. Grasshoppers whirred through the grass. Weeds poked out between the flat stones of the walkway, and though the lawn needed scything, it was tidy.

The children seemed unaware of his approach. Tanner set his burdens on the ground and crossed the last few yards to stand behind them. Their heads reminded him of stepping-stones; the tallest one, a girl, came no higher than his chest; the next girl was a head shorter, and the boy a head shorter than that.

"What's takin' you so long?" one of them whined.

Tanner wondered the same thing. Had she gotten stuck? Propping his hands on his hips, he called, "You need any help up there?"

Startled, the youngsters spun around. Above, the branches rustled, then shook violently. A shrill scream cut through the air.

Tanner's smile faltered. He clamped his hand atop the

boy's head, unconsciously using the short form as a post to whip himself around, then sprinted forward.

He saw the root too late. The toe of his boot hooked on the obstacle. Arms outstretched, Tanner pitched forward, hoping still to catch her as she dropped from the branches. He flinched when he fell short of his goal and she hit the ground with a sickening thud.

Chapter Two

NO SOONER DID Tanner scramble to his feet than he heard a hardy young voice bellow, "Don't you touch her! Don't you touch her!"

The breath whooshed from Tanner's lungs as he felt himself tackled from behind. His knees buckled; something that felt like a head slammed into his thigh.

Tanner reached behind his back and, grabbing a pair of suspenders, swooped his attacker off the ground. Forty pounds of fire and fury and fists dangled wildly in the air.

"Settle down, Maverick." Tanner tried soothing the youngster. "I aim to see if she's hurt."

It didn't calm the boy a bit. Legs no higher than boot sleeves pumped harder, arms skinny as rifle barrels flailed wilder. A heel caught Tanner in the groin. He doubled over with a grunt and nearly dropped the kid.

Gasping in pain, he tightened his hold on the elastic bands but still got clobbered half a dozen more times in the few seconds it took to reach the woman's side. He had just curled his arm around the boy's waist to try to keep him still before he did any more damage, when a blaring chorus of "Lemme go! Lemme go!" nearly ruptured his eardrums.

Tanner maneuvered his arm across the boy's scrawny chest and clapped a broad hand over his mouth, smothering the noise. Or most of it anyway. Garbled *Mm-mm-mm*s vibrated repeatedly against his spit-moist palm.

The boy restrained, Tanner braced his weight on the balls of his feet and lowered to the woman's level. One thing was sure, he noticed first off, she wasn't ugly as a two-headed heifer.

She had thick black hair that billowed around her head in loose waves. Her face was the lovely oval shape of a cameo, with twin circles of pale rose on cheeks smooth as polished ivory. Fine-lined lids twitched spasmotically. Dusky lashes curled outward, then fluttered.

Her eyes opened.

And Tanner sucked in a deep breath of air so humid, it made his lungs sweat. Or maybe the moist summer heat had nothing to do with the sudden tightness in his chest. This woman would steal breath from a dead man.

Through those long dark lashes, a pair of eyes peered up at him, their shade so soft a green he swore they whispered.

She stared at him, bewildered and vulnerable, arousing within him a primal need to shield and to comfort. But deeper down, a more carnal need kindled, one that crossed the boundaries of honor and decency.

Tanner swallowed roughly. She was pretty in the quiet, untouchable way that turned saints into sinners. Tanner always knew he'd be a lousy candidate for sainthood anyway, but never more than at that moment.

A sharp elbow to Tanner's gut jolted him to awareness. Shifting the squirrelly child to his thigh, Tanner mentally upbraided himself. What in tarnation was he doing gawking at a poor young lady? She could be teetering on the edge of her own death and here he was, practically drooling over her like a hound dog over a ham bone!

With his free hand he delved beneath a thick skein of hair to search for a pulse. A steady beat throbbed against his fingertips. He closed his eyes. *Thank God.*

"Miss, can you hear me?" he finally asked her, his voice dropping an octave lower than normal.

* * *

She'd landed so hard, it felt as though her lungs had exploded from her chest; her back stung from her neck to her waist; her limbs seemed useless flesh and bone, dulled to everything but grains of sand embedded in the pores; and an ache at the base of her neck was spreading across the back of her skull.

For a moment Eden feared she *had* broken her fool neck!

She quelled the panic soaring inside her and forced herself to relax.

From a distance, muffled sobbing reached her. And from very close, an oddly recognizable scent penetrated her numbed senses.

Eden tried to get a grip on her disorientation, for she could almost swear she detected the musky essence of a man, and more distinctly, the smell of . . . chicken feathers?

"Miss, can you hear me?"

The words blended together like a thousand echoes, yet the voice, laced with worry, compelled her to focus on the source. Eden blinked rapidly, clearing her cloudy vision.

Dappled afternoon sunlight was blocked by a pair of shoulders so wide, they could belong only to a man. His features were concealed by the shadow of a wide-brimmed hat. Thick buff cotton trousers molded muscular thighs, and a leather vest hung stiffly over a loose white linen shirt. And tucked in his arm was . . .

Eden tensed. Every muscle coiled.

Get up, Eden! He has your son!

Nothing moved, not her arms, her legs, nothing.

It sickened her to realize that her body wouldn't cooperate with the protective instinct charging through her.

She forced herself to relax, to think rationally. Her son appeared in no danger; certainly if the man meant harm, he would not bother lingering around.

That realization lessened her gripping fear.

Just then, the hat that had been shielding his face was suddenly whisked from his head and tossed negligently aside, "Miss, are you hurt?"

Awestruck, Eden opened her mouth to respond; no words came forth.

The tumble from the tree must have knocked the talk right out of her, for she couldn't find the power to speak. In fact, she seemed incapable of little more than gaping at the man crouching over her.

At the streaked blond hair falling just above his shoulders.

At the clean contours of his face, the masculine jawline softened with kindness.

At the narrow dun-colored mustache between his straight nose and smooth lips.

Rich green eyes regarded her intensely. "Are you feeling any pains?"

She shook her head dumbly. No, she felt no pain other than the mild headache, yet something stirred to life low in her womb, flurries similar to those she'd experienced carrying each of the children.

Only different somehow.

More alarming.

Abruptly Eden swung her head to the side. Scanning her surroundings, she spied Ruthie a few yards away, wide-eyed and whimpering. Lissa stood beside her, pale and silently anxious. What a fright she must have given them!

Mustering her strength, she inhaled two feeble breaths, then dragged in a sustaining one, and raised herself up on one elbow. Stars swirled in her head. Her lungs expanded. Eden bowed her head and waited for the sensations to pass.

"You shouldn't move just yet," he chided, jerking forward to support her back with his hand. Goose bumps skittered down her spine at the contact.

"I'm fine," she whispered. She had to let the children see that she was hale and hardy. They were insecure enough after losing their father. She didn't even want to imagine what losing their mother so soon after would do to them.

"Miss, what I know of doctoring wouldn't fill a bullet casing," the man declared, "but that was quite a drop. You might have hurt something inside that I can't—owww!" A pained howl shattered the tense atmosphere as Little Seth clamped his teeth down on the palm of the hand covering his mouth. The man sprang to his feet; Seth tumbled from his lap and escaped behind Lissa.

"Son of a bug," the man hissed under his breath while vigorously shaking his hand in the air. "The little hellion *bit* me!"

"It was probably the only way he knew to get you to remove your hand," Eden remarked quietly.

He glanced up from examining the neat row of blood-drawing teeth marks. "Couldn't he have just said so?"

Eden almost laughed at his comical expression. "Not with your hand over his mouth."

"He was screeching in my ear!"

"You had him trussed up in your arms."

"He was attacking me!"

"He thought I was in danger—" Suddenly Eden's eyes narrowed with suspicion. "Where did you come from, anyway, mister?"

Even in her muddled state, she knew they'd never met before. Yes, she'd visited so many places that she'd lost count of them all, but she would have remembered crossing paths with this man. His favorable features would have been hard to forget.

He dropped his hand to his side and gave her a quizzical look. "Missouri," he replied after a brief hesitation.

"No—I meant, how did you come to be in our front yard?"

"I saw you in the tree on my way into town. I . . . uh, thought you might need a hand. . . ." His face went faintly ruddy.

"You saw me—" Eden's stomach knotted as a wave of dawning and bleak despair rolled through her. "Would you mind keeping what happened here today to yourself?"

"What, admit that I startled the daylights out of you and caused your fall?" He shoved his hands into his pockets and gave her a bashful grin. "Believe me, it's not something I'm ready to brag about."

Mesmerized by the crooked slant of his lips, Eden's

heart beat a little faster. Unsettled, she lurched forward to a full sitting position. A wave of dizziness crashed upon her. Eden groaned and flattened her hand across her forehead.

The stranger dove to his knees beside her. In a voice tight with anxiety, he said, "I better send for a doctor."

A sensation so foreign she could not find a name for it filled her. Never once in her life had anyone shown such concern for her well-being.

Eden choked on a humorless chuckle and brushed her matted hair away from her face. "The closest thing to a doctor in Dogwood Springs is the undertaker, Aaron Arnold. I have no use for that scavenger. As far as I can tell, I'm not dead. Just had the wind knocked out of me."

Muttering something about stubborn women, he scooped his arms beneath her knees and behind her back. "I am at least going to get you settled somewhere comfortable."

Eden gasped as he lifted her in one smooth motion.

"You can rest on the porch for a while." Then, addressing Little Seth, he waved toward the well at the side of the house. "Maverick, you go on and get her something cold to drink."

Although his tone was kind, it left no room for debate, as if he were accustomed to taking control. Eden couldn't say if it surprised her more being hauled into his arms, or watching Little Seth immediately obey his order.

His stride brisk and confident, he carried her through the tall grass across the yard while the girls followed, their astonishment reflecting her own.

Eden wanted to object, to insist that she was perfectly capable of walking on her own. But his firm hold warned her that protesting would gain her nothing, just as his voice brooked no arguments. With her arms looped around his neck to keep herself from slipping, Eden bit her tongue, part resentful of his interference, part grateful. For in spite of her claims, her body still hadn't quite recovered from having a ten-foot fall abruptly halted.

Her side buffeted against his chest with each step he took. The muscles hidden beneath his thin shirt were unyielding, and the friction of their bodies rubbing together made her feel like a pond with a pebble skipped over its surface. All shimmery and fluid and distorted . . .

The distance to the porch seemed to take hours to span instead of seconds. He set her down in the rocking chair. She freed her arms and sank onto the hard seat, her legs as unsteady as her heartbeat, her hand shaking as she took the cup of water her son had waiting.

"You still look a little peaked. Are you sure you don't want me to fetch someone with a little more experience than me?"

Eden shook her head. There really wasn't anyone to fetch.

There never had been.

"All ri-ight," he deferred in a shrugging tone as he straightened his back. He arced a glance behind him. "Then you just sit there while I see what can be done with that swing."

Eden started to tell him that it wasn't necessary, but he forestalled her with a raised hand.

"No arguments, please. It's the least I can do." He flashed a guileless smile to the children. "Who wants to show me the way to the tree? I don't think I can find it by myself."

What a ridiculous statement, Eden thought. Not only was the live oak the only tree in the forepart of the yard, but it stood well over a hundred feet tall.

At the same time, though, it was touching that he made an attempt to include the children, in spite of Little Seth biting him, which he seemed to have quickly forgiven. Their father had always seemed to forget they existed at all.

Ruthie looked to Eden for approval.

She didn't have the heart to refuse.

Receiving Eden's reassuring smile, Ruthie shyly offered, "I will." Her braids bounced against her back as she traipsed along at his side, her head no higher than his hip.

Indecisively, Little Seth loitered behind for a second before chasing after them.

A warm glow spread through Eden when the man

slowed his steps and waited for Little Seth to catch up. He glanced at both their dark heads, saying something Eden couldn't hear, then gave a curt nod. The three took off in a run, the man obviously checking his pace so the children would win the impromptu footrace. His laughter when they reached the live oak ahead of him made the blood ripple in Eden's veins. It reminded her of his scent, his laughter did. Masculine and warm. Bold yet smooth.

And the curiously faint odor of chickens she'd detected merely added to his earthy essence. His clothes were ordinary, giving no indication of what he did for a living, but a man's scent often hinted at his livelihood. Too, the tight muscles and the exposed skin below his wrists and above his collar bore a dark tan that suggested he spent a vast amount of time outdoors.

Perhaps he's a farmer, Eden speculated. *Either that, or he has horrible taste in cologne.*

"I thought we weren't never s'pose to talk to strangers."

Startled to awareness, Eden swept her lingering study from the trio to Lissa, who had remained at the base of the steps. Her brown eyes glowered at their backs and her mouth was set in a grim line.

Eden collected her wits. Searching her mind for an explanation, she was remiss in correcting Lissa's grammar. "You children must steer clear of strangers for your own protection—but I am an adult. It's different."

"Why? A stranger is a stranger. You don't know that man any more than I do. He could be one of those bad men you're always warning us about. One who wants to hurt us because Pa put him in jail."

Eden scrutinized the man who was now shimmying up the oak. Her son's and daughter's cheers carried to her ears as his lanky form navigated each branch with enviable ease. When he reached the branch she had fallen from, his blond hair remained visible through the ripe forest of leaves.

How could she make Lissa understand that she sensed *this* stranger meant them no harm? Eden frowned. She didn't understand herself. So what if he had appeared genuinely concerned about her? And so what if he cavorted with the children? It wasn't like her to so readily accept another person into her life, no matter how harmless he seemed.

She could attribute it to intuition, and yet, her instincts had failed her before—and often enough to teach her not to rely on them. So why, *especially* after the years with Seth, was she breaking a cardinal rule and permitting this . . . this outsider to breeze into her yard, risking her babies. . . .

Eden splayed her fingers across her brow. It was a complex question that she didn't know how to answer. "Please, Lissa, can we discuss this later? I'm not up to this right now. My head is still spinning from my fall."

"Well, you shouldn't have climbed that tree in the first place. Pa wouldn't have. He woulda used the ladder."

"I haven't replaced the cracked rungs yet," Eden sighed.

"Pa woulda fixed the rungs then fixed the swing."

Eden closed her eyes. Seth wouldn't have done any of those things. She had a score of items needing repair around the house, things he had always promised to get to. But there had always been WANTED posters to tack up, leads on criminal activity to follow, records to file, deputies to train. . . .

The children and the stranger approached, saving Eden from traveling again down the same dead-end road with Lissa.

"Now, that was a pleasure," he exclaimed, brushing tiny bits of bark from his clothes. "I haven't climbed a tree since I was a boy. I used to have this fort way back in the woods—"

"You had a tree fort?" Little Seth interrupted in awe.

"Sure! Don't all young boys build themselves forts?"

"Not Little Seth," Ruthie said. "Mama won't let him go into the woods *or* climb trees. It's a rule."

"How old are you, boy?"

Little Seth held up five fingers. Ruthie reached over and closed his thumb. "He's really only four. He's gonna be five next month. Mama says he'll be old enough to go to school with me and Lissa when he's five."

"Congratulations!" he told Seth, who revealed two crooked bottom teeth with his proud grin. " 'Course, there are still lots of days of summer left to while away until then. I haven't settled in town yet, but as soon as I do, maybe we can talk your ma into letting me and you do a little fort-building."

"You'd really help me build a fort?"

"Sure. Old men like me don't get many chances to climb trees anymore, but secretly?" He leaned low and winked. "I use all the excuses I can come up with."

Eden stared at him, unblinking. If all old men were built like this one, they'd consider themselves lucky. She placed her hand to her fluttering stomach. No, he was far from being old, as he claimed. Beneath his plain clothes she recalled all too well feeling the power of a man in his prime.

Her gaze darted away to the worn toes of his black boots, then to her tightly clenched fingers. "I appreciate your kindness, but the children know the rules in our household are not to be broken. They are set for good reason."

Although he studied her with a queer expression, she neither owed him an explanation nor gave one.

He inclined his head, seeming to accept that. "I beg your pardon. Reckon I've done enough damage around here today. So I'll just be on my way." Pinching the brim of his hat between two fingers and his thumb, he gave a casual salute. "But if you ever do need anything, send word to town. The name's Tanner McCay."

Dogwood Springs was much like a dozen other towns he'd seen on his journey south. Mothers chatted to one another as they pushed hooded baby buggies along raised wooden walkways flanking the main road, stopping now and then to peer through the windows of various shops that had been erected parallel to the railroad tracks. Benches scattered about beneath shady trees in the park were occupied by aged or weary or idle souls who had finished their errands, and now sat shooting the breeze. Steel on iron rang

from Moley's Carriage Repair, and through the open dou-
ble-doors of Pratt's Livery, a fire glowed from the horse-
shoeing pit. The scent of fine grain dusted the air in front of
Deidrich's General Store as a farmer loaded fifty-pound
sacks of oats into the bed of his wagon. Across from the
train depot, Hannah's Home-Cooking Cafe attracted those
with a hunger for the catfish supper that only Hannah herself could fry to melting perfection, so the sign claimed,
and racing children dodged the many droppings left by
horses now standing at hitching rails or pulling conveyances
out of town.

It appeared a peaceful community. Tanner never
would have guessed that nearly a year ago it had been the
scene of a violent crime unless he'd been told.

"As I said, there will be a formal election in the square
at ten A.M. sharp."

Giving Tiny Ellert his undivided attention, Tanner
pushed away from the window and lowered himself into
the wobbly desk chair. When Tiny had first walked through
the door twenty minutes earlier, Tanner thought one of the
wild hoydens from outside was seeking a hiding spot inside
the two-celled jail.

But the five-foot-tall figure standing before the scarred
desk could never be called anything but a man. A short
man—the shortest Tanner had ever met—but a man
nonetheless, with a shock of thick brown hair, fashionably
long sideburns, and a loose-fitting three-piece suit that
made Tanner sweat just thinking about wearing it in this
heat.

"I thought my position was cut and dried," Tanner
said, picking up a pencil and tapping it end over end on the
tidy desktop.

"The election is simply a formality," Tiny replied.
"The local authorities have already approved your employment. But we must abide by council policy and have the
vote publicly counted before you are officially appointed."
He returned to the sheaf of papers in his hand. "In addition
to providing a safe environment for our citizens and issuing
summonses or warrants and collecting bills if necessary, it

will also be your responsibility to maintain the jail quarters and see to any prisoner's health and welfare. Three meals a day, fresh water for drinking and bathing, medical attention if needed, and in the event of a prisoner's demise, burial costs."

Tanner grinned wryly. "If any prisoners have to depend on my cooking or doctoring, they'll wind up in a coffin."

"The previous marshal's wife attended to some of those details."

"I'm not married, though."

"Then it is your prerogative whether you provide those services yourself or hire outside help. You may petition the council for reimbursement of the expense; however, I do not guarantee the extra funds will be available. As it stands, you may wish to supplement your thirty-five-dollar-a-month income by bringing in wanted criminals and collecting on the rewards." Tiny waved toward the desk. "In the top drawer you will find a packet of posters."

Tanner slid the drawer open and peeked inside. Under a large ring holding keys to the cells, a sketching of a sour-faced "Pistol Pete, Horse Thief" glared up at him, as though insulted by the paltry fifty-dollar reward issued for his capture. Amused, Tanner shut the drawer and leaned back in the slatted chair.

"Those rewards cannot be counted on with any regularity, though," Tiny went on. "Most of those offenders have long since moved on to western pastures, such as New Mexico or farther. They change their names, sometimes their appearances, and no one is the wiser to their criminal activities unless they strike again."

How well Tanner knew that. His father and brother had gotten away with their crimes for years using all the tactics Tiny Ellert spoke of.

But even professional outlaws got sloppy and wound up paying the price. Fain and Terron's ten-year prison sentences proved that no one could escape the long arm of the law.

Once more Tiny referred to the papers in his hand,

muttering things he'd already covered as his pudgy finger skimmed down the list. "I believe I have covered everything."

"What about the house?"

Tiny's stout body went taut. "The house?"

"I have a letter from a Mr. Hollis Clark that says lodgings are included with the job."

Tiny ran a finger around the starched collar of his shirt. The unflappable bookkeeper assigned to brief him of his duties suddenly seemed nervous, and Tanner wondered why. But he bided his time until Tiny's eyes stopped darting around the jail quarters, finally settling on a spot behind Tanner's head.

"Mr. McCay . . ."

"Call me Tanner. Or Mac."

Tiny ignored the informality. "Mr. McCay, normally the council would provide you with accommodations," he explained, "but the house that comes with the position is . . . ah, presently occupied, and will be for the next several months. The council did not anticipate your expedient arrival and therefore did not prepare the widow who resides there for eviction."

Eviction. What a cruel word. Picturing a doddering old woman kicked out on her bustle, Tanner grimaced.

Hastily Tiny inserted, "But if you are insistent, the council will see that the proper measures are taken to rectify—"

"I don't need a house," Tanner interrupted, cutting his hand through the air. "I can bed down in one of the cells."

Clearly relieved, Tiny propped a brown felt bowler hat atop his head. "Then, if there is nothing else—"

"Just one more thing. You've been around here awhile haven't you?"

"With the exception of several years to attend an eastern college, I have lived here all my life."

"Then maybe you could tell me a little about the people." One person in particular, but Tanner refrained from speaking the thought out loud.

"Most are industrious, law-abiding citizens who make

their living farming cotton, working their business, or are employed by the railroad or one of the mills. Although, as in every town, we have our share of miscreants, which is why we maintain the protective services of men such as yourself."

"What happened to the last marshal?"

"After four years of devoted duty, he unexpectedly met his demise at the hands of nefarious villains."

Tanner didn't recognize all the big words Tiny used, for he couldn't boast of the same amount of schooling, but he got the gist of them. "How?"

"He was shot down defending the train from being robbed."

It was one of the risks of being a lawman, Tanner realized. No doubt the last marshal had been aware of that, too, when he took on the job. "He leave any kin behind?"

"A young wife and three small children."

Tanner's mouth fell open, and he pitched forward. "Not the family living down by the bend in the road!"

"In the two-story structure, yes. Marshal Page's sole surviving relatives consist of two daughters, a son, and his wife, Eden."

Glory be, she was a *mother*? He would have guessed a sister maybe, or a governess, but not a mother! Not only did she look too young to have borne children, but she didn't have that maternal look about her—no worry lines seaming her brow, no fatigued circles beneath her eyes.

"How long ago did Marshal Page die?" Tanner asked absently, turning to stare out the large front window.

"Ten months, fourteen days."

Ten months. Tanner grinned to himself. That was a long time to be without a husband.

The chain of a timepiece plinked against the buttons of Tiny's vest, and a second later the lid clicked shut. Out of the corner of his eye, Tanner caught the bookkeeper sliding his watch inside his coat then shifting from one foot to the other. "That's all, Tiny. You're as jittery as cold water in a hot skillet, so I reckon I'm keeping you from something."

Tipping his bowler, Tiny opened the door. "Very

good, Mr. McCay. I will leave you to become acquainted with your new surroundings. Should you require my assistance further, you may find me in my apartment above the barbershop. Otherwise, I shall see you in the morning," he said over his shoulder as he walked out the door.

A heavy silence fell over the empty room.

So her name is Eden. A beautiful name to go along with that beautiful face, that beautiful body . . .

He felt a pinch of hunger in his middle, but with his mind on Eden Page it took him a moment to realize it was his stomach rumbling with want of food. Tanner kicked his feet off the desk. The chair scraped against the floor as he pushed backward to rise. Scouring the jail, he discovered that the cupboards beside the potbellied stove across the room were empty, the three shelves on the wall beside the smoke chute likewise bare. Hannah's catfish sounded tempting, but he figured he better make his meager coins stretch rather than splurge them all on one meal. He'd spent most of his money just getting out here, and had about enough funds left in his pocket to buy a week's worth of supplies. Hopefully after that he could arrange for an account at one of the general stores to last him out until his first payday. If not . . .

His glance slanted toward the crate in the corner behind the front door. Myrtle was curled up into a fat white ball, her beak tucked beneath a wing. Nah, he couldn't do that. In fact, he didn't think he could eat another chicken as long as he lived, not without wondering if he was eating one of Myrtle's kin.

Grabbing his carpetbag from beside the desk, he headed for the left cell. Tossing the gripsack on the narrow cot, he strode across the bare slab floor toward the small square cut high in the stone wall, needing to occupy his thoughts with something other than his empty stomach.

Tanner pressed his face to the vertical bars and spotted the enormous oak standing out from all the other trees lining the road. She had gumption, he'd give the widow that. Climbing ten feet in the air to tie a silly rope was not something just any woman would do. Then to go on as if the fall never happened . . .

A staticlike sensation crept throughout his veins at the memory of how perfect she had felt in his arms, her curves fitting pleasurably snug against him. Impulsively, Tanner tucked his nose against his shoulder. Yep. Traces of her fragrance still clung to the fibers of his shirt. Morning glories and honeysuckle soap warmed by the sun.

"Ten months, huh?" he mused, an idea taking shape. Would Eden welcome him if he came a-callin'? She hadn't sneered at him, or cowered at his touch. Those were good signs. In fact, the way she'd gazed at him with those whisper-green eyes made him wonder if it was possible that she could have felt a little attracted to him.

The thought startled him. Humbled him. A pleasured grin stole across Tanner's face.

Then his spirits sagged. Heck, back home, women wouldn't give him air if he was in a jug. Why should Eden be any different? Tanner would hardly blame her. What woman in her right mind would want to associate herself with a man related to two of the most notorious outlaws Flat Fork, Missouri, had ever seen?

Tanner clasped his hands on the narrow sill and rested his chin on his knuckles.

This isn't Flat Fork, though.

He'd come here to put his past behind him. To start fresh. No, he hadn't envisioned his new life including a woman, but maybe a higher power had it arranged that way. Maybe he *did* have a chance with Eden, after all.

So what if she already had kids. Truth be told, the idea of kids and a tree swing and a white picket fence—and a woman waiting for him at the end of each day—had always floated in the back of his mind. He didn't indulge in that fancy often, given his rotten luck with the ladies and the dangers of his profession. And yet, just because he would be wearing a badge didn't mean he wasn't a man, with a man's needs and hopes and desires.

And even though he didn't know much about how to raise youngsters, he knew how *not* to raise them. He wouldn't try blackmailing them into doing things out of some warped sense of obligation. He wouldn't force them into going against their beliefs.

Giving it serious thought now, having a family of his own sounded more appealing than ever. Especially, Tanner grinned, if the woman waiting for him at the end of each day was Eden Page.

Maybe he could invite her out for a stroll, or to supper once he had a few dollars to spare. They'd get to know each other, at least. After almost a year without a husband, she might be entertaining thoughts of being courted again.

Maybe, Tanner contemplated, getting this job held more than he'd expected.

Chapter Three

EDEN BENT LOW and kissed her daughter's forehead. "Good night, Ruthie. Sweet dreams."

"Good night, Mama," she replied, scooting down into her quilt. "Mama?"

Her hand curved around the fluted lantern globe, Eden delayed blowing out the light to give a Ruthie a questioning look.

"That man was nice, huh?"

Lissa snorted from beside her sister. "He was a stranger."

"Yes, Ruthie, he was nice," Eden agreed. "But Lissa is correct. He is a stranger, therefore you must not speak to him again."

"But he's not a stranger anymore. We know his name. It's Tan McCrary."

"Tan*ner* Mc*Cay,* you dimwit!"

"Ma-maa, Lissa called me a dimwit!"

Eden's lips quirked in wry exasperation. "Go to sleep, girls. Save your energy for tomorrow's squabbles."

She extinguished the lamp, then quietly shut the door behind her. There had to be an effective way to convince her daughters to stop their constant bickering. One of these days she would figure out what it was.

After peeking in on Little Seth, who snored gently

from his bed in the next room, she entered her room across
the hall. Eden slipped out of her dress in a soft glow of
lamplight, then flicked the stifling widow's garb carelessly
across the trunk pressed against the bed's simple pine foot-
board. Wearing only a black shift, she strolled barefoot to
the open window, then settled on the sill with her knees
drawn up to her chest and fixed her eyes on a large patch of
bare wood on the outside of the house. The paint had flaked
off from many seasons of Texas heat and rain and looked
more cream-colored than yellow in the daylight, but the
morning glories she'd planted helped dress up the exterior.
Twining up trellises on either side of the front porch, the
web of vines and spade-shaped leaves at least partially hid
a need for a fresh coat. Too bad they didn't reach all the
way up to the second floor balcony, though. She really
needed to fill the gap left by the two missing rungs on the
railing.

It wasn't exactly a castle of girlhood dreams, but she
had long since realized that dreams were a waste of energy.
Wasn't she richer now than she'd ever been in her life? The
house might appear a bit weathered, but the roof didn't leak
and the floors were real wood instead of dirt and the structure was sound. And it belonged to her.

Eden sighed, then nibbled on her lower lip. *For now,
anyway.*

She knew she was only postponing the inevitable by
coming out here—the juggling of the budget. But she could
recite the numbers in her sleep already and knew a few
minutes of stalling wouldn't make any difference. Peace
was such a rare luxury.

By the time she answered John Sullivan's summons to
meet with him first thing in the morning, she'd have her
projected expenses for the next month itemized. That had to
be the only reason the banker had sent the message earlier.
And no doubt she'd have to endure an hour-long lecture of
his reminders that the year was almost up.

As if she needed reminding.

If only she could move, put this bad chapter of her life
behind her and begin anew somewhere else.

But she was stuck here. On borrowed money, in a borrowed house, living on borrowed time. Eden massaged the tensing muscles of her neck. That was the worst of it, not being able to plan the future. Having goals with no way to attain them and still keep Lissa, Ruthie, and Little Seth safe.

She knew she must remain strong, and yet . . .

Sometimes she felt crushed by the weight of her burdens.

Sometimes she wished she had someone to confide in.

Sometimes she yearned for a strong shoulder to lean on.

Unbidden, the image of a broad, vested body and a carefree smile slipped into focus with startling clarity.

"I think he's sweet on Mama."

Hearing the whispered comment, Eden stilled.

"No, he isn't," Lissa contended.

"Sure he is. He said something about her when he was fixin' our swing."

Tanner McCay? Fully alert, Eden sat straight up, hissing when the top of her head cracked against the bottom of the window frame.

"What did he say?"

Yes, what did he say? Eden mentally urged, rubbing the sore spot. It wasn't right to eavesdrop on the girls, yet she couldn't bring herself to stop listening.

"He said, 'It takes a spit-and-polish kind of woman to climb a tree and still look like a lady.' "

A spit-and-polish woman? Was that a compliment or an insult?

"What's that supposed to mean?"

"How'm I s'pose to know? But you shoulda seen how he was looking at her when he said it. Kinda like how you were looking at the chocolate cake tonight before you finished your stew. Only he wasn't drooling."

Eden smothered her laughter with her hand.

"Oh, what do you know, Ruthie," Lissa scoffed. "You're just a baby."

"I am not a baby!"

"Are too. And so what if he's sweet on Mama?"

"Am not. And so if he's sweet on Mama, and Mama's sweet on him, maybe he'll be our new pa."

"You shut your mouth, Ruth Rosemary! We already got a pa!"

"Not anymore we don't. But even if Pa didn't get kilt, I'd still want Tan McCrary to be our pa 'cause I like *him* better."

"His name is Tanner McCay, no-brains, and you don't even know him."

"I like him anyway. He plays with me and Seth."

"Well, you just better listen to Mama and stay away from him if you know what's good for you. Just because he told us his name don't mean he's not a stranger. Now go to sleep. We have lots of chores to do in the morning before we go into town."

Leaning her head back against the window frame, Eden stared at the multitude of stars for a long time after the girls quieted, her thoughts centering on Tanner McCay rather than on the meeting with John Sullivan. Honestly, why couldn't she get him out of her mind? Whatever happened to her deeply rooted caution regarding strangers? But she'd been thinking about Mr. McCay throughout the evening—same as her daughter, it seemed. Any little thing that happened after their short encounter had made her recall some detail about him.

Fetching water from the well, she thought of his considerate attempt to make her comfortable on the porch. Another debate with Lissa made her wish she had his knack for authority. Listening to Ruthie chase Little Seth upstairs to bed stirred images of him letting them win the race across the yard.

For pity's sake, she couldn't even wipe off the kitchen table without remembering the feel of his hard, muscled chest beneath her palm. Eden grimaced at her own foolishness.

And just when she'd finally banished him from her mind, Ruthie and Lissa pushed him right back in.

She swung her feet over the sill and slid onto the balcony. Inhaling deeply, even the pine- and cedar-scented air of the woods nearby reminded her of him. Of how he smelled. Like a sturdy hope chest, where a maiden stored all her treasures, all her dreams for the future.

Eden frowned. What a silly comparison. She was no longer a maiden, and he'd smelled more like chickens than trees. Besides, none of her buried dreams had involved a tall, blond stranger. How odd that she could, that she *should,* recall so much of the man. That she had noticed such intimate details to begin with.

And yet, no man had ever looked at her the way he had. Even Ruthie noticed it.

Had he really said she was a spit-and-polish woman? Must be some Missouri phrase, because she couldn't recall hearing anything like it anywhere else. She decided it was meant to be flattering, and she was . . . well, flattered.

Pressing her fingertips to her suddenly warm cheeks, Eden was startled to find herself smiling. How about that, she thought, more awed by the discovery than disturbed. It was the first time anyone besides the children had made her do that in a long, long while.

Dread coiled in Eden's stomach when, on the other side of the huge mahogany desk, John Sullivan did not quite meet her eyes. A man in his late forties, the banker took exceptional care of his appearance. He wore a starched suit of deep burgundy tailored for his fit frame. The black silk tie around his neck didn't have a single wrinkle in either the bow or the long strings down the ivory shirtfront. Every strand of thinning coal-black hair, the temples slightly graying, had been slicked into place, and every whisker of his jaw-framing sideburns ran in perfectly even lines.

He slid one paper behind the others, dipped his pen into the inkwell and wrote something she couldn't read, returned the pen to the stand, then leaned back in his thick-cushioned chair.

His actions told her this visit would not bode well.

Eden gnawed on her bottom lip while watching his

fingers drum upon the arm of the chair. A beam of sunlight caught on the ruby ring gracing his pinky finger. The nickel-sized jewel glittered, a blatant display of the difference in their status.

The whole office, in fact, reflected his financial security and her lack of it. No comfortably worn brocade sofas here, Eden noted, but settees and lounge chairs covered in the finest burgundy leather. Neither would Sullivan dare settle for a simple sideboard of pine, decorated with hand-crocheted doilies and collections of pebbles in clay dishes. Instead, crystal liquor decanters and priceless figurines adorned intricately carved tables sitting about the spacious office, and one entire wall boasted leather-bound books on ceiling-high shelves.

She glanced away from Mr. Sullivan to the children, who were seated on a bench just inside the door, sucking on a rare treat of peppermint sticks. Thankfully, they knew to conduct themselves around the lavish surroundings. It would take her a lifetime to pay for one broken item.

Finally giving her a speculative look that intensified her sense of doom, Sullivan framed his chin with his fingers. "I'm going to be candid with you, Mrs. Page. The citizens of Dogwood Springs owe your husband a mammoth debt. Seth Page prevented an incident that could have very well devastated this town when he foiled the attempted train robbery last September. More important, he saved the lives of six innocent people, including mine, at the expense of his own life. Allowing you and the children to remain in the house, and provide you with a small stipend for one year, is hardly adequate thanks. If it were up to me—"

"Please, Mr. Sullivan, get to the point." It was the same old grueling story she'd heard since Seth's funeral.

He dropped his hand suddenly. "Very well. The year is almost up. Come October first, the Sullivan Financial Institution will require that you begin making rental payments on the property or remove yourself from the premises."

Insulted but not surprised, Eden stiffened her spine. "I have never wanted or expected charity, Mr. Sullivan. I will gladly pay the required—"

"It is twenty dollars a month, Mrs. Page."

Eden's mouth dropped open. "Twenty dollars a month! For pity's sake, the house is made of wood, not gold!"

"It is not an unreasonable amount, considering the house sits upon ten acres and the leaser is entitled to the borrowed water rights."

"But the widow's stipend doesn't even amount to that much!"

"Which is why I am giving you advance notice so you can make preparations."

"I cannot afford to move, Mr. Sullivan, and you very well know that."

"Then what will you do?"

He sounded like he would rather she put her children on the street than live in the bank-owned house. But the streets were not easy. They were rough and unmerciful and uncertain. If it took her last breath, she vowed never to expose her children to that sort of lifestyle.

No matter what depths she had to sink to.

Casting her eyes downward, Eden drew the drawstring of her fringed reticule between her fingers. She resented Seth now more than ever for the position he'd put her in.

Tears stung, of anger and humiliation, and frustration. "Until another house is available, I have no choice but to continue living in the one we presently occupy."

"How will you pay for it?"

"I will find a job, of course."

Eden thought she saw a glimmer of sympathy in his slate-gray eyes, but she must have been mistaken. Bankers were second only to lawmen when it came to utter lack of compassion. Of emotion, period.

"I know I have been refused employment before," she hastened to explain, "but surely there is someone in this town willing to hire me in spite of the fact that I must have the children with me until they start school. My daughter is almost eight years old, and a hard worker, and Ruthie and Little Seth will not be burdens." She waved toward the three small figures sitting still and quiet a short distance away. "You can see how well they behave. And they would be willing to attend to small tasks—"

"As long as they remain within your sight," he finished for her. He leaned forward and sighed. "I understand your predicament and empathize with your fears regarding the children's safety, but I cannot force any of the townspeople to change their views. They believe that you would not be fully devoted to your duties as long as your three youngsters are tied to your apron strings. And frankly, Mrs. Page, I tend to agree. The entire town is aware of your obsession with the children—"

"I am not obsessed," Eden ground out, "I am simply concerned for their safety. You of all people know how many enemies my husband made as marshal. As a mother, I have every right—"

"I am not disputing your maternal rights, Mrs. Page. I am only stating a fact, and how it has hindered your employment prospects since the passing of your husband." He clasped his hands together. "Do yourself a favor, Mrs. Page. Find yourself another husband. Let him take care of these matters. An attractive young widow such as yourself should have no trouble marrying again."

Eden's throat burned with such fury, she didn't trust herself to speak. She knew people gossiped about her, and it had never much mattered. She didn't give two hoots about other people's opinions about the way she raised her babies. No one, not even Mr. High-and-Mighty John Sullivan, had any right sticking their noses into her private business.

The patronizing mask on Sullivan's lily-white face changed to irritation.

"I apologize for offending you, Mrs. Page. That was not my intention."

Horsefeathers, Eden thought.

"But as president of this institution, I am entrusted with all transactions. The first of October, you will be required to sign a lease, promising to pay twenty dollars a month for one full year for rental property belonging to this bank. If you are not gainfully employed at that time, I will

have no recourse but to put personal feelings aside and dis-
qualify your tenancy."

Although her lips were pressed so tightly together she
lost all feeling in them, Eden contained her rage and rose
from the chair. Without a sound she walked to the door,
silently motioning the children out of the cloying office.

Years of learning to control her emotions paid off
when she stepped outside behind them without stumbling
and suffering further degradation.

She could not believe she had actually trusted John
Sullivan. *That weasel!* Eden silently railed as she pulled the
sheer black veil over the crown of her hat so it would cover
her face. How easily he dismissed the pledge he'd issued
the day after Seth's funeral, that she and the children could
live in the house for as long as they needed. Wasn't robbing
the children of their father enough? Was his greed so deep
that he could steal their home away too?

And *then* he had the gall to tell her to "find herself a
husband"! As if she were not perfectly capable of handling
her own affairs, her own family. And as far as husbands
were concerned, she'd tasted enough grief and misery from
one to know she wasn't in any hurry to have another adding
to her difficulties!

"Mama, how come we don't never hang up
buntings—hey, there's that man! The one who fixed our
swing yesterday!"

Immersed in her own thoughts, Eden had paid no attention to the mass of humanity packed thick as hops in
Spring Park, nor to the vibrant red, white, and blue banners
strung from second-story balconies in preparation for the
upcoming Fourth of July celebration.

But startled by Ruthie's declaration, Eden jerked her
head in the direction her daughter pointed to.

The blood drained from her face. Recognition of the
man standing on the platform in the center of the park,
looking for all the world like a king towering over his sub-
jects, sent a piercing shaft of disbelief through Eden's core.
The crowd below him was applauding. Eden heard nothing
above the hollow roaring in her ears.

"I didn't know he was gonna be our new marshal!" Ruthie exclaimed.

Reeling, Eden watched a beam of sunlight reflect off the five-pointed badge attached to a leather vest. She'd witnessed this same scene before, nearly four years ago, when Seth Page had been officially pinned marshal of Dogwood Springs, Texas.

Only it wasn't Seth receiving the shiny star of a lawman.

It was Tanner McCay.

Chapter Four

"MAMA, YOU CUSSED!"

Eden tore her eyes from the spectacle of Tanner McCay raising his right hand as he was sworn in by Hollis Clark, the burly owner of Clark's Sawmill. "What?"

"You cussed!" Lissa repeated.

"When?"

"Just now. You said 'damned tin man.' "

She couldn't have. On occasion she reverted to color-ful words learned in her youth, but only when she was seething mad, and even then, never within hearing of the children. "Lissa, I don't want that kind of talk coming from your mouth," Eden scolded. "It's vulgar."

"But *you* said it!"

Eden yanked on the lacy cuff of her gloves. "Then I was wrong. But that doesn't give you permission to repeat my mistake."

"Whatsa damn tin man?" Seth asked, tugging on her sleeve.

Her hands upon his shoulders, Eden steered him in the opposite direction. "Never you mind, Seth Daniel Page." Mercy, she had to watch her tongue in the future, she thought, prodding her son forward.

Eden could not resist one last glance over her shoulder at Tanner McCay. As though he felt her eyes upon him, he searched the crowd until their gazes locked. Eden's heart missed a beat when his face lit up. Never taking his eyes off her, he spoke briefly to Hollis, shook his hand, then vaulted off the raised stand.

For a moment Eden lost sight of him as the mob surrounded him, but he appeared again, weaving between female figures in gingham and calico dresses and gentlemen in frock coats. His smile touched upon man and woman alike, his hand touched the head of every small child.

But his eyes remained focused on her alone, and realizing that he was heading straight for her, Eden knew an insane urge to run.

Checking the impulse, Eden swung around and began to walk away, growling between her clenched teeth.

How could she not have known? Usually, she could spot one of his kind a mile off! They all walked in the same cocky manner. All had the same stern jaws, and noses tilting so far up in the air that they would drown if it rained. . . .

Why hadn't she noticed those traits in him before now?

I should have noticed. . . .

I should have known. . . .

Her shock gave way to an anger so deep and harsh, it scored her soul.

"Wait!" he cried.

She quickened her pace. She would *not* stop, not for him. He had some nerve! Coming around to her house, giving her that hammering-heart smile, pretending to care that she could have killed herself falling out of the tree, pretending to truly enjoy racing her children across the yard, when he could not possibly feel *anything*. She *knew* he couldn't! He was a damned, empty, emotionless criminal-catcher with only a damned tin star pinned to his shirtfront to tell him apart from the damned ruthless killers and thieves he'd spend every precious minute of his damned worthless life tracking down. . . .

"Wait!"

Her heartbeat surged, her throat constricted. Only a

few paces separated them now; his shadow met with hers on the parched dirt road. If she could only make it to the house . . .

Tanner McCay fell into step beside her. "Where's the fire?"

Not pausing her pace, Eden shot him a venomous glare. He could not have seen it, she knew, with the veil shielding her face.

"I'm glad you made it to the ceremony. I was almost sure you were going to miss it, until I saw you standing there in front of the bank."

Eden didn't bother correcting his mistake as she marched onward. If she'd had the slightest clue of what was taking place in the town square, she would have rescheduled the meeting with Mr. Sullivan. To her frustration, Tanner matched her swift strides.

"Aren't you even going to stop so we can talk a bit?"

Finally Eden stopped so fast that it took him two extra steps before he realized what she'd done and he back-tracked. "Children, hurry on to the house. I'll be right there."

They spared only a moment to look at her in confusion before obeying. Eden gave thanks that Lissa paid heed to the urgency in the command and knew well enough not to argue.

When they were out of range, she demanded, her nostrils flaring, "Say what you have to say, *Marshal* McCay."

He laughed at her unintentional rhyming.

Eden kept her eyes trained straight ahead and her back rigid.

With a perplexed rise of his brows, he asked, "Are you angry with me?"

She ground her teeth until her jaw hurt. "Don't you have someplace else to be?"

"I'm supposed to meet a few members of the council for a little celebration at Avery's saloon, but they can wait." He cocked his head. "I take it you've recovered from yesterday."

Oh, yes. She'd recovered. The fall might have temporarily knocked her brain loose, but getting smacked in the face with the truth had certainly set her straight this morning!

After a moment of enduring her stony silence, he shifted from one foot to the other. "Actually, I was planning on paying you a call, even if you hadn't shown up in town. I didn't realize who you were when we met." He coughed into his hand. "I'm sorry about your husband, Mrs. Page."

I'm not, she wanted to counter. But she checked the spontaneous reply and forced another between her lips. "I neither need nor want your sympathies."

"The little ones are doing well, I hope."

She stole a sideways glance at him. Didn't he understand a rebuff when he heard it?

"No more fretting over their mama?"

When she didn't answer, he gave her a bashful smile that she swore was a calculated maneuver to put her at ease, no matter how natural it seemed. But it wouldn't work on her, Eden convinced herself. No, he could flash that little dimple in his left cheek until the moon turned to cheese, and she wouldn't relax her stand where he was concerned.

He swerved in front of her and raised his brows. "No more broken ropes? No more damsels in distress?"

Eden, don't let him wheedle his way into your good graces. As if answering an unspoken plea, he straightened, and her eyes followed the trail his fingers made up the edge of his worn vest, over his heart, to the five-pointed badge.

The waning flame beneath her rage instantly blazed again.

"You know, Mrs. Page, I've met some mighty fine women by peculiar means," he chuckled, "but I've never had one fall at my feet before. I have to admit, it's a quick-certain way to gain a man's attention."

Eden bristled, then whirled on him, the lid blowing off her boiling cauldron of fury. "What arrogance! How dare you presume that I even *want* a man's attention!" It was the second time that morning she'd heard a comment of that ilk, and it made her nauseated—especially coming from him.

The swathing of her veil nearly strangled her, she spun away so fast. Sure, he was attractive in a wholesome, earthy way. Denying that would be pointless. No doubt that charming grin and those twinkling forest-green eyes had persuaded other women to make utter fools of themselves to catch his notice. And now that he sported an emblem of the law, many would think him dangerously appealing, Eden conceded.

But she was *not* other women! She didn't need a man, handsome or otherwise. Specifically not some two-bit thrill-seeking marshal.

Somewhere deep inside she had a shred of self-respect left.

The last hundred feet to the house elapsed in a blur. Passing through the gate, Eden's heels clicked on the stones of the walkway and weeds pulled at the weaving of her skirt as she stormed toward the house. And yet, realizing that she had been just as taken in by his looks, his guile, came the dawning that a fool was exactly what he'd made of her.

No, she couldn't blame that on him.

That's what really galled. She'd done that quite well all on her lonesome.

The last thing she wanted was for him to follow her, but that was just what he did. Mounting the top porch step, she swiveled around to face him again. "I suggest you leave my property at once." No matter what the future held in store, the property did still belong to her. For a few months more, at least.

"But I was ho—"

"And don't bother coming back." Eden whipped open the door. "Your kind is not welcome here."

"—we could—"

The door slammed, punctuating her statement.

"—celebrate my victory," he finished lamely.

Stunned, Tanner stared at the empty porch. *His kind?* All he'd wanted was to break through that layer of ice she'd developed overnight. Did one bad joke make him a lecher?

Or . . .

Nah. He shook his head. She couldn't have learned the truth about him this fast. It had to be something else. Something personal.

But what? He knew he hadn't mistaken that flash of interest in her eyes yesterday. He'd honed his observation skills to an art, so when the day he became a lawman arrived, no one could say he did sloppy work.

The longer he tried to figure out where the conversation had gone awry, the more puzzled he grew. Tanner threw his hands in the air. "What in tarnation does 'my kind' mean?"

"Mama says you're a damn tin man."

Taken aback at getting an answer to a question he hadn't expected anyone to hear, Tanner searched the area below, and glimpsed a dark head disappearing beneath the stairs. He stepped off the porch, following an almost inaudible scratching sound. Peeking in the dark hollow beneath the house, he spied the little hellion hunched between cobwebbed beams and musty earth, scraping a twig in the dirt.

He bit back a grin. "I don't suppose you know what she meant by *that* remark."

Seth shrugged. "Nope. Just heard her say you were a damn tin man."

Clearly the boy knew little more than he did. Even so, Tanner lingered beside the porch, reluctant to leave. He surveyed the cramped space. Eroded mounds of sand and clay banked up much of the area beneath the house itself, but the small figure looked quite comfortable in his spot under the stairs. "This is a pretty nifty hideaway, Maverick."

"It's my fort. I can't have one in a tree, but this 'un's okay."

"You come here often?"

He waved the twig at the nothingness. "I was talkin' to my friends."

Tanner instantly understood the rules of make-believe. "Care to introduce me?"

He pointed in turn. "That there's Joe. And that's Patch, and that's Amos. They don't talk much, but they listen real good."

Emotion clogged in Tanner's throat as he recalled the imaginary faces of his own childhood pals. He nodded to each of the boys, who existed only in the child's mind. "Pleased to meet you, Patch. Amos. Joe."

"And my name's Seth. 'Cept my mama and my sisters call me Little Seth, even though I ain't little no more. I'm big." Swiftly he added, "But you can keep callin' me Mav'rick if ya want."

"And I'd sure like it if you called me Mac. You boys enjoying yourselves under here?"

Seth shrugged again. "We were fixin' to make mud pies." With a sly glance, he asked, "Want one?"

Tanner nodded. He sat at the open end of Seth's fort, since fitting his five-foot-eleven-inch frame inside with the rest of the "boys" looked like an impossible feat, and accepted the glob of dripping mud Seth scooped from a bucket at his side and plopped in his hand.

"Thank you. I'm so hungry, my stomach is touching my backbone," Tanner declared. He faked filling his mouth and chewing, taking care that Seth didn't catch him disposing of the mud behind his back.

"My pa use to say that. He useta be a marshal too. Wore a star just like yours."

Tanner sucked in. Tiny had told him how the last marshal had been killed, but he wasn't sure if he should say anything to the boy. How much did Seth know about his father's death?

As if reading his mind, Seth said, "He died savin' lotsa people from some bad men who were trying to rob the train." He cast an innocent brown gaze toward Tanner. "Are you gonna save people too, Marshal Mac?"

Tanner swallowed, and let the mud pie slide from his hand. "I'm going to try."

Seth nodded seriously. "Me too. I'm gonna be a marshal when I grow up. And Joe and Patch and Amos are gonna be my deputies."

Tanner hoped when that happened, there would be someone sharing the occasion with him. Having a door slammed on his moment of glory after he'd worked for ages to achieve it had taken the edge off his triumph. "I think all of you will make fine lawmen."

"Ruthie wants to be a dog when she grows up."

Tanner choked on his laughter.

"Lissa told her she can't be a dog, but Ruthie doesn't care what Lissa says. Mama says we can be anything we want, long as we try." A sudden calling of his name from above stole his attention. "I gotta go. Lissa's hollering."

And in a blink, he had scrambled out the other end of his fort.

Craning his neck, Tanner caught a glimpse of mud-caked boots and soiled trouser bottoms skimming up the steps.

"You been eating dirt again, Little Seth?" Tanner heard. "Mama's gonna tan your—"

The door shut, cutting off the rest of the sentence.

Shaking his head, Tanner rose, and wiped his hand on his thigh, leaving grubby streaks across the denim pant leg. Poor kid, he thought. It was bad enough losing a father without having to reckon with a houseful of females—*although,* older and a tad bit wiser, Tanner didn't think it such a dismal prospect.

Resisting the temptation to brave Eden Page's frosty attitude just to see her again, he glanced one last time at the closed door before ambling down the walkway. Hollis and Tiny and the rest of the council had been kept waiting long enough.

And maybe Tiny would have a few answers.

The attempted robbery was still a big issue in Dogwood Springs, Tanner discovered a short while later as he sat in on the conversation taking place in the jailhouse. He listened intently, his fascination about the unsolved murder of Seth Page running a close second with learning everything he could about the marshal's family. Hopefully they'd drop some tidbit of information that would shed light on why Page's widow wanted no part of him.

"He always was a hard-nosed man," Hollis related, hitching his thumbs in the expansive waistband of his trousers, "but that day, as he rode hell-bent-for-leather toward the railcars, I thought his face would crack plaster. Bullets were flying every which way and he didn't even duck."

"Didn't matter that women and children riding on the train could have been killed by those wayward bullets, they just kept hollerin' at the top of their lungs and firing shots at Seth." Micaleb Brandenburger raised his whiskey flask to Tanner.

Tanner declined the hotel owner's offer, preferring his morning coffee black and bracing rather than dosed up with liquor. "And with all the witnesses present, not one can identify his killer?"

"They always keep their lower faces covered with blue kerchiefs and their hats tipped low over their eyes," John Sullivan replied. "One witness from Marion County testified that he saw yellow hair under the hat of one man when they hit the Daingerfield bank, but no one has collaborated his story."

" 'Bout all we do know for sure is that the two bandits responsible for shooting Seth are of average height and weight," Micaleb added, "built much like you, Mac."

Tanner scowled, hoping Brandenburger was merely making a comparison and not an insinuation. "That doesn't narrow it down much, does it? A group of men are able to attack trains and banks, yet no one can give a firm description?"

Sullivan cocked a brown eyebrow. "It does bear investigating, though. You can simply eliminate small and large men with hair any other color than blond."

"Are you all sure the robbers were men?"

Hollis guffawed. "I think I can tell the difference between a man and a woman."

"We formed a posse and went after them, but they dis-

appeared with nary a sign, same as when they hit trains at
Clay Ridge and Jefferson, and banks in several other
towns," Micaleb reported. "We thought about hiring us one
of those Pinkerton fellas like they done for the James gang
up north, but crops were poor last year and no one 'round
here had that kinda money. And the railroad wouldn't do
nothin' 'bout it 'cause no money was taken."

"However, the council decided that it would be in the
town's best interest to hire another marshal in the event
they returned." Sullivan's brow lifted at Tanner, as if measuring his worth. "We trust that you are capable of defending our citizens in the same manner should the need arise?"

What a coldhearted son of a bug. "Not exactly," Tanner said. "I don't plan on getting myself killed."

As if aware of the sudden tension in the room, Micaleb rolled his shoulder away from the wall. "Well, Rosalyn's gonna fill my hide with buckshot if I don't get back
to the hotel and mind the front desk. I wish you success filling Seth's boots, Mac."

"Yeah, I best get on back to the sawmill," Hollis said.
"Jist hired me Widda Tilly's boy and he wouldn't know
beans if his head was in the pot."

Sullivan, too, stated that he was needed at the bank,
and all three men filed out.

Sifting through the information he'd gleaned, Tanner
lifted Myrtle from her crate and stroked her soft neck. She
rocked her feathered body, folded her bony feet beneath her
wings, and settled contentedly in his lap. "You haven't
strung more than two words together since we got here,"
Tanner said to Tiny. "You have any idea who could be responsible for trying to rob the train and killing Page?"

"I believe it was a spontaneous perpetration committed by desperate criminals to expand their coffers, rather
than a premeditated strategy."

"Tiny, who does your laundry?" Tanner chuckled.

"I do. Why?"

" 'Cause I think you're putting too much starch in
your shirts. You can relax around me, you know."

Wary, Tiny tilted his head.

Tanner sighed. "Look, I get the impression we'll be spending a lot of time together. But those ten-dollar words you keep spouting are much too high-priced for my ten-cent education. If I have to carry a dictionary around just to translate your speech, it's gonna take me forever and a day to understand what you're saying."

When Tiny wavered with indecision, Tanner encouraged him. "Relax, okay? Pull up a chair, kick up your feet, and make yourself comfortable. I give you my word I won't tell anyone."

Tiny hesitated before leaving his post near the banister dividing the office from the cells, and stiffly lowered himself in the chair. "How may I assist you, Marshal McCay?"

"You can start by calling me Mac. Or better yet, call me Tanner."

"As you wish . . . Tanner."

"Tiny, I've been doing some thinking. Even though this is a small town, there might be instances when I'm needed in two different places at the same time. I can't be everywhere at once. I'm gonna need a deputy."

"I can provide you with a list of capable gentlemen from which to choose."

"I was hoping you would consider the job."

Deep-set blue eyes widened with astonishment. "Me?"

"Sure. You have a better idea of what this job entails than I do."

"Misters Clark, Sullivan, and Brandenburger are also quite informed, among others."

"Yeaaah," Tanner hedged, arcing his head, "but I don't get the feeling they would be as dependable. You were the one to take time out of your schedule to welcome me. You were the one considerate enough to show me around town."

Tiny swallowed. "They have familial obligations and establishments to oversee," he explained.

"What about you?"

"I have only myself to care for."

"You seem familiar with the legal system. Can you shoot a gun?"

"I am proficient in firearms, yes."

"Then why are you trying to pawn the job off on someone else?"

He hesitated for a long while before answering. "I simply feel another may suit the requirements of a deputy marshal much better than I. Perhaps you should delegate the duty to someone with a more . . . commanding presence."

Suddenly, it dawned on Tanner what Tiny was trying to—but couldn't—spit out. "It's because you're short!" He laughed at the absurdity. "Where'd you get the idea that a person's size decides what job he is capable of handling?"

"I am not alone in my perceptions."

"Ahhh." Tanner nodded. "Folks giving you a hard time?"

He evaded Tanner's knowing look.

"Well, I don't believe in judging anyone by physical appearance. You'd be the perfect deputy, and if you think about it, your size could be an asset."

He reminded Tanner of a little kid when he glanced back, his expression both dubious and hopeful.

"Sure!" Tanner contended. "What outlaw would feel threatened by someone in such a small package? They'd underestimate you, see, and by the time they figured out just exactly how much havoc you could wreak, it would be too late!"

Tiny sat up a little straighter and cleared his throat. "I am honored by your confidence in me. I should like very much to become your deputy."

Wasting no time lest Tiny change his mind, they both stood and Tanner had him raise his right hand to swear him in. "Now that that's settled, let's get down to the next order of business." Rubbing his chin, he said, "Looks like I landed myself in a barrel of pickles. Think we should start jogging some memories tomorrow. There's got to be someone who saw something that day. Maybe they just thought it too minor an incident to have mentioned before."

Taking his new status seriously, Tiny brought out a notebook from an inside coat pocket. "I would suggest waiting until the Fourth of July. The celebration draws rural citizens as well as townspeople. Since you will be patrolling the town, you will have an opportunity to reach a broader base of witnesses that may have been present the day of the robbery attempt."

Tanner wagged his index finger in the air. "Good point. It's only a couple days away, and anyone who doesn't show up, I'll catch another time. I also want to talk to employees of the East Line and Red River Railroad. They must have kept records."

"I will collect the names posthaste," Tiny said, making a note.

Needing to stretch his legs, Tanner unfolded himself from the chair and walked to the stove. The cozy aroma of hot coffee saturated the air as he refilled his cup.

"You are quite intrigued by Marshal Page's demise."

The pot made a hollow clink on the cast-iron burner. "One thing you should probably know is that I don't have much tolerance for loose ends. I like having things tied up. Finished." Lifting the cup to his lips, Tanner mused aloud over the steaming rim, "I can't help wondering about his family, though. How they're adjusting and all."

"I did notice you chasing the widow Page down the street earlier."

Tanner gave him a chagrined look. "Yeah, you and the rest of the town."

"Do you have romantic inclinations toward her?"

Flushing, Tanner wished he didn't have one of those faces that revealed his every thought. He strode toward the window with his cup in his hand and looked out the dingy panes. "For all the good it does me. I don't think she likes me much," he said over his shoulder.

"She does not ally herself with anyone. In her four years of residency in Dogwood Springs, I cannot recall her ever taking an active position in the community. After her husband's death, she became almost a full recluse, venturing into town only to conduct necessary errands."

"Don't seem healthy to me, cooping yourself up all the time."

Tiny shrugged.

"Don't you wonder why? I mean, she's a pretty lady, and a widow at that. I'd venture the men in this town would have at least tried to woo her."

"She is in mourning."

Tanner might have believed the simple logic if yesterday's incident weren't still so fresh in his memory. But the news made her even more mysterious. And if there was anything he found irresistible, it was a mystery.

Chapter Five

TANNER SPENT THE next hour being escorted around town by Tiny who introduced him to several of the citizens. At Tanner's suggestion, they wrapped up the tour at Hannah's cafe.

Hannah seated them at a window table and took their orders. She was an easy woman to look at, generous in figure, with a pleasant smile and a mop of frizzed brown hair, slightly streaked with gray, tied back with a ribbon.

In fact, she reminded him a lot of the cafe she ran. The flowered paper on the walls was faded but intact, the tables and benches scarred but inviting, and the wonderful aroma of food mixed with the clean scents of summer heat and beeswax polish.

While they waited for their meal, Tiny lost a bit of his stiff formality and filled Tanner in on the quirks and accomplishments of the people they'd met.

"I had a little visit with the Page boy earlier," Tanner said, subtly steering the conversation to the family who interested him most.

Flagging a napkin across his slap, Tiny asked, "How did you accomplish getting past Widow Page to actually converse with one of her children? She is fiercely protective of them."

"I noticed."

"But to the extreme that she will not let them stray from her sight for an instant. Not even to avail herself of a position."

At Tanner's blank look, Tiny simplified the terms. "She cannot find a job."

Hannah returned, giving Tanner a chance to organize the riot of questions Tiny's bit of news bred.

She set two plates, each heaping with a crusty fillet of catfish, greens, and biscuits big enough to sleep on, in front of them. "Eat up, fellas. Your stomachs are growlin' so loud, I thought a thunderstorm was blowin' into my diner."

"I appreciate you starting a tab for me, Hannah."

"Nothin' to it, Marshal. I've been here for five years now, but I remember what it's like getting settled into a new town. Until the railroad came through, I could barely rub two nickles together. Y'all just let me know if you need anything else, y'hear?" She flipped at a strand of hair near Tanner's ear and winked at him. "And I mean *anything* else."

Tanner guessed that many a bachelor had fallen prey to the sultry invitation in her big black eyes. And though he eyed the provocative sway of her hips as she strolled off, she left him feeling nothing more than mildly entertained.

Unlike another, who turned him inside out with just a glance.

Thankfully, Tiny made no comment about Hannah's shameless flirtation, instead, devoting his attention to his meal while Tanner's thoughts reverted back to their interrupted conversation.

Finally losing the battle with his curiosity, he prodded, "Are you saying that in a town this size, no one will hire Mrs. Page?"

After swallowing, Tiny replied, "Not under the conditions she sets. She has been offered employment several times, but she steadfastly refuses to work unless she is permitted to bring her children with her."

Tanner whistled between his teeth. "It can't be easy for her, losing her husband and being forced to raise three young'uns alone."

"I am not saying I condone their stance, I am simply stating their position."

Tanner frowned. He couldn't shake the feeling that Eden Page's reasons stemmed from something a whole lot more serious than an aversion to working. And that "something" was also related to her ordering him off her property.

Pushing his plate away, Tanner rested his elbows on the cleared spot and leaned forward. "I once bought a stallion from a mustanger I knew who captured wild horses by 'creasing' them. He'd fire a bullet into the animal's neck, grazing the cord to daze it so it could be caught. That stud was the finest mount I ever owned, but the experience left him gun-shy. Just the sight of my Peacemaker sent him into a frenzy."

In the process of cutting his fish into manageable bites, Tiny paused for a moment and tilted his head questionably.

"The point I'm getting at is that people tend to react a lot like animals when they feel threatened, particularly mothers who believe they are protecting their offspring. It sounds like Mrs. Page might have had an experience similar to the one my horse did."

"Not that I'm aware of. However, neither does the widow take me into her confidence." Tiny shrugged and set the knife in motion again. "In any case, I am given the distinct opinion that she is having a difficult time of it now."

Tanner smoothed his mustache thoughtfully. "I wish there were some way I could help—wait a minute. Didn't you tell me she used to cook and clean for the prisoners?"

"When her husband was marshal, yes."

Tanner grinned, reckoning he knew just how Samuel Morse felt thirty-some years ago when he heard his telegraph wires sing for the very first time. "Then I think I just might have a solution to her problem."

He found her sitting on her knees in the large garden in the backyard, bent over a thinned row of carrots.

Tanner watched her from the concealing shadows at the rear of the house. He'd rehearsed what he planned to

say the entire night before, but now that the time had come
to talk to her, he couldn't remember a single practiced line.

As his admiring gaze swept over her, his mind turned
to mud, his mouth felt like chalk, and son of a bug, sometime in the past few minutes a band had wound itself
around his chest and was getting tighter by the minute.

Tanner could almost hear his mother's voice again,
calling someone a spit-and-polish woman, the highest form
of praise Ina ever gave to one of her gender. Eden Page fit
the description better than anyone he'd ever met. Even with
her hands plunged into dirt, her hair in disarray under a hat
brim the size of a wagon wheel, and large damp spots on
her dress between her shoulder blades, she still managed to
look every inch a lady.

And she plumb took his breath away.

Sucking in a deep draft of air, he forced himself to remember why he was there in the first place. The job. Yeah,
that was it. He was supposed to be offering her a job at the
jailhouse.

Now he had only to figure the best way to approach
her. She didn't look busy exactly. Just intense. Tanner
wiped his hand down his pantleg. He couldn't recall a time
when anyone had made his palms sweat—leastwise, a female anyone. But he swore there were still gashes on his
face from the slicing looks she'd thrown at him yesterday.
He had no doubts that if he didn't choose his words carefully, her temper would rise higher than a cat's back, and
he'd wind up paying a visit to Aaron Arnold to have the
spade at her side removed from his chest.

He supposed he had a right to a little nervousness.

Well, hiding behind the corner of the house, spying on
her like a fox ready to pounce on his last meal, wouldn't
remedy either of their situations, he reminded himself.

Squaring his shoulders, Tanner strode toward her,
hoping he looked more confident than he felt. "Mrs. Page?"

Eden froze.

Before thinking, she swiped at the hair drooping along
her cheeks and felt her gloves leave a trail of grime under
her eye. Wiping at the patches of dirt on her skirts only

ground the soil in deeper, and she was keenly aware of the sweat stains under her arms and in the valley of her bosom.

Eden closed her eyes. That he should see her like this . . . menial and filthy . . .

"I don't mean to bother you, Mrs. Page."

Her lips flattened, and she cursed her traitorous heart for leaping at the sound of his voice. What did she care what Tanner McCay thought of her appearance? She hadn't invited him. Didn't even want him on her property. As a matter of fact, she wanted to forget he existed at all.

Battling the urge to turn around and look at him, she finally said, "I thought I told you not to come around here, Marshal McCay."

"I wanted to apologize for upsetting you yesterday. If I said something, or did something—"

Eden ripped another scrawny carrot from the soil and flung it into the basket between the rows. "I don't want your apology. In fact, I want nothing to do with you at all. Now, go."

"All right. But before I do, I'd like just a minute of you time. Truth is, I came for another reason too."

"I'm not interested."

Silence followed.

Somehow, she wasn't surprised that he'd ignored her.

Craning her neck, Eden glanced behind her and demanded, "Are you hard of hearing?" Her eyes widened when she noticed the downward direction of his gaze.

She jumped to her feet and spun about, her face hot as a chili pepper, her fists clenched in the folds of her skirt. "Of all the nerve! I don't care what title you go by, mister, you have no right gawking at my . . . at my . . ." Eden snatched a bunch of carrots from the basket and hurled them at the lecher. "I am *not* an object to be ogled!"

"Wait!" He held his hands up as if to ward off the attack. "I'm sorry. I couldn't help myself." He grinned helplessly. "You just have the nicest—"

She grabbed the entire basket and raised it above her head.

"Skirt! I was gonna say skirt!"

Her voice low and trembling, Eden threatened. "If you don't leave this instant, I'll make you *really* sorry!"

"But I haven't yet told you what I came for!"

"I don't care *what* you came for, I told you I'm not interested."

"But I want to offer you a job!"

In spite of herself, Eden gasped. *A job?*

She could pay the rent. She would be independently earning her own income. She could wipe that high-and-mighty smirk off John Sullivan's face and feed it to him on a platter.

Her thoughts tumbled over one another like apples rolling down a cider-pot chute. "What kind of job?" she found herself asking.

Slowly lowering his hands, he explained, "I've been told I have to feed and doctor anyone I take into custody. I have very little experience doing either chore, so I need someone to take over those duties. Think you'd be interested?"

"Why me?"

"I was told that you once tended to the prisoners—"

He didn't say "when your husband was alive," but Eden knew it was on the tip of his tongue.

Instead, he swiftly added, "I would pay you, of course. Regular each month." He darted a cautious glance over her shoulder and pointed. "You still planning on hitting me with that?"

Her gaze shifting to the side, Eden noticed she still held the woven basin poised high as though it were a lethal weapon.

Eden's face blanched. She'd thrown carrots at him.

She'd almost slung the whole bushel, basket and all, at him.

Years and years of mastering her reckless tendencies . . . in one split second, wasted.

Eden dashed the basket to the ground and, wheeling away, jammed her fist on her hip. Her chest heaved, her eyes misted over. Damn him for making her lose control!

"What gives you the idea I even need a job? Or why I'd ever consider working for you?"

"Marshal Mac! Marshal Mac!"

"Tan McCrary!"

Little Seth and Ruthie barreled through the back door and across the yard, cutting short any reply he might have made. Eden's pulse quickened as she realized they were rushing straight for the marshal.

His face brightened, and a smile split his features from ear to ear. "Hey, Maverick! And my little sweet potato too!"

"What are you doing here, Marshal Mac?"

"Did you come to play with us again?"

"Wow! Is that a *real* gun?"

"Will you come and see the new dress Mama made for my doll?"

Angry tears seared Eden's lids when he laughed at the barrage of questions. His whole face lit up from within, and there was that dimple again.

Oh, he was good. How long had it taken him to perfect this act of sincerity?

But damn him, he had no right—*no right*—duping innocent children into believing he was truly glad to see them.

The sight of Little Seth's hand reaching for the holster buckled around the marshal's lean hips seized Eden's attention.

At the same instant she commanded, "Seth leave that gun be," the marshal plucked her son's fingers away.

"Sorry, Maverick, you aren't allowed to touch that," he said. "It's a very powerful weapon, used only for defense. . . . Here, I brought you something else."

Digging into his pants pocket, he withdrew a penny, then hunkered down. "Look. See those numbers? They say 1882. That's this year, and this is a brand-new penny, fresh from the mint."

"What about me, Tan?" Ruthie bounced as though her feet were made of springs. "Did ya bring somethin' for me too?"

"Huh?" he gasped in mock horror. "I don't know . . . I might . . ." Reaching behind his back, he pulled a cotton cap no bigger than a teacup from his back pocket. "Well, glory be! How'd that get there?"

"A bonnet for Annie! Oh, it will go just fine with the dress Mama made for her!" Her arm wound around his sturdy neck, and her lips smacked against his smooth-shaven cheek. "Thank you, Tan."

Resentment filled Eden at the familiarity, the openness, in which they greeted the marshal. It was a mistake to let them accept the gifts. She knew she should make them return the items instantly. And yet, hearing Ruthie's unrestrained joy and seeing Little Seth's fascination after so many months of solemnity, she just couldn't find it within herself to make them give the presents back. They got gifts so seldom.

Oh, why did he have to have such a deceitfully endearing way about him? Why did he have to involve her children? And what would happen when he grew tired of this game, as he surely would?

He'd leave her to pick up the pieces of their shattered hearts, that's what.

"And here. I have a very special mission for the two of you." From inside his shirt pocket he revealed a dainty white collar of Irish lace and handed it to Ruthie. "This is for your sister. Can you see that she gets it?"

"Lissa's gonna love this!"

Over Ruthie's head he continued their suspended discussion. "I promise to behave myself, if that's what's worrying you. No more ogling."

"What's ogling?"

Tanner curved his fingers like claws and with a mock growl, tickled Ruthie's sides. "It's a little creature that hides under bridges just waiting to tickle little girls!" he teased over her delighted squealing.

Eden bowed her head, hating herself for even considering his offer.

But she was so tempted . . .

He snatched her son in one arm, her daughter in the

other, and lifted them high into his arms as though they belonged there. "You can even bring these little scamps with
you if it bothers you having someone else watching them
while you work."

Her gaze shot to his face. Did he know? Had he heard?
His hopeful expression gave away nothing, so either the
gossip of how she raised the children had not yet reached
his ears, or he knew and was pretending that he didn't. Yet,
what did it matter if he knew or not? He was the only one
in all of Dogwood Springs who hadn't discounted her because of her so-called queer obsession.

Damn him for being the only person in this town willing to accept her strict conditions!

"You don't have to give me an answer now, Mrs.
Page. Just promise me you'll think about it, all right?" Set-
ting the children down, he tousled Seth's hair and chucked
Ruthie beneath her chin. "Be good, young'uns."

"But ain'tcha gonna stay and play?"

"The marshal has duties to attend to, Ruthie. He's a
busy man," Eden managed to say over the lump in her
throat.

He stared at her for a long while before his gaze fell to
her daughter. "Your ma's right, sweet potato. I just stopped
by this morning to say hello. I do need to get back to
town."

"Yeah, he's gonna go catch bad men!" Seth declared.

"Yes," Eden flatly repeated. "The marshal *must* go
catch his bad men."

Eden rested the back of her head against the chair and
closed her eyes. From behind her lids appeared a picture. A
girl; lank-haired, sunken-cheeked. A petticoat made up
mostly of patches and a threadbare dress hung on her thin
frame. Poor she was. Poor and pathetic and doomed to a
life of loneliness. Unwanted. Unnecessary. Slowly the fire
in the girl's eyes dimmed, leaving her to stare vacantly
back at Eden, much like the subject of a photograph stared
at a camera lens.

Except Eden was not the lens. She was a mirror in

which she saw a reflection of her own past, and a distinct image of Lissa and Ruthie and Little Seth's future.

Unless she took control.

Her eyes snapped open and she jerked forward. The figures in the ledger had not changed, had not magically multiplied while she took a mental journey backward in time.

Eden uttered a mild curse, then flung herself out of the chair.

Damn Seth for putting me in this position! she railed, pacing her bedroom.

Always before, she'd been completely independent, relying only on herself for the basic necessities. Until she'd hitched up with Seth Page, who believed that a woman's sole purpose in life was to cater to his every whim and bear him a dozen strapping sons to follow in his footsteps.

But when she'd finally delivered him his son, he still wasn't content. Only in the thrill of chasing outlaws had he and satisfaction met head-on. Eventually, his consuming passion had also gotten him killed.

And cast her into the difficult role of being both mother and father to their three children.

Eden dragged her hands down her face. In truth, there wasn't that much difference between the past ten months and the past nine years. She still had to maintain order and discipline, keep house, tend the garden, cook meals, wash and mend clothes . . .

But now, on top of all those responsibilities, she had to find a way to support them financially. Otherwise, there wouldn't be a house to keep.

In less than three months' time, the allowance set aside to provide for her family in the event of her husband's death would be used up.

The town council called it a widow's stipend.

She called it charity.

Either way, it grated on her pride to accept the financial support. But the galling fact remained that she and the children would not have survived this long without it. Even with the allowance, she'd had to sell everything worth selling. Seth's horse, his guns, the wagon, half the furniture.

But what would she do when that money ran out? She'd planned to sell what vegetables she could spare from her own garden, but she couldn't expect the pitiful sum the produce would bring to cover the costly amount John Sullivan demanded to keep a roof over her children's heads.

She needed a job. Desperately.

And into her yard strolls Tanner McCay, offering her one. One she knew how to do. One she'd been doing for almost nine years, here and there—tending to the lawbreakers the marshal brought in. He'd even answered the plea no one before him seemed to have heard—that a job not separate her from her babies.

With a sudden sinking feeling she knew she'd have to take up Tanner McCay on his offer, even if it meant swallowing the last of her pride.

She had no other choice.

"Good day, Marshal."

Pausing at the door to the jailhouse, Tanner tipped his hat at the town spinster shuffling down the boardwalk. "Good day, Miss Percy. That red bonnet is mighty fetching on you. In fact, I wonder if there isn't a law against a lady stepping out looking sweet as cherry cobbler."

Miss Percy's laughing blue eyes all but disappeared beneath the wrinkles brought on by her crooked-toothed smile. "Oh, you young rake. If'n you charm the rest o' the gals the way you charm me, you won't get no work done 'round here 'cause they'll be follerin' at your heels like a shaddaw."

Tanner chuckled, wishing he'd get that lucky with one woman, anyway. "So where are you heading this afternoon?"

"I'm in the direction of Ruddy Deerpot's down t'end of the road. We got to get started on bakin' for the Fourth of *Juu*-ly celebration."

"I'd be the envy of every man in town if you'd let me walk down to the Deerpots' with you," he offered.

"Naw, you go on, Marshal. No sense in wastin' time with stale waters like me, though I'm obliged for the thought. But if'n it gets any hotter, I'll wind up meltin' sure as I'm standin' here jawin', so I best get movin'.'"

He waited for Miss Percy to pass by before entering the jailhouse, leaving the door ajar. Any breeze, even a sultry one, would be welcome about now. Wiping the back of his neck with his kerchief, Tanner stuffed the damp cloth back into his pocket and hung his hat on a peg in the wall.

Other than a minor scuffle at the saloon, it had been a quiet afternoon, no one besides the spinster willing to brave the heat. Walking her to the other end of town would have been a welcome distraction from the thoughts of Eden that had hounded him all day. But another part of him was glad Miss Percy had turned him down. In case Eden showed up, he didn't want to miss her visit.

"I got you some corn, Myrtle," he called, heading for the chicken's crate, shaking the paper sack in his hand. He found the wooden cage tipped over, the door flipped open. A quick sweep of the room told him nothing else had been touched while he'd been out and about meeting the barber, the undertaker, the saloon keeper, and the grister, yet his pet was missing.

"Myrtle?" Tanner turned full circle. Other than an egg lying atop some papers on his desk, there was no sign of her. "Heeere, chicky-chicky." Heck, how did a body call for a hen anyway?

Moving farther into the room, Tanner searched the corners, under the stove, in the cupboards, but she was nowhere to be seen.

In the cell he'd temporarily taken over for his own, he figured he was getting closer when he had to sidestep the little "gifts" she'd left all over the floor. "Myrtle, where are you hiding?"

A round white head popped up from the pillow on his bed. Tanner shoved his fists on his hips. "Now, Myrtle, let's get something clear here. I treasure our friendship. I truly do. But friends is all we'll ever be, got it?"

Rising, Myrtle puffed out her breast and fluffed her

feathers, then gave him a naggish look that he read to say, "Finally home?"

Tanner slid her off his pillow and she half hopped, half flew off the cot. "I suppose I should rig up a pen for you somewhere." He eyed the bird droppings on the floor. "Outside, of course. But until then, stay off my bed, all right?"

Tanner quickly cleaned up the mess on the floor with newspaper, then scattered a handful of ground kernels at the far end of the cell, knowing it would be useless to try to stuff his feathered friend back into the crate. She'd only escape again. He could hardly blame her. If not for the window—bars aside—in the cell, he doubted he could tolerate such close confines either. Even as a kid he'd craved freedom. Ina once told him even sleep never stopped him from wandering toward open spaces. He'd never hurt anybody or anything with his sleepwalking, but he used to wonder what he did and where he went. *Well, that was a long time ago, Mac*.

Returning to the desk, he stored Myrtle's egg in the desk drawer from which he withdrew the pile of WANTED posters. Beneath them he also found a number of files.

With no pressing matters requiring his time, he figured that instead of dwelling on whether or not Eden would accept his offer, he might as well familiarize himself with as many particulars about the robbery as he could before interviewing witnesses.

Soon he had the desktop covered with newspaper clippings from all over East Texas. Each time even a vague description of the outlaws that had been plaguing the area for the past two years appeared, he sifted through the posters, looking to match the sketchy detail with a face or specific criminal's past record or a pattern that would link them to the attack on the E.L. & R.R. train pulling out of Dogwood Springs last September.

Tanner pored over the mountain of material fanned out upon his desk until his eyes went blurry and his brain swelled from the parade of faces and letters being absorbed into his memory.

"I just don't get it," he muttered, planting his elbow on the desk and plowing his fingers through his hair. "Nobody seems to know what the slugs look like, or where they'll hit next. There isn't any rhyme or reason to the attacks, and no way to track them once they leave the scene. It just doesn't seem possible that someone can lay in wait near a busy depot town, try and rob the train, kill the marshal in cold blood, then leave without a trace."

Tanner shook his head with complete bafflement and slammed the file folder shut. The robberies, rather than being a string executed by one group of men as he'd first assumed, appeared more of a rash outbreak in the same area by several groups imitating each other. But the case— or cases—reeked of a familiar foul odor he couldn't place. And it wasn't Myrtle he smelled.

He toyed with the star pinned to his vest, feeling the nubs at the end of each point, the engraved title "Marshal" across the front, and beneath that in the shape of a smile "Dogwood Springs, Texas."

Protecting and serving law-abiding citizens. Enforcing the law. Solving cases. Bringing outlaws to justice. It was all a part of his job. The people expected—no, trusted— him to do no less.

And yet, he didn't have a clue who had struck near this particular town in broad daylight and stained the road with blood.

Strutting in front of the desk, Myrtle clucked several times and tipped her beak in the air.

"I know," he sighed. "I shouldn't let it trouble me. This is only my first week on the job, but that's the whole thing," he explained to Myrtle as he brought out his harmonica. "This isn't just a job, just a regular wage. This is my one and only shot to make a difference."

Tanner blew into the instrument. The first six sliding notes of "Dixie" filled the silence with each blow-draw-blow. He paused, his lips brushing warm metal as he spoke his thoughts aloud. "If I fail at proving my worth to these people before they connect me to Fain and Terron, I won't get another chance. No one will ever believe I'm not a crook like them. In fact, I'm not fully convinced some folks don't believe that now."

Most of the folks at the ceremony had seemed genuinely glad to watch Hollis swear him in, but there had been a few odd, almost wary glances, and an undercurrent of distrust. He'd felt that like a clammy hand in a dark alley.

John Sullivan topped the list.

Tanner knew that actions spoke louder than words. He could spout his innocence until his face turned blue, and there would still be skeptics. No, the best way to prove his honesty and goodwill toward these people was to arrest the murdering, thieving bandits.

Pocketing the mouth harp, Tanner sighed with frustration, then reopened the file.

Chapter Six

Eden drew in a deep breath. Upon its release, she marched through the doorway of the jailhouse. Nothing had changed in her husband's absence, she immediately noted. The same dingy white walls and forbidding iron-barred cells greeted her, almost mocking in their appearance. Odors of dust and gloom had settled in every nook and cranny. Not one touch of humanity softened the stark and sobering purpose of the building.

She'd thought herself prepared for this confrontation with her past. But now inside the familiar quarters, the dismal aura closed in on her, making it hard to resist bolting for the warm comfort of home.

Eden forced her stiff legs to move, each click of her heels sounding like gunshots in the oppressive silence. Standing before the cluttered desk, she frowned. Even the seat of authority was still occupied by a man little more than a stranger.

He just had a different face.

Smoothing her veil back over her hat crown, Eden waited for Tanner McCay to raise his bowed head. His hand framed his unshaved jawline, and strands of his sandy hair poked between his fingers. He gave no sign of being aware of her presence.

Her gaze landed on the posters and newspaper clippings holding his attention. Nausea rose inside her as she recognized every single scrap of paper stacked in front of him.

Apparently, he couldn't wait to bury himself in his work, and just like Seth, he became so caught up with the deeds of felons that he was oblivious of anything or anyone else around him.

Well, let him waste his life, she thought, squashing a seed of unreasonable disappointment before it had a chance to flourish. What Tanner McCay did with his time was none of her business. She was there to work for him only until something else came along, not enter into a lifelong commitment with the man.

And she might as well get it over with.

Eden wound her purse-string around her hand until her fingers turned white, then cleared her throat.

"Mrs. Page!" He shot out of the chair so fast, it tipped over and clattered to the floor. Scrambling to right it, his feet tangled in the legs and he nearly wound up having splinters driven into his gums.

Mouth aslack, Eden watched as he regained his balance. Nonchalantly, he yanked his vest from beneath his armpits so it fit around his torso as it was meant to, and he grinned, wide and sheepish. "Guess I haven't quite gotten the knack of standing yet."

She said nothing. Couldn't. This man was their new marshal? For pity's sake, Eden thought, how did he catch outlaws? By tripping over them?

"I didn't expect to see you so soon."

Her mouth shut with an audible snap, and it took her an instant to remember why she'd come to the last place on earth she ever wanted to be again. But the image of three trusting faces that flashed inside her head made her reason vividly clear. Eden cleared her throat and tilted her chin. "For twenty-five dollars a month I will take the job."

This time his mouth fell open.

Recovering quickly, he waved toward the ladderback chair beside the desk. He repositioned his own chair, and they lowered into their seats at the same time.

He didn't take his eyes off her. The clock on the shelf by the stove ticked off several awkward moments. Eden glanced out the door, where the children waited. She licked her lips. The drawstring cut into her knuckles. Wasn't he going to say something?

Apparently not. He just sat there watching her, his green eyes aglow.

A warmth stole into her blood, and her arms went all tingly. Wringing the reticule in her hands like a dishrag, Eden fought the unwelcome sensations. Judging from the awe she read on his face, one would think that she was the only woman he'd seen in decades. "Marshal McCay, I would appreciate it if you would stop staring at me so that we can discuss business."

Visibly jolted, he shook his head. "I just can't believe you're here."

Neither could she.

"You really want the job?"

"For twenty-five dollars a month."

Falling backward against the chair frame, he whistled between his teeth. "That's a lot of money, Mrs. Page."

Eden forced down the swell of guilt. She told herself that his earnings would barely cover her costly fee. But how he paid her was his problem. She couldn't afford guilt just then. She had enough problems of her own to worry about.

Before he recovered from his surprise, she forged ahead. "I shall come in on Tuesdays and Fridays between the hours of one and five to tidy up. I would appreciate it if you could find something to keep you busy elsewhere during that time."

"I expect I could," he said, nodding thoughtfully, "but if I take in any prisoners between those days, I'll need you here more often. 'Course, it wouldn't be any trouble just to come on by your place—"

"No!" Tempering her sharp tone, Eden said, "I don't want you coming to my house for any reason. In a town this size, rumors would begin flying."

"But how I am supposed to let you know when to bring meals for them?"

Eden pulled a red-and-brown flannel cloth from her reticule and laid it on the desk. "Tie this to the post outside the boardwalk. When I see it, I will know that you have taken someone into custody. Once the prisoner has posted his bond, or paid his fine, or has been dealt with by the circuit judge, remove the cloth until another is arrested."

He stayed quiet for several minutes, stroking his mustache. Eden held her breath at his close scrutiny. He'd changed his mind about hiring her. She knew it. All those before him had once they realized she would not compromise her demands.

"You don't like me much, do you, Mrs. Page?"

Caught off guard, Eden's first impulse was to tell him she would rather lie in a nest of vipers than have any association with one of his ilk. But so much rested on his decision. She pondered the question carefully before answering. "I will not be paid to like or dislike you, Marshal McCay. I will be paid to perform a service."

She couldn't tell from his frown if he was disappointed by her reply or if he was fixing to deny her the job. She wished if he planned the latter, he would do it quickly, while she still had a shred of dignity left instead of putting her through the agony of waiting.

He caught his bottom lip between his teeth, and just as she neared the brink of weeping her despair, he slapped his thigh and his grin broadened into a wide smile. "Well, I reckon you'll do a fine job, Mrs. Page. Tuesday is the holiday, so why don't you start next Friday? I wouldn't want you to miss out on the festivities."

"I prefer to begin Tuesday and earn a full month's wages."

He inclined his head. "As you wish."

"And I still have your permission to bring my children?"

"That goes without saying."

The heavy load she'd carried tumbled off her shoulders. Rising, Eden let out her pent-up breath and released the death grip on her handbag. She'd done it. She'd put herself at his mercy without resorting to begging and had gotten a job working for him in spite of her stringent rules.

Perhaps a handshake would be fitting to seal the arrangement, Eden contemplated, yet the last time she'd touched him, a stream of shameful yearnings had shot clear to her bones. She recoiled at the memory. If she'd known then who he was, he never would have affected her so strongly. She would not have allowed it.

He followed her outside, where the children were seated on a bench to the right of the doorway, swinging their feet, and watching the town come alive. Now that the midday heat had somewhat abated, folks had ventured outside to set up for the Fourth of July festivities. Signs of the holiday were visible everywhere. Vibrant banners were looped from balcony to balcony, and more were being strung around windows. The raised platform the marshal had stood on two short days before was also being dressed for the occasion, and a pair of sweat-soaked lads were replacing the wicks in lamps hanging from poles, so the square would have sufficient light to dance by at evening time.

At the sight of Tanner, Little Seth and Ruthie jumped up, but Lissa sent him a glower hot enough to reduce him to ashes. In spite of the hostility she didn't try to hide, Tanner confused Lissa by giving her a gentle smile.

Seth tugged on his shirtsleeve. Tanner bent low, and into his ear Seth whispered loud enough for Eden to hear, "Patch tried to steal my penny."

Startled, Eden frowned. Who was Patch?

Tanner seemed to know. His lips twitched, but his brows came together in what was clearly feigned seriousness. "Maybe you should find someplace to hide it, then."

"Do you hide your special 'longin's?"

The marshal peeked at her above Little Seth's head.

Eden averted her face, swallowing with difficulty. *'Longin's* was just a mistaken pronunciation of "belongings." Yet the shortened version of the word scored a tender spot.

"Sometimes," Tanner answered, the weight of his gaze still on her. "But sometimes I find greater joy in sharing them with someone."

"You think I should share my penny with Patch?"

"That's up to you, Maverick. People have to make their own choices in life."

Eden grabbed her son's hand and tugged him away. "We've taken up enough of the marshal's time, Little Seth. Ruthie, Lissa, come along. We've supper to put on the table."

"But, Mama, I want to watch," Lissa said. "Those men are fixin' to rake the road."

"You can see well enough from the house."

Lissa groaned, then dragged herself off the bench. "Why'd I even hafta come to town if all I was gonna do was sit on a dumb ol' bench while you talked to the stupid marshal?"

Though her voice faded as she trailed behind her mother and siblings, Tanner caught the sullen words. The eldest girl had taken an immediate dislike to him, and he couldn't for the life of him figure out why.

But it seemed the acorn didn't fall far from the tree. Eden treated him with the same unfriendliness.

Tanner leaned against the doorjamb with his arms folded across his chest. Ruthie and Little Seth, holding tight to Eden's hand, turned and waved, while Lissa scuffed her feet against the ruts in the road, glancing wistfully behind now and then at the decorations. When he waved back, the two littler ones skipped ahead of their mother.

"Did she accept the position?"

Tanner slanted a downward look behind him. He thought he'd smelled Tiny's cologne. It was some musky foreign scent, pleasing to the nose. "Where'd you come from?"

"Bacon and Bligh's, down the fairway."

He must have noticed Eden leaving the jail on his way home from the joint-owned cooper and tinker shop, Tanner surmised. Although he worked out of his apartment, Tiny made frequent trips to several of the businesses in town, since he kept their accounts. As usual, a collection of ledgers was tucked under his arm.

With a droll chuckle, Tanner said, "You aren't going to believe what I just did."

"Why shouldn't I?"

"Because I can hardly believe it myself. I have some coffee on the stove. Feel like joining me for a cup?"

Tiny glanced at his pocket watch, more out of habit than anything, Tanner guessed. Then Tiny nodded. "I will confess that I am not in any haste to decipher Mr. Bligh's mistabulated records."

While Tanner topped a pair of mugs to the rim with the thickening brew, he filled Tiny in on Eden's visit.

Tanner handed a cup to Tiny, then lowered into the opposite chair and stretched his legs across a corner of the desk, crossing them at the ankles. "I don't know what surprised me more," he finished, plucking at the rag Eden had left behind, "her showing up here or all those rules she spouted."

"Especially her fee," Tiny gasped.

"I reckon those kids need the money more than me. If you would have seen her . . . that lady's got more pride than a hedgehog has spines. If it was for herself, I don't think she would have come to me if she was naked in a snow-storm and I had the only fire alive for miles. But for those kids . . . It was the most selfless act of love I've ever seen." Fain could have learned a few lessons from her.

"It does not sound as though she was very grateful."

"Hah!" Tanner's head bobbed back. "I think she hates me now more than ever. But I can't tell if it's me person-ally she hates, or if she just resents me for taking over her husband's job." He swallowed a mouthful of coffee then shook his head. "She's a hard one to figure." Lowering the mug he added, "I have to give her credit, though. She's as clever as she is comely. She predicted every avenue that might throw us into each other's company and built a brick wall to head me off at the pass."

"And this is the woman you have set your cap for. Tanner, pardon my boldness, but there are other ladies in town who would be more than willing to settle with you if it is a family you desire."

"But she's the only one who stirs me"—Tanner patted the left side of his chest—"right here. When I look at her, my heart starts galloping like a Thoroughbred and my hands get all sweaty and I seem to grow two left feet." He felt himself turn red at the admission.

"Perhaps you have the ague," Tiny drawled with what could almost pass as amusement.

"No," Tanner laughed. "I guess I'm just smitten with her."

"Do tell. Only one struck with Cupid's arrow would comply with all her demands. You are aware that nearly every cent you earn for your regular duties will go to the widow."

"Yeah, well, it might be tough going for a while," Tanner admitted. "But things worth having don't come without making sacrifices. I'll just have to make up the dent to my income the way you said. Rounding up a few renegades."

"I do admire your ambition, Tanner, but in the meantime, you must eat. Keep in mind that seventy-five percent of accused criminals in this country never meet prosecution. Our justice system cannot prevail when they so easily evade the authorities. Seth Page's tragic murder is a prime example."

"Oh, I'm not closing his case yet. And don't worry about me eating. I've been fending for myself for a long time now."

The discussion veered toward the investigation, and Tiny suggested a few people that Tanner might interview at the celebration. Though he made notes of those to contact, Tanner could not rid himself of Eden's image. A germ of an idea had latched itself in his head.

No sooner did Tiny walk out the door than Tanner returned to the stack of records with a spurt of renewed determination. Salvaging what good there was left of the McCay name wasn't just for his personal satisfaction anymore. It wasn't to gain the respect of the townspeople either.

No, it had gone beyond that.

Catching the lowlifes that had killed Eden's husband was going to make her look at him in a new light. He'd see that it did.

Four days later Eden ushered the children inside the jailhouse. She was relieved to find it empty, she told herself. The last thing she needed while she worked was her new boss getting underfoot, distracting her.

Halfway into the drab room, a splash of color on the desk seized her notice. Eden came to an abrupt halt and stared. On a cleared spot between neatly stacked files lay a small posy of bluebonnets tied with a green ribbon. Attached to the ribbon was a small card with her name written on it in bold square letters.

Astounded, Eden set her basket on the floor and slowly reached for the flowers. Midway, she drew her hand back, then inched forward again. She brought the tiny petals to her nose, inhaling the faintly sweet scent. Unfolding the card, she read aloud, "Welcome to your first day. Tanner."

A giddy rush of delight warmed her cheeks, and she buried her nose in the blossoms. She'd never gotten flowers before. Not ever.

"Where'd you get those, Mama?"

Eden dropped the posy and whirled around, her hand over her speeding heart.

Ruthie climbed onto the chair and swiped up the bouquet. "Where'd these come from? Hey, they have your name on 'em. Did Tan McCrary give 'em to you?"

Eden's gaze veered away. "I . . . uh . . ." Damn him. He'd done it to her again. Knocked her off balance. Granted a secret wish. "Enough of this dillydallying," she stated brusquely. "We need to get started." She was here to work. Nothing more.

Reaching into the basket of cleaning supplies, she shook out a long apron and tied the strings around her waist. "Ruthie, could you help Little Seth fill the buckets

with water? And, Lissa, would you mind tending the
stove?"

On her way out the back door, Ruthie leaned toward
her sister and taunted, "See, Lissa! I told you he was sweet
on Mama!"

Lissa snorted as she grabbed the shovel and began
loading ashes from the stove into the cinder bucket.
"They're just stupid weeds he prob'ly picked in the field.
Pa woulda brought her somethin' that smells a lot prettier.
Like roses."

And cows flew, Eden thought. Seth would have been
the last person to give her bought flowers, much less go out
of his way to pick them. Even though the bluebonnets were
no better than weeds, they'd been tenderly plucked and
bound with a ribbon to match her eyes. That alone made
them worth more than the most expensive bouquet money
could buy—even if they had come from the marshal.

For the next half hour she kept busy sweeping, dusting, and directing the children to various chores. But when
she caught herself humming a romantic ballad as she
stripped the cot fragrant with Tanner's distinctive earthy
scent, the ridiculousness of her actions hit her.

Eden wound up the sheets in a tight ball. For pity's
sake, what was she doing? How could she let herself become charmed by a silly token? Flattered by the unexpect-
edness of the gift? She knew lawmen. Had spent half her
childhood being carted off in cuffs by the unfeeling bas-
tards. But she hadn't learned her lesson then. No. She'd
gone and committed herself to eight more miserable years
with one.

The flowers, no doubt, were just a sign of an ulterior
motive, Eden thought, stuffing the laundry into a pil-
lowslip. She'd often seen men perform sweet gestures for a
woman, but it usually happened when they wanted something from her.

Her mouth set in a grim line, Eden flung the bundle
over her shoulder and strode to the desk. She snatched up
the posy. Crushing the fragile stems in her fist, she tossed it
into the trash bin.

She didn't know what Tanner McCay wanted from her, but if his intention was to soften her up to get it, then he was in for a disappointment. She had nothing left to give.

"Seth, empty the wastebasket in the fire pit out back," Eden said, dropping the laundry beside her basket to take home for washing. "Lissa, throw out the dirty water and rinse out the bucket. Make sure you leave the door open so I can hear you, and you watch your little brother. Ruthie, you get clean sheets from the closet and make up the bed in the far cell."

No sooner did the children leave than the front door opened.

"Come on, Billy Joe."

Eden twirled around at the entrance of Marshal McCay pushing a stringy-haired man through the opening. Close to her own age, he wore saggy brown britches and a soaking-wet linsey-woolsey shirt. And he stank of liquor.

"But I didn't do nothin', I tell ya! It was Bobby Jack's fault!"

"And you just reckoned that he needed a good dunking in the horse trough."

"Shut up his mouth, didn't it?"

"Almost drowned him was more like it."

Tanner saw her and nodded a greeting, but continued guiding the staggering lad into the empty cell. "Just make yourself at home, Billy Joe. Your pa can pay the fine in the morning and you'll be free to go home."

"In the morning! But I'm gonna miss the fireworks!"

"The way you been tossing those bottles back, you would have missed them anyway. At least here, you'll be safe instead of passed out in some dank alley."

Eden barely listened to the debate. She blinked, certain her weary eyes were playing tricks on her. Attached to a leash that was tied around Tanner's left wrist was a chicken bringing up the rear. Docile as a lamb, it not only tolerated the tether but seemed to enjoy it.

The door clanked shut, and a groaning Billy Joe Bentley collapsed onto the unmade cot. With the bird prancing behind, Tanner ambled back around the banister and slipped the large rings of keys into the desk drawer.

Pointing, Eden stammered, "That's a . . . that's a chicken!"

He grinned that dimpled grin. He scooped the pullet up with one broad hand and stroked her arching neck. "Kinda cute, wouldn't you say? Myrtle, meet Mrs. Page. Mrs. Page, meet Myrtle."

"Myrtle? You keep a hen for a pet?"

"She took a shine to me and I couldn't resist."

There was that boyish glint in his eyes again.

Helpless against the giggles bubbling inside, Eden covered her mouth with her hand. She staunched the eruption of laughter, but her shoulders quaked and her eyes watered from the effort.

Afraid she'd burst into a fit of laughter, Eden sought concealment between the wall and the stove, but she couldn't get the sight of the very masculine marshal and his scrawny feathered companion out of her mind.

"Why, Mrs. Page, are you laughing at me?"

Attempting to compose herself, Eden didn't realize he'd come up behind her until his cool breath tickled the nape of her neck. "Of course not. I—the Bentley boy reeks of whiskey. The fumes . . ."

"You can't lie worth beans," he cut in, his eyes sparkling like dew-kissed grass.

Eden cleared her throat. "Do you know how ridiculous you look, walking a chicken like a dog?"

"I built her a coop out back, but she kept flying out of it and following me. We didn't have any problems until some mutt started chasing her. A wagon almost hit her when she flew under the wheel."

"Try clipping her wings," she said, dismayed at the breathlessness of her voice and hoping he didn't notice. They were talking about *chickens,* for pity's sake.

"I tried that a couple times with the chickens on my mother's farm, but never managed to cut them right. The little biddies still flew."

His mother's farm—no mention of a father, which left

open the possibility that she and the marshal had something in common. That the marshal and her children had something in common. A knot formed in her stomach. "The trick is to spread the wing like a fan and snip the feathers at an angle close to the skin. They can still fly, but not very high."

He relaxed his shoulder against the wall and folded his arms. "You know a bit about poultry, then?"

He stood too close for comfort. His body heat warmed her back, his manly scent embraced her. Flustered by his nearness, Eden toyed with the top button of her blouse. "A bit."

The ensuing silence increased her agitation.

"You're staring at me again, Marshal McCay." She didn't have to look at him to know. She could feel the pressure of his gaze. Tugging, beckoning.

"Maybe it's because you're prettier than bluebonnets on a hill." Softly he added, "Did you like the flowers?"

Eden brushed past him to grab the cinder bucket. It was time this conversation ended. "What are you doing here, Marshal? We had an agreement."

As though understanding that he'd entered forbidden territory, he took her cue and put distance between them. "I had to break up a pair of brawling brothers before they killed each other. Don't mind me. As soon as I write up an arrest report, I'll be out of your way."

Eden jerked her thumb toward the occupied cell. "What about him?"

"Those are sturdy key locks on the doors. I checked them myself, so you'll be perfectly safe."

"But I haven't made up the cot with fresh sheets yet."

From the cell came a rumble of snores, and Tanner gave her a lopsided grin. "I doubt he cares. He'll be out cold till tomorrow. In fact, I'll be surprised if he even remembers how he got here."

"Marshal McCay, I will not return just to make up one—"

"Tan!" Dumping the bedding she carried, Ruthie

dashed around the railing and bounded into the room. "Hi, Tan!" She threw herself at Tanner, hugging his legs.

"Hi yourself, Ruthie," he chuckled as he rubbed her back.

"Are you gonna play with us today?"

"I'd love to—"

"Some other time." Eden pried her daughter off the marshal. "Take this outside and empty it."

"But Ma-maa!"

"Ruth Rosemary, don't give me any sass now. Just do what I said so we can finish up here."

Crestfallen, Ruthie took the cinder bucket and trudged toward the back door. At the gate in the divider, she stopped and gazed at Tanner. "Can you come play tomorrow?"

Her eyes were so wide and hopeful, he knew he'd give her the moon if she asked for it. But he knew he'd better not make any promises without discussing them with Eden first. "I'll try, sweet potato."

Eden avoided his eyes as she knelt to gather the sheets. She had them in her arms and in his cell before he could even lend his help, so he wandered over to his desk and dug through the drawer for the arrest forms he remembered seeing.

Tanner pretended deep concentration in writing the report, but he was aware of every move Eden made. From beneath his lashes, he watched her make up his bed. Her arms lifted as she flipped the sheet over the mattress. A dress never looked so good on a woman. All black, with lacy pleats down the front bodice, it molded to her figure like skin. Down her slender arms. Across her high breasts. Around her small waist. From there, the gathered panels of her skirt and apron fell around her hips to her ankles. And when she leaned over to tuck the linen, with her knee in the middle of his bed, he licked his dry lips. Her bottom wiggled and swayed with her movements in a rhythm that did wild things to his bloodstream.

The pencil snapped in two between his fingers. Tanner glanced down, unaware that he'd been squeezing it that tightly. But when he glanced back up, Eden was disappearing outside. Tanner scrambled to his feet, stubbing his foot against the desk leg in his haste to follow. At the door he caught the tail end of a tense exchange between Eden and Lissa. Tanner tucked himself behind the door and shamelessly listened.

"Because I must stay home with Ruthie. I cannot leave her in the house alone."

"Why do I have to miss out because of her? Why can't I go see the fireworks by myself?"

"You know why. Must I constantly remind you?"

"It's not fair! Pa wouldn't care if I went."

"*I* care. I love you, Lissa Caroline, and I'm not about to risk losing you again. Not even if they shot all the fireworks made in China."

Tanner peered around the door. Lissa's eyes were hard, her mouth set in a defiant line. He couldn't see Eden clearly, but imagined her expression was just as intense.

He stepped from his hiding spot out into the open. Lissa spied him and bolted, and Eden, her hand on her hip, watched the girl go. He felt sorry for both of them.

Doffing his hat respectfully, he said softly, "Mrs. Page?"

Her head swung in his direction, then away. Her hand shot to her nape where her fingers plucked at wispy strands of hair.

"I couldn't help but overhear. I'll be at the celebration on patrol all day and night. If you'd like, I could watch over your daughter. That way she wouldn't miss out on all the fun."

Her spine stiffening, she replied, "Lissa knows the rules, just as she knows they are enforced for good reason."

Eden said that so often, he was beginning to wonder just what reason she had for keeping the kids under such close guard. Tiny hadn't exaggerated her obsession. Prisoners had more freedom than the Page children.

But Eden's face was tight with the warning that he'd best just keep his mouth shut about it. And yet he couldn't just let the subject drop. He'd bet his last dollar that Lissa needed someone in her corner.

Searching his mind for words that wouldn't seem like an attack on the widow, Tanner studied her children. Lissa sat on a crate, her arms folded tight across her chest, while Ruthie and Little Seth solemnly stirred ashes and paper in the stone-lined fire pit. "They must really miss their pa. It might do them good to get out of the house for a while, away from all the reminders, and I'd be more than willing—"

She sighed in a way that convinced Tanner his opinions weren't welcome, no matter how gently they were delivered.

"Marshal McCay, we are doing our very best to adjust. I think that outside interference will hinder what progress I have made with them."

"I don't want to interfere," Tanner clarified, smothering a flash of irritation. "I just want to help."

She brushed past him. "We don't need your help."

He followed her into the jail. "Well, how about my friendship? Seems to me like the kids, at least, might enjoy a little of that."

"Friendship is the last thing any of us needs from another damn tin man."

Tanner slowed his pace. It wasn't just the words, it was the scathing tone she used that made him feel like a swarm of bees was stinging his heart. "What does that mean—*tin man*?"

Grabbing a mop in one hand and a pail of water in the other, she paused with an impatient sigh. "It means that I work for you, Marshal McCay. That's all, nothing more. If you are looking for friendship or needy causes, then perhaps you should look elsewhere."

He got the feeling she was purposely evading the question. Pinching the brim of his hat, he circled it in his hands. "Mrs. Page . . ." He frowned. "I think you've formed an opinion about me that I really don't deserve. If you got to know me, you'd realize that I'm—" The stubborn lift of her chin told him words were a waste of breath.

Tanner sighed, then adjusted his hat on his head. The only way she was going to believe he had honorable intentions was for him to show her.

After he had wound the leash around his wrist and left with his chicken in tow, Eden pressed her face to the large windowpane, the bitter pill of regret dissolving in her mouth. Whether the taste was there from the defensively harsh words she'd thrown at him, or at the emotional injury she'd seen on his features, she couldn't say.

But she certainly hadn't expected him to take her advice so soon. There he stood on the boardwalk, up the road, his head thrown back as he laughed with a buxom lady standing beside him beneath the HANNAH'S HOME-COOKING CAFE sign.

The knot that had been in her stomach for most of the day twisted, and Eden clutched the mop handle close to her breast. She wished that *she* felt as free, as open to laughing with him like the other woman . . .

He strolled away from the restaurant, drawing attention with his unusual pet. Children followed him as though he were the Pied Piper, and elders pointed at him while they chuckled. And women—of all ages—paid no attention to Myrtle. Instead, they watched him as he passed by. He was not a towering man in height, but the way he walked, so proud and straight, gave one the impression that he was ten feet tall. Combined with his wholesome good looks and ready good cheer, he was a presence hard to ignore, and even harder to hate.

Was she misjudging him?

When he did something sweet, like leave flowers for her to find, or make a spectacle of himself leading a chicken around town as he was doing now, or show a kindness to one of her children, she could almost forget who he was, and a sliver of weakness would creep into her convictions.

But then she would see the shining badge on his vest, the gun at his side, and she would remember all over again.

Eden sighed forlornly, her breath fogging the glass. If

by some queer stroke of fate she was mistaken about his character, then it really made no difference. She still couldn't allow the attraction she'd felt for him the day she'd met him build into something deeper, more meaningful. She'd only be letting herself in for more pain. Lawmen were a breed unto themselves. Driven. Preoccupied. Unmerciful. Eventually, those facets of a born personality would shine through in him too. A case would arise, and he'd be off and running without a backward glance. And he'd be gone for days and days. . . . And when he returned, he would either waste the night away celebrating a successful capture with his friends, or laze around the house, sullen and snappish because he didn't get his man.

If those inevitable truths weren't enough to sway her, there was a cemetery at the end of town with a dozen headstones marking the graves of marshals and deputy marshals.

Any way she looked at it, she would lose. The children would lose. They would all suffer. And they'd had enough suffering to last a lifetime.

Chapter Seven

At eight in the morning the clear piercing cry of the train's whistle roused Tanner from a light slumber. He stood, stretching his arms high to loosen the kinks that sleeping in the chair had put in his joints, and yawned. His lips were still numb from sliding his mouth harp across them half the night, and his ears still rang with the clang of spoons, the grating of a washboard, and the rapid click of sticks beating against the walls.

Stepping outside, Tanner picked his way across the tangle of human bodies passed out on the boardwalk. The acrid smell of powder still hung in the thick air. The cupboard beside his desk was bursting at the seams with Peacemakers, Remingtons, and derringers of every size and caliber. He hadn't minded the men getting a little rowdy once the fireworks signaled the finale of the celebration, but when they'd started recklessly shooting off weapons, he and Tiny started hauling them two at a time into the cells and claimed their irons. Most were harmless souls, a little too drunk and a little too dumb, just trying to have a good time, but one thing Tanner wouldn't tolerate in his town was stupidity with a firearm. In the first place, it was against ordinance to carry a gun in town, but firing bullets into crowds was as stupid as a body could get, no matter how innocent the intention.

But neither did he expect he could lock up a dozen sotted fools in two small cages without a few of the more wild ones coming to blows. So he'd pulled out his harmonica, hoping some slow tunes would lull them to sleep. It hadn't worked that way. They'd grabbed what they could from the cells to use as instruments—from his cell mostly, because he had taken out only his personal effects and sharp objects, leaving the rest. And before he knew it, music rang through the walls as the amateur musicians packed in both cells resulted in a crude but enthusiastic band. A team of folks curious about all the commotion were drawn to the jail. When they heard the music, they'd stayed, stomping to the songs, hollering their requests, singing at the top of their lungs until just before dawn.

Tanner hooked his thumbs in his back pockets and, leaning his shoulder against the post, balanced most of his weight on one leg. Yeah, it had been a wild night, all right. They'd all be gone soon, though. Already, wives were marching down the sun-drenched road to collect their husbands and fathers, their sons. Some family members wore expressions of disgust, others of amusement.

Rosalyn Brandenburger was one of the latter.

Tanner grinned with admiration as she approached. He had to admit that Micaleb's choice in a woman wasn't too shabby. From the big city of New York, Rosalyn could pose for one of the fashion plates found in ladies' magazines. She always dressed in the height of fashion, from the silken spokes of her frilly deep-purple parasol to the toes of her polished high-ankled boots. And every layer of flounce dripping from her printed mauve walking gown complimented her hourglass figure. Even her chestnut hair reflected a true sense of upper-class style, pulled away from her lean face with combs so that fat sausage curls fell over one shoulder only. She wore none of the cosmetics ladies of society often used to bleach their skin, didn't need them. Her complexion was fair, her lips naturally a deep red, her lashes long and spiky. And when her brown eyes twinkled with good-natured humor as she scanned the men sprawled on the boardwalk, she looked like an impish girl of twenty instead of a mature woman twice those years.

Lifting a dark, winged brow, she waved her gloved hand in an arc above the slumbering heads. "Are one of these mine? Or did you stick my Micaleb in the calaboose?"

"He insisted I put him inside. Said he'd be safer in there once you realized he didn't make it home last night."

"After twenty-four years of marriage, a woman learns to accept in her man what not even the Lord Himself can change. But let's us just keep that betwixt ourselves, hmmm?"

A few minutes later Tanner had to literally wipe the grin off his face when Rosalyn emerged with Micaleb in tow.

"Ouch-ouch-ouch . . . woman, that hurts!"

"I'll give you hurt, you sorry gutter rat." She nodded regally at Tanner, as though it were perfectly normal to be hauling a six-foot, two-hundred-twenty-pound man out of the jailhouse by his ear. "Good day, Marshal. Remember, supper will be served promptly at six."

Tanner tipped his hat brim, mutely confirming the invitation he'd accepted from the couple the previous evening. Then he gave his attention over to others claiming their loved ones.

By noon the cells were empty, the boardwalks once again cleared as folks sought whatever shelter they could find from the climbing heat. Wiping sweat from his neck with his bandanna, Tanner recalled once hearing someone say that God had made Texas when He was a small boy wantin' a sandbox. A land where wells dried up and a spur striking rock could set the endless plains of thirsty buffalo grass into a raging sea of fire.

Spit-shining his badge, he examined the thick evergreen woods beyond the town limits. No, he hadn't found the desert wasteland he'd been told to expect, but it was going to take him awhile to adjust to these sweltering temperatures that made a body feel that hell was just a mile away.

Who knows? Tanner thought, smacking a mosquito on

his arm as he crossed the threshold into his office. Maybe it was too late. Maybe his brain had already been baked to a crisp. Otherwise he wouldn't be considering going against Eden's wishes and paying another visit to her house.

Tanner set the list of those he'd arrested the night before on the desk. Peeking from beneath a paperweight of quartz rock was another list, the one he'd had in his pocket up until a few hours earlier. On it he'd made notes next to the names of those he'd talked to about the day of the robbery.

Some had responded to his inquiries with open friendliness, others were wary and closemouthed. How much was due to him and what gossip had reached their ears, a common reluctance to talk with someone wearing a badge, or just a blocking out of the tragic day, he couldn't decide. Even so, begging their pardon for dampening their cheer, he pursued his plan to jar some memories.

He frowned as he read the notations. He hadn't gotten nearly as much information as he would have wished. Many of the witnesses had kept their eyes locked on Page rather than on the bandits, others had taken cover the minute Page had said, "Scat!" and hadn't seen a thing. But the few that could remember watching the drama fully played out gave details so foggy they were about as useful as rain in a flood.

The only one on the list he hadn't spoken with—not counting railroad personnel—was the victim's wife herself.

Seized with inspiration, Tanner stuffed the sheet of paper into his shirt pocket and sauntered out the door. He stopped short, then detoured around to the rear of the building. Myrtle was pecking at the ground corn scattered on the floor of her coop. The instant she spied him through the wire, her newly trimmed wings flapped her excitement and she half flew, half skated toward Tanner.

"Feel like going for another walk?" he asked, pulling her close to his chest. "You made quite an impression on Mrs. Page the last time she saw you, so you and me together will go pay her a visit." Myrtle nudged his open hand and nibbled at the calluses on his palm.

After tying Myrtle to her leash, Tanner headed toward

the widow's house with a spring in his step. It was the perfect excuse. He'd tell Eden he needed *her* accounting of what happened the day of the robbery.

He supposed he could wait until she came to work on Tuesday to interview her—*nah*. Why put off for the weekend what could be done today? He wanted to keep her flustered. The way she'd been hunched between the wall and the stove, trying to hide her laughter—and her fascination. Though her mouth said one thing, her body language told Tanner quite another story. She was as taken with him as he was with her. The only difference was, Tanner wasn't fighting *his* feelings.

Lissa was sweeping the porch when he strode up the walkway. The instant she spotted him, she bolted inside the house.

His shoulders slumped. Getting her to warm up to him wasn't gonna be easy. He wanted to tell her he understood what she was going through. His father wasn't dead, no, but until he'd finally been sent to prison, Fain had up and left him and his mother so many times, he might as well have been dead. Having lived under similar conditions as Lissa, Tanner knew the difficulty of learning to trust people again.

Sighing, knowing he had a bumpy road ahead of him where she was concerned, he tugged Myrtle's tether. "You be on your best behavior now," he warned, wagging his finger at her after they'd climbed the steps.

He waited, thinking it pointless to knock if Lissa had gone to fetch her mother. But a few moments passed with no one arriving to greet him. He knocked.

Another few minutes passed.

Shifting from one foot to the other, Tanner raised his fist to rap on the door again, when it flew open, and Eden stood in front of him. She looked plumb exhausted. Bruised crescents darkened the creamy skin beneath her eyes and lines of fatigue were grooved into the corners of her frowning lips.

She folded her arms across her bosom and thrust her hip to the side. "What do you want, Marshal?"

"Did the party keep you awake last night?"

"What gives you that idea?"

"You just don't look like you got enough sleep."

"If you came here to discuss my appearance, then you have wasted both our time."

She started to shut the door, but Tanner stopped her with his hand flat against the wood. "I'm here on official business."

"I can't imagine what sort of 'official business' you could possibly have with me," Eden sneered.

"I'm investigating your husband's murder."

The color drained from her face, and her spine went taut. He stepped forward. She stepped backward. And before Tanner knew what she intended, she slammed the door in his face.

Tanner yowled when the wood bounced off his nose. Stumbling, he doubled over from the sharp pain lancing between his eyes, his hand cupped protectively over the throbbing bridge, his eyes watering like a leaky spigot.

"Marshal McCay, are you all right?" Eden cried, rushing toward him.

She tipped his head up, and Tanner barely saw her through his blurry vision.

" 'Sakes alive, you're bleeding!"

He brought his hand away. Sure enough. Blood was gushing out of his nostrils and onto the heel of his hand. He fumbled with the knot of the kerchief around his neck. "I'm dribbling all over Lissa's clean porch."

"Come into the house."

She didn't give him a choice. She grabbed him by the elbow and steered him through a wide entryway into a room on the left, then shoved him into the first chair within reach. "I'll get some rags." Hurrying away, she called over her shoulder, "Keep your head tilted back and that bandanna pinched over your nose."

He tried obeying, but his mouth filled with the gagging taste of copper.

When Eden returned and saw that he was still sitting upright, she scolded, "You are supposed to be keeping your neck bent and your nose in the air."

"I can't. The blood feels like it's clotting between my eyes and dripping down my throat."

He heard her set a few things on the dining table. Then she approached him from behind.

"It's the only way I know of to stop the bleeding," she said, packing his nose with a folded wad of soft flannel and pulling his head back.

With a second cloth dampened in water, she wiped his drenched mustache clean. The display of concern surprised him. Mockery, or even scorn, seemed much more the norm with her. But he felt neither in her gentle touch.

Tanner closed his eyes. The stinging needles of pain were forgotten as a novel sense of contentment flowed into his soul. Was this how a man felt when he found the woman he'd been longing for? Or was he just so starved for the companionship of a female who didn't cringe at the prospect of coming within an arm's length of a McCay that he was willing to put himself at her mercy—even if she loathed the ground he walked on? He didn't think he was that desperate. But he had to admit, he could get used to this kind of fussing.

Heck, if he would've known getting hurt would bring about such a change, he would have thought of it long ago and saved himself some frustration!

"You are a vicious family," he teased, his voice muffled from his closed nasal passages. "I've shed more blood in the past week than I have my entire life."

"I am sorry, Marshal," she whispered repentantly, bowing over him. "I didn't mean to hurt you."

An apology was the last thing he expected to hear from her.

Tanner opened his eyes, and after a minute the moisture in them evaporated. In the awkward position of having his neck bent over the chair frame, he was given an upside-down view of Eden. With a will that amazed him, Tanner ignored the heat of her breasts cushioning the back of his head and concentrated on Eden's face. Sensing his regard, her lashes swept down, curling away from her lids so that they cast a delicate shadow on her tightly drawn cheekbones. He curled his fingers into his palms to keep from smoothing away the lines etched into her brow.

"Had I known the festival was going to make you lose sleep, I would have forbidden it," he said, instead touching her as tenderly with his voice as he knew how.

Eden's lips twitched, and something spiraled in his chest.

"Only God or an act of war could prevent the celebration of a national holiday," she replied. "In small towns like Dogwood Springs, parties under any circumstances are the only time folks find relief from the routine of their toiling days."

Tanner wondered, then, why she hadn't sought the same relief. But hesitant to destroy the conversational mood with questions that would clam her up, he quipped, "I wouldn't dare claim being God, but I *have* been accused of being an act of war."

"I think you know as well as I do that if you would have tried to stop their jubilee, they would have ridden you out of town on a rail."

"It would have been worth it. Not only would it have saved me a whole lot of paperwork, but you wouldn't have been robbed of a good night's rest."

"It wasn't the festival," she sighed, rinsing the cloth. "My daughter had a bad night."

"Lissa? Is she still upset about not seeing the fireworks?"

"No, it was Ruthie."

Tanner sat up in the chair, his brows snapping together, his injury forgotten.

"Get back here. Your nose hasn't stopped bleeding yet."

"Hang my nose! What's wrong with Ruthie?"

"Loud noises—" She broke off suddenly and her eyes narrowed with wariness. "What concern is it of yours?"

"Do you find it so hard to accept that I care?"

"Frankly, Marshal McCay, that is precisely what I find hard to accept." With her hand upon his shoulder, she shoved him back down into the seat. Though she resumed wiping his face clean, her caressing touch had become almost scouring.

His thoughts remained troubled over Eden's daughter, but Tanner realized that the fragile spell had been shattered. He glanced around the nearly empty room, hoping to find a safer topic for discussion to recapture the mood. His gaze landed on two draped objects hanging above a plain pine sideboard, on walls painted a homey shade of pink. He knew without looking beneath the brown broadcloth coverings that the objects were mirrors. It was a familiar practice of superstition to cover mirrors in rooms where a loved one has died, lest the next person to see their reflection also meet their end. In fact, he'd followed the practice himself when his mother passed on. But then and there it gave him an eerie feeling, sitting in the same room where the local hero had been laid out.

Eden saw the direction of his gaze, and pulled slowly away from him, her bright eyes dimming.

And Tanner thought he finally understood her reactions a little better. "Did you love him very much?"

With sudden jerky movements she plunged the rag into the blue-rimmed basin on the table, wrung out the water, then wiped the blood tracks alongside his mouth. "I thought you were here on official business, Marshal."

"Kinda hard to keep my mind on business when I've got a pretty lady washing me down."

Twin patches of color rose in her cheeks before her lips formed a prim bud. She took his hand and pressed the rag into his grasp. "Then perhaps you should wash yourself down and tell me exactly how I fit into your investigation. It seems more likely that you would speak with John Sullivan, or the other passengers who were on the train."

Tanner withdrew the wad of flannel from his face, even though his nose still felt swollen and moist inside, then sat straight in the chair. "I already have, but I was hoping you could tell me what you saw that day."

"I saw my husband murdered."

"Mrs. Page, I understand that it's difficult to talk about, and that you'd probably just as soon forget the whole thing."

Tanner leaned forward with his arms resting on the table. "But it's important that you recall every detail of what you saw so your husband's killers can be brought to justice."

She swallowed and clasped her hands together in her lap. Tanner couldn't decide if it was grief or guilt stealing the color from her cheeks. But it was one or the other. Of that he was sure. "That *is* what you want, isn't it?"

Abruptly, Eden stood, and began gathering the basin and cloths together to take to the kitchen. "Fine. You want to know what I saw? I'll tell you. But take notes, Marshal, because this is last time I will discuss it."

While Eden took the items to the kitchen, Tanner patted his pockets, searching for his pencil and notepad. She'd already started her recanting when he found them, and he had to scribble madly to get her words on paper.

"We were in town that afternoon, the children and I, picking up some odds and ends from the general store. I had just come from the jail to get money from Seth, so he was in his office right before we'd gone into Deidrich's—"

"What time was this?"

"Around one o'clock. We were inside for approximately fifteen minutes." Eden came to stand inside the doorway between the two rooms. She leaned her shoulder against the frame while wiping her hands on her apron.

One o'clock. The train would have just been pulling out of the station at that time, heading east for Shreveport, Louisiana. "Go on," Tanner urged.

"When we came out, I saw that the door to the jail was open. We passed by, but Seth wasn't there. I remember thinking it strange that he would leave the door open, because he had a habit of locking it anytime he left the building. There used to be a cabinet beside the coatrack, filled with his guns—some of them were very valuable. Anyway, I glanced around, looking for him. That's when I heard a commotion near the depot."

"What kind of commotion?"

"Yelling. Yipping."

"Did you hear anything before that?"

Eden frowned, as if searching her mind for a memory.

"Nothing out of the usual—except the train whistled three times. But then, there were a lot of people about, and wagons coming and going, so I thought something was blocking the tracks."

"No shouts, no gunshots . . ."

"No." She shook her head firmly. "Not until later."

"I'm sorry to keep interrupting. Please continue. You heard a commotion near the depot. . . ."

"Yes. We had nearly made it home when I told the children to go into the house, because I had this horrible feeling that something was about to happen. I looked back, and there were people milling around the depot. That's when I saw them—three men. They wore long linen usterettes—dusters—but their faces and heads were covered. They had their guns drawn on the people grouped together, like they were standing guard. Somebody fired into the crowd, it could have been Seth—I don't know—and killed two of the men. People were screaming, others were diving under benches and such. The third man ran.

"I was still looking for my husband, when a group of townsmen raced past me out of town. I began to chase after them, but the road became very congested, with people and horses and wagons, all, I would assume, trying to escape the melee."

Though she remained composed, her hands were linked together at her stomach, as if cradling a pain inside. "The caboose finally came into sight, and just as I'd thought, the train had stopped. People raced ahead, running faster, taking me along with them. I heard shots then, but could not see clearly with all the horses and people and wagons . . . so I pushed my way between them, and as they ducked to avoid the bullets— the next thing I knew, my husband lay in the road with a bullet hole in his stomach." She sighed with finality. "Much later I learned that a young man had witnessed the robbers lying in wait, and had ridden into the depot to warn Seth of what was happening."

"Yeah, fourteen-year-old Joseph Briggs, who bled to death last winter when he cut his foot off chopping wood."

"I never knew his name."

"Unfortunately, he was about the only soul who could identify the killers." Tanner tossed his pencil on the table with aggravation. "There has to be something else. Something left out . . ." It was the same story—more or less—that he'd heard a dozen times already. Swoop and hurrah. Then gone.

"I've told you everything I know."

"Was there nothing else that stands out as odd, or memorable?" he nearly barked.

"Marshal McCay, why don't you tell me what it is you are asking for?"

"What did they look like? Did they use their left hands to shoot, or their right? Did they talk with an unusual accent?"

"Horses."

The out-of-the-blue word halted Tanner's verbal train of thought. "What?"

"Horses. I saw horses when I ran toward Seth. It was just for an instant, but I saw four of them, galloping out of a ravine along the tracks. All were brown and very fine. One had a white stocking on its rear leg."

"I know about the hor—" He turned startled eyes toward her. "A white stocking? Are you sure?"

Eden recognized the zealous gleam in his eyes as he scrambled to retrieve his pencil and make note of the information. Even as she nodded, a chill climbed up her spine. The flesh-and-blood man she'd treated was gone, and in his place was the cold, consumed official.

Oh, why did he have to be a lawman? She glanced over his head, out the window to the road that led to town. Why couldn't he have just been a simple farmer? Or a merchant? Those professions were safe. Ordinary. Nonthreatening. As a farmer, at least for part of the year he would have a bit of idle time on his hands. Or as a merchant, once the shop closed for the night, so did the man detach himself from a day of business.

But crime never stopped. It was like a living, breathing thing that brought out the worst in humans on both sides of the law. It pulsed like a heartbeat, growing stronger with every thrilling twist. And complications fed it, that wild beast within.

Biting back tears of unreasonable disappointment, Eden wished she never had met Tanner McCay. Witnessed those endearing sides of him that she used to hope to find in her husband. More, she wished he wouldn't throw her crumbs of kindness, then reveal what she knew all along. That deep down he was no different.

But then, wishes were worthless anyway.

In a subdued manner she said, "If that's all, Marshal, then it's time you were on your way."

He tucked his pencil and tablet into his pocket and, dabbing beneath his slightly enlarged nose with the kerchief, unfolded his lean body from the chair. "Thank you, Mrs. Page. You've been very helpful."

The statement was issued offhandedly as he shuffled toward the hallway. And though it didn't surprise her that she'd been forgotten so quickly—after all, she had obviously given him a fresh lead to a stale case—the sting she felt at his absent dismissal did give her cause to wonder. She'd thought herself over and above such hurt.

Hugging her middle, she strolled after him and found Lissa standing in the hall, glaring at his back.

"What's *he* doing here?"

Eden moved toward the door and held the screen partly open as she, too, watched him descend the porch steps. "He had some questions about your pa," she answered truthfully.

"Did you tell him it was none of his business?"

"No, I . . ." Eden left the sentence hanging when she spotted Ruthie and Little Seth bounding around the side of the house into the front yard, with Myrtle, leash trailing and wings spread, in hot pursuit behind them. "What on earth . . . ?"

She stepped outside onto the porch, letting the screen door slam shut.

"Mama! Mama! Look what we found!"

Tanner's head jerked up at the sound of Ruthie's excited cry, and a devastating smile broke out on his face. "Myrtle!"

"We found it on the porch!"

"Yeah, it was just sittin' there," Seth added, "and look what it givved us!" He proudly held up a small brown egg as though it were a rare jewel.

"*Gave*, Little Seth," Eden corrected her son. "And the hen belongs to Marshal McCay." She pointed down the walkway.

As though just realizing his presence, Ruthie and Little Seth twirled around.

"Tan!"

"Marshal Mac!"

"It's your chicken?"

"Where'd ya get her?"

"Can Little Seth keep the egg?"

Laughing, he retraced his steps to the base of the stairs, where the children had finally come to a stop. Their eyes were glittering like the specks in a piece of sandstone. From their discovery, yes, Eden thought, but brighter because of the marshal's visit.

"So you found my wayward friend, did you? I guess I must have forgotten to tie her to the porch." He lifted the hen in his arms and ruffled her feathers as she cradled against his broad chest. "Thank you for taking care of her for me."

Earnestly, Seth declared, "Oh, she wasn't no trouble. She's been follerin' us all over the yard—"

"And she already ate her lunch. I gave her some corn from Mama's garden," Ruthie said. "Hey, what happened to your nose? It's big and red."

He touched his nose, then glanced up at Eden with amusement. "I had a little accident."

Embarrassed heat filled her neck and cheeks.

Ruthie slid her hand into Tanner's. "You came to play with us, huh? Just like you promised."

Again his eyes rose to hers, and the same blast of entrapment that showed in his eyes coursed through Eden's heart. She stared back at him, until a mutual discomfort at being put on the spot transformed into a current that had

nothing to do with the children. It became an intimate exchange of awareness, of him as a man, and her as a woman.

Disturbed by the leaping of her pulse, the swelling of
her breasts, Eden severed the visual contact. It was simply a
physical response to an attractive male after so many
months of being widowed and alone. Yes, that sounded reasonable. Improper, but reasonable.

She'd just bury her feminine desires as she had so often
before. She'd mastered the ability during the years as Seth's
wife.

Except . . . Seth had never awakened sensations of this
degree. How was it that Tanner McCay could with just a
look?

Alarmed at the possibility that she might not be as re-
sistant to the marshal as she'd first resolved, Eden sucked in
her breath and struggled for yet another excuse to sway
Ruthie and Little Seth from his company.

But she made the mistake of looking into the children's
faces: her daughter's held such hope; her son's, such eagerness . . .

And she was lost.

"I believe the marshal was heading back to his office,
but he might be able to spare a few minutes."

"Heck, I've got the whole afternoon!" he quickly as-
sured them. "Maybe we can talk your mama into all of us
going fishing?"

Ruthie bounced up and down with glee, and Seth
punched air with a loud "Yippee!"

Tanner's expression implored her to agree. Eden
closed her eyes and nodded, unable to refuse. She supposed
it was the least she could do after clobbering him with the
door. At least by fishing, she could keep a bit of distance between them.

"I just have to take Myrtle back to her coop and let my
deputy know where I'll be. I shouldn't be long, but why
don't you go on ahead and I'll meet you?"

"Follow the creek behind the bank upstream until you
reach the fork. Take the left branch, and just beyond the

split oak, you'll see a wooden bridge. That's where you can meet us."

Once Tanner and Myrtle headed for town, Eden collected their gear from the closet beneath the stairwell while Ruthie and Little Seth scampered to the garden and dug for worms, and Lissa sullenly packed a basket of food to snack on.

Fishing had never held much appeal for her when they'd gone in the past, to give their diet a bit of variety, but neither had she and the children done so for the sheer pleasure of it.

Eden told herself that that was the cause for her anticipation as they tromped through the woods on their way to the best catching spot by the bridge. It had nothing whatsoever to do with Tanner McCay's joining them.

A half hour later Tanner missed Little Seth's squeals of delight at the thirteen-inch catfish whipping at the end of his line. An hour after that, three fat catfish had been strung on the line, but there were no triumphant cries, only questions of what was taking "Marshal Mac" so long. And fifteen minutes after that, two more fish had joined their scaly brothers, but Seth and Ruthie no longer cared. There was still no sign of Tanner.

And though it had dawned slowly as Eden and the children scanned the banks of the shimmering creek, vainly searching for his lanky form as they'd been doing for nearly two hours, she finally realized what a fool she'd been to believe he'd show up at all.

He wasn't coming.

He'd made up his own excuse.

And the bastard . . . she clenched her fists around her pole . . . the bastard was leaving her to deal with her children's disappointment.

Chapter Eight

"You are terribly late, Tanner," his deputy notified him, glancing at his timepiece.

"I know." Having donned a clean shirt, he shrugged into his vest then adjusted his gun belt. "But she was once married to a marshal—I'm sure she'll understand when I tell her Old Man Washburn was beating on his wife again." Tanner grabbed the pole he'd borrowed from Hollis on his way back to town from the Washburn place.

"There aren't any laws against that."

"I know that too. That's why I brought the miserable bum in for skipping out on that fine he owes for shooting up Widow Tilly's barn." Tanner spared a glower for the filthy, bearded brute standing with his hands gripping the cell bars and his eyes cold as ice on a rusty water pump. "Won't keep him long enough, though. He'll be home before you know it, and probably light into the missus worse than he did today." That was the frustrating part of this job. Just because a person did something morally wrong didn't mean it was illegal. "Anyway, thanks for keeping an eye on him for me, Tiny."

"I shall keep myself occupied with Bacon and Bligh's accounts while you go about *wooing* the widow." Tiny grimaced as he made himself comfortable in Tanner's chair.

Tanner settled his hat on his head. "You don't approve of me courting Mrs. Page, do you?"

"I simply feel your pursuit of her will result in failure."

Checking the attachment of the hook at the end of the line, he peered at his deputy from underneath the rim of his hat. The sun pouring in from the window brightened the dim room, but sure didn't shine any light on Tiny's reason for such a cynical remark. "You ever get a gut feeling about someone?"

"Intuitive perception? Occasionally."

"Well, I have a gut feeling about her," Tanner stated, winding the line around the pole. "It's like she's locked herself up. Closed herself off from life. And she's keeping her young'uns in the same prison. I aim to show them what they've been missing." Throwing the door open, Tanner winked. "And I don't aim to fail."

Swinging the bucket at his side, Tanner whistled as he crossed the dusty road, pole propped against his shoulder. He nodded to folks along the way, but even the odd looks he received now and then couldn't dampen his high spirits.

It was an afternoon made for leisure. The steamy spell of weather that had lasted all this long week while he settled into his new home and position had finally broke a short while ago. Judging from the quick drop in temperature, the scratchy clouds above, and the clarity of the train whistle earlier, the chances were high for some rain later tonight. But for now, a pleasant breeze freshened the air with scents of a day in the full bloom of summer. And Tanner could think of nothing more enjoyable than spending it with Eden and the children. Tiny knew where to find him if he needed him, which—Tanner hoped to God—he wouldn't.

He kept a brisk pace as he rounded the rear of the red-brick building. Dried pine needles covered many a root, and mimosa plants reached out their fernlike branches to swat him in the face. He inhaled deeply of the greenery, of the spring-fed water of the tumbling creek, and savored the sounds of mockingbirds imitating one another and squirrels scampering from limb to limb.

He found the fork, and following it to the left, soon spied the oak split nearly in two from rot, its bald branches reaching out like the charred arms of a scarecrow. A smile broke out on his face. The bridge waited a hundred feet ahead, where Eden and the kids would be . . .

Leaving?

No, Tanner thought, picking up his pace. Maybe the shade cast from the surrounding trees was just making it appear like they were packing up. Leastwise, he hoped.

But the closer he got, the clearer it became that they were, indeed, getting ready to leave. Eden was lifting her ever-present basket, while Ruthie took Little Seth's cane pole from him so he could bend over the banks to grab hold of a line of fish from the water. Lissa rose from the bed of needles, where she had been sitting under a tree, and brushed off the back of her paisley-printed dress.

Guilt assailed him as he crashed through the under-brush. He shouldn't have taken it for granted that they'd hold out for his arrival. She hadn't been exactly willing to go on this outing with him to begin with.

At that moment the twigs snapping beneath his heavy tread alerted Ruthie to his arrival. Her head snapped up, her mouth fell open, her eyes sparkled her joy at seeing him.

"Mama! He made it! He made it!"

Then she raced toward him, and Tanner spread his arms to catch the calico-clad bundle of glee leaping at him. Little Seth, chasing after his sister, also jumped toward Tanner. He shifted Ruthie into one arm and caught Seth with the other.

"Hi, scamps."

"We didn't think you were comin', Tan. Mama said you prob'ly got sidewinded."

"Side*tracked,* doo-doo head," Lissa corrected Ruthie with scorn.

"I caught two catfish," Little Seth boasted. "One's as big as Ruthie—oh, no, I dropped 'em in the grass!"

Tanner barely heard the claim, barely felt the boy scramble for his freedom to retrieve his abandoned prize. Tanner focused on Eden alone. He couldn't tell if she was angry—and rightly so—or just indifferent. She stood on the bridge, her arms hanging limply at her sides, the basket in one hand an inch off the ground. Her face was empty of expression.

His boots scuffed the planks of the bridge as he closed the distance between them. Seth was busy scouring the grass for his lost fish; Ruthie had attached herself to him, with her arms looped around his neck and her legs wrapped around his hips, just above the gun belt he wore. And Lissa—as usual—made sure no less than five feet remained between herself and him.

But all he could think about was the excuse Eden had made to explain his delay. Reaching her, he threaded his fingers through the glossy black hair pulled over her ear and plaited into a long braid. "Did you really think I wouldn't show up?"

"It didn't matter either way, Marshal McCay," she said with a shrug. "If one doesn't expect, one does not get disappointed. That is my outlook, anyway."

The careless movement of her shoulder was in complete contrast with her rigid posture. She hadn't rejected his touch, though. The sign was encouraging.

"*Would* you have been disappointed?" he asked, a sliver of hope making its way into his heart.

"*I* never expected. The children, on the other hand . . ."

"Eden." Her beautiful name rolled off his tongue like warm honey, leaving a sweet taste in his mouth. He savored it for a moment before continuing. "I would never make a promise to you—or them—that I had no intention of keeping."

At last she seemed aware that his hand intimately cupped the side of her head. She tore herself away. "So what kept you detained—no, let me guess. You suddenly remembered that you had a stack of summonses on your desk that had to be delivered."

"Close." Tanner set Ruthie down and leaned against the railing. "Washburn mistook his wife for a sparring partner. I couldn't arrest him for beating her, but I did manage to find a warrant on file so I could lock him up. I hurried as fast I could to get here." He sensed she didn't want to hear excuses or apologies, but he hoped the latter showed in his eyes. "Did I miss the best hours of fishing?"

"Lissa and I each caught one, Little Seth caught two." She slung the basket over her arm again. "Actually, we were just packing up."

Tanner stayed her with his palm against her shoulder. "Think we could try for a couple more?"

"Can we, Mama? I didn't catch any fish yet," Ruthie reminded her.

Eden wavered.

"We can't have Ruthie going home empty-netted," Tanner pressed.

"Oh, all right," she sighed.

"Goody!" Ruthie cried. "Seth, we git to stay!"

"But we've been here for more than two hours and the children are tired, so we can't stay much longer."

The crooked grin he responded with tugged at her heartstrings, but Eden vowed that no matter how charming he looked when his lips curved in that disconcerting way and his dimple slashed his cheek, she wouldn't forgive him. She'd endure his company, that was all. For the sake of the children. He owed them this time, and they deserved it for waiting.

"Hey, Tan?" Ruthie called after they had all settled along the bridge's railing and cast their lines into the water. "How come birds fly south for the winter?"

"Well, I s'pect it's because they like the warm weather."

"No, silly. 'Cause it's too far to walk!"

Ruthie's joke prompted an avalanche of giggles, and Little Seth piped in, wanting his own glory. "What time is it when a moose sits on a fence?"

"Time to get a new fence," Tanner told Eden out of the corner of his mouth. But to Seth he said, "I don't know. Four o'clock?"

"Time to build a new fence!"

Tanner actually looked surprised that he'd guessed the answer. "Okay, okay, I got one."

"Marshal *McCaaay,*" Eden cautioned. She knew what kind of jokes grown men tended to tell.

"It's clean!" He shifted from one leg to another and recast his line. "This fellow from Missouri and this fellow from Texas were sitting in a sal—ah, barbershop, boasting about how much land they owned. The Missourian says, 'I have me a farm on five acres,' to which the Texan replied, 'Oh, yeah? Well, I can get on my horse at sunrise and ride until sunset, and *still* be on *my* farm.' The Missourian thinks about this for a minute. Then he finally says, 'Yep. I had me a horse like that once too.' "

In spite of herself, Eden's lips twitched. Ruthie and Little Seth, however, merely gave him blank frowns.

The next half hour passed by as he entertained them all with delightful stories, "Jack" tales, and humorous jokes designed for the children that almost made Eden laugh out loud. And though she was able to hold back her laughter, she could not quite prevent herself from relaxing and inwardly enjoying his company.

He hooked two more fish, and the expression on his face was so like her four-year-old son's that she once more found herself doubting years and years of ingrained opinions.

Then Tanner did something that left her completely flabbergasted. Something she had never seen a lawman do. Something that her husband would have died before doing.

He unpinned the star on his vest and tucked it into the small pocket below.

Unprepared, Eden reeled from the act. For this afternoon, this glorious summer afternoon, she and the children didn't have to share him with anyone. He wasn't the preoccupied marshal ready to desert them at a moment's notice—he was just a man taking time out of his demanding schedule to fish with a family he barely knew.

Her strictly maintained convictions were laid bare, open and raw and vulnerable to his influence.

He wasn't supposed to be human.

And Eden floundered, suddenly overwhelmed by the frightfully powerful flood of emotion. She swallowed the lump in her throat. It was time this little farce ended before she did something really stupid.

Like fall for his country-boy appeal.

"Children, it's time we called it a day." She wondered if he was even aware of what he'd done and hoped he didn't notice how it affected her. "Lissa, would you mind—"

But Lissa was no longer sulking at the opposite end of the bridge, where she had taken up a militant stance from the moment the marshal arrived.

Eden scanned the banks on either side of the river. "Lissa? Lissa, where are you?"

"Maybe she's just hiding from me," Tanner suggested with a note of wisdom. Her daughter's unconcealed animosity toward him obviously hadn't escaped his notice.

Grabbing Ruthie's and Little Seth's hands, Eden marched off the bridge. Lissa's frequent rudeness was difficult enough to contend with, but this disappearing act went beyond Eden's tolerance. "I mean it, Lissa, you come out here this instant!"

She was hardly aware of dragging the younger children along while she ducked beneath low-hanging branches, tramped over ferns and saplings, and crunched pinecones beneath her boots. She explored every shadow that moved, checked every nook and cranny under the braces of the bridge. The glare of the sun upon the shallow creek made her eyes burn from staring at it for any sign of her child frolicking in the water—or, worse, floating on the surface.

Grappling for the anger that was quickly losing strength, Eden fought the building pressure in her chest. She shouted Lissa's name until her voice went hoarse, each call distantly echoed by the marshal. But the longer they searched, the more difficult she found it to breathe. No answers met any of their biddings. Only an eerie silence. Even the birds had stopped singing.

After endless minutes of combing the woods along the creek, Tanner on one side, Eden on the other, the panic she'd tried so hard to keep at bay clawed its way into her veins. Wild-eyed, she met Tanner at the bridge and clutched at his shirtsleeves. "Where could she be?"

Tanner crushed Eden's quaking frame to his chest, trying to hide his own anxiety. Hot terror radiated from her every pore, fairly scorching him. "Eden, calm down. We'll find her."

"But we've looked everywhere! *Everywhere!*"

Ruthie and Little Seth looked on with fearful worry while Tanner held their mother, sliding his hands up and down her back. "Maybe she just went home."

"But she wouldn't just leave! She knows better!" Eden's voice broke on a sob, her tears soaking his shirt-front. "Someone has taken her, I just *know* someone has taken her!"

He tucked his chin against the top of her head. She was irrational with worry, didn't know what she was saying. "Let's just check at the house before we go jumping to any conclusions."

And if Lissa wasn't there, he'd cut straight to town and collect as many of the townspeople as he could. They'd form a search party. Not one twig would go unturned until they found Eden's daughter.

He didn't speak any of his thoughts aloud to Eden, but as they quickly gathered their belongings and hastened toward the house, he mentally listed all those he would enlist for help.

Tiny and Micaleb and Rosalyn. Hollis and Hannah. Who else knew the area well? Oh, yeah, Billy Joe and Bobby Jack. And Simon Pratt from the livery. Tipp Avery from the saloon . . .

When they reached the house, Tanner's knees went weak with relief at the sight of Lissa, sitting on the back porch, holding Ruthie's corn-husk doll to her chest.

But Eden stormed full speed ahead as though she were ready to strangle her daughter. "Lissa Caroline Page, you and me are fixing to tangle."

She seized the girl by the upper arms, shaking Lissa

once so hard that Tanner thought her head would snap clean off her neck.

"What do you mean, running off like that without a word to anyone?"

"I was tired. And I was hot after sittin' in the sun for hours waitin' for"—she jerked her thumb Tanner's way—"Mighty Mac over there."

"That's no excuse! You *know* better than to ever leave without telling me—"

"Eden, take it easy—"

"*You* mind your own business!" she lashed out at Tanner. "She knows the rules! She . . ." And suddenly she dropped to her knees and enveloped Lissa in a bone-crushing hug. "You know the rules, Lissa." Eden began to weep. "You *know* the rules."

"I'm sorry, Mama."

"I thought I'd lost you. Oh, mercy, I feel as though I've aged a hundred years." She clutched Lissa tighter to her, wildly stroking her braids. "Don't you ever, *ever* do anything like that again, do you hear me?"

"Yes, ma'am." Lissa nodded rapidly and sucked in a sniffle.

Pushing her back, Eden gripped Lissa's arms. *"Do you?"*

Sensing that Eden's anger was again mounting, Tanner wrested her hands away. "Leave the girl be, Eden. Can't you see she's truly sorry?"

She looked at him, and the lingering terror in her eyes made Tanner shudder. He kept his gaze steady on Eden as he softly said, "Lissa, honey, why don't you go on to your room. Your ma's had a bad fright, and she's real shook up right now, but I think once it soaks in that you're safe, she'll come talk to you."

Lissa didn't hesitate to obey.

Ruthie and Little Seth passed by, shock and worry and fear plain on their faces. Tanner gave them an assuring nod, silently urging them to seek out their big sister.

Once the children had gone inside, Tanner guided Eden to the porch. He sat her down on the bottom step, where she gazed vacantly over the line of the pine trees, into the distant horizon painted light orange. Her face had become gaunt and weary after Lissa's disappearance, with a sort of tragic beauty that made him want to spend the rest of his life protecting her.

Loving her.

A swift and powerful dawning swept through Tanner. He'd known her for hardly more than a week, but he knew without a shred of doubt that he was falling in love with her.

For all the good it did him.

If she hadn't already learned of his shady background, she would soon enough. And even the slim chance he might have of building something with Eden would be ruined.

Yeah, he really needed to confess his past to her, but it would have to wait. This was not the time. She still hadn't fully recovered from the ordeal with her daughter.

He settled down on the step above her, flanking her with his legs, and laid his hands on her stiff shoulders. "You want to talk about it?"

She tensed further beneath his touch. "Talk about what?"

"You reacted pretty strong just now."

"My daughter disobeyed, Marshal McCay," she responded flatly. "Should I have patted her on the head and acted as if it were all right?"

"I'm just not sure hollering at her did any good."

"Do you have children?"

"No—"

"Then what gives you the right to judge how I should or shouldn't react?"

"I don't have young'uns of my own, but I remember what it was like being seven going on forty." Tanner squeezed her shoulders through the thin black fabric of her widow's weeds. "She's just a little girl. A lot of things have happened to her that are turning her world upside down. She's lost her pa. Her brother and sister probably get on her nerves. She doesn't know what to make of me. . . ." He let the sentence dwindle while he absently massaged Eden's neck, searching for words that wouldn't offend her. He had no business telling her how to raise her kids. And yet he wished he would have had someone sticking up for him while he'd lived under the shadow of a wastrel father and a mother who'd just up and quit on living. "I think she's trying to find out what her purpose in life is, and sometimes she acts out her frustration in ways that test your limits. She just needs a little time to herself now and then to sort things out. To cope with all that has been thrown at her."

"Are you insinuating that I am denying her that privacy?"

"Would it be so hard to give her a bit of freedom?"

"Yes," Eden whispered so softly he barely heard her.

"What's the worst that could happen?"

"I could lose her."

Tanner watched the thickening clouds for a long while before he spoke again. "There is more than one way to lose someone you love. Years back, I knew this boy. He had a wild streak in him a mile wide and his ma was bent on ridding him of it. She kept him on a leash so tight it pretnear choked him. One day he just up and headed down that long road to bad. She never saw him again."

Eden shrugged free of his hands and moved to stand several feet away, rubbing the back of her neck where his thumbs had been kneading the knotted muscles.

"I guess what I'm trying to say is that sometimes our best intentions go awry. Lissa is amazingly bright, and a bit high-strung. She might reach an age, and be so hungry for independence, she'll run as fast and far as she can."

"So what am I supposed to do?" she cried. "You seem to have all the answers. You tell me. If I allow them to break rules, I risk putting them in danger. But if I enforce the rules, I risk watching them repeat my mistakes."

Her mistakes? What had she done, run away from as strict a home as she kept? Struck out on her own to prove she was her own person?

It was only a hunch, but if he was right, then they had more in common than he'd ever dreamed. He had his own proving to do. That he was stronger and more honorable than his father. That he could not be romanced into a life of crime like his brother had been.

'Course, nothing would have made Fain McCay prouder than to have *both* his sons follow in his footsteps. A chill took hold of Tanner when he recalled how close he'd actually come to doing just that before he'd finally escaped.

But not all families were as corrupt as his. Surely if Eden's family knew what dire straits her husband's death had left her in, they would want to help.

"Eden, I doubt that any loving parent wants to see their children make mistakes, especially the same ones they did. Your parents probably felt the same way when they were raising you."

"I wouldn't know. My parents couldn't be bothered with raising me at all. They dumped me at the side of a road in the middle of nowhere when I was barely a year old."

Tanner's breath caught in his throat. "My God," he gasped, "you were just a baby!" Just when he thought he was beginning to figure Eden out, she'd gone and scrambled his theories. Given how closed she was about her personal life, the last thing he'd expected was for her to reveal such a staggering bit of information. It was almost too cruel to believe. What would make someone do such a terrible thing? "Maybe . . ." His throat worked down a thick lump of emotion. "Maybe they didn't leave you on purpose. Something could have happened—"

"Why must you try to paint a pretty picture of what they did?" Eden barked over her shoulder. "They abandoned me. It's as simple as that."

"Who raised you, then?"

"I raised myself."

"No, I mean, who found you? Where did you live?"

He watched her as she stared at the horizon. His pulse gave a shameful leap at the sight of her, but glory be, she was so pretty. Boldly, the setting sun kissed her face. Her cheeks. Her lashes. Her chin and her neck and her hair. He wanted to be the sun right now. That big ball of fire that shone down on the land, making everything it touched blossom and come alive with its warmth.

"I was told that an old freight driver found me half dead in the ditch and took me to the closest orphanage. Undernourished, they said." She swallowed heavily, but her level voice gave him no hint to her feelings. "For several years afterward, I was too sickly for anyone to adopt. Then the War Between the States broke out, and there just weren't enough families nearby who were willing or able to take in all the children. So they herded us onto a train like we were cattle and shipped us West. Some got lucky and were placed in decent homes, while others were taken in by folks wanting a cheap means of labor."

Wow. He never would have guessed that Eden hadn't been brought up in some well-to-do family. She seemed so educated, so poised. "Which of those took you in?" Tanner asked, dreading her answer.

"Neither. I wound up going back to the orphanage."

He didn't need to ask why. No one had chosen her. Even though she had the blood-heating curves of a mature woman, she was still so thin, a body would have to shake the sheets to find her. So it seemed a safe guess that as a child recovering from near starvation, she hadn't given anyone the impression of a sturdy worker. And if she was as reserved then as she was now, she wouldn't have won over any hearts with a bubbly personality.

"But I survived," she said, her chin jutting out. "And I did what I had to do to get by until I married Seth."

He didn't even want to imagine what she'd done "to get by."

No wonder she watched her children like a hawk. They were all that she had. She probably feared if she didn't hold on tight to her kids, she'd fail them the same way her folks had failed her. And she had no one to confide her fears in, no one to compare mothering skills with. There hadn't been anyone to teach her.

Yeah, a lot of things were beginning to make sense now. Why she kept to herself all the time—he didn't much

blame her for not trusting people—and why she had agreed
to work for him when she clearly didn't want to.

Fury boiled inside him at the thought of the people
who had tossed her away and hardships she'd faced because of their cruelty. It seemed that he and Eden shared a
common bond. He found a strange comfort in the revela-
tion; maybe she wouldn't judge him too harshly when he
did tell her about his blood ties to the boy who'd been lured
off the straight and narrow.

Tanner pushed himself off the stoop. Reaching her
side, he tipped her chin toward him, and the anguish in her
eyes made his chest hurt. "You have got to be the most
amazing, most courageous woman I have ever met. My
mother would have called you spit-and-polish. Fighter on
the inside, elegance on the outside."

She opened her mouth as if to shush the praise, but
Tanner pressed his fingers to her lips to stop her. "I am
truly sorry that your childhood wasn't all rainbows and
sunshine. If I'd had the power to spare you from that suffering, I would have done it"—he snapped his fingers—"like
that."

Her lashes shuttered down over her eyes, but not before he noticed a flare of skepticism in the deep green
depths. And when she tilted her head away with a sour
frown, he shoved his hands into his pockets, using every
last ounce of restraint to keep from wrapping his arms
around her. Back at the bridge she had sought comfort from
him. Right now, though, there seemed to be a wall between
them thick enough to stop a bullet.

"If you think about it, though," Tanner said at length,
"a lot of good came out of those blows you took. So maybe
you have regrets." He lifted one shoulder in lazy dismissal.
"Maybe you think you made some bad decisions. Don't we
all? Life is filled with forks in the road and we each have to
choose our own paths. If you would have taken any of
yours differently, you might never have married your husband, might never have borne those three terrific
young'uns."

"Are you always this optimistic?"

"Hardly," he quipped. "It takes practice."

They stood together for several minutes, she so close yet so far away. The wind picked up, ruffling the tops of the cornstalks in the garden, and the damp scent of impending rain filled the air.

Eden rubbed her arms and turned toward the house. "I need to be getting inside."

Tanner nodded. "Yeah. I need to make sure Old Man Washburn is all settled in. I take it that I don't have to tie that scarf around the pole for the next couple days."

"No, it's not necessary this time. I'll see that his meals are delivered."

She took a step away; he took a step away. Then they both stopped and spoke at once.

"I had . . ."

"I would . . ."

Then Tanner chuckled.

Eden licked her lips.

Silence stretched between them. Finally Tanner said, "I just wanted to tell you that I had a nice time earlier."

"Yes. It was a pleasant afternoon, before—well, before . . . you know." She gestured to the upper story of her home. Hesitantly she added, "Would . . . would you like to join us for supper? It seems only fair, since you helped catch the fish."

"I'd enjoy nothing better, but I'm afraid I already made other plans for this evening." 'Course, he would have broken his dinner engagement with Rosalyn and Micaleb in a heartbeat if Eden had sounded sincere. But like everything else, the words seemed dragged out of her. "Besides, you and Lissa probably need to hash some things out. I'd only be in the way."

With a tip of his hat, his long strides carried him out of sight.

Watching him go, Eden wondered if his other plans included a buxom restaurant owner. She quashed an unsettling seed of envy and loaded into her arms the fishing gear that had been scattered across the yard. It meant nothing to her what he did with his time. Although she wished she would have thanked him for helping her search for Lissa, she was glad to see him go. Glad he hadn't accepted her invitation. He knew more about her now than any other living soul, and sitting across a dinner table from him would have been decidedly awkward.

The clouds rolled in, releasing a swift shower of rain just as Eden threw open the back door. Mercy, what had possessed her to spill such private, utterly humiliating details of her childhood to him, a virtual stranger? He had coaxed the words from her simply by listening.

And asking questions as though he were honestly interested.

Without criticism. Without contempt.

If he had any inkling of how unruly she'd been growing up, how often she had deserved the stones that had been thrown at her and her bags being tossed out front doors, he wouldn't be calling her a "spit-and-polish" anything. He'd be calling her a hopeless wretch. Troublesome baggage.

Eden's step through the hallway faltered and she shut her eyes. Why was he always so nice to her? There had to be a reason. She certainly didn't encourage his kindness. No matter what she did, he remained calm and reasonable, or he came back with a humorous quip that made her ashamed of her own behavior. If he had any idea how badly she thought of him half the time, he wouldn't be so nice.

Shoulders slumped, she started down the hall again. A drop of moisture plopped onto her cheek. Eden glanced at the ceiling. Dammit, the last thing she needed was for the roof to spring a leak. She couldn't see any telling cracks in the overhead structure. She freed one of her burdened arms and curiously brought her fingers to the wet spot. She tasted it.

It wasn't a raindrop. It was a teardrop. Hers.

Chapter Nine

LONG AFTER THE children had fallen asleep to the gentle melody of crackling rain against the window, Eden remained on the edge of the girls' bed. Little Seth had curled up at the foot of it and dozed off before she could take him to his own room, Lissa's hands were folded beneath her cheek, and Ruthie lay next to her sister with her thumb in her mouth and the corn-husk body of Annie tucked close to her chest.

Bone weary, Eden's tired body urged her to catch a few winks herself. She couldn't make herself leave, though. Not yet. She just wanted to sit for a little longer, close to her babies, where she belonged. Today had been a brutal reminder of the price one could pay for negligence.

Eden smoothed the gentle auburn waves of Lissa's hair away from her face. She might have lost her today. Yes, this time Lissa had simply wandered off; the two of them had discussed her complete disregard for the rules until Lissa had grown too drowsy to talk.

But Lissa hadn't been the only one to break the rules. Eden knew she was equally guilty, if not more so. A good mother would have been paying more attention. A good mother would have known exactly where her children were at every given second. Would never have taken her eyes off any of them for an instant. Hadn't she been taught that lesson long ago?

Hadn't the devastation of losing Lissa once before been enough? Apparently not, Eden berated herself, for instead of being a good mother, she'd let herself become distracted by Tanner McCay. His smile. His laughter. His open affection toward Ruthie and Little Seth and his patient understanding with Lissa.

Her traitorous attraction for the man could have cost her one of her babies.

Would it be so hard to give her a little freedom?

Eden closed her eyes in remembered agony. He had no idea how hard. Or how much pain was involved. But she knew; it haunted her every breathing moment.

It didn't haunt the tin man's.

Of all the things Rosalyn could have picked to serve for dinner, she had to choose chicken. Baked golden brown. Sprinkled with green flakes of some kind of herb.

Just the sight of it sent Tanner's stomach turning.

He pushed the cut-up breast around on the pretty china plate in front of him. Hopefully, if he mixed the meat in well with the snap beans and diced potatoes, his hostess wouldn't notice that he wasn't eating.

For the umpteenth time, he wished he wouldn't have promised to spend the evening with the Brandenburgers. What if Ruthie had a bad night again? What if Little Seth hadn't found a safe place to hide his penny from Patch?

What if Lissa was still crying?

What if Eden needed him?

The way she'd looked when he'd left her, so quiet and withdrawn . . .

". . . ain'tcha, Mac?"

Tanner's head jerked up. "I'm sorry, Micaleb. What's that you were saying?"

"Well, Rosalyn asked if something was wrong with your food and I said you were prob'ly just done in from last night." The sturdy oak chair Micaleb leaned back against barely fit his lumberjack-sized body.

He glanced guiltily at Rosalyn, who sat at the opposite end of the dining table in the couple's private quarters. Tanner's gaze was drawn to the ivory cameo pinned to the throat of her high-necked blue blouse. It must have cost a fortune. He'd never be able to afford something so fine. A peace officer's salary barely covered the basic necessities. And now that he'd hired Eden, it would take him forever and a day to save up enough money to buy something half as nice as the brooch.

The idea of loving Eden suddenly sounded downright scary. He had so little of value to offer her. Was he the fool Tiny accused him of being? Heck, he'd never fallen in love before. He didn't figure there was much to it except to just let it happen. But what if he did it wrong? What if Eden found him lacking?

What if she couldn't learn to love him back?

He couldn't say how long Rosalyn waited before he remembered his manners. Shamefaced, Tanner shifted uncomfortably in the chair. "I beg your pardon, Miz Rosalyn. It's not the food. I guess my mind just wandered."

"See, woman, I told you it wasn't the food. No one can pass by this place without sampling Mellie's chicken. We got ourselves the finest cook in the state."

Rosalyn cast her husband an exasperated smile, but as she removed their plates to a serving table nearby, she gave Tanner a sympathetic look that held a volume of wisdom.

"So, had a busy first week, did ya?" Micaleb asked, removing bits of food from between his teeth with a slender steel toothpick.

"Nothing unusual," Tanner replied, thankful for the diversion. "Chased a loose cow back into its pasture Saturday, and Ruddy Dearpot thought she had a prowler in her house Sunday night. Turned out she just forgot to close her front door and the wind kept slapping it against the frame."

"Vern Tilly said he saw you over at the sawmill Monday, too."

"Just went by there to pick up some scrap lumber Hollis said I could have to finish my chicken coop. Caught him just as he was locking the doors for the night."

"Hollis always closes the mill 'bout five, though."

Quizzically, Tanner nodded. What did that have to do with anything?

"That's funny," Micaleb said with a frown. "Vern swore he saw you there 'round ten o'clock."

"At the sawmill?" Tanner shook his head, baffled. "Couldn't have been me. I was back at the jail by nine." Yeah, he'd been absorbed with Eden a lot lately, but it seemed he would at least be able to recall a trip to Hollis's place at that hour. Unless he'd been sleepwalking. He hadn't done that since he was a little scrapper, though, and the problem hadn't resurfaced—that he knew of, anyway.

"The fella was wearing a hat and trousers just like yours."

"It was probably someone else, then. In these duds"—Tanner swept his hand down his best homespun britches—"I don't exactly stand out in a crowd."

"Micaleb," Rosalyn cut in, "the Tilly boy is well-meaning, but you must admit he is quite scatterbrained."

"Only 'bout some things. He's real good 'bout remembering people."

Her blue eyes flashed with disapproval. "You are insulting our guest, husband. If Marshal McCay says that he wasn't at the mill, then he wasn't at the mill. In the dark, how could Vern tell the difference between the marshal and half the other men in this town?"

Shoot, Tanner thought, he'd been hired to break up spats, not start them. Especially between a husband and his wife. "Then again, I could have judged the time wrong," he said, hoping to smooth over the awkward moment. "I had to sell my watch to buy supplies for the trip down." But the explanation he gave rang hollow in his ears. Yeah, he'd given the town a quick once-over, same as he did every night. But Mondays were slow, Monday nights even slower. He knew for a fact he'd been at the sawmill at five, because Hollis had been on his way home. And he'd definitely been back at the jail by nine. He recollected glancing at the clock on the shelf just before turning in. "Speaking of time," Tanner said, unfolding himself from the chair, "it's getting late. I'm much obliged for supper, Miz Rosalyn. Guess I wasn't too hungry."

"Now, I've told you before to just call me Rosalyn," she admonished.

In the large reception area, Tanner adjusted his hat on his head. Rosalyn and Micaleb lingered in the parlor, and though Tanner couldn't make out the words, he got the impression that Rosalyn was scolding Micaleb for chasing him off.

Next time, Tanner thought, he'd keep his ears open and his mouth shut.

As Tanner stepped down off the boardwalk fronting the hotel, his gaze strayed toward the house at the end of town.

Rosalyn slipped up behind him and curled her hand around his elbow. "It's the widow, isn't it?"

He nodded shortly. He didn't even try to lie about it. His face would give him away. It always had.

"I cannot say that I know her well, but take a bit of advice from someone who understands what you are going through. Give her a little time. It took me three years to convince Micaleb that he couldn't live without me before he finally realized the error of his ways. So don't give up. I've found that the best things in life are worth waiting for."

Tanner had to laugh. They had a very odd marriage, Rosalyn and Micaleb did. She dragged him around by his ear in public, told him off in private, and yet it was clear even to Tanner that after twenty-four years of marriage to the big lug, she still considered Micaleb Brandenburger the best thing since figgy pudding.

Would he and Eden ever share that kind of love? If so, how long would *he* be forced to wait until she came around? Months? Years? That was an awfully long time to be patient.

Rosalyn's last words hit him hard. Instinct told him Eden was worth anything. She had so much love inside her, and no one but those kids to lavish it on. Did Seth Page know how lucky a man he'd been when he'd married the little orphan?

A little time, huh? "I'll wait," he decided out loud. A lifetime if he had to.

Several days passed. Then a week. Then two. During the third week, as Eden darted a glance inside the jailhouse window on her way to Deidrich's General Store, she told herself that she simply must stop looking for him around every corner. It was obvious that the marshal was avoiding her. Wasn't that what she'd wanted? What she'd asked, almost demanded, of him? To leave her and the children alone? The reminder didn't soothe her as she hoped it would. Tanner's prolonged absence left a keen emptiness in her days that no amount of work could fill. She just didn't understand herself anymore.

The children hadn't gone unaffected either. Lissa remained the same, and Eden found perverse comfort that her eldest daughter couldn't be swayed, but Ruthie continually asked about him. Where he was, why he didn't come visit them, why he was never in his office on the days they went to clean it or to bring meals each time the scarf flapped from the post. Eden had no answers.

Then there was Little Seth. The boy spent more time beneath the porch than she deemed usual or healthy. Often she'd hear him whispering, but whenever she glanced under the house, she saw no one but her son.

Eden pursed her lips and quickened her pace down the boardwalk. The way the younger two had been acting since they'd gone fishing a full three weeks ago was exactly why she hadn't wanted them getting involved with him. He hadn't promised to be a vital part of their lives, not in words, but nonetheless he'd given them that impression. They had become very dependent on his attention in the short time they'd known him.

And she couldn't help but feel to blame for their disillusionment.

How could she tell them that he'd been kind to them only to get to her? It all boiled down to his job. Didn't it always? Marshal McCay thought she knew something about the robbery. All his sweet talk and coaxing smiles had been an act to get her to speak. When he learned that she could tell him nothing more than anyone else in town, he must have realized the futility of entertaining children starved for a father figure, to pump their mother for information she didn't have. It didn't matter to him that three—no two—innocent hearts were bruised by his thoughtlessness. Then again, Tanner McCay was just another lawman. So, of course, it *wouldn't* matter.

The bell tinkled above the door. Heat had settled inside the store like a fog, and all the scents clouded around her. Tangy vinegar from the various barrels of pickled eggs, beets, and pigs' feet lining the floor in front of the counter; the inviting sharpness of store-ground coffee beans, locally-grown tobacco, and cowhide footwear; the homey comforts of herbal packets for teas, sacks of cracked corn and cornmeal, and bottled vanilla. Just about anything necessary to supply a small community could be found in Deidrich's.

The girls headed for the display of painted porcelain dolls and fabric bolts while Little Seth wandered over to the weaponry and leather items exhibited in and on glass cabinets. Today was his fifth birthday. All he'd been able to talk about lately was how he hoped he would be given a gun just like "Marshal Mac's." Eden cringed at the thought of her only son growing up to be one of the enemy. She'd almost been sick the first time she'd caught him acting out the role of a marshal. She'd heard him through the kitchen window while putting up vegetables. His drawling commands to "reach for the sky, pardner," then the imitation gun pops as he shot at "bad men" from behind the rain barrel had nearly sent her flying out of the house in a fit. Only the fact that he was just an innocent little boy kept her from scolding him.

It reinforced her decision to keep herself and her children away from the living product.

"Mornin', Widda Page. How's the job workin' out at the jailhouse?"

"Just fine, Mr. Deidrich." Browsing through rows, she offered nothing more to the curious merchant. Good or bad, she wouldn't tell him. Gossip spread like volcanic lava in Dogwood Springs, hot and slow, but eventually reaching every corner of the town. The less said, the better.

"Marshal Mac back from Shreveport yet?"

The tin of baking powder she'd just pulled from a shelf nearly dropped to the floor. Eden caught it with a shaking hand, then let it tumble into the basket on her arm. "I haven't seen him," she answered truthfully.

"He left over two weeks ago. How long does he plan on stayin' away?"

He'd been gone two weeks? Then how . . . ? But the scarf, she'd seen it just yesterday. . . .

As much as Eden despised gossiping, she suddenly realized it did have its advantages. "I'm sure he will be returning any day."

"Hope so. No insult meant to Tiny Ellert, but that fella don't amount to poot in a whirlwind when it comes to protecting this town—beggin' your pardon for my language, ma'am. Never will understand what Marshal Mac was thinkin' to make him his deputy. Who in their right mind would be scared off by a midget?"

Her lips pinched together in disapproval. People should not say things about other people who were not present to defend themselves. "Apparently he has taken over Marshal McCay's duties quite well during his absence."

"That's only 'cause he gets Hollis to cast a shadow over him when he has to bring someone in. But Hollis cain't keep leaving the sawmill. Vern Tilly done jammed the gears once and busted a blade plumb in two the second time. Hollis says if he had a dime every time the boy broke something, he'd be a rich man."

In an area abundant in timber, Hollis Clark was no doubt already rich beyond compare. With the exception of John Sullivan, that is. Deidrich rattled on about people Eden scarcely knew and cared even less about. She blocked out the sound of his nasal voice as she shopped for the ingredients she lacked to bake Little Seth's birthday cake. Thoughts of the marshal weren't so easily banished.

At least she now knew why she hadn't seen him

around. But what on earth had compelled him to go to Louisiana? He could at least have left word. It was highly irritating to learn of his whereabouts through another person. After all, she was the one who worked for him. And he owed her almost a month's wages.

The bell alerted her to the entrance of another customer. Eden instantly looked for Little Seth and the girls. Seth had his nose pressed against the glass of the gun cabinet, and the girls were admiring from a safe distance a pretty doll with long cornsilk curls and a frilly dress. Glancing back at the doorway, Eden felt a little silly when a fashionably attired woman and a young girl wearing a smaller cut of the same lemon silk dress walked in. Corrina Sullivan and her daughter Annabelle were hardly threatening. Reassured that her children were safe from the gilt-haired pair of females, Eden relaxed her guard.

Annabelle, of the same age as Lissa, wandered to the front counter and popped a gumdrop into her mouth while Corrina handed a slip of paper to Mr. Deidrich. The girl's bored gaze swept the store, then landed on Lissa and Ruthie. Suddenly she broke away from her mother and made a beeline toward the dolls. Without regard to the expense of it, she grabbed the one with the cornsilk hair and frilly dress off the shelf, raced back to the counter, and slammed it down hard enough to smash the fragile face.

Lissa gasped and Ruthie hid her face against her sister's side. Then, once she recovered from her astonishment, Lissa curved her arm protectively around Ruthie's shoulders and advanced toward the girl, a look of fury on her face.

"My sister was looking at that doll, Annabelle. You had no right just walking up and taking it like that. That's rude."

Eden's eyes widened in surprise at Lissa's quick defense of Ruthie. She searched for Annabelle's mother but found the woman engrossed with a mail-order catalogue at the far end of the store.

"I can take it if I want to. Mother is buying it for me."

"How do you know we weren't gonna buy it first?"

"You could never buy this doll! Everyone knows *you* have no money. My father said your father left you so poor that soon you won't even have a house to live in."

Lissa shoved Ruthie behind her and balled her hands into fists. "You take that back, Annabelle Sullivan."

Oh, mercy, Eden thought. All they needed right now was for Lissa to get into a fight with the banker's snotty daughter. They'd be out on their rears by morning, lease or no lease. With a bright smile pasted on her face, Eden purposely stepped between them before Lissa let her fist fly, and addressed her own daughters. "Girls, did you decide which doll you liked best?"

The fire in Lissa's eyes changed to fleeting confusion. Then, with a wisdom beyond her tender years, she understood the silent message. "We *thought* we wanted that one. But we changed our minds. We'd rather pick one different from anybody else."

"Then why don't we browse through the catalogues? Perhaps one in there will strike your fancy."

Annabelle glared at them as they made a big show of oohing and aahing over the selections pictured in a mail-order book. Eden would have enjoyed their pretense in front of the spiteful girl if her heart didn't feel so heavy. Her children deserved better than this.

Once the pair left, Eden and Lissa dropped the pretense and they both sighed. Looking at each other, they burst into giggles.

"We showed her, didn't we, Mama?"

Hugging Lissa, and feeling closer to her daughter than she had in ages, Eden whispered, "We sure did, sweetheart."

"Are we gonna order that little Indian doll?" Ruthie asked.

Tears of regret stung Eden's eyes. "I think your Annie would be dreadfully hurt if she had to share you with another, don't you?"

Ruthie nodded seriously, then smiled. "But it was fun looking!"

"You may continue looking while I finish my shop-

ping as long as you do not move from this spot." Eden
pinned Lissa with a uncompromising look. "Not one inch.
Is that understood?"

"Yes, ma'am."

Eden left the girls to flip through the catalogues a little
longer while she paid for her meager purchases, glad that
her son had been so completely awed by the weaponry that
he hadn't given their foolery any notice. The ruse would
have been harder for Little Seth to understand. He was such
a quiet boy, content to just sit under the porch and play in
the dirt. Until he'd taken up imitating Tanner McCay, he
hadn't engaged in games of pretend.

Turning away, she almost ran into Rosalyn Brandenburger. "Pardon me, Mrs. Brandenburger."

"Hello, Mrs. Page. Not a very pleasant child, is she?"

Oh, no, Eden silently groaned, looking away. Her
cheeks flamed with embarrassment that one of the most
prominent women in town had overheard the exchange
with Annabelle.

"John spoils her dreadfully. Mark my words, he will
come to regret not taking a paddle to that little behind—oh,
forgive me. Bluntness has always been one of my many
faults."

Eden wouldn't know. She and the hotel owner had
shared little more than passing pleasantries in the past four
years.

"Your girls are certainly growing up into darling
young ladies. Are they excited about school starting again
soon?"

"Lissa is. Ruthie prefers being outdoors more, though,
and it's Little Seth's first year, so naturally he is excited."

"I'm afraid that my Micaleb and I missed out on such
events." Sorrow entered her vivid blue eyes. "We had a
daughter ourselves once, but she was stricken down with
polio when she was three."

Eden felt her heart go out to the woman. They shared a
common bond. She'd come close enough to losing Lissa to
know that some things were equally as painful as death.
"I'm very sorry for your loss."

As if uncomfortable discussing such a private tragedy, Rosalyn gave a strained smile and reached over to finger a bolt of apple-green cloth. "This shade would look very pretty on you, with your dark hair and light eyes. . . . I envy you your coloring. You can wear pastels without looking sallow."

Truth to tell, she envied Rosalyn's pale elegance. She felt like an Indian paintbrush among roses beside the stately woman.

"It hasn't been a year yet," Eden said softly.

"A year for what?"

"I am still in mourning—"

"Oh, pooh. That silly restriction might be socially acceptable back East, but out here it is commonplace for a woman to shed her mourning clothes early. How is she expected to catch herself a man if she cannot play up her assets?"

Eden pursed her lips. Why did everyone assume she was in the market for a husband?

"Speaking of men," Rosalyn added with a feigned innocence that didn't fool Eden, "has the marshal returned from his trip yet?"

The gossip mill had certainly been whirring overtime. Didn't anyone have anything better to talk about than the town marshal?

Still a bit peeved that Tanner had announced his departure to everyone but her, Eden caught herself before she retorted that she hadn't been hired to play Tanner's keeper. Instead, she said, "I am certain that everyone in town will know the instant he steps off the train."

"Yes, I do believe they will," Rosalyn chuckled. "You know, Mrs. Page, the Ladies' Literary Society will start meeting again every Thursday afternoon once school begins. Perhaps this year you will accept my invitation to come read with us. We've just gotten Constance Fenimore Woolson's novel *Anne*. It's about the life of a young orphan. Fascinating reading."

Eden felt herself pale. As always, the word "orphan" struck a cord of bitterness deep inside. How different her life could have turned out if only her parents would have given a darn.

"Thank you, Mrs. Brandenburger. I will give your invitation some thought." *When cows grow fins.* And give any of those women a chance to see beyond her thin veneer of respectability? Not likely. If they had even an inkling that it was simply a closely guarded sham, they'd oust her out of town. Her future here was already fragile at best, thanks to Sullivan's decree.

"Good. Then we shall look forward to seeing you. Be sure to bring a wad of cotton for your ears, or you will get quite a headache from Mrs. Dearpot's bellowing. She cannot hear her own voice without that hearing horn of hers, but she refuses to use it!"

In a flurry of silk petticoats, Rosalyn Brandenburger whirled out of the store. Shortly afterward, Eden gathered the children and also left.

"You made me very proud back there," Eden softly told Lissa as they strolled homeward, "watching out for Ruthie the way you did."

"Is it true what Annabelle said, Mama? That we won't have a house to live in anymore?"

"No, Lissa, it's not true. We will always have a house."

"But we are poor, aren't we?"

Eden considered the question before answering. "There are many definitions of poor. We may not have as much money as the Sullivans, but come what may, we have love for each other. And if you could measure that in coin, why, we'd be the richest family in the world."

Lissa seemed satisfied with the explanation. The gnawing guilt in Eden's middle couldn't be as easily appeased.

They covered the rest of the distance home in relative silence. A mockingbird swooped from a pine tree bough to peck at the ground before diving back to its nest. The jangle of horses' harnesses competed with the yap of a stray dog bounding down the road.

The instant they reached the beginning of the fence line, an alarm went off inside Eden's head. She slowed her steps and directed the children behind her as she took in the change that had occurred during their short absence. The grass that had grown almost to the top of the pickets had been completely hacked to the ground, and the fallen reeds lay in great mounds over half the yard. Tiny bugs and dandelion seeds hovered aimlessly; the scent of grass was sharp. Eden came to a full stop, listening cautiously.

Phwack, shhhee. Phwack, shhhee.

Bwuck-bwuck-bwuck.

Eden's heart climbed into her throat.

The marshal was back.

Chapter Ten

SHE FOUND HIM attacking the knee-high growth below the morning glories while his hen pecked at the ground alongside the porch, clucking her contentment.

The lump in Eden's throat seemed permanently lodged there as she watched him swing the scythe back and forth. He'd discarded his shirt, his vest and its accompanying badge, and his gun belt was nowhere in sight. His bare back, speckled with pieces of weeds, shone with sweat. Every ripple of muscle caused a like effect in her stomach. Tighten, relax. Tighten, relax . . .

Eden absently handed the basket of groceries to Lissa. Her feet seemed to have developed minds of their own as they brought her closer to Tanner. Ruthie and Little Seth recovered from surprise much faster than she did. They scampered over the freshly cut yard, the individual names they had for him exploding from their mouths.

The scythe halted in mid-swing. He turned. Standing before her was a powerful man in all his breath-stealing glory. Not only was his back a sight to behold, his chest seemed a wall of solid muscle and sun-tanned flesh. A narrow trail of fine, tawny hair began at his navel and disappeared inside the damp waistband of worn denim trousers; the bottoms were tucked into sturdy black boots. A hammer, secured into his belt, hung against his hip.

Eden slowly grew aware that her son and daughter were clinging to his legs, wearing smiles so wide they looked painted on. His broad hands rested across their backs.

"You came back just in time for my birthday, Marshal Mac!"

Ruffling her son's brownish-red mop of hair, he said, "You didn't think I'd miss such an important occasion now, did you, Maverick?" Eden saw the slight lifting of his brows, though, and knew he'd had no inkling that her son's birthday was July 26. She certainly hadn't told him.

"Mama's gonna make Little Seth a cake with his favorite chocolate icing. Do you like chocolate icing, Tan?"

"Children, go inside and help your sister put away the groceries."

"But—"

"Don't sass me now, Ruthie. Seth, go on with your sister while I have a word with the marshal."

Smiling wide, Tanner told them, "Myrtle left you each a present on the rocking chair. Your mother could probably use them in the cake."

The mention of a present sent them both up the steps, and with twin squeals of delight, they hurried into the house, each clutching a small brown egg in their hands as if they were gold nuggets.

"What are you doing here?" Eden asked.

He darted forward to pluck his shirt from the porch railing and slipped his arms inside. He left the buttons undone. Eden mustered all her willpower to keep her gaze from dipping down to the flat nipples on his exposed chest.

"Well, I figured if this yard didn't get cut soon, the kids would wind up getting lost in the grass. It's no kind of work for a lady, so I'm here to lend you my labor. Thought I'd mend the fence when I'm through with the lawn."

"You must have just returned from your trip. I'm sure you have other work to do at the jail."

He mopped at his chest with the kerchief he'd taken from his pocket. "I caught up on my paperwork after I got in last night."

Eden lost the struggle. Her eyes watched every dab he made with the rag.

"Would've been back sooner, but I had me an unexpected run-in with a poster man on a hustled horse."

Her tongue thick, her mouth dry, she croaked. "You could have told me you were leaving."

"Didn't think it would matter to you." He shoved the kerchief back into his pocket and Eden's gaze shot back to his face. "I thought about you while I was away."

"You didn't have to."

"Think about you?" His eyes twinkled brighter than ever.

"Do the yard," she said sternly.

"It needed doing."

"I know, but—"

"Eden, I *like* doing things for you. Is that so hard to believe?"

Her heart swelled with an emotion she found too distressing to examine. She could not let him see how deeply moved she was that he'd gone to all this trouble. For her.

She tilted her chin stubbornly. "Maybe it is. I've been doing for myself for so long that when someone suddenly does something for me, I can't help but wonder what they want in return."

A kiss would be nice, Tanner mused. God, more than anything in the world, right now he wanted to kiss that cynical mouth. Feel her lips beneath his own. He'd dreamed of it for two long, lonesome weeks. That, and more. Seeing her now, her cheeks rosy from the morning sun, wisps of her glossy black hair framing her face, the urge was almost too powerful to resist.

He reckoned he deserved a medal for controlling himself when temptation in the flesh stood so close he could smell it. Taste it. His throat felt lined with sandpaper when he managed to say instead, "I just wanted to see you. I meant to come by and make sure that you and Lissa had made amends, but the trip was unexpected."

In a way, the telegraph he'd received had been a blessing. Not two days had gone by before his resolve to give

Eden time had cracked. Within a week, impatience got the best of him. In fact, he'd been working on another excuse to visit her when the reply to his request for an interview with a shareholder of the East Line & Red River Railroad had been delivered.

The shareholder had been frustratingly tight-lipped. An assistant engineer of the E.L. & R.R. train had let an interesting bit of news out of the bag, though. Tanner longed to share his discovery with Eden, but since any mention of his work got her dander up, he decided to hold off.

"I will admit that the yard looks very nice. But, Marshal McCay, I must insist that you stop coming by here whenever the whim hits. What will people say?"

"Do you really care?"

Her eyes clouded over. She lifted her chin. "It isn't easy making a home in a town where everything you do or say is up for public censure. And it's usually the children who wind up paying for an adult's indiscretions."

"I can't see anything wrong with a man working on a widow's yard. Glory be, Eden!" he declared with a short laugh. "Where I come from, folks expect a fellow to offer his help when someone needs it. It's called being neighborly."

"When the man is unmarried, and the widow has been without her husband for quite some time, people may believe she is inviting him to work on much more than her yard." She left him to think on that while she disappeared inside the house to bake her son's cake.

And think Tanner did. He thought until the wicked ideas her words planted in his head made him dizzy with wanting.

As she helped Little Seth pick eggshells from the cake batter, Eden couldn't help but wonder what Lissa found so interesting beyond the dining room window. She'd been standing in front of it, staring through the pane, for the last ten minutes.

Then her head began swinging back and forth, her

braids waving across her shoulder blades. "I hope you have lots of bandages handy, Mama."

"What do I need bandages for?"

" 'Cause the marshal just stepped on the rake and whapped himself in the head with the handle and now he's picking up the scythe. No telling how much harm he's gonna do to himself with that."

She'd been watching Tanner McCay all this time? "Ruthie, stir this gently." Bewildered, Eden wiped her hands on her apron and strolled toward the window. From beside Lissa, she pulled the tatted white curtains aside.

Sure enough, the marshal had the curved tool in his grip and was heading for the overgrown section of the yard. "Why, that stubborn fool," Eden muttered. Then she let the curtain fall back into place. "Well, if he wants to blister his hands, then that's his decision," she said, returning to the kitchen. "We have more important things to do than stand around watching him."

An hour later, a golden brown cake sat cooling on the windowsill. The kitchen smelled of heaven and heat. The counter was filled with sticky dishes that needed washing before the batter had to be chiseled off. The girls were upstairs wrapping Little Seth's gifts while he sat at the table, his face hidden by the bowl he was licking clean. "Seth, I'll be back directly. I'm going to the well for water to clean up this mess."

Bowl and all bobbed up and down.

Her purposeful pace faltered when she spied Tanner at the well cranking up the bucket, a dipper in his hand. Her fingers tightened around the handle of the pail she held. Once again shirtless, he threw his head back and brought the ladle to his mouth, quenching his thirst. Water streamed along his mouth and down his chin, down his solid chest, the tanned flesh burned bronze by the sun. If it had been any other man performing a completely ordinary and mundane ritual, Eden knew she would have turned away without hesitation. Yet there was something mysteriously compelling about watching this man, bare-chested and utterly masculine, that kept her motionless. Breathless.

As though sensing her presence, the dipper lowered and he dragged his wrist across his mouth while his fixed gaze measured her approach. The muscles in her stomach contracted. Eden averted her eyes. Was it her imagination? Or had the temperature climbed ten degrees in the last few seconds?

"Marshal." She nodded once.

He moved to give her access to the well, but did not leave. She wished he would. Wished he would take the highly appealing scents of earth and summer and salty sweat with him too.

"I've got only the area in front of the big windows by the porch and the side yard left to do." He tipped the bucket resting on the stone ledge, filling her pail.

"You've worked more than enough. I can manage the rest."

"I don't hold with leaving a job half done. I should have it finished within the next couple of hours."

"Perhaps you'd have an appetite for hot beef sandwiches and cake." The words were out before she could stop them.

"I was sure hoping you'd ask." He grinned. She almost dropped the bucket. "I smelled your cooking clear on the other side of the house, and my stomach started rumbling like a wooden bridge with a team of wagons rolling over it."

Eden almost smiled at the vision he conjured. "I wouldn't want you to cancel any previous plans."

"And I wouldn't want to spoil a family celebration."

Eden tugged the heavy pail off the ledge. Water sloshed onto her dress.

He immediately reached for the handle. "Let me take this in for you."

A current skittered up her arm as his hand curled around her knuckles. She jerked free and whirled away, her braid slapping against her back as she strode toward the back porch. "S-S-S-Seth . . ." Damn, now he'd reduced her to stuttering—and swearing! "*Seth* would be thrilled if you stayed."

"I don't have a gift for him."

Though he trailed several steps behind her toward the back porch, it seemed she could feel his warm breath tickling the skin of her neck. "The girls made him a drum from a small cask we found in the cellar, and I have sewn him a new shirt, so he will not lack for presents."

"Still, it is his birthday. I don't feel right barging in empty-handed."

"Just your being there will make him happy," she said with a note of irritation. "He's taken quite a liking to you."

"Yeah, he's sorta grown on me, too." He opened the back door for her and set the bucket on the floor. Then, shoving his hands into his front pockets, he leaned back against the counter and crossed his ankles. Why he tarried, Eden couldn't imagine. But strangely, she wasn't in any hurry to chase him off.

"You ever hear of Jesse James?" he finally blurted out.

Eden glanced at him curiously, then looked away. "Who hasn't heard of him?"

"Did you know that James was reported to have robbed a train a few miles from here?"

"You sound surprised," Eden said, scraping leftovers from the plates into the slop bucket. As long as she kept busy, she could keep up the pretense of normalcy. Except there was nothing normal about holding a conversation with a half-naked man in her kitchen.

"I am. I haven't heard a peep from anyone about it. I'd have thought a robbery so close to town would have been big news."

"It was for a while." She began stacking the dishes. "Dogwood Springs was swarming with federal marshals, rangers, railroad investigators, and fortune hunters. Then, when nothing turned up, the railroad told people it was probably a hoax."

Without being asked, he emptied the water from the pail into the kettle on the stove then knelt to stoke the fire. "I was told that they wanted it kept quiet because it was bad for business."

Suddenly annoyed with him for rousing her interest,

Eden propped her hands on her hips and demanded, "Why don't you tell me where all this is leading?"

"All right," he sighed. "I went to Shreveport to follow a possible lead on the near robbery your husband was killed in. Thought I was wasting my time until I talked with the engineer, who showed me records that a strongbox was stolen during a second robbery that happened not three months ago in Jefferson. Credit's been given to the James gang."

"You don't believe it?"

Tanner turned on the balls of his feet. "Jesse James was shot and killed this past April by Robert Ford."

When Eden offered no comment, the absence of conversation gradually developed into an uneasy silence. His leg muscles bunched as he straightened. Eden studied him covertly when he passed by her, glancing away the instant their gazes met. He was built nothing like her late husband. Seth had been forty-four when he died. He liked sitting. At the office, at home, when he traveled—be it by horse or train—he sat. He had acquired a paunchy middle and wide rump with all that sitting. The same could not be said about Tanner McCay. He was firm where it mattered, with defined muscles in all the right places, and he obviously used them often.

"Do you need anything else before I get back to work?" he asked gruffly.

I need to stop thinking of you. "No," she croaked, shaving lye soap into the basin.

He opened his mouth to say something, then shook his head as if he'd changed his mind. "I best get out of here before—" He turned and ran into the door frame. "Son of a bug," he hissed, rubbing his shoulder on his way outside.

Slapping her hand to her brow, Eden rocked her head back and forth. Hard to believe such a strong, well-built fellow could be such a clodhopper, but every time she saw him, he was either tripping over or knocking into things. His clumsiness made him human, though, and that in itself was frightening.

The water hadn't yet come to a boil, so Eden trudged

up the steps, checked on the girls, then went to her own room. She changed from her wet outfit to a gray shirtwaist that pleated above her breasts and a full skirt the shade of charcoal. Dull colors, Eden frowned, but proper for a woman in mourning.

Her glance landed on an edge of forbidden pink ribbon peeking from the crack in the top drawer of her dresser. Did she dare? Eden checked over her shoulder. The hallway stretched empty; no one was looking. The ribbon tempted. Eden bit her lip. It would be such a little thing. Just a sprig of color around her collar to brighten the dreary outfit. Hardly noticeable.

At last, with a regretful sigh, she settled for simply tucking it into the pocket of her skirt.

Ruthie and Little Seth were as thrilled as she'd expected they would be when she announced a few minutes later that the marshal would stay for the birthday party.

Lissa was another matter. "Why'd you have to invite him?" she asked.

As Eden poured hot water into the dishpan, steam clouded the air. "It seemed the right thing to do since he's worked so hard on the yard," she replied.

"Nobody asked him to."

"Even so, I expect you to behave yourself. I am not overly fond of the marshal either, but if I can put aside my feelings, then so can you. For your brother's sake. It is his birthday, after all."

Other than a sullen glare, Lissa kept her thoughts to herself.

Eden tidied up the kitchen, whipped up the icing, and was pulling a wide, blunt-edged knife from the block to frost the cake when a knock sounded on the back door.

Tanner peeked inside without waiting for permission to enter. "Am I too late?"

"We've eaten already, but I left a plate for you on the table. Help yourself while I finish up here."

Hearing his voice, Ruthie leapt off the bench and dragged him by the hand to the dining table. On the way through the kitchen, he hooked his hat on the peg near the door, then slid into the chair at the head of her table as if he'd been doing it all his life.

Eden stole glances at him as she smeared chocolate frosting on the cake. He'd washed up. Clumps of brown streaked the sandy strands of the damp hair brushing the top of his shoulders. He'd parted it on the side and combed it back, exposing the clearness of his evergreen eyes, the sloping lines of his scrubbed face. Beads of water were trapped in his mustache.

What would it feel like to kiss a man with a mustache? Would the bristles be stiff and scrape her lips? Or would they be lush and sensuous?

Alarmed at the bend her thoughts had taken, Eden spun away just as Lissa's sneaky fingers came out of the bowl. "Why don't you get the candles from the cupboard instead of swiping all the icing?"

Sucking on a chocolate-smeared finger, Lissa rolled her eyes. Eden carried the plate to the table.

"How come you was gone so many days, Marshal Mac?"

"I had to talk to a man who works for the railroad."

"Did you get to ride in the train?" Ruthie asked.

"Did bad men try to rob it?" Little Seth asked eagerly.

"Yes, I rode the train, and no, nobody tried to rob it."

"If they woulda, you woulda skeared 'em off, huh, Marshal Mac?"

The glass of cold tea paused at his mouth. He sought out Eden with a helpless raise of his brows. Tense, she waited for his reaction. "I'm thankful I didn't have to worry about that," he finally said. "Tell me what you did while I was gone. Were you good for your mother?"

"Little Seth lost his shoe in the well, but it landed in the bucket so we got it back out and I lost another tooth." Ruthie proudly displayed the widened gap of her lower gums.

"You keep that up, sweet potato, and you won't have any left to brush."

The pleasant buzz of conversation and laughter

wrapped around Eden. Tears pricked at her eyes. This was what she'd always imagined her family would be like. What she'd seen looking into homes when she'd lived on the streets. A mother. A father. A room filled with the sounds of children and the coziness of sharing life's trivial happenings.

"And you, Lissa, what did you lose?"

His innocent question was greeted with a sharp, "I lost my pa."

He stopped chewing the bite he'd just taken of his sandwich to shoot a quick, wary glance at Eden. "I know you did, honey. And I'm right sorry about that."

Eden's heart nearly melted there on the spot at the deep compassion in his voice.

"But Tan'll be our new pa, won'tcha, Tan?"

The room went suddenly quiet; the silly sentiments in her mind instantly fled. She set the knife down with extreme care. "Lissa, fetch the matches from the box by the stove, please."

"Don't bother," Tanner said, digging into his pants pocket.

Her chest tightened as he neared, cupping a small tin with leaves engraved on the lid. He pulled out a match.

Lissa stabbed five beeswax candles into the center of the cake. Seth scooted down the bench so that the cake was just beneath his nose. Ruthie clapped her hands.

"Don't forget to make a wish, Little Seth," she cried.

The match flared to life and Tanner touched it to each wick. Little Seth eagerly scrambled to his feet on the bench. Just as he leaned over to blow out the flames, the bench tipped beneath him.

Eden and Tanner both lunged across the table for him.

"Mama, the cake!"

She dimly heard Lissa's warning as Tanner's weight propelled her forward. He managed to catch Seth by the arm and save him from falling at the same time she felt the single layer collapse and squish beneath her bosom.

Once the surprise of being tackled wore off, she became aware of the solid length of man flattening her against

the table. The sheer sensuality of his lean body fitted
against her bottom and back shocked her so, that a moment
passed before Eden realized that a sharp stench was infest-
ing the kitchen. "Something's burning."

The weight on her back disappeared. Tanner hauled
Little Seth up onto the bench Ruthie had quickly righted,
then yanked Eden to her feet. "It's your hair!"

Eden squealed, and batted wildly at the fire eating her
braid like a starving animal.

Reacting just as quickly, Tanner scooped a handful of
cake from the table and ground it into the plait lying against
her bosom. "The tail must have landed on a wick."

Long after the danger passed, his palm remained on
the heaving swell of her breast. Their eyes met. A swift
current of awareness passed between them. Powerful and
frightening. Elemental.

"The fire's out, Marshal," Eden croaked.

"I'm afraid not, ma'am. It's just started taking hold."

As if the respectful title could soften the boldness of
his words, his touch. She recognized the glint of desire in
his eyes and hated herself for responding to it. To him.

"You're enjoying this, aren't you?" she asked stiffly.

"I'd enjoy it a whole lot more if there weren't three
sets of eyes studying our every move." And of all the gall,
he winked.

Taking her hand in his free and clean one, he helped
her to stand. He took his sweet old time letting go of her,
too.

"Glory be, you about went up like dry tinder. Did you
get burned?"

A strong odor of singed hair and melted wax lingered
in the air. Eden examined the frizzled end of her braid and
a brown-edged hole in her apron bib. He'd doused the
flame before any real damage had been done. "No, I—" A
fat glob of chocolate frosting and yellow cake plopped
from her front to the table, where the rest of Little Seth's
dessert had been mashed into an unrecognizable pulp.

She curled her lips in disgust. "Oh, no. Look at this
mess. Seth's cake, my clothes."

Tanner started it. His mustache quivered and he choked on a laugh. Then Ruthie giggled. Lissa snickered.

Woebegone, Little Seth cried, "I didn't get to blow out the candles. Now my wish won't come true!"

Tanner whisked him into his arms and tickled his sides. "You don't need to blow out candles for your wishes to come true. In fact, there might even be a couple of them wrapped up. How about you open your presents and see?"

He scrambled down, about to chase after Ruthie and Lissa. Tanner caught him by the suspenders. "Ho there, Maverick. Let your sisters get your presents. You can go wash up outside. And while you're out there, check if Myrtle is still on the front porch, where I left her."

Little feet thudded on the stairs as the girls rushed up to their room for Seth's gifts, and Seth left to check on Myrtle.

They were alone. Eden was acutely conscious of that. "I need to change. I look a fright."

"You look good enough to eat." With a crooked finger he lifted a mound of frosting from her apron bodice and popped it into his mouth. Devilry danced in the green pools of his eyes.

Eden whipped the garment off over her head. Lips pressed together, she stalked into the kitchen. Tanner seized her by the elbow and turned her to face him.

"I shouldn't have done that, Eden."

"Stop calling me that. I have not given you permission to call me by my first name."

"But it's such a beautiful name. I like saying it."

"You don't have that right."

"I want the right." He pinned her to the counter with his gaze alone. "And I want you. Have since the second I laid eyes on you."

Tense, unable to move, Eden watched his head dip, his mouth descend, fearing he would kiss her. More afraid he wouldn't.

He laid his hand just above her hip, and his fingers gently pinched her waist. Hot fingers. Strong fingers.

The touch of his lips upon hers was so light, she barely

felt it. She kept her eyes open, and he, his. So green they were. Like still ponds during the first thaw of spring. The gentle brush of his mustache beneath her nose sent a shiver down her spine. Soft and tickling, she discovered. Her chest swelled and her heart stopped when his partly open lips tasted her again. And then again.

She couldn't do anything about her shallow breathing, but she kept her mouth rigidly shut. She wouldn't give in to him. If it took every last ounce of strength she possessed, she would not give in to him.

She remained unyielding when the tip of his tongue sampled the corner of her mouth. Her jaw. Her . . .

Earlobe. He drew it into his mouth.

No, she wouldn't . . . *ohhh*.

Give in . . . *mmmm*.

To him.

A whimper caught in Eden's throat. His mouth landed on the cord of her neck. He sucked the sensitive spot.

Her arm went around his neck, draping limply across his shoulders, and she tilted her head to the side. He raised his. Gazing into those hypnotic eyes, a spell wove around her, that of denied hopes, secret longings, forbidden hungers. Eden swayed forward, her lids drifting down.

Damn him for making her surrender.

Chapter Eleven

TANNER SLID HIS hands around her hips, holding her close. She opened her mouth for him. His tongue made a quick foray between her parted lips. "You've been dipping into the cake batter too, haven't you?" he murmured against her lips between kisses. "You taste just like I knew you'd taste. Like sugar and butter and vanilla, all things sweet."

Her fingers on his back clutched his shirt, her nails bit into his skin. Deepening the kiss, Tanner pulled her to him, folding his arms around her waist. She still wasn't close enough. He bent a little, then straightened, driving his lower body against hers.

Oh, God, they'd been made for each other. There was no way she could mistake what he was feeling just then, not when he was holding her curves tight to the point of breaking against him. She made a noise—half moan, half sob. Was he being too rough?

He cupped the sides of her head in his hands and pulled her back. Those beautiful eyes of hers stared back at him, glazed. Her lips were swollen, moist. She looked soft and willing. So desirable. "Eden."

Crushing her to him again, need making him shake, he covered her mouth with his. It felt like the first time he'd ever kissed a woman. Wanted a woman. Only better. Because it was Eden. The reason his heart galloped and his palms sweated and his gut tied itself in knots and he couldn't walk straight anymore.

Breathing harshly through his nose, his fingers raking through her hair, he took everything she gave and returned it with lusty greed. He was too grateful to be surprised. Too desperate to ask why. It was enough that she was finally in his arms, almost choking him with the hold she had around his neck, meeting each of his tongue thrusts with one of her own.

"Is Tan done kissin' Mama yet?"

Tanner released Eden so fast that her knees buckled and she tumbled against him. Panting, he spun around, one arm curled behind him to hold Eden steady. Lissa stood in the doorway, glowering at them. One of her hands covered Ruthie's eyes, so all that could be seen was a pair of black braids, a gaping grin, and the big object she held in front of her, wrapped in rumpled newsprint.

Eden gave a little cry and bent over the counter with her face buried in her hands.

In his lifetime he'd faced crazed mobs. Wild horses. Blazing bullets. All without a second thought to the outcome, all without a shred of fear.

All seemed like a stroll in the park compared to facing this little girl whose mother he'd just been mauling in the kitchen.

Lissa lowered her hand from Ruthie's eyes, but the rigid line of her mouth told its own story. Tanner shifted uncomfortably. "Your ma had something stuck in her eye."

"Very original, Marshal," Eden muttered. He heard her inhale, then blow out a trembling breath. "Girls, find Little Seth so he can open his presents."

Taking Ruthie's hand, Lissa eyed Tanner for several very long seconds before she obeyed.

When Eden made to follow, he grabbed her fingers and held her back. "Eden, I didn't mean for the kids to catch us ki—"

"Don't." Her cheeks turned a bright pink, but she wouldn't look at him. "Please don't say it. I'd just as soon forget anything ever happened."

Tanner grinned mischievously. "Whatever you say, Mrs. Page."

Each squeak of the well crank echoed the screams of protest in Eden's strained muscles.

One thing she'd definitely have installed in her new house—if she ever got one—was an indoor water pump. Hauling twenty buckets of water was the last thing she felt like doing after the day's upheaval, but the children needed a bath. She needed a bath. Mercy, she swore she had icing stuck in her ears.

The memory of how the icing had gotten there prodded at Eden. She pressed her lips into a grim line. Tanner had only been trying to weaken her defenses, that was all. Why, she hadn't figured out yet, but it would lead to no good. Of that she was certain. The sooner she accepted that, the sooner she could forget today's folly and the better off they all would be.

Resolved, Eden swiped a tangled strand of hair out of her mouth and grabbed the rope handle, tugging the full bucket onto the ledge. Her brows puckered. "What on earth?" Cautiously, Eden pinched the waterlogged cowhide pouch attached to the handle between her fingers and studied it from all sides. The children? Why would they have stuck a pouch in the well bucket, though? And where would they have gotten it in the first place?

Pulling on the thong tied to the rope, Eden tugged the opening apart and peeked inside. Then she emptied the contents into her hand. She recognized the marshal's engraved match tin, and her bewilderment grew.

The tiny drawer slid open, and inside lay a small, folded piece of paper. She set the pouch beside the bucket and tilted the note toward the lantern light spilling out the kitchen window. "Meet me tomorrow by the bridge. You bring the children and the basket. I'll bring the food. . . ." Eden lifted her face to the moon, bringing the note to her throat. "Tanner," she whispered, then hastened to read the rest. "P.S. I lied. I'd forget my own name before I'd forget the best welcome-home I've ever gotten."

Eden came dangerously close to crying. Why was he doing this?

Finding him shoveling out a half-built chicken coop behind the jail the following morning, she slapped the pouch against his chest. "Let's get something straight right now, Marshal McCay. If you think your little sweet-talk notes will pry more information from me about my husband's death, then think again. I've told you everything I can remember."

His brows shot all the way up his forehead as he gaped at her. "I wasn't planning to pry anything from you," he said. "Eden, don't you know when a man is trying to court you?"

"Is that what you're doing?" she scoffed. "You expect me to believe that you want to saddle yourself with a widow with three children?" Courting her, hah! Did he think she was that gullible? Well, she had news for him! She'd spent too much time on the streets to have gone through life ignorant of a man's machinations.

"Why not? I'll admit that I'm probably not very good at this courtin' stuff." He sounded put out. "I've never done it before. But after what happened in your kitchen, I figured I must be doing something right."

"What exactly happened that would give you that idea?"

The shovel handle flew one way, the pouch another as Tanner reached for her, a sly glimmer in his eye. "Care to be reminded?"

Eden deftly sidestepped his touch. "For pity's sake, it was just a kiss, not an invitation. It meant nothing."

He leaned back and folded his arms across his chest. "I think all that tripe is easier for you to believe than the truth," he charged with a note of superiority. "You liked kissing me as much as I liked kissing you and you're just too afraid to admit it."

The challenge hung in the air. Looking at him, scenes from yesterday blinked before her eyes. The way she'd bared her neck to his mouth, his breath hot against her damp skin. The feel of his thick hair between her fingers. The raw hunger that had gripped her when she'd been in his solid embrace.

"Fine. I liked it." She lifted her chin defiantly. "Does it boost your ego to hear me say that, Marshal McCay?"

"Don't you think you could call me Tanner?" he asked, laughter lurking in those green depths.

"No, I don't. No matter what I call you, it doesn't change who you are."

"Oh? Who am I, Eden?"

"The marshal," she hissed.

"You say that like you've got something against all marshals. Would you rather I be an outlaw?"

"I'd rather you stayed out of my life! If you have so much time on your hands, why don't you spend it tracking down my husband's killers?"

"I plan to. After you agree to go on that picnic with me."

She gave him what she hoped was a withering glare. "Absolutely not." It was the right answer. Eden knew it was. So why did it leave such a bitter taste in her mouth?

He leaned low, and with a wicked glint in his eye whispered, "Bet I can get you to change your mind."

The scoundrel had blackmailed her.

He must have known she would not be able to resist those innocent little faces. Ruthie's big green eyes, her pouty mouth, her hands clasped in front of her as if in prayer. "Please, Mama? Pretty, pretty please?"

And Little Seth, attached to her back, his arms tight around her neck, promising to clean his room for "eighteen-ten days" if she said yes.

Lissa had shrugged as if she didn't care one way or the other, but Eden noticed a yearning just beneath the indifferent façade.

The marshal simply stood back and waited, a small smile playing at his lips and his eyes twinkling deviously, until the children wore her down.

It had been blackmail, pure and simple.

Eden did admit that it was a good day for a picnic, though. He'd found the perfect spot, at the base of a gently sloping hill. A strong breeze ruffled the treetops on either side of the glade where they'd spread their blanket. Below, Ruthie and Little Seth played water tag with the marshal in the creek while Lissa seemed content to crouch at the bank with Myrtle and look for pebbles to add to her collection.

Squeals of delight mingled with husky laughter and splashing water. Eden lay down on the blanket. Blocking the sun from her eyes with her arm, she listened to the pleasant sounds. She just didn't understand him. Why wasn't he chasing squatters off land? Tearing down Pop Downing's moonshine still? Searching the back roads alongside the train tracks for bums who often jumped inside railcars? Those were things a marshal ought to be doing in the middle of the day.

No, she didn't understand him at all.

A while later, footsteps approached. Eden opened one eye a crack and peeked out from beneath her arm. Three wet pairs of bare feet and calves stood nearby among a smattering of dandelions, and a set of wrinkled yellow claws high-stepped through the grass.

"Shhh. She's sleeping," the marshal whispered to the children. Then he lowered himself on all fours and crawled to the picnic basket.

"Get out of that basket, Marshal."

Caught red-handed stealing a flaky apple fritter left over from their meal, he gave her a look of complete innocence. "A growing boy's gotta eat."

"If Seth eats any more he's going to burst," Eden chided, shutting her eyes again.

"I was talking about me." The fritter disappeared in three bites.

Thief, she thought, her lips twitching in spite of herself.

The children plopped down beside her to snitch goodies from the basket and bathe in the sun after their afternoon of hard play. Myrtle clucked deep in her throat, hopping from one lap to another until she reached Eden's side. There she squirmed and wriggled, then lowered into a big lump of snowy feathers. Eden hand-fed bits of ground corn to the lovable bird curled at her hip, feeling more at peace than she ever had before.

No financial worries plagued her; no guilt for neglecting the endless chores at home spoiled the day. She simply lay on the blanket, relaxed and serene, listening to the rustle of nature, the soft chatter of children, the beguiling chuckles of the man two feet away. . . .

This was what she'd been searching for all her life.

Soon Tanner brought out his mouth harp. After the first musical stanza of "Goober Peas," he added the lyrics in a steady tenor that curled Eden's toes.

Ruthie and Little Seth caught on to the chorus quickly. "Peas! Peas! Peas! Peas! Eating goober peas! Goodness how delicious, eating goober peas!"

"I brought my drum," Seth cried. That came as no surprise. He carried it wherever he went. Unfortunately, Little Seth was not a musician. His uneven pounding echoed in the air, even scared a bird out of a tree.

"Try *tat-tat-tattattat*." Tanner demonstrated the beat. "Keep that up."

Smooth harmonica and slightly offbeat drumming combined to play popular songs from the gold-rush decade, among them "Oh Susannah" and "Blue Tail Fly," which Ruthie and Seth knew by heart and sang with gusto. Myrtle hopped around as if dancing to the tune. Lissa simply lay quietly on her stomach, her chin propped in her hands, her feet swishing through the air as she sorted her stones.

Laughter at the song's end made Eden open her eyes, and she saw Tanner watching her. She stopped the tapping motion of her foot instantly. He didn't say a word. But a self-satisfied grin stayed on his face as he taught Ruthie and Seth a rollicking love song. He drew out the first parts of each phrase, while the kids contributed the maiden's name. "Get along hoooome . . ."

"Cindy, Cindy!"

All together "I'll marry you someday!"

Tat-tat-tat.

"Do another one, Tan!"

He held his hand up in protest. "My lips need a rest before they fall off."

That would be a shame. The thought took Eden completely off guard. Needing to keep her hands busy, she brushed away the crumbs on the blanket while Ruthie and Seth clamored onto Tanner's stomach.

He opened his arms and cuddled them close.

The sensation building in her chest nearly smothered Eden. She couldn't remember a single time when the children had felt comfortable enough with their father to climb into his lap. Even if they had, she doubted Seth would have allowed it.

But Tanner McCay had such a way with them. It was as if he intuitively knew what each of them needed. He didn't push himself into their lives, rather invited them to come to him with his soothing voice and easy nature. Neither did he force Lissa to accept him, but he didn't ignore her either. He seemed to understand Lissa—better than she did sometimes—while waiting for her reluctance to crumble. And it was crumbling. Had he heard her daughter softly join in on that last part of the "Cindy" song? Eden had.

"These two are falling asleep, Eden."

"We have been here longer than I expected." She started to get up.

"Let's stay. Just a little longer."

"It is peaceful," she conceded. "All right. Just a little longer." Kneeling, she helped roll first Ruthie, then Seth, from his arms onto the blanket.

"Thanks. My arms were getting numb." He rocked forward and sat up.

Eden cocked her head to the side and discovered his face very close to hers. So close that she could see tiny lines beneath his eyes, the pores on his nose, the brush of whiskers above his lips. And when he turned to look at her, he didn't move, he didn't breathe. The green depths of his eyes beckoned her. Lashes lowering, lips parting, Eden drifted closer as if pulled by an invisible string, wanting . . .

"I've got twenty white pebbles, thirteen brown, eight black, and two blue."

Eden sat back abruptly. Lissa had been so quiet, Eden had forgotten that she was still awake. But thankfully Lissa had been so engrossed in sorting her stones that she remained unaware of her mother's weakness.

Her eyes strayed back to the marshal. He wore the same blue cambric shirt as the first time she'd seen him, and it stretched taut across his back as he bent forward to pluck a dandelion gone to seed from the grass. Entranced by the sight of him twirling the stem between his rough fingers, she remembered again how those fingers had touched her, coaxed responses she'd tried with all her might to ignore, and even harder to deny. In spite of the warnings in her mind, he'd awakened yearnings for so much more.

She pressed her fingertips to her feverish brow. Mercy, the man picked flowers. He liked children. He held intelligent and tickling conversations. And yet he wore a badge and strapped on a gun. Where was the logic in that?

"Is it all right if I look for more pebbles?" Lissa asked.

Eden licked her lips, struggling to regain her wits. "Just don't wander away."

"Yes, ma'am."

Lissa ran toward the creek with Myrtle chasing after her.

Tanner leaned back on his elbows and stretched his legs in front of him. "God, this place is almost as pretty as you are."

The stripes on her dark maroon skirt suddenly became very fascinating. "I thought there was some code of honesty that lawmen had to uphold."

"You're even prettier when you blush like that." His dimple flashed as he handed her the fuzzy-topped stem.

Even if her life were at stake, she couldn't have stopped herself from accepting it and bringing the feathery ball to her nose.

"Little Seth calls them blow-wishes. You're supposed to make a wish and blow."

"That's silly."

"Haven't you ever blown dandelion seeds into the wind?" he asked, his brows arching in shock. "Go ahead. Just pretend it's a candle on your birthday cake."

Against her will, her eyes grew moist. She swung her head away. A lavender butterfly lighted upon a smattering of tiny white flowers growing wild nearby, but the magic of the day had turned to a bittersweet memory.

"Eden, honey? What is it?" He scooted closer to her, so close that she felt his hair brush her cheek. "You never had a birthday cake, did you?"

He was much too perceptive.

"When's your birthday?"

"In June." It was as good a month as any.

"You don't sound very sure."

"Nobody *knew* for sure," she replied, blinking rapidly. "Only that I came into this world at the beginning of summer."

He tipped her chin toward him and looked past her weakening defenses into the secret heartaches of her soul. "Then pretend today is your birthday, and that dandelion is your candle. Make a wish, take a deep breath, and blow."

"What's the point?" she asked, unable to keep the dejection from her voice. "Wishes don't come true."

"They do if you believe," he insisted with such compassion that she nearly burst into tears. "Come on. Take a chance. What could it hurt?"

He had no idea. Every chance she'd ever taken had hurt in one way or another.

"Eden, the worst failure is never trying at all."

Searching his eyes, she found the promise of understanding.

I'd never make you a promise I couldn't keep.

A tiny germ of hope unfurled inside her. Closing her eyes, Eden let all the wishes she wouldn't let herself wish before form in her mind. One stood out above all others. She blew, and the dandelion seeds pulled free of the stem, scattering into the wind carrying them away.

The hope died as Eden watched them sink uselessly to the ground.

"What did you wish for?"

Feeling completely foolish, Eden dropped the weed and rubbed her palms against her skirt. "A safe place to raise my children. A home of our very own that can never be taken away from us."

"You already have a home."

"It isn't a home," she said crisply, watching Lissa scoop her hand through the water at the creek bank. "It's a house that the town council provided when Seth took the job here. After Seth died, we were allowed to live in it until my widow's stipend runs out at the end of September. After that, John Sullivan has generously agreed to let me rent it for a small fortune each month. One of the benefits of being a marshal's widow, I guess." She grimaced at Tanner. "Needless to say, I had to find a job before he would agree to that much."

The following silence made Eden squirm. For the first time since she'd met him, she could not quite read his expression. He looked almost . . . violent.

Chapter Twelve

Tanner stormed past the lines of folks waiting to conduct bank business, ignoring their looks of astonishment as he headed straight for the office at the end of the building.

The house that comes with the position is . . . occupied . . . did not prepare the widow . . . for eviction. Everything clicked. One of the many doddering old widows from town didn't live in the house he was supposed to have gotten as part of his employment agreement. Eden and the kids did. And since he'd turned it down, the bank had started charging her rent.

The closed door didn't stop him. He threw it open, startling the banker and Hollis Clark, who sat in a chair nearby.

Vaulting across the desk, Tanner grabbed Sullivan's immaculate silk tie and twisted it in his fist. "How much, you son of a bitch!"

"Mac, what in tar-nation . . . ?"

"Stay out of this, Clark," Tanner ground out, never taking his eyes off John Sullivan. He jammed his knuckles against Sullivan's windpipe until his ash-white face turned a mottled red. "How much are you charging the widow Page to live in that house?"

"T-t-twenty d-d-dollars."

That accounted for the high wages she charged to clean the jail. "Why, you thievin' weasel. Where I come from, stealing is still a hangin' offense."

"I have the authority!" he claimed with righteous indignation. "Each day she inhabits that house, this bank loses money."

"What kind of fool do you take me for? My contract spelled out clear as daylight that the house went with my job. If I'd taken it, you wouldn't have made diddly. But when I turned it down, you decided to rape Eden."

"I have never laid a hand—"

"Moneywise, you crooked snake." With one last vicious twist, Tanner released his hold and lowered his face until they were nose to nose. "Guess what? It's gonna stop. Right now. I'm laying my claim to the house."

"You . . . you are claiming the house?" A flash of chagrin crossed Sullivan's face. He glanced at Hollis, who shrugged. Tugging his suit coat and straightening his rumpled tie, Sullivan said, "I will have the eviction papers drawn up immediately."

"No, you won't. I want the house, but Eden Page and her kids will stay in it."

"Your contract does not make—"

"My *contract* doesn't say beans against it, either. Who I choose to let live there is my decision. Fight me on this and I'll bring suit against you for breach of contract."

"What am I supposed to say to the widow?"

"You won't say a word to her," Tanner growled. "Go on ahead. Charge her a gold mine for living there. But you know what you're gonna do with the money? You're gonna open up an account in her name and stick every stinking penny in it that she pays you so she has a little nest egg put away should anything happen to me." With a bruising whack to Sullivan's collarbone, Tanner demanded, "Got it?"

Sullivan's head bobbed up and down. Tanner retreated a few steps, then left the office before his wrath got the best of him. A lot of good he'd do Eden rotting in prison for killing the town banker.

Marching down the boardwalk, Tanner wished Sullivan wouldn't have given in so easily. Had the banker fought him, it would have been a perfect excuse to rearrange that pompous face of his.

The violence pumping through his veins stunned him. He hadn't felt such helpless fury since he was ten years old—until Eden told him about Sullivan's deceit. He'd hid the rage erupting inside him behind a forced smile. Couldn't even remember what excuse he'd made when he'd left her place after walking them home. All he could think about was righting the wrong that had been dealt to her. He wasn't a powerless ten-year-old kid anymore, standing by while another laughed in the face of the legal system. He was a grown man with the law on his side.

Before he realized it, he was taking the steps up to Tiny's apartment two at a time. Tiny barely opened the door to the sound of his pounding fists before Tanner barged inside. "I thought you were my friend, Ellert."

"Tanner! I was about to pour myself some tea—"

"Why didn't you tell me that Eden was the widow living in the house I refused?"

Shutting the door, he said after a long pause, "I feared you would use the information to your advantage to ingratiate yourself with her."

"I'm in no mood to unravel your fancy words, Ellert. Talk in plain English."

Sighing, Tiny waved Tanner to a thick-cushioned chair, one of a pair flanking an octagon table where a soot-stained lamp cast a wan glow on several open ledgers. A curved pipe lay smoldering in a glass dish, tobacco smoke lending a spicy aroma to the dim and musty room.

Tanner refused to budge. He had some answers coming, and by God, he wouldn't take them sitting down.

Rocking back on his heels, his hands around the striped suspenders denting his stiff white shirt, Tiny nodded once. "All right. At first I did not credit the importance of who resided in the house. Then, once you displayed such an interest in the widow, I had concerns that you would pursue the clause in your employment contract to perhaps . . . compromise her."

"As in force myself into the house, maybe into her bed?" Tanner threw his hands in the air. "What would I have to gain other than a warm body that I could buy for a heck of a lot less than twenty dollars a month?"

"Information."

"About what? The train robbery?"

Tiny averted his face and went to remove the whistling pot from the stove.

Openmouthed, Tanner watched his every move without twitching a muscle. "That's it, isn't it?"

His guilty silence as he poured hot water through the sieve atop his cup gave Tanner all the answer he needed. "You think I'm planning to seduce Eden for information so I can finish the job?" His deputy hadn't worried about Eden, or the kids, or even about Tanner getting hurt for caring about her. Tiny had worried that Tanner would make another raid on the town. Only one thing could have given his friend, his partner, cause for doubts.

Almost numb, but not quite, Tanner dragged his hat from his head and held it limply at his side. "Just how much did you dig up on me?" he asked flatly.

"I did not have to dig, I merely scraped aside a bit of topsoil." Keeping his back to Tanner, Tiny pulled a crock from the shelf. "The McCay name has earned a place on the front page of every newspaper along the Missouri borders. I daresay it has competed with the James gang on frequent occasions." Turning around, Tiny stirred a teaspoon of sugar into his tea with aggravating leisure and faced Tanner squarely. "You and your brother were born in 1861 on a farm in Flat Fork, Missouri, to Fain and Ina McCay. In 1862 the farm was nearly destroyed by Union guerrillas who suspected Fain of harboring members of Quantrill's Raiders. From that point on, it is alleged that he participated in several raids with them, including the attack on Lawrence, Kansas, in 1863.

"After William Quantrill's death two years later, Fain McCay made headlines, not only for the banks he had begun to larcenize, but because his accomplices were his two small sons who, despite their young age, were as proficient in staving off armed men at pistol point as seasoned professionals. Once his fame preceded him, Fain McCay turned to holding up trains and stagecoaches, much in the boisterous manner of his outlaw neighbor and fellow raider Jesse Woodson James, until his incarceration eighteen months ago."

"It seems you know more about me and my kin than I ever reckoned."

"God's teeth, man!" Tiny slammed the cup onto the bare table in the kitchen area, spilling tea onto the polished surface. "It's the council's duty to learn as much as possible about the person they depend on to protect this town. Did you expect that you could keep your activities concealed indefinitely?"

"I never expected that I'd have to defend myself to my own partner." That's what hurt.

"Had I wanted you to defend yourself, I would have made my position clear the day I accepted the status of deputy marshal. Had I not believed you were en route to amending past transgressions, no power on earth could have persuaded me to work with you. However, I am only one member of the town council."

"Meaning?"

"Others on the council may not be so inclined to concede my summation of your improved character."

His confusion must have shown, for Tiny said, "I believe you have become genuinely committed to your profession."

Tanner squared his shoulders. "You didn't at first, though, did you? You thought I'd been involved in last year's attack, since the bandits were never caught. And the rest of the council still wonders." Tiny nodded reluctantly. "Why did they hire me, then, if they don't think I can be trusted?"

"Because only two men were foolish enough to apply for the job."

"Oh, yeah? Who was the other fool?"
"Me."

Night shadows had invaded the small, one-room apartment Tiny occupied above the barbershop, and the stale smell of fish filtered in through the open window that looked down upon Hannah's restaurant. Two cats screeched and hissed in the distance, and falling kindling in the woodstove made a muted thump.

Sipping his third cup of tea, Tiny sat in one of the matching russet chairs, the only furniture beside a neatly-made bed in the corner, a sturdy chest of drawers, and the two tables, one of which served as a desk. "I was a fool to think my law degree would guarantee me clients," he confessed. "Or at the very least obtain me the position as a peace officer of the community of my birth. Even an eastern education is no match for prejudice."

Although he had the face of an average thirty-five-year-old man, he had the body and build of a stocky adolescent boy. If anyone ever bothered to look past that, Tanner mused, they'd be amazed at the amount of know-how packed in that stunted body. According to Tiny, no one ever bothered.

"So," he concluded, "I set about keeping accounts for the local citizenry, suppressing my desire to practice law in any form."

Tanner rested his head on his linked hands, trapping his knuckles against the back of the plush chair, and stared at the splash of lamplight on the ceiling. The boyish eagerness, the thrill he'd felt at getting elected as marshal, came back to mock him. "I guess I was the bigger fool, then, for thinking I could keep my past a secret. Or if word did get out, that folks would still give me the benefit of the doubt. It explains all the odd looks I've been getting. Guess everyone is just waiting for me to knock off the bank or hold up the train."

"To my knowledge, only Clark, Sullivan, Brandenburger, and myself are aware of the stigma attached to your surname, and only because of the standard policy to research any applicants. The remaining citizens are simply wary toward you because of the alleged curse."

"What curse?" Tanner scoffed.

"Haven't you noticed how many peace officers Dogwood Springs has gone through over the years?"

"A lot of lawmen die. It's a hazard that comes when you wear a badge."

"Thayer got trampled by his own horse, Myrick drowned when he fell through the ice over Hollytree Pond, and, of course, you are aware of how Page died."

"So they figure a bunch of accidents amount to a curse on the town?"

"People are highly superstitious, and the coincidence merely fuels the fire. Every time word spreads of another marshal dying, folks become more convinced that they should be prepared to make burial arrangements for anyone who holds office in Dogwood Springs. That is why you were hired, in spite of your family."

"Should I feel flattered that they'd rather have a two-bit crook whose life is disposable than a midget with a law degree?" he shot back.

Tiny had the grace to overlook the insult. "The rationale was to hire a thief to catch a thief."

Suddenly weary, Tanner pressed his thumb and middle finger into his eye sockets. "I'm not a thief, Tiny. And I owe that to my mother. No matter how much grief Pa gave her, she refused to let him drag me along on his 'adventures.' Because of her, I escaped that sort of life before I got sucked into it too deep. But I've had to live with an exaggerated reputation because my pa and brother weren't as obliging."

"I have already reached that conclusion. I believe I can say the same for Clark and Brandenburger."

"But not Sullivan."

"Your family's reputation preceded you. As president and owner of the bank, he has more at stake than any of us, and I'm afraid the incident with the train bandits has left him calloused against you."

"I sure didn't give him cause to think otherwise."

Tanner stintingly explained what had happened in Sullivan's office a short while earlier. Tiny gasped when he heard the price Eden was being forced to pay to hold on to the house, and Tanner believed his surprise was real. "Seth Page might have been a hero, but he wasn't much of a provider as far as I'm concerned. What kind of man leaves his wife and kids at the mercy of a shark like Sullivan?" Even Fain, for all his dirty dealings, hadn't left Ina completely destitute. Sure, the money had belonged to others, and his mother had cringed every time she'd spent a cent of it, but she'd used it to buy only the barest necessities. The rest of it was probably still hidden somewhere in the farmhouse. She'd never returned it to the rightful owners for fear that they'd accuse Tanner of the robberies.

"A man who feels he is invincible."

"Well, I know the risks of this job. It's one of the reasons I never started a family. But I can't help what I feel for Eden. I want to make sure she never again has to blister her hands scraping up money to live on."

"Then why not confess your knowledge of her financial burden? Not only might your honesty save her the labor of working for you, but it may earn you her gratitude."

"Because she's too proud! If she knew I stepped in and took over her affairs, she'd never forgive me. She'd think that I doubted her ability to care for those kids." That, and a bit more selfishly, the ties binding them would be cut. As long as Eden worked for him, there was a thread linking them together.

"You are going to great lengths to provide for a woman not even your wife."

"We may not have exchanged vows, but she's mine. I feel it"—he hit his balled hand against his chest—"right here. She just doesn't know it yet."

"That is an arrogant assumption."

"My only other choice is to let her go. And I can't do that." Tanner unfolded himself from the chair and rocked his hat on his head until it fit right.

"You may have no choice if she cannot accept the man you once were, and the man you hope to become."

"Point taken." Though the idea of living the rest of his life without Eden and the kids filled him with an emptiness he couldn't explain, not to anyone—least of all to himself. "But even if she never returns my feelings, I still aim to protect her." In case Tiny had any doubts, Tanner stressed his next words. "Anyone who thinks to ever hurt Eden or her children again will have me to reckon with."

He strode to the door with a somber Tiny following him. Opening it, Tanner paused on the threshold. "Just out of curiosity, what made you change your mind about me?"

"You had faith in me when nobody else did."

Steam rising from the washtub left beads of moisture on Eden's face as she scrubbed Little Seth's trousers against the ribbed board. Every washday she found herself wearing holes in the knees of his trousers trying to get out the ground-in dirt. "Seth, you have got to stop crawling around under the house. Don't you know that spiders and snakes hide under there?"

Lissa clipped another sheet to the line. "Yeah, big fat hairy spiders and long slimy snakes that eat runty little boys."

"Stop teasing him, Lissa."

"It's my fort," Little Seth said, lining the clothespins up like soldiers on the porch step. "Marshal Mac says it's nifty."

Ruthie carried over an armful of wood to feed the fire beneath the washtub. "He plays with his friends under there."

Eden's arms stilled. She gave Ruthie a puzzled look. "What friends?"

"Patch and Amos and Joe," she answered.

"Seth?" Eden fought to keep the alarm from her voice. "Have you been inviting neighbor children over without my permission? Where did you meet these boys?"

Little Seth and Ruthie exchanged a secretive glance, guilt written all over their faces.

"Lissa, what do you know about this?"

But Lissa, staring past Eden's shoulder, seemed not to have heard the question. "Mama, isn't that the lady from the hotel?"

Eden looked back, surprised to see Rosalyn strolling toward them. She rubbed the kink in her back as she rose from the bent position. "We will discuss this later," she told the children. Wiping her hands on her apron, Eden called, "Hello, Mrs. Brandenburger."

"Oh, do call me Rosalyn. Hello, children." Her smile revealed teeth as white as the fringe on her parasol. Turning back to Eden, she said, "I ran into Tanner on the way here and he asked me to deliver this to you." From the gingham-lined basket on her arm, Rosalyn withdrew a paper-wrapped object and handed it to Eden.

Eden frowned as she took the package. It had the shape and smell of a loaf of bread. She flipped open the attached note and read it silently: "The ducks are starving at Bass Ridge Pond. Let's go feed them tomorrow morning. Tanner."

"That man is stone deaf," Eden muttered aloud, a small smile playing on her lips.

Ruthie dashed around the washtub and clasped her hands under her chin. "Is Tan givin' you another present, Mama?"

"Another?" Rosalyn asked with an amused lift of her brow.

"It's not the first one."

"I do believe the man is sweet on you," Rosalyn sang.

"Hmph. If he would devote as much time to catching criminals as he does pestering me, the outlaw plague would be cured by now." Her claim held less bite than she intended.

"That's a new word for it, pestering. In my day they called it courting."

"Pestering, courting—it's all the same to me." Eden forced herself to fold the note and hand the loaf back to Rosalyn. "Could I impose on you to return this to him?"

"With a message or without?"

Eden pondered the question. "Tell him to look up the word 'no' in the dictionary. He hasn't yet seemed able to grasp its meaning."

"There is something to say for persistence, Eden."

And he was persistent. Eden gave him that much. In fact, he wouldn't leave her alone. This was the fifth invitation he'd sent since their picnic after her son's birthday. And though she'd refused every one, he still hadn't given up.

"You said that you were on your way here, Mrs.— Rosalyn."

"Oh, yes, I almost forgot. I brought something for the children, too." Rosalyn dug back into her basket.

Lissa peered between the freshly washed sheets hanging limply from the clothesline. "For us?"

"What is it?" Ruthie cried, Seth following close at her heels.

"Well, we raised enough funds at the hug social to purchase new slates and chalk for all the school-age children—"

"Hug social?" Eden interrupted, her polite smile falling flat.

Rosalyn paused in doling out the slates and chalk to the children. "Tanner said he had invited you."

"Yes, he did." It had been the third invitation, actually. "But I thought it was a joke."

"Oh, no. Every year we hold a fund-raiser for the church or the school. This year we decided rather than a box supper, we'd have a hug social. We made it so that it cost ten cents to hug anyone between fifteen and twenty, five cents to hug someone from twenty to thirty or two old maids, and one dollar to hug another man's wife. We raised over twenty dollars total."

Don't ask, Eden. You don't care. You don't— "Did the marshal hug anybody?"

"Oh, he certainly did!"

The redheaded restaurant owner. Eden knew it.

"He paid a full ten cents to hug that hen of his!"

* * *

The next Friday morning passed at a crawl, but just before the noon hour it seemed to have sprouted wings. Eden rushed about the house, searching every room's nooks and crannies for Seth's shoe. The child was constantly taking his shoes off, then misplacing them. Just as she entered the living room for another exploration, something shattered in the kitchen and Eden wondered what Ruthie had broken this time.

"Mama, my socks have a big tear in them. Can you sew them?"

On hands and knees in front of the sofa, one of the only pieces of living room furniture she hadn't been able to sell, she told Lissa, "Just find another pair. And go see what Ruthie broke, would you please?" *Ah-ha!* She dragged out the worn and warped leather object that matched the one on Seth's left foot.

When Eden rose, she noticed Lissa still standing in the doorway, frowning. "Go on now, Lissa. I can't be late for work."

"What are you wearing that for?"

Eden glanced down at the forest-green skirt and navy-blue rose-and-leaf print shirt she had on. Self-consciously she brushed off the bit of dust clinging to her shoulders. "What's wrong with it?" In fact, it was one of her better outfits.

"You're s'pose'ta wear black."

"It's a thousand degrees outside and black just absorbs the heat." She rose and started past her daughter to check on Ruthie herself.

"You always wore black before the new marshal started coming around."

The accusation scored a point that she refused to acknowledge. Eden mustered as much composure as she could dredge up. "What I wear has nothing to do with Marshal McCay. If I take the time to change, I'll be late." She wasn't going to examine why she was in such a hurry to get to work either. It couldn't be that she might—*might*—run into him. That would be as good as admitting that she was letting him get under her skin.

"You're forgetting about Pa, aren't you, Mama?"

I'm trying. She didn't say that, of course. It would only upset Lissa more than she already appeared. Instead, Eden knelt and looked into eyes a swirling blend of brown and gold. Too observant. Too astute. Her baby girl was growing up so fast. Where had all the time gone? Eden willed away the knob in her throat and summoned a smile. "I could never forget your pa. I see him every day when I look at you and your brother. You both are so much like him." She drew her finger across Lissa's bangs. "But almost a year has passed since he died. Would it make you happy if I wore black forever?"

No answer.

Eden sighed, then sat on the bare floor, her skirts billowing around her thighs, and pulled her reluctant seven-year-old into her lap. Belatedly she sensed that what she wore had nothing to do with her choice of clothing. It had everything to do with insecurity—a feeling of which she was very familiar. Wrapping her arms around Lissa, she gently urged, "Tell me about your pa."

Lissa's surprise made Eden feel ashamed that she hadn't thought to ask before. "He was big."

"Yes, he was," Eden concurred.

"And strong."

"I agree."

"And handsome."

"Oh, yes." Eden nodded. "I noticed that the first time I saw him."

"Where was that?" Lissa asked with a curious tilt of her head.

"At a stage depot in Fort Worth. He was standing outside the ticket counter"—*demanding to know why the stage was late*—"talking to the clerk. The instant I alighted from the stagecoach, he turned, and I knew he was the man I would take as my husband."

"Did you feel all warm inside when he looked at you?"

"I felt something for him." *Obligation.* "We were married a week later."

Lissa sank against Eden's front and sighed. "I bet you were so happy."

It was gushing down rain. Standing in front of the dour-faced justice of the peace, she'd been shivering in her soaked calico dress from cold and fear. There were no flowers, no tender touch of his hand to ease her qualms, not even a ring until afterward. And Seth'd had a fit parting with the two dollars the tarnished band had cost him at the pawnbroker's shop. Eden smiled sadly at the memory. "I was even happier when you were born."

"Was Pa?"

Eden silently sucked in a breath of dread, then let it creep back out. Seth had been furious when he'd finally come home from tracking a pair of horse thieves and learned she'd delivered him a girl child. "He swore you would be a boy. The minute he saw you, though, he didn't care what you were." An old pang of bitterness returned full force. He'd taken one look at their newborn daughter and hadn't cared at all.

"Tanner McCay's nothing like my pa."

She took a long time to respond. "No, sweetheart, he isn't."

He was walking out of the jailhouse, about to tie the scarf around the beam to signal another prisoner, when she and the children arrived. Though he looked haggard and mussed, his face unshaven and his clothes rumpled, his eyes glowed when he saw them approach. Eden realized in that instant that she was coming to expect—to even secretly savor—that particular expression.

"Hey, if it isn't my favorite family!" He greeted Ruthie and Little Seth with the same open affection as always when they rushed toward his legs and pelted him with exuberant questions.

Yet his eyes never left her.

A shameful warmth rippled through Eden as his appreciative gaze skimmed up and down her body, as if reading every secret concealed beneath her clothing. Likewise, the sight of him quickened the flow of her blood.

Funny how the days had passed so slowly during his short absence. He'd had to leave again for two days after receiving word that Mad Dog Owens, a teenage rapist, had been spotted in the area. Now that he was back, time seemed to stand still. Each second seemed to go on forever, yet disappear in a blink. Eden knew it didn't make any sense, but nothing had made sense since the day he'd strolled into her yard.

He couldn't sense how he made her feel, could he? All confused and eager and flustered. It was bad enough that she couldn't subdue her reaction to him when she was alone, when uncontrollable dreams hounded her at night. To Eden's utter dismay, the dreams were of a terribly wanton nature, involving naked flesh and wild caresses and greedy mouths, and she would awaken confused, feverish, and aching for something just out of grasp.

Tanner wouldn't leave her alone, not even when she slept.

And that petrified her, because she wasn't so sure anymore if she wanted him to.

Hiding a fresh wave of turmoil, Eden avoided his eyes and gestured to the scarf he'd stuffed into his pocket. "Another mouth to feed? I hope it isn't Owens."

"No, I took Owens to county. It's Washburn again." Marshal McCay's severe tone told her that she need not even ask why he'd been arrested; Washburn was a notorious woman-beater. The marshal had certainly been busy. " 'Fraid this time I'm gonna need you to take a look at him."

"What happened?" Eden led the way into the jail.

"He, uh, had a little accident with the butt of my gun."

Glancing between the bars, Eden could see that. A crusty trail of blood marred the side of Mr. Washburn's hardened face, along his eye and down his jaw. She set her basket down in front of the desk, noticing but paying little attention to a towel-wrapped object lying on top of it. "I'll need water to clean that wound."

"I'll fetch it, Mama."

"No!" Eden startled them all. Her chest felt banded in

panic. Her hands trembled. She curled her fingers into her palm, hiding the fact, hating that she was back to fighting hysteria, when until Lissa had wandered away from the creek she'd had it under control. "No," Eden repeated. "Just . . . stay in here and shovel out the stove."

The marshal's too-observant gaze remained on her.

"Did ya shoot him, Marshal Mac?" Seth asked, staring at the huge man sitting on a cot behind bars.

"No, son. Just conked him over the head to settle him down. I'll get that water for you, Mrs. Page. There should be some bandages in the kit in the bottom desk drawer."

Eden remembered. That was where Seth always kept the medical kit too. As she retrieved the small metal box, glad for the diversion, she felt thankful that Washburn needed only a minor bump tended instead of a bullet removed. She'd dug shot out of bodies more times than she cared to recall, and the last time . . .

The realization that she could be treating the marshal—this marshal—made her weak. She braced her arms on the desktop, breathing deeply in an effort to calm herself.

He found her like that a few minutes later, dropped the bucket, and rushed to her side, flinging his arm across her back. "Eden? Are you all right?"

She nodded mutely.

"If you aren't up to doctoring him, I'll fetch Arnold."

"No, no. I—it's nothing."

" 'Nothing' wouldn't make you turn white as bleached cotton."

"I said it's nothing." She ducked away from under his arm, away from his concern, and took the medical kit with her to the cell door. After he unlocked it, he drew his gun and made to enter with her. Lissa, Ruthie, and Little Seth had stopped their individual tasks—tasks that were so routine by now that it was unnecessary to direct them—to stare at the marshal with a combination of surprise and awe. "Is that really necessary in front of the children?"

"Yep," was all he said.

He was an intimidating figure, leaning against the

wall, his low-tipped hat brim shadowing his face, his arms folded across each other, the barrel of his Peacemaker resting across his left biceps, his five-point badge reflecting inner power. This was a side of him she hadn't glimpsed until then, yet she felt comforted and protected having him at her side, in this role, more than she would have if he'd been the awkward charmer with the knee-buckling grin.

And as she began cleaning Washburn's face with a trembling hand, it struck her that Tanner McCay seemed to have the ability to do what her husband and other lawmen she'd met never could—separate the man from the occupation. That prospect had been easily unacceptable before; there had been no visible comparison. Now, as a firsthand witness to the changes that came over him when he worked, Eden could no longer deny fact. Tanner McCay and Marshal McCay were distinctly, unmistakably different.

But how long would it last before the two—man and profession—merged into one brute force?

Eden refused to examine the emotions warring inside her. There were too many of them colliding at once. Instead, she sponged the gash behind Washburn's temple with iodine and covered the wound with a bandage.

The marshal reholstered his gun as soon as they cleared out of the cell and his prisoner was once more locked in, and though his expression resumed its usual, wholesomely appealing guise, traces of his alter ego lurked just below the surface. A little bit of hardness, a whole lot of caution.

He's good at his job, she thought with an odd, intuitive conviction. "How long have you been a marshal, Marshal?" Eden asked, taking the broom from the closet and joining Ruthie in the next cell.

He grinned bashfully from the doorway. "About a month."

"I mean, not counting Dogwood Springs?"

"About a month," he repeated.

Eden halted the broom to gawk at him. "Are you serious?"

"As a snakebite."

"But you seem so . . . experienced."

"I rode with a couple of posses, was even a deputy once. But until I got elected here, that's as far as I got."

"Always the bridesmaid, never the bride?"

"Don't think I cotton too much for that analogy, but yeah, that about sums it up."

She linked her hands on top of the broom handle and rested her chin on her knuckles. "I must say that I'm surprised that the town council would hire you without more proof that you could handle the duties."

The innocent remark brought back the memory of his conversation with Tiny. Tanner's lip curled. "I guess you could say they found my skills fitting for the job." The presence of Little Seth at his side distracted him. He ruffled the boy's hair. "Hey, Maverick, what's that thing on my desk?"

"I don't know, sir."

"Hmmm. The only time I ever see something wrapped up is around a birthday—you just had a birthday, didn't you?"

"Yes, sir," Seth whispered, holding his breath as he stared at the object.

"Wonder if the birthday fairies left that here for you. . . ."

"For me?"

Tanner wandered to his desk and picked up the gift he'd found for Little Seth several days before but hadn't had a chance to give him until then. "It feels like a five-year-old's present." Bringing it to his nose, Tanner said, "It smells like a five-year-old's present. Hey, aren't you a five-year-old?"

A slow nod of bated anticipation was his answer.

He tossed it to Little Seth. "Maybe you best open it and see."

Catching the bundle, Seth immediately peeled open the towel wound around it. His face brightened. "Wow, my wish came true and I didn't even blow out the candles!" Seth pulled the angled stick from an old threadworn holster and fit it in the palm of his hand, his index finger slipping into the odd loop nature had made for a trigger guard. All Tanner'd had to do was saw off about a foot of rot from the part that made the barrel. "It looks just like yours!"

Tanner couldn't help grinning like a mule eating cactus at the pure joy on Little Seth's face. He'd known the minute he saw the unusual piece of branch that he'd found the perfect gift for the boy. Seth's reaction was worth getting lost in the woods, stepping in a cow patty, falling into a bog, getting eaten alive by mosquitoes, slicing his ankle on an old tin can, and finding a tick in his britches when he finally made it back to town.

"A gun? You gave my son a gun?"

Eden's ashen face, the horror in her voice, pulled the plug on his pleasure, and Tanner's broad smile fell.

Chapter Thirteen

"WHAT WERE YOU thinking to give him such a thing without first checking with me?"

Little Seth running around, pretending to shoot at invisible outlaws with his finger, that's what, Tanner thought.

Shifting uncomfortably, he replied, "He's been eyeballing my Peacemaker. Until he's old enough to learn how to handle a real gun, I thought he'd have fun playing with a fake one."

"What kind of house were you raised in?" she gasped.

Tanner sucked in his breath, the words a cannonball to his gut.

"He is a five-year-old boy!" Her fingers went bone white around the broom handle. "He has no business with a gun!"

"It's a harmless toy—"

"Harmless?" She advanced toward Tanner, looking as if she wanted nothing more than to take a swing at him with the broom. "Guns are not harmless. They kill people!"

"A careless person with a gun kills people, Mrs. Page," Tanner corrected her, feeling a rare mounting of temper. "Unless a boy is taught at an early age to use a weapon safely, sure as God made little green apples there's gonna be grief in his house. The day's gonna come when he'll be expected to feed his family, or have to protect himself in order to survive. Would you honestly turn him out in the world defenseless?" The thought plumb gave him the willies.

She glanced around. Washburn had passed out in a drunken stupor, but the kids were hanging on every word. Her voice lowered to a harsh whisper. "At least I have no intention of poisoning his mind."

"That wasn't the idea at all—"

"Oh, no?" Her slender brows arched. "Silly me," she mocked, slapping her forehead, "how could I forget? I'm talking to a marshal here! Slinging a gun is romantic and dashing. It isn't a statement to kill or be killed."

"Look," he argued in a matching tone, "if I hadn't learned to respect my weapon, hadn't learned how to use it proper, I might have shot Washburn today out of pure reaction. A rush does that to you, whether it's out of fear or anger or whatever. You don't think, you just pull the trigger—unless you learn that there are other choices."

"Are you speaking from experience?"

He might as well be spitting into the wind for all the good reasoning did him. Eden refused to be reasoned with. "In a manner of speaking."

"Well, so am I." Her eyes blazing with the fire of contempt, she hissed, "You crossed a line, Marshal McCay. You had no right giving him such a gift without my consent. You are not Little Seth's father nor are you his guardian, you are my boss. Perhaps it would do you well to remember that in the future."

"Eden?"

Jerking her head up from her arms, Eden spied Rosalyn standing in the open doorway, a closed parasol hooked over one arm, a covered basket over the other.

"Why are you crying?"

Eden turned her face away to wipe the wetness from her eyes and dab her nose with her apron. "I'm not," she quickly denied, but knew her thick voice gave her away when Rosalyn sailed toward the desk.

Ruthie and Little Seth, who had been helplessly patting Eden's back since she'd burst into tears, stepped aside to make room for the woman. Rosalyn set her things down, then lifted Eden's chin and looked sternly into her eyes. "What is it? And don't tell me it's nothing, because I won't believe you."

Oh, why did this woman always catch her at the worst times? Eden silently bemoaned.

"The marshal made her cry," Lissa tattled, handing Eden a glass of water.

"Tanner?" Rosalyn cried in disbelief. "What did he do?"

"He gave my brother a gun for his birthday."

Rosalyn gasped.

"Not a real gun," Eden clarified, avoiding Lissa's glower for defending Tanner. "A branch shaped like one."

The concern lines evaporated off Rosalyn's high forehead. "Oh, *that* gun."

"You know about it?"

"Everyone knows!"

Eden groaned.

A husky laugh escaped from Rosalyn as she lowered herself gracefully into the chair. "If you could have seen the look on his face when he came tramping out of the woods holding that scrawny stick—why, you would've thought he'd just found the cure for tuberculosis!" She shook her head in amusement. Fat chestnut curls, secured on one side of her head with a diamond comb, dragged to and fro across the top of her shoulder. "He sanded it down until it was smooth as glass, then scoured this town until he found someone willing to part with an old holster," she continued, unaware that she was rubbing salt in Eden's open wound. "It was the sweetest thing I've ever known a man to do."

"Mama got mad at Tan."

"She hollered at him," Seth added.

"I accused him of poisoning my son's mind," Eden confessed, her eyes again filling with remorseful tears.

"Oh, dear." Rosalyn frowned. "And what did Tanner say?"

"Nothing. He walked out."

"Talk to him, Eden," Rosalyn urged. "Straighten this out. You'll find that you will feel much better once you've cleared the air."

"I don't know if he will listen."

"Then cuff him to the nearest pole and make him listen."

Fool woman. *Bang!* The hammer hit the nail head and drove it in. How could she be so blasted narrow-minded? It was just a cotton-pickin' toy, for pete's sake!

Tanner took another nail from those clamped between his teeth and set the point to the wood. Glory be, didn't she get it? Boys played! They pretended they were cowboys or Indians . . . *bang.* Gold diggers and stage-coach drivers . . . *bang, bang* . . . bankers and train engineers . . . lawmen or outlaws . . . *bang, bang, bang!* Heck, he and his brother used to play games like that all the time.

After Tanner had nailed in one end of the roosting rod in Myrtle's unfinished coop, he was breathing heavily with frustration. He crossed the coop to affix the other end. Wooden pole screeched against inner frame as he wedged it into place. The sound startled Myrtle, who had perched on his shoulder, and she dived off to pace at his feet.

"Howdy, Mac."

Tanner glanced behind him and nodded absently at his visitor. "Hollis."

He wasn't much in the mood for company, but Hollis didn't seem to notice. His pot belly dipped low over his belt as he sat spread-kneed on a nearby tree stump and stuffed his cheek with chaw.

"Whooey, it's hotter'n love at haying time out here," he declared, mopping sweat from his face with a kerchief. "How can you stand it?"

Tanner squatted to check the straightness of the bar. "It's even hotter inside," he replied. In more ways than one. But even though his temper had reached the breaking point, Tanner couldn't bring himself to leave Eden and Washburn alone in the same room. In case she needed him, he was only a holler away. Not that Eden would ever need *him*. She'd made that clear as daylight.

"Came to see if you were goin' to the council meeting at Avery's tonight."

Satisfied that the rod looked even, Tanner rolled another nail into place and set the hammer swinging. "I'm the marshal, not an alderman." And if he ever forgot his place again—*bang, bang, bang*; iron sank into wood—he could sure count on Eden to remind him of it. According to her, he was just a walking mind-poisoner. A gun-slinging dunce. A dang tin man. Whatever the heck that meant.

"Reckoned you would on account o' Sullivan talking all week about pressin' charges against you for pret-near strangling him." Hollis's chuckle hinted at admiration. "Remind me never to get you riled."

Bent over the wood, his mind filled with Eden, a minute passed before the comment registered. Even then Tanner's brow puckered in confusion. He swung around to face Hollis. "What did you say?"

"I said, remind me—"

"No, before that."

"That John's wantin' to skin your hide for almost strangling him?"

Tanner's fist tightened around the hammer handle. "Why, that conniving—what does he aim to gain by pressing charges against me? I can't very well throw myself in jail."

"Heck, he prob'ly figures if he needles you enough, you'll turn in your badge and hightail it out of his hair."

Falling back against the coop wall, Tanner groaned and pinched the bridge of his nose. Dang. This was turning out to be one of those days when a body wondered why he bothered to get out of bed. First the argument with Eden, now this.

Tanner squinted up at the dull blue sky. This fight to make something decent of himself was getting awful tiresome. It wasn't the first time he'd found himself locking horns with a man like John Sullivan, who'd like nothing better than to see him fail. This was the first time he'd had anything to lose, though. He'd stood up for Eden—who he doubted would be very grateful—and now his job was on the line.

A mirthless sound burst from his lungs. If he had to do it all over again, he knew he'd do the same thing. Even if it meant going up against the town's wealthiest, most powerful alderman. He'd be a poor excuse for a man if he'd stood by and done nothing while Sullivan swindled a helpless woman and her young'uns. Folks might claim he was a lot of things; he wouldn't add coward to the list.

"Reckon I better show my face at this meeting after all," Tanner said decisively, returning to his work. Let that highfalutin carpetbagger try and drive him out of town and job.

"Yep, well"—Hollis hoisted his bulk off the stump—"you might want to think about finding yourself a lawyer."

He stood just inside the chicken coop with his arm raised high against the frame, his face hidden in the bed of his elbow. At his side a hammer dangled loosely in his grip.

He looked . . . vulnerable. The urge to go to him, to lay her cheek against his broad back, to wrap her arms around his waist and beg his forgiveness nearly overwhelmed her.

She tried to remember who and what he was, but the reasons she wanted nothing to do with him kept getting clouded by pictures. . . .

Of Tanner rambling through a field of bluebonnets, wearing snug denims and his old leather vest, his muscled body flexing each time he bent to add another flower to the bunch already in his fist.

Of him sliding his mouth across his harmonica, then singing so loud and bold that she could feel the music all the way down to her soul. The energy. The life. The simple, sweet pleasure.

Of Tanner cuddling the children . . . leading a chicken around by a leash . . . giving her blow-wishes . . .

Eden shut her eyes.

Suddenly, the sound of iron hitting wood wrenched her from her thoughts. She opened her eyes just in time to see a hammer ricochet off the coop wall, then fall soundlessly into a pile of hay. With his back to her, she watched Tanner whip off his hat and clench it tightly. His shoulders rose and fell rapidly.

Eden cast a quick glance behind her at the children seated just inside the doorway, gaping at Tanner. "Practice writing your letters until I get back," she told them.

"Yes, ma'am," they replied, then bent over the paper she'd given them.

Crumpling her apron in her fist, Eden approached Tanner. "Marshal McCay, I'd like to talk to you."

Startled, he jerked halfway around. Eden winced. No gentle smile of invitation welcomed her. No dimple flashed in his cheek. In fact, she thought he looked kind of pale.

As if to escape her presence, he moved away to fetch the thrown tool. "You've said plenty already, Mrs. Page."

Remorse weighed on her like ten layers of wet wool. He'd wanted only to please Little Seth, and she'd all but spat on him for it. Eden guiltily lowered her gaze to the ground. "I want to apologize."

"You don't owe me any apologies. I'm just the boss, remember?"

He wasn't making this very easy. Had she pushed him past his limits? Tanner was one of the most even-tempered men she'd ever met, but once crossed . . . well, it was obvious that he could be a force to reckon with. But now that she'd built up the courage to face him, she couldn't let him chase her away, not even if that courage was disintegrating piece by piece. Her fist twisted the crisp fabric. "If you only understood—"

Cut off abruptly when he rounded on her, the wounded anger in his features wrenched Eden's heart.

"How the heck am I supposed to understand anything when you won't talk? Am I supposed to read your mind? Pull answers from thin air? Dammit, I'm not magic! I'm just a man."

Suddenly, his shoulders slumped, as if his rage had

grown too heavy to bear. "Just a man who's trying to grab hold of the best that life is giving me."

"And I," Eden countered, her voice unsteady with emotion, "am just a mother trying to hold on to the best that life has already given me."

Myrtle's soft clucking filled the brief void meeting that statement as they stared at each other. Finally Tanner said, "Then maybe we're both doing it wrong." He slid his gaze away. "Look, Eden, this isn't a good time to talk about this. I've got a lot on my mind right now."

He started to walk away, and Eden knew deep in her soul that if she didn't stop him now, he'd walk away and never come back. There would be no more flowers, no more songs, no more laughter.

Cuff him to the pole if you have to, but make him listen.

Her heart thudded painfully in her chest. She'd never have the courage or physical strength to cuff Tanner to anything, but Rosalyn was right; she had to make him listen.

"Seth used to brag that no one ever fooled with him because he was a marshal, as if his guns and his badge made him immortal." Her voice sounded abnormally loud to her own ears.

He straightened, but wouldn't look at her.

Mercy, this was hard. Eden opened and closed her hands, struggling for words to explain her behavior. "It was a game to him. A contest that he'd won for so long that it was inconceivable that he would ever lose."

"It *is* a game. Like a wild ride on a bucking stallion. The thrill comes from pitting yourself against a beast you have no control over but are compelled to tame."

"I don't want my son playing games like that—"

"Eden," he cut in, her name a short, dry laugh. "I hate to be the one to break it to you, but he plays them all the time. What do you think he does under the house?"

"He . . . just sits there."

"He pretends he's a lawman, and three imaginary little boys are his deputies."

"How do you know this?"

"He told me. He also told me that he wants to grow up and be a marshal, a hero like his pa was."

Eden inwardly recoiled as she remembered Little Seth caressing the toy in wonder. Holding it with reverence. How naturally the handle had fit in his palm, as if it were an extended part of him. She recognized the signs; she just refused to acknowledge them.

"Heck, I can't blame him. I don't know of a boy who hasn't wanted to be a hero sometime in his life."

"I suppose you want that too," she said sadly.

"Yeah," Tanner admitted wryly, "maybe I do. The fellow riding in on a big white horse, six-guns strapped to his hips, sweeping you off your feet . . . But all I got is threadbare blue, a scrawny chicken, and a rusty old Peacemaker." He shook his head at the humor in it. "I don't exactly live up to the image, do I?"

"Haven't you realized that that's all it is?" she whispered. "An image used to lure men away from their homes and families, and eventually into the grave?"

"Are you telling me you don't believe in heroes?"

"I can't believe in something that doesn't exist. And I don't want Little Seth believing in them either. The thought of him winding up like his father . . . it just tears me apart."

He studied her face silently for a long while. "What do you want me to do, Eden? Do you want me to take the gun back from him?"

Eden's lips rolled back over her teeth and she closed her eyes, wrestling with inner demons. Destiny had played a cruel trick on her. The more she tried to avoid lawmen, the more they were thrown into her life. "I can't do that. He's wanted one for so long, it would break his heart if you took it back now." Tonelessly she added, "Besides, as you pointed out, weapons are a necessary fact of life." A shudder passed through her. "But perhaps you"—she cleared her throat and turned pleading eyes to Tanner—"perhaps you could find the time to teach him, you know, the difference between a toy gun and the real thing."

He drew his finger along her jaw and gave her that endearingly crooked grin. "I'll make the time."

"Marshal Mac!"

Eden and Tanner both turned just as a gangly, tow-headed boy in his mid-teens came speeding around the corner.

Coming to an abrupt halt, Vern Tilly panted, "You gotta come quick, Marshal. Billy Joe done went and tied Bobby Jack to a telegraph pole and he's fixin' to set him on fire."

"I'm tempted to let those boys just kill each other and be done with it," he muttered.

"Marshal Mac, hurry!"

Eden hid her disappointment at the intrusion behind a forced smile. "Go on. Duty calls."

He glanced at Vern, then back to Eden, as if torn between the promise he'd just made to her and the commitment he'd made long ago to his sworn duty. Sworn duty won out.

She turned away slowly. She knew he had a job to do, yet she couldn't suppress the stab of jealousy. This is how it would always be if she let her heart rule her head.

"You're late, Tanner," Tiny said out of the side of his mouth.

"I know. Sorry, fellas." Tanner tipped his hat to the group sitting around the table in Avery's saloon. "Had me a little trouble down at the jail."

"You get those boys settled down, Mac?" Hollis asked.

"After they about tore each other's heads off in my cell. Finally had to cuff Billy Joe to one side, Bobby Jack to the other."

"Shoulda put one in with Washburn," Micaleb said. "He'd'a put the fear of God into either of those young whelps."

Sullivan glared at him, Tiny, and Hollis in turn, then snarled at Tanner. "If you are through with your tea party, let's get down to business."

Tanner moved to stand in a corner near the table, where he leaned against the smoke-stained wall. Soon a smile was itching to break out over his face. He discovered a perverse enjoyment in watching Sullivan squirm.

After he'd managed to wrestle the torch from Billy Joe's hands, drag him off to the jail, then untie Bobby Jack from the telegraph pole and drag him off to the jail, Tanner had taken up Hollis's suggestion and sought advice from the only lawyer he knew.

Watching Tiny stand up in defense of him three hours later made him glad he'd done so. Armed with that fancy law school degree of his, he had Sullivan sputtering and spitting in no time at all.

"He attacked me in my place of business!" Sullivan cried, leaping from his chair, which jarred the round table and sent Micaleb's tumbler of whiskey spilling over the edge. "Clark was there, he can vouch for McCay's hostile conduct."

Hollis missed the way Sullivan jerked a thumb in his direction, for he had leapt to his feet to avoid getting his lap soaked with liquor. Micaleb, too, jumped out of his chair, trying to save his drink.

Tiny remained unruffled. "Correction—in the privacy of your office. Which reduces the charge from public to simple assault, a misdemeanor which in this state carries a fine of no more than one hundred dollars. In view of the fact that you attempted fraud against Mrs. Page, I believe I can convince the judge to release Marshal McCay with a verbal reprimand. You, on the other hand, could be charged with a felony."

Sullivan paled, then flushed a deep, inflamed red. "I knew it was a mistake to hire you," he snapped at Tanner. "I should have listened to my instincts. You are no better than that convict that sired you." He jabbed his finger in the air toward Tanner's nose. "I'll warn you now, you might have fooled this town into thinking you're some kind of champion riding around on that fancy roan at all hours of the night—"

Tanner's arms slowly unfolded from across his chest and fell to his sides. "What in fire's fury are you talking about, Sullivan?" he interrupted. "I don't ride a fancy roan."

"Deny it all you will, but people have seen you checking locks and windows of half the stores in this town, and canvassing the streets on an unmarked horse."

"I'm one of those that saw you," Micaleb claimed. "You were riding behind Deidrich's last Sunday night."

"Then you made a mistake," he countered with deadly calm, his gaze never leaving Sullivan's face.

"Uh, Mac, I saw you too," Hollis put in reluctantly. "Down at the depot just the other morning on my way to the mill. Asked if you needed help, but you waved me on."

"I don't ride a fancy roan," Tanner insisted, dread clawing its way up his spine. "For that matter, I don't ride any horse, not since I lost mine on the trip down."

"You'd like us to believe that, wouldn't you?" Sullivan smirked. "A bit difficult when two witnesses are sitting right here."

"You wouldn't be calling me a liar, now, would you, friend?" Tanner asked directly, his voice low and ominous.

"I am a bit more careful in choosing my *friends,* McCay. You are not one of them." The chair screeched backward along the sawdust-coated floor. "I don't know what you're planning, but mark my words, you won't get away with it." Sullivan slammed his hat on his head and abandoned the meeting.

"Whew," Hollis breathed, breaking the tension-filled silence Sullivan left behind. "Feel like I was the dirt in a cockfight pit during the first round. I need a drink."

"Think I'll join you."

Clark and Brandenburger escaped to the bar.

"I get the feeling Sullivan just threatened to expose me."

Tiny collected the few papers and books he'd brought with him and stuffed them into a thin leather case. "John's family has wielded uncontested power and influence in this community for many years. He takes it as a personal affront when that status is undermined." Tiny looked up at Tanner with consternation. "His testimony can be very damaging. I hope you are prepared for the results should he make your records a matter of public appraisal."

"I'll get to the bottom of this before it goes any further. There's an explanation somewhere." Withholding his thoughts, he summoned a weak smile and flat-handed Tiny on the back. "Thanks for standing up for me. For such a little fellow, you pack quite a wallop."

Tiny shrugged one shoulder. "It was a simple case, easily reconciled."

"You're being modest." Tanner picked up his linen duster and slung it over his shoulder. "It's a shame you don't open up a practice here. I can see it now." Forming his hand into C, he drew an imaginary line through the air. "Tiny—what's your real name?"

"Chandon, but—"

"Chandon Ellert, Attorney-at-Law. Has a nice ring, huh?"

"Tanner, I have told you before, people are very narrow-minded—"

"Then I reckon they need their minds broadened."

Tiny cleared his throat. "Yes, well, let us fight one battle at a time, shall we? I have a premonition that this one has only just begun."

Tanner wholeheartedly agreed as the doors swung behind him. He passed by Deidrich's and Hannah's, the meeting playing itself over in his mind. *Was* he guilty of Sullivan's accusations?

The question hounded him all the way to the jail. He hung his hat and duster on the wall peg, then unbuckled his holster but kept his gun. With both cells full and blissfully quiet, Tanner settled into the stiff-backed chair. A fifteen-year-old conversation echoed in his head.

Ma, I didn't sneak out to meet no one. I was asleep all night.

Don't you lie to me, Tanner David McCay. I got one son raisin' hell all over the state, I won't have me another.

I ain't lyin', Ma!

You 'spect me to believe you're walkin' in your sleep?

Hard as he tried, he never could remember what he'd

done during those lost hours, yet Ina had always told him he acted wide-awake and perfectly normal. Nobody ever got hurt; nothing ever got stolen. Still, he'd always found grass stains on his pant cuffs and clumps of soil on his boots.

Though he hadn't done so in years, he'd been under pressure lately and it might have triggered the sleepwalking again. It would at least explain the new round of late-hour prowling he was being accused but had no memory of.

A few minutes later he propped his feet on the desk. His socks were sun-bleached white, not a speck of fresh dust on them. On the floor beside the desk lay his boots, scrubbed shiny and clean. He had to know. If he awoke in the morning, grass blades clinging to his soles, or red Texas dirt staining the bottoms of his socks, then he'd have evidence that the nightly sightings were him after all.

But a little detail still nagged at him—where'd he get the horse?

Chapter Fourteen

LITTLE SETH DASHED from cover to cover, whipping his toy gun from the holster secured around his waist with a piece of rope, shooting at poor Myrtle, who'd unwillingly become the stagecoach robber Seth was bent on capturing dead or alive. Ruthie, of course, determined that she would not be left out of the game, and played her brother's deputy. Tanner acted as a judge some of the time, but filled in as a horse when the need arose, which it seemed to now.

He bucked and made a whinnying noise. Grabbing his hair, Ruthie giggled.

God, he loved this time with them. Keeping his promise to Eden, he visited as often as his duties would allow. Sometimes she helped him and the kids as they painted the fence, made a new ladder, and replaced the rungs on the upstairs railing, but mostly, she and Lissa did their own chores a short ways away from wherever he and Ruthie and Little Seth were working.

But every now and then he'd get the feeling that Lissa was watching from a distance, yet all he ever saw was a dark blotch of shadow that disappeared as quick as it took shape.

They were the bright spots in a dark and uncertain future.

Suspicion had settled like a storm cloud over the town,

bringing the threat of his professional ruin, especially after
he'd been sighted again the day before, in broad daylight,
supposedly trying to break into Moley's Carriage Repair—
for what, he couldn't imagine. He didn't even own a carriage.

Rosalyn encouraged him to hold his head high; Tiny
advised in that fancy vocabulary of his to look for the light
at the end of the tunnel.

It was growing dimmer and dimmer, though, and Tanner often wondered why he bothered staying in a place
where his welcome wore thinner.

"Marshal McCay, what on earth do you think you're
doing?" Eden scolded, emerging from the house onto the
front porch.

Tanner wrenched his mind from his troubles. "Why,
I'm the horse, ma'am," he said in a deep, exaggerated drawl
from his hands-and-knees position. "I'm supposed to be the
judge, but Deputy Ruthie's horse went lame, so I'm filling
in."

"You are supposed to be teaching Little Seth the difference between reality and make-believe."

"He's learning pretty fast, don't you think? Don't recall ever seeing a boy make believe better than Marshal
Maverick here." He winked.

She folded her arms across her breasts and gave Tanner
a disapproving look. "I meant you should be teaching him
gun safety, not encouraging him to shoot everything that
moves."

"But Myrtle is armed and dangerous!" he cried. "The
boy's only defending himself."

"Come on, Mama," Ruthie cheered, bouncing on his
back as if she sat on the real thing. "Come play with us. You
can be the damsel in a dress!"

Her laughter came without warning. The sound, un-
tamed and husky, set Tanner's blood to pumping like a
plunger in a butter churn. Amazed, he simply stared at her
for a long while before finally rising from the ground,
Ruthie sliding off his back.

"You better be careful, Eden," Tanner warned, brushing the dirt off his knees. "Laughter like that does crazy things to a man's insides."

She ducked her head shyly.

He smiled. It was still gonna take awhile, but her frozen emotions were slowly thawing.

"When are you gonna be our pa, Tan?" Ruthie asked, leaning so far back in the swing that the tails of her black braids dragged in the dirt. Seth sat on her lap, leaning the opposite way, hanging on to the ropes for dear life.

He should have known they'd get to a "when" question, Tanner thought, shaking his head. They'd already covered why birds fly, where trees come from, what makes grass green, and who tucks in Mrs. Sun when Mr. Moon wakes up. But pushing Ruthie and Little Seth on the tree swing while Eden went into the house to get them all something to drink helped get his mind off his troubles. "Oh, sweet potato, I'd like that better than anything in the whole wide world. But your ma has to marry me before I can be your pa."

"What's marry?" Little Seth asked.

Out of the corner of his eye, Tanner noticed a shadow move near the corner of the house beside the porch. He tilted his head forward for a better look, wanting to confirm his suspicions that Lissa was the one who had been spying on him lately. The shadow darted back. "It's when a man and a lady go in front of a preacher and promise to love each other for the rest of their lives," he answered Seth, pretending ignorance when the shadow stretched out again.

"We got a preacher!" Ruthie announced. "Let's get married."

Amused at the simple logic, Tanner said, "It doesn't work like that. Your ma has to agree first."

Ruthie didn't wait for the swing to stop moving before she jumped off, dumping her brother in the dirt. She grabbed his hand and yanked him to his feet. "Come on, Little Seth. Let's go tell Mama to marry Tan so he can be our pa."

Tanner caught them gently by their collars and hauled

them back. "Whoa there, you two. Your ma won't marry me just because you tell her to. She's gotta want to."

Ruthie rolled her eyes in a comically childlike way. "But we got her to go on a picnic."

"And fishing," Seth added.

"Only because she couldn't resist you little scamps."

Suddenly an idea began taking shape. *No,* Tanner thought, trying to rid himself of the tempting notion, he couldn't. He shouldn't. It was too naughty, too underhanded. . . .

But if the kids could use their wiles to give their mother a nudge in his direction, if Eden could see that they all belonged together . . . "Maverick? Sweet potato? How'd you like to be part of my posse?" With their heads close, Tanner knelt to whisper his plan.

"Ruthie, did you stock the wood box like Mama asked you to?"

Ruthie whirled around, and bouncing like she had springs in her feet, cried, "Lissa! We're gonna get Mama to like Tan so he can marry us!"

Lissa sent Tanner a stunned look. "You're gonna marry my mama?" she whispered as if it were something he should be ashamed of.

Knowing no other way to answer her except with honesty, Tanner shrugged. "I hope so—someday."

"But you're a tin man!"

There was that word again. Tanner cocked his head to the side. "You don't like tin men, do you?"

"They take people away! And we don't ever see 'em again!"

Ah, now it was beginning to make sense. "Honey, I don't want to take your ma away."

"Yes, you do!" Lissa argued, her voice panicked, her hands balled at her sides. "Mama says that tin men care only about themselves. That they don't need nobody. And that we're not s'pose to trust 'em, not ever!"

Tanner rubbed his mustache thoughtfully. "Have you ever seen a tin man before?"

She bit her lip and frowned anxiously. "No."

"Then how do you know that's what I am?"

Glancing down at his vest, she stated, "Because you wear a star." Then, cupping her hands behind Ruthie and Little Seth's necks, she steered them toward the house. "You two are always runnin' off when we got a zillion chores and now you're gettin' out of 'em again. . . ."

Her voice faded, but her words echoed in Tanner's head. Shoot, didn't the girl know that her father had worn a star too?

Then again, kids didn't think in those terms. At her age, he hadn't made any connection between how his father supported them and who he was at home. Fathers were simply fathers.

Sure, he'd known that thieves existed. That didn't mean his father was one. The day Fain had made him and Terron hold guns on all those people in the First National Bank of Davis when they were ten years old had opened his eyes, though. Up until that incident, Tanner had held only the horses, completely unaware of what Fain did out of sight.

Not that Seth Page was anything like Fain McCay. Shoot, his name alone was tied with sainthood. Little Seth wanted to grow up and be like him. Ruthie was so hungry for a father's affections that she'd take any man willing to give her any that came close. Lissa was afraid that someone might step into his shoes and steal her mother's love, and Eden . . . Eden had lost her faith in heroes. Because her own hero had gone and died on her?

Well, one thing Tanner knew was that Saint Seth Page's death was tearing his family to shreds. And he had no idea how he should go about mending the rips when he was hanging on only by a thread himself.

Eden had put Ruthie and Little Seth down for their naps, and while Lissa snapped beans for supper, she and Tanner sat on the porch drinking cold tea, he on the bottom step, she in her rocking chair. Eden studied his profile, wondering at the cause for the deep lines etched into his brow.

"You are unusually quiet, Marshal."

"Just thinking."

"Does it hurt that bad?"

"What?"

"You have this pained look on your face."

His laugh was short, almost forced. "Eden"—he rubbed his palm against the seam of his trousers—"what would you do if someone insisted that you'd done something you couldn't prove you didn't do?"

Stunned that anyone—least of all a man—would ask her opinion, Eden pondered the question carefully before answering. "I suppose that would depend on what it was. Are you talking something illegal?"

"No, not illegal. Peculiar and this side of shady, but not illegal. Not yet, anyway."

"And you accused me of not making sense?" She gave him a sideways smile.

He stood up and began to pace. "Shortly after I came to Dogwood Springs, I was seen chasing someone away from the sawmill. I don't see how that's possible because I was in my own bed, sound asleep. Another time I was seen behind the general store. If I remember correctly, that was the same night I'd returned from Shreveport. Again I went straight to the jail, so tired I almost sawed logs right at my desk. That's just the beginning. I've also been seen checking locks on all the stores and riding a horse around town. Problem is, I don't own a horse."

Once the astonishment of his confiding in her wore off, Eden sifted through all the factors. "Is this person certain it was you?"

Tanner shrugged. "It's not just one person anymore, it's half the town from what I hear, and they all swear to their stories."

"If you are not the one people keep seeing, then who else could it be?"

Dropping to a crouch, Tanner picked up a stone and studied it thoughtfully. "Someone who wants everyone to believe it's me."

"An impostor?"

"Or a decoy."

Eden frowned. "Who would go to all that trouble? And just as important, why?"

"Somebody with something to gain."

"And so it begins," she whispered.

"What was that?"

"Nothing. Only that you've been in town just a short while and you've already acquired an enemy."

"The only enemies I ever made are already in prison."

"At least you didn't bring any with you like my husband did."

"Your husband made himself quite a few, huh?"

Eden grimaced, the only sign of how deeply his words had affected her. "I think it's a requirement. Do you think Washburn is behind this?"

"He was the first on my list, but he spent the night in the cage the time I'd been spotted at the train depot, so I scratched him off."

"You made a list? Who else is on it?"

He mounted the steps and stood against the porch railing. "John Sullivan."

"John Sullivan? Tanner, I admit he can be difficult, but what would he have to gain?"

"My resignation."

"I thought he supported your election."

"Let's say we've had a difference of opinion since then."

"Must have been some difference. So you believe he is plotting your downfall," Eden concluded.

"I can't be sure without proof." He tossed the stone into the yard and squinted at the cluster of pine trees beyond the fence. "That's what bothers me."

She'd never seen him so troubled. Hesitantly, she rose from the chair and closed the few feet separating them. "Is there anything I can do to help?"

He hung his head and sighed, and Eden could have kicked herself for offering. Hadn't she learned by then that no matter what overtures she made, they would be rejected? An old pain welled up inside her, reminding her what it felt like to be shut out. Shunted aside. How could she have expected anything less?

Stung, she started to turn away when he caught her hand and tugged her close. The press of his lips against her knuckles sent sparks dancing up her arm.

"You just did. More than you know."

His touch, so tender, his words, so sincere, caught her unprepared. Eden had no idea how to respond. Mute, she gazed at the top of his bent head. Gilded strands weaved with ginger blond; the pattern repeated in his spiky lashes. And his eyes, when he looked at her again, shone with his special brand of whimsy, yet just underneath she detected a gray unrest.

Sunlight and shadow. Mystical and mysterious.

"Eden." Tanner stared into her eyes. "I'll be leaving in the morning for Austin. The governor's called a meeting with all available agencies and officers to talk about how to best protect towns from the wave of crime hitting the state."

He was leaving? A sense of loss unraveled through her at the news. "You just got back, though."

"I'll be gone only as long as I have to, but I'd hoped you'd do me a favor before I leave."

She swallowed dully. "What favor is that?"

"Kiss me good-bye."

Eden wavered between despair and desire. It was dangerous to let herself be swayed by Tanner McCay's persuasive charm. And yet she couldn't lie to herself; she'd been longing to kiss him again ever since Little Seth's birthday. Throwing reticence to the wind, Eden glanced up and down the empty road, then pulled him into a dark corner of the porch. She wrapped her arms around his neck, combed her fingers through the hair at his nape.

He met her halfway, slanting his lips across hers. Hands she'd thought of so often slid around her waist until he'd enveloped her in a body-fusing embrace. The kiss deepened, awakening cravings unlike any she'd ever felt until he came into her life. When he stroked his tongue against hers, she stroked back because she wanted to. When he tightened his hold, she tightened hers because she needed to. And then, just before he pulled away, Eden swore their souls had touched.

"You don't know only how to welcome a man back, you know how to send him off, too." A slow, sensual, very satisfied smile spread across his face, stealing what breath she had left. "Bet the time with you in between is bliss."

"Be careful," Eden nearly pleaded.

He rubbed his nose back and forth across hers. "Always."

Then he backed up and fell down the porch stairs.

"Is not!"

"Is so!"

"Lissa, stop wiggling before I stick you in the leg," Eden scolded, her mouth full of pins. She jabbed another pin in the let-down fabric of Lissa's best red calico dress. "And, Seth, stop running through the house," she commanded when he flew through the kitchen doorway into the dining room then out the hall doorway.

Lissa stomped her foot. "But Ruthie keeps saying—"

"You two have been squabbling all evening, so I'd rather not know what this argument is about. Just hold still so I can finish this hem. I still have to attach the ruffles." Little Seth careened around the table, knocking the sewing basket off the bench. Spools of thread rolled every which way across the floor. Eden snatched the pins from her mouth. "Seth Daniel, if I have to tell you again to stop running through the house, you'll find yourself tied to the chair."

"Mama, this dress is old and ugly. Everyone's gonna poke fun at me. Why can't you make me a new one?"

"At fifteen cents a yard for material? You know I can't afford that right now. I'm afraid you'll just have to start school with what you have."

"Pa would make sure I had new dresses for school." Lissa pouted belligerently. "Fancy ones like Annabelle's pa orders from the catalogue, too."

Eden breathed an irritated sigh. "I'm doing the best I can."

"When Tan's our pa, he'll buy us all the dresses we want."

"Mama, tell Ruthie that Tanner McCay is not gonna be our new pa!"

"Is so!"

"Is *not*!" Lissa turned to Eden desperately. "I don't want you to marry the marshal! I don't want a tin man for a pa. I just want my old pa back!" Lissa bounded off the chair and raced from the dining room, wailing. "Why can't things be like they used to?"

Rapid clomping grew distant as she sped upstairs, then a door slammed.

Recovering from shock at last, Eden turned to Ruthie. "Wherever did you get the idea that the marshal would be your new father?"

"Tan McCrary said so. He said if you knew how good he was, you'd like him and would go see the preacher with him, then I can call him Pa. He even made me and Seth his 'possums to help you like him."

Eden gawked incredulously at her daughter first, then her son, who had scrambled under the bench Ruthie sat on. Now she knew why her younger two had been raving about Tanner lately, as if he were the best thing since peppermint sticks—he'd coerced them into helping him get into her good graces. He'd been gone for ten days, and during that time she'd felt as if Ruthie and Little Seth had ganged up on her. She merely had to mention that something around the house needed repair, and one or the other instantly remarked: "Just ask Tan McCrary/Marshal Mac to fix it, he can do anything." Or if she wore one of the articles of clothing packed away since Seth's death, she'd hear, "Oh, Mama, Tan'll think you look pretty as a posy in that." And around the supper table, the two would shake the plaster with loud, off-key renditions of the "Cindy" song, bringing to Eden's mind the day they'd gone on their picnic and she'd made her first blow-wish.

Between her conspiratorial offspring and her own internal tug-of-war, the pressure weighed her down so that she could hardly think clearly anymore. Yes, she admitted that the affection Tanner McCay gave to them freely impressed her, but often, as she watched her son, she had to fight alarm. Under Tanner's lively encouragement, Little Seth had grown bolder in his games of pretend. Her quiet and shy young son was changing before her very eyes into the same wild hoyden she'd been as a child, with the same unseemly traits that had earned her a lifetime of contempt. And the wiser, more cynical voice inside Eden urged her to beware.

"Ruthie, sweetheart, listen to me," Eden entreated. "I know you've become very attached to the marshal. But he made a mistake telling you something that isn't true." She'd take that up with Tanner as soon as he returned, too.

"But it is true! I saw you kissing. And holding hands."

That was another thing they never let her forget—as if she could. "That doesn't mean that I will marry him."

"You have to, Mama! I want Tan to be my pa." Ruthie's eyes filled with tears. "Otherwise he'll be a stranger and then I can't love him no more!"

A stranger. Eden averted her face. Tanner had wormed his way into their lives and entrenched himself too firmly to ever be called a stranger. He filled a void she'd become used to, brought laughter into a home where it had been lacking . . .

But marry him? Eden mentally shook her head. A future looked very bleak without him now, and yet, given Ruthie's sentiments, Eden knew the decision she'd been struggling with since he'd left had been made for her. She had to put a stop to their association. If she didn't, she would be risking the children—and herself—to the perils of making Tanner a vital part of their existence; it would only get worse as time wore on. Where a lawman went, danger followed. She'd had enough of looking over her shoulder every minute of every day—growing up, during her marriage, and most especially after Lissa had been used as a pawn in a wicked game of revenge.

Even if by some miracle her family remained untouched by enemy forces, she didn't know if she had the courage to accept the obsession again. She hadn't missed that determined thrill in Tanner's eyes whenever he talked of finding Seth's killers. He would not stop searching for the train robbers. Nor would he give up on finding his impersonator until that mystery was solved. And then there would be more robberies, more mysteries to feed that insatiable appetite, until at last he was the slower draw, or instinct failed, or he simply allowed himself to become too arrogant.

And just as he'd stolen into her tightly guarded life, made them all start believing that wishes could come true, he would go away and take all that was merry and bright and special with him.

"It's best you don't love him now, Ruthie, because if you do . . . if you do"—she turned away and whispered, anguished—"he'll only break your heart."

"Always thought Governor Roberts was too busy building all those schools to give a care about all the outlaws moving onto Texas soil," Micaleb commented as the stagecoach bounced over another rut in the road. "Guess I was wrong. Glad you asked me to join you."

Staring out at the countryside with his elbow on the window, his hand framing his mouth, Tanner shrugged. "I figured crime isn't just the marshal's problem, it's the whole town's problem."

Micaleb sifted through the new packet of WANTED posters Tanner had gotten from the governor's office. " 'Specially in light of these new robberies springing up all over. Makes my spine prickle knowing that the towns are scouted before the thefts. Never thought much about it when new blood moved into the area, but now I'm beginning to wonder about this fella everyone keeps sayin' is you."

"I tried telling you that wasn't me." The day there had been a sighting near Simon Pratt's livery had laid all Tanner's doubts to rest; his feet and boots were as clean that morning as they'd been before he'd turned in for the night. "Tiny and Hollis seem to accept my innocence. John is the one who won't listen to a word I say."

"Can't blame John for being wary, though. He used to own an iron foundry with one of those fancy blast furnaces until the Confederates swiped it out from under him to make bullets during the war. Pulled 'im right off hobnob hill and into the poorhouse. He scraped and scratched and built the savings and loan, swearin' nobody would ever take away what belonged to him."

"You mean he wasn't just born ornery?" Tanner scoffed.

"Nah, hard knocks pounded that into him. He would've lost everything all over again if Seth hadn't stopped that train from being robbed. Ain't no way John'll take a chance on something like that happening a second time. But at least if anyone says they saw you in the last couple weeks, I can vouch that it ain't."

That's something in my favor, Tanner thought. He still wasn't convinced that Sullivan wasn't out to lift his badge, but after what he'd heard from Oran Roberts, a sick feeling gnawed at his gut. As much as he wanted to ignore the possibility, it was sounding more and more like Dogwood Springs had once again become the target of renegade bandits.

"Hope we make it home afore those clouds bust open."

Tanner glanced up at the swirling charcoal sky. "Me too." But it had nothing to do with getting a little wet. He missed Eden and the kids so bad his teeth ached. He'd thought of nothing but walking up to her door and kissing Eden senseless the minute she opened it.

By the time the stage finally arrived in town later that night, the storm had attacked full force. Tanner stopped by the jail to drop off his baggage, make sure that Myrtle had been moved into his cell out of the rain, and briefly scan the report Tiny had left on his desk. Impatience got the best of him, though. He stuffed the paper into his desk drawer.

Trees doubled over with the force of the wind that tore at Tanner's hat and duster, and stinging pellets of rain drove into his skin as he fought his way to Eden's house. A bright fork of lightning zigzagged between the treetops to his right and a roar of thunder came up behind him, ending in a ground-jolting clap.

The sound of a scream, high-pitched, pierced Tanner's

soul. He froze at the gate to Eden's house, feeling the walls
of his heart tear.

It was a child's scream. Of a terror so deep, so profound, it smothered him. He didn't know how he recognized
it. Instinct. Intuition. Whatever. But he did.

His feet ate up the distance between the fence and the
house in loping strides. He leapt over the steps onto the porch
and flung the front door open; it crashed against the round
table behind, snapped back, and the sound of shattering pot-
tery echoed in the air long after he bounded up the stairwell.

Another thunderclap, muffled by the walls, and another
scream, closer now that he had reached the second-floor
landing. Tanner traced the terror to the farthest room on the
left and burst through the door.

Eden's head jerked up. As if in answer to a silent plea,
Tanner stood in the doorway, one hand gripping the knob,
the other curled around the frame. His duster stuck to his
pant legs, his hair was plastered against his skull, and his
eyes reflected crazed alarm.

She did not fear his presence. She welcomed it.

Needed it.

Ruthie whimpered against her breast and Eden rocked
her baby girl as she had done dozens of times, through other
storms, be they of nature's making or those of imagination.
Tears welled in her eyes for the combination of both forces
assaulting her daughter. For her own helplessness . . . "It's
the thunder," she told Tanner, choking on the rage she felt
toward the imagined threats to Ruthie. "Loud sounds
. . . thunder, guns, fireworks . . . she remembers her father."

He lowered his hands and stepped carefully into the
room decorated in soothing pinks and girlish flowers. So
manly, so overwhelming among the faded floral bedspread
and curtains and table skirts.

"Did she see—"

"No." Eden shook her head in adamant denial. "But
they brought Seth back here, bloody and dying. I did my
best . . . I couldn't stop the bleeding . . ."

"He was gut-shot, Eden. There was nothing you could do."

"All the same, he died from a gun wound. She's made a connection between the loud noise and his death. That's why I forbid guns from being anywhere near her, and keep her away from celebrations. I can't control the weather, though."

The tender compassion on Tanner's face nearly broke Eden's fragile composure.

"May I try?" he asked, reaching for Ruthie.

Eden looked at his hands, so big, so gentle. Hands that held those deadly guns strapped to his hips were now offering to comfort her innocent, precious child.

She gave a soundless nod, and passed Ruthie to Tanner. He brought the little body close to his chest. Ruthie's arms went trustingly, naturally, around his neck, the ruffles of her nightgown sleeve pale against his rain-washed flesh. The soothing noises he crooned to her as they lowered onto the mattress held Eden spellbound.

"Hey, sweet potato, your eyes are leaking."

"Tan, you're back!"

"You know how we stop leaky eyes?" He balled his hands beside each of her ears, and made a rolling motion with his fists.

"Make it go away," Ruthie sobbed. "Please make it go away."

"Make what go away?"

A faint droning erupted into another splitting pop, and Ruthie scrambled tighter into Tanner's arms. "It's gonna get me!"

"Aw, honey, don't you know what that is?" he asked, rocking back and forth. "That's just God having a little fun up in heaven with his angels. He's got a great big wagon wheel that he gives a little shove. The wheel goes round and round and round, and whoever can get it to go the farthest wins." As if on cue, another roll began in the distance. "Listen, can you hear Him?" Ruthie clutched at Tanner until his neck went red, and Eden tensed right along with Ruthie as the noise grew louder. "Here comes the wagon wheel . . ."

Tanner said with false brightness. "It's going farther. And farther . . ."

Rubbing Ruthie's back, Eden anticipated screams when the thunder crashed.

"Wow," he exclaimed when it did. "I reckon God just made a point!"

The screams didn't come. Ruthie remained tight as a bowstring, but she made not a sound.

"Who do you think is winning?" Tanner asked.

She shrugged in his arms.

"Is my pa an angel?"

Startled, Eden and Tanner both glanced across the other side of the bed where, until now, Lissa had been lying quietly. It was the first civil thing Lissa had ever said in Tanner's presence, and neither grown-up knew how to react.

She raised her head from the folded hands beneath her cheek. "Is my pa one of the angels God's having fun with?"

"I'm sure he is," Tanner finally answered.

Lissa lay back down. "Then he's winning."

It took time, but eventually Ruthie relaxed, even released her terrified grip on Tanner's neck to listen to the thunder.

Tanner's and the girls' hushed voices carried to Eden as they tried to guess what far-reaching city the thunder wheel had finally landed over, and who made that particular score.

Eden remained silent, awed and grateful, even a bit envious that he'd been able to accomplish in one night what she hadn't been able to do in twelve months—dim Ruthie's fear of loud noises.

After a while Ruthie drifted off to sleep in Tanner's arms, and when he tucked her beneath the lightweight coverlet, Eden noticed that Lissa, too, had fallen asleep.

By mute communication, she and Tanner tiptoed from the room.

"Would you like a cup of coffee?" Eden asked when they reached the kitchen door.

"Do you mind if I hang my coat somewhere to dry?"

"Oh. Certainly." Preoccupied with Ruthie, she'd completely forgotten that the clothes he still wore were soaked.

He shrugged out of the duster. Eden took it and hooked the collar over a peg by the back door. "I could probably find something of Seth's for you to wear if you'd like to get out of those wet clothes too. You'd probably swim in his trousers, but—"

Tanner held up his hand. "Thanks, but I'll change when I get back to the jail." Then he leaned his hip against the counter.

Not so long ago he'd stood in that very same position. Had talked with her, shared his troubles, and here she was sharing hers. What was it about this kitchen that drew them together? It seemed to hold a magical connection for them, make her aware of the man behind the badge.

Achingly aware.

Eden hastened to the stove, where the inner cavern was filled with tinder and newsprint awaited a match. With trembling hands Eden lit the paper and watched the orange-blue flames writhe to life. Staring at them, she realized that Tanner had the same effect on her banked desires. One look, one touch, and need twisted inside her.

"How do you do it?" she whispered in confusion.

"What, calm Ruthie?"

Eden latched on to that much safer, much wiser straw. "I've spent more nights than I can count trying to ease her fear of loud noises, to no use. I mean, a good mother would know what to do for her child, and yet, I'm lost. . . ."

"I don't think it's the loud noises that she fears as much as it is the memory of death. By giving the sound of thunder something less threatening to compare it with, she can find peace. I know of no other more peaceful being than God."

"You believe in God, then?"

"A body has to if he wants to play with the angels," Tanner winked at her. "What about you?"

"Once upon a time." Before God forgot about her. And yet, deep down inside, she recognized the blessings in her life. Lissa, Ruthie, Little Seth . . . Tanner.

Rising, she busied her flustered hands grinding coffee beans. The pungent smell filled the cramped kitchen, the sound of crunching gave her something to think on besides the rain beating on the shingles. "You certainly seem to have a special touch with children."

"Not all of them."

"With mine you do."

"I like yours."

The gears stopped whirring. "Even when they aren't very nice to you?" She mentally included herself.

"Lissa doesn't trust me. She figures she'd better drive me away before I can leave, so she won't feel the pain she felt when her pa died."

"You think she feels responsible for Seth's death because she trusted him?"

"It's possible. She's probably mad at him for leaving. But since she can't tell him that, she takes it out on everyone and everything else around her. She feels in control with her anger; she can't feel in control with her fear."

After measuring grounds into the pot of water, Eden took a half loaf of bread and a jar of raspberry preserves to the table. Tanner followed lazily. What he said made sense. The first time she'd been arrested for stealing an apple from a vendor's cart, she'd fought and cursed, then kicked the policeman between the legs—all because she'd been afraid of going to jail.

Then later with Seth, her anger at his being there for everyone but her, had turned inward but no less fierce, all because she'd been afraid he was rejecting her.

"I try to understand Lissa, and be patient with her, but Seth was never around enough to be any kind of father to the children. Not the kind of champion she makes him out as, anyway." Funny how good, how *right*, it felt to talk about her worries with Tanner. How easily he listened, put things in perspective.

"Maybe the way she makes him out is what she always wanted but never had."

"All right, sage one, what about Little Seth, then? He's not angry, he's withdrawn—around me, anyway. Around you"—her mouth curled downward—"he's the invincible lawman."

Tanner chuckled and Eden shot him a mildly scathing look.

"I'm sorry." Tanner struggled to maintain a sober face as he lowered himself onto the bench beside her. "It's just that, that boy of yours . . . he could be me all over again."

"How's that?"

"Pretend friends, in a hurry to grow up and be somebody folks look up to, that sort of thing."

"And why were you in such a hurry to grow up?" She tore off a piece of bread and slathered it with jam. "You don't talk about your own family much."

Tanner squirmed. He couldn't have been given a better opening to tell her the truth about his family. Tanner knew he had to. She would find out sooner or later, as fast as word was spreading around town. Subtle, odd looks that had once been directed his way had become unmistakably distrustful. Shoot, some folks were downright rude. He'd expected it in the wake of Sullivan's threat, but it still stung that people could be so quick to judge without any hard facts. They'd begun treating him like a maggot in a stew pot.

Yet when his mouth worked to form the confession, the words stuck in his throat. Selfishly, he wanted a little more time with her. And somewhere deep inside lived the hope that maybe she'd never know, would never find out, about the McCays.

And he'd never lose her.

"There's not much to tell. I have a brother, but we live separate lives. My mother died last year, and my father wasn't around much even before that."

"Is that why you spend so much time with my children? To somehow make up for your own father not being there for you?"

Tanner clasped his hands in front of him. "I never thought about it, but yeah, I suppose. That, and maybe I remember how hard it was for my mother to raise me and my brother on her lonesome. I wonder if you find raising your kids alone as hard."

"No, I think I find it more challenging." She tilted her head and smiled whimsically. "A contest of wits and wills. Around them I must remain sharp. Alert. It's sort of . . . adventurous, I think."

Tanner propped his elbow on the table, rested his chin in his hand. "And do you find adventures gratifying?"

His eyes smoldered.

"Fulfilling." Eden rose and strolled away from him. From his compelling gaze. She went to pour their coffee but found the pot only mildly warm. "By the time this pot brews, your clothes will be dry." Eden turned to smile at him . . .

And caught him staring at her behind. There was a feverish gleam in his eyes that stirred up all those secret longings she'd tried so hard to hide, to bury.

Heat spread as his gaze traveled from her feet to her waist, to her breasts. There it stopped, then continued.

Their eyes locked.

"You're staring at me again, Marshal McCay," she notified him breathlessly.

He dropped his sultry gaze. "I'm sorry, Eden. Maybe this wasn't such a good idea."

He pushed himself away from the table and stood.

Eden's heart started pounding frantically. Her palms went clammy. It was too soon for him to leave. She'd only just begun feeling safe with him. How could he give her the gift of hope, then snatch it away before she'd had the chance to tell him . . .

Tell him what? Thank you? No, that wasn't right.

She'd wasted so much time running from him. Now he was running from her.

Just say it, Eden. Say the words you would never allow yourself to say before, because if you don't, he'll walk out the door, out of your life, maybe for good, and you'll be left with nothing again.

"Don't go."

Chapter Fifteen

SHE REACHED OUT. "Don't go."

He glanced over his shoulder as if expecting someone else to be standing behind him. Eden chuckled softly, her heart nearly overflowing with tenderness for this extraordinary man.

"Eden, if I don't go now, you might have to chase me away with a rolling pin."

Oh, how she'd missed him. His humor. His strength. His sensitivity. She needed that now. Needed him. So much for her decision to cut him from her life.

Her skirts lapped against her legs as she glided over to him. His eyes narrowed to slits. Through thick black lashes she peered up at him. "Would you leave me without a proper good-bye?"

"There isn't anything proper about the thoughts running through my head right now."

She watched his throat work. His broad hands had balled into white-knuckled fists. She took one of them, rubbed her cheek across the hard knuckles. His hand opened, fingers slid into her hair. One by one, pins made tinny *ping*s onto the floor. The coil loosened, then tumbled down, her unbound hair fanning around her shoulders.

Tanner weighed a thick skein in his palm, bunched it, wound it, reeled her in even as his mouth descended. Then all she felt was his lips on hers, the faint brush of his mustache beneath her nose. They rested a moment, their mouths touching, their breaths mingling, neither pulling back.

He opened his mouth slightly, closed over hers, then again, moist, inviting, coaxing. Reaching behind her, he pressed her lower back closer to his solid frame. Restraint hummed through every corded muscle, hesitance quivered through his every nerve.

Arms that had hung limply at her sides came up to wind around his slim waist.

The storm outside raged. Inside, another brewed. Like the distant thunder, Eden felt sensations roll through her, become more distinct as he sucked her lips, then crash down upon her when his tongue thrust into her mouth. She responded, mating with him, drawing him tighter against her curves.

Without warning he jerked himself from her arms.

"Okay, that's enough, I've reached my limit." Retreating a step, he rammed the back of his knees against the bench. He stumbled, then awkwardly regained his balance. Sweat had bubbled up on his forehead, his chest lifted and lowered with labored breaths.

She kissed the side of his neck, feeling him wince, tense. Brushing her lips across his damp skin, she whispered, "Stay with me tonight."

A groan rumbled from low in his throat. "Eden, I've dreamed of you . . . ever since I first laid eyes on those beautiful legs of yours, but I don't think you're ready—"

Eden shushed him with her finger to his lips. "I'm ready." She took his hand and led him down the hallway, up the stairs, into her bedroom. No sounds came from the other rooms; the children were sleeping deeply in spite of the storm raging outside.

The door clicked shut. In her plain room of dull yellows and worn browns, he stood out like rugged mountain amid a lonely prairie. Natural, commanding, awe-inspiring.

"I have a confession to make," she said.

"Let me guess—you've never done this before."

Her brows rose, and Eden released a short, nervous gust of laughter at his teasing. "No. 'This' is how I bore three children. I have the scars to prove it." Her small smile shrank. "I did lie to you, though."

"About what?"

"Remember when you kissed me the first time, and I went to the jail and told you it meant nothing?"

He nodded.

"It meant something."

His fingertips rested beneath her chin. Willingly, Eden tipped her face to receive him. "You could very likely grow heavy with a fourth after tonight."

"I'll take my chances."

After another long, drugging kiss, he peeled off his shirt and bared his chest to her. Broad, sleek, a solid wall of golden flesh and masculinity.

Next went his gun belt, which he looped around her bedpost. Only when he began unfastening his trousers did she feel a cutting edge of apprehension. Not counting climbing the tree, this was the most daring thing she'd done in nine years.

She sat on the side of her too-wide, too-long-lonely bed, slowly pushing the buttons on her bodice through each hole, from the modest high neck, down . . . five, six, seven . . . Eden concentrated on the mushroom-shaped buttons as though her life depended on freeing each one.

The mattress sank and rose several times as Tanner crawled across it. "Are you afraid, Eden?"

She hesitated. Was she afraid? Mercy, yes. She was terrified. Admitting that to herself, she nodded.

"Of me?"

Dropping her hands and twisting her fingers together, Eden shook her head no. Then yes. Then shrugged and bowed her head. "I'm afraid of what you make me feel."

"Adventurous?"

"Yes."

"Reckless?"

"Very."

"Selfish?"

"Extremely."

He didn't laugh at her. He didn't ignore her. He didn't tell her not to be afraid. He simply said, "Let's just take everything one step at a time." Then Tanner took one of her agitated hands and laid it flat over his chest. "Can you feel that? That's what you do to me."

The steady slam of his heartbeat. Warm, bare skin. Life. Tenderness.

And in his eyes, undisguised desire.

Her breathing turned shallow.

The release of the ninth button felt as if the door to a prison had been thrown open. Eden's doubts flew away and she rose, facing him boldly, without reserve. Since the day she'd met him, he had confused her. Made her feel as if she stood in a room of mirrors, all capturing reflections of her in the past. A wild hoyden, a solemn reject, a prim bride, a neglected woman . . .

But at that moment he made her feel as though she stood on the threshold of something wild. Unpredictable. Exciting. If this even came close to what a lawman felt like chasing fugitives, then she understood how it could easily become an obsession.

Shrugging her shoulders in turn, Eden peeled away the gown, revealing her black muslin chemise. He watched every move she made. The darkening of his eyes, the slumberous lowering of his thick lashes, gave her a freedom, a courage she'd forgotten she'd ever had.

And she liked it. Embraced it like a lost friend. Her dress fell in a puddle of midnight fabric to the floor. He licked his lips, his gaze taking in the sight of her shamelessly clad in her sheer black undergarments and net stockings.

His bare chest rose and fell with deep breaths. His stomach was flat and hard, and just below his navel, the top button of his trousers had been left undone. *Mercy, the man should be illegal.*

Two steps and Eden stood before him, flanked by his wide-spread knees. She peered at him through half-lowered lids as she framed his cheeks with her hands. Lifting his face, she lowered her head, covered his mouth with hers. Eden parted her lips at the first sweet caress of his tongue, matching his leisurely strokes, indulging in the flavors found within his mouth. He tasted of rain and wind. Of hopes and wishes. The brush of his mustache upon her lips felt like temptation itself. His arms curled around her in a possessive embrace, and falling backward onto the bed, he dragged her with him.

Coaxing, seductive kisses erased the very last thread of hesitation.

He wedged his hands between them and shucked off his damp britches. The awkward rolling motion of his hips sent shafts of hot delight clear to her spine as he squirmed beneath her, pressed himself against her belly, swollen and eager.

Soon after, her drawers joined his britches somewhere on the floor. Rough palms seared the backs of her thighs through her black net stockings, from the indentation of her knees, past her garters, finally coming to cup her bottom beneath the hem of her chemise. His lips ceased moving, his moist breath came in ragged gusts as he nuzzled his nose back and forth against hers. "I have to stop."

"No," Eden protested. If he stopped now, she'd die. She'd just die.

"Eden, honey"—he chuckled self-consciously—"if I don't stop for a minute, this is gonna be very disappointing for the both of us."

The meaning was clear. She touched his hair, swept the sandy strands away from his tightly drawn cheeks, drowning in the liquid depths of his eyes. That he cared enough to put aside his needs for the sake of hers moved her beyond words. She'd never felt so cherished in her life. "May I look at you?"

"Yes, ma'am," he whispered hoarsely.

Eden looked her fill and more. He lay still and stiff beneath her while she learned where his collarbone indented, where the cords of his neck met the swells of his shoulder muscles. She counted four tiny moles on his upper right arm, noticed that the hair grew thickest between his elbows and wrists. She found a small arrow-shaped scar above his left nipple that he couldn't remember how he'd gotten, nor did she think she would remember if he could tell her, for her mind had gone numb from studying the utter beauty of him. Of the way they fit together, of the way his skin was so much browner than hers, of the way he waited, restraining himself with visible effort until she finished her examination.

Pressing her lips to his throat, she inhaled his scent; it nearly rose from him like steam. Musky, virile, moist. Like heaven and hell in one body.

"May I touch you?" she mouthed against his salty skin.

"Please do," he croaked.

Eden found unabashed power in lying atop this gentle man. Liberation in roaming her hands wherever she wanted. Awe in watching him respond to her light touch. With each flash of lightning through her window she marveled at the rapture on his face, the drowsy eyes, the parted lips and clenched teeth. It didn't seem possible that she could arouse him to this degree. She, who had never had anybody want her. She, who had been cast away so often that it felt almost normal.

A forbidden coil of desire blossomed, unfurled inside her, and she allowed it.

Her brazen fingers skimmed down the length of his lean body, down his hard chest, his taut abdomen, following the narrow line of fine blond hair from his navel to his groin. Curious, questing, she traced the crease between his thigh and hip—

With a shout, Tanner jerked his knee to his chest.

Eden squealed. Her hands flew off him. "I hurt you! I'm sorry."

He seized her wrists and flipped her onto her back. "You didn't hurt me."

Wide-eyed, Eden searched his honest eyes. She hadn't hurt him?

He shook his head slowly, as if knowing her thoughts.

"But . . . but you yelled."

"You *tickled* me."

"I what? You're ticklish . . . down . . . there?" The last came out in a squeak. "I had no idea a man was—"

Amusement lurked in his dark green eyes. "Neither did I."

Now she was truly confused. "But how could you not know? Surely you've done this sort of thing before." Hadn't he? Mercy, she'd never heard of an almost thirty-year-old virgin man! He seemed so practiced. Knowledgeable.

"I didn't know"—his eyes darkened to a dusky pine, his voice dropped an octave—"because a woman has never explored my body the way you have."

Hot color flooded her face, matching the heat surging through the rest of her body. "Oh."

He dipped his head and pressed a kiss to the racing pulse below her ear. "I'm honored that you are the first," he whispered against her skin. "The only."

A shy smile tugged at her lips.

He unbuttoned her chemise, folding the plain edges back and exposing her breasts. Subtle as a spring breeze, his fingers glided across the top of each mound, making them tight and heavy with anticipation. Her lungs burned with the inability to breathe, her breasts ached to have him suck her.

Entranced, she watched him lower his mouth and latch on to one pert bud. Eden nearly shot off the bed at the intense sensation, bucking into him, crying softly, "Tanner-TannerTanner" over and over again, his name a song on her lips.

She gripped his head between her palms as feverish desire built, spreading from her knees to her neck, everywhere he touched, yet centering somewhere very, very close to her heart. . . .

He rose over her. Linking their fingers together, he brought their joined hands above her head. "I love you, Eden. So you don't regret lying with me, I want you to know I'll never hurt you. Not now, not ever. I promise you that."

"Don't make me any promises, Tanner," she said, anguished.

"I already have."

Then he entered her. Moved inside her. There was no awkwardness, no fumbling, nothing but fluid grace in his sure and steady strokes that brought more pleasure than she had ever dreamed was possible for her to feel. He allowed her to decide the pace, gave her unlimited control over their movements, which she found heightened her pleasure.

A heavy pressure unfurled inside her, frightening yet exhilarating, growing more intense. Eden ground herself down upon him each time he drove himself inside her . . . whimpering, clutching the sheets, his shoulders, his hair, tossing her head from side to side, biting her lip to keep from crying out.

Reaching fulfillment together, spots swirling in her head, Eden silently pleaded, *Don't ever leave me.*

When their rasping breaths once more returned to a normal rate, Tanner turned to his side, carrying her with him. Eden fit her sated body into his, finding strength in his solidness, yet feeling weakened by his gentleness. "You are like no man I've ever known."

He hugged her close and sighed contentedly. "Lucky me."

"I'm the lucky one." He was so heart-wrenchingly gentle, surrounding her with his essence, like a velvet cloak around fragile glass. "I never thought men like you existed, especially considering what you do for a living. The only lawmen I've had any contact with were harsh, unforgiving machines. No emotion. No depth."

"You've been in contact with the wrong ones, then."

"How"—she swallowed, finding it hard to ask what she found harder to believe—"how do you know that you . . . you know . . . feel that way about me?"

"How do I know I love you?"

Eden nodded, so grateful that he understood what she couldn't put into words.

"I just do. Every time I see you, my heart jumps into

my throat. I don't think about other women. I find excuses to be near you. And when we're together, like this, I feel whole."

"But why? Why me?"

"Eden," he chuckled, "I can't pick just one reason. It's all of them together. The flash of stubbornness you get in your eyes when you've made up your mind. The way you protect those kids of yours. The habit you have of wringing your hands when you're nervous." Running his hand down her thigh, he wiggled his brows. "And the way you look in black net stockings sure doesn't turn my stomach."

Eden glanced down and noticed she still wore her gaping chemise and stockings. "Ah, I knew it was something gallant."

His fingers traced the length of her arm, from her elbow to her wrist, to her knuckles, then back up again in reverse. "Are you tired?"

She nodded. It was a pleasurable, satisfied kind of tired, though. Did he realize that he was romancing her? "But it's been so long since I've talked to anyone over seven years old that I can't remember the last time."

"What about your husband?"

She emitted a sound between a laugh and a sob. "Seth Page didn't talk; he never stopped moving away long enough to utter more than 'Later, Eden.' After a while it seemed a waste of time to try." Flatly she said, "Later never came. And then it was too late."

Tanner remained quiet for a long while. His nearness, his lazy caresses, were like balm to a stinging gash.

"Why did you marry him?" he whispered.

A blush suffused her cheeks. She ducked her head. "You don't want to hear about this now."

"Yes, I do. Why did you marry him?"

She flopped over to lie on top of his stomach, propping herself up on his chest with her forearms. "Have you ever wanted something so desperately that you ached for it? Felt incomplete without it? That you were willing to risk anything to get it?"

Tanner studied Eden intently. Her. He wanted her that

desperately. More desperately than he wanted a decent reputation, an honest name, a noble identity. Every time he
and Eden parted ways, he hurt in places he never knew
could hurt, felt empty clear to his soul, was willing to risk
his heart—his dreams—his very future. Especially now, in
the aftermath of their loving, with her soft hills and valleys
crushed against him from shoulder to knee, her sugar-and-
spice scent filling his nostrils, the husky lilt of her voice
bathing over him like a summer breeze. "What did you
want, Eden?"

"A name."

"You married your husband for a name?"

"A last name." She laid her cheek upon his chest. "I
never had one, never knew what mine was. I can't even be
sure that Eden was my first name, but at least I had that
much. The mistress of the orphanage said that when I got
placed in a home, I'd be given a last name. I remember
being very excited the day the orphan train pulled out of the
station. I thought, at last, I'd belong to a family and get a
name. But no one wanted me because I'd been so sickly."

Having confessed that much, she plunged ahead. "I
ran away when we got back to Chicago. Often. The police
kept bringing me back to the orphanage, many times in
handcuffs because I fought them. I was labeled a truant and
a petty criminal. In the two homes I had been placed in, the
parents decided I was either too much trouble or that I'd set
a bad example for their other children."

It was the strangest thing, curling up in the bed,
spilling all her long-buried secrets to a tin man—no, he
wasn't tin. He was flesh and blood, warmth and sunlight.

"When I was sixteen I saw a handbill from an agency
advertising for brides. They matched me up with Seth. He
sent the money for a stagecoach ride. I came to Texas, and
married him a week later."

"So you didn't even know him."

She shrugged. "He was Marshal Seth Page. It sounded
honorable and respectable. And it was a fresh start. I'd been
reckless and defiant in the past, so I vowed that I would be
the epitome of purity and faultlessness. That way he wouldn't

cast me out too. On my way to Fort Worth, I watched the ladies in the cities so I would know how to act. It took a while, even after Seth and I were married, for me to perfect my ways. He never noticed. I thought that maybe he would see me differently if I were smart. I read everything I could get my hands on. He never noticed that either. But I had my children—my own family. It was enough."

Tanner shut his eyes and gave thanks. She'd said "*was* enough."

He must have dozed off, for the next thing Tanner knew, the bed was jostling. He cracked open one eye. Eden was half draped over his arm, her face snuggled into his chest. Just over the delicate rim of her ear he spied a cap of black hair silhouetted by predawn light coming through the window beyond.

He lifted his head. "Maverick?" Tanner whispered so not to disturb Eden. "What are you doing up so early?"

"I couldn't hold it no more."

"Did you wet?"

Little Seth nodded shamefully.

"Why didn't you go to the outhouse?"

"I'm not s'pose'ta go out by myself. It's a rule. And Mama wouldn't wake up."

Eden and her silly rules. "Go on back to your room. I'll be right there to help you change."

As soon as Little Seth left, Tanner eased away from Eden and got out of bed. Glancing at her, he knew he would give her anything she asked. But would she take it? He pulled on his trousers, then walked barefoot to the room across the hall. Little Seth never asked why he'd been in his mother's bed, nor did Tanner make any excuses as he first stripped the boy of his wet sleeping gown, then the narrow bed of its linen.

He handed Little Seth a soapy cloth to wash himself with, rinsed him down, then helped him redress in a clean set of clothes. "Next time you gotta go and you can't wake your ma, just try and make it to the chamber pot."

"You ain't gonna tell Lissa, are you, Marshal Mac?"

" 'Course not. Why?"

" 'Cuz she calls me a baby."

"It'll be our secret, then," Tanner promised, tugging the suspenders over Seth's shoulders.

"Marshal Mac?"

Tanner raised his eyebrows in question.

"Does Mama like you yet?"

He couldn't stop himself from blushing. "I reckon she just might."

Downstairs, they readied the stove and set a pot of coffee on to brew.

When Tanner returned to Eden's room, she'd already begun to stir. He bent over and sucked her neck. " 'Mornin', beautiful."

A languid smile stretched across her face, then suddenly she stilled and her eyes snapped open. "What time is it?"

"Early."

"Tanner, you have to leave."

"Without my coffee? You do live dangerously."

"Don't joke," she ordered, scrambling out of bed and throwing a cotton wrapper around her nudity. "You have to leave before the children wake up."

"Too late. Seth's already been in here."

She gasped. "Did he say anything?"

Tanner grinned. "He just asked if you liked me yet."

Her nose wrinkled, her lips twisted to the side. "Hmmm. Well, maybe just a little." Then she shoved his shirt, boots, and gun belt into his arms, crammed his hat onto his head, and pushed him around the foot of the bed. "Now, go on, get out of here."

"Eden, the door's the other way."

"I know. You have to climb out the window so no one will see you leaving the house."

"Climb out the—" Tanner planted his feet, refusing to budge another inch. "Eden, I've climbed up trees, I've climbed off a horse, I've even climbed a mountain once, but I've never climbed out of a lady's window."

"Tanner, please. If not for my sake, then do it for the

children. Think of how people will treat them if they see you walking out my front door at sunrise, looking"—she regarded him with her head tilted to the side—"absolutely, adorably mussed."

"People wouldn't think anything if I had every right to be here in the first place."

"Huh?"

He'd thought about it for half the night after she'd fallen asleep in his arms. It was a risky proposition, but he found himself asking anyway. "You said that all you've ever wanted is a last name. What about mine?"

"What are you saying?"

He dropped to one knee and held her left hand. "Marry me, Eden. Be my wife."

Chapter Sixteen

HER FACE WENT ghostly pale. Her head shook from side to side. "I can't marry you," she finally answered, her voice unusually thick, her eyes suspiciously bright. "That's asking for more than I can give."

He forced a smile he didn't feel. "I reckon I gotta accept that—for now." Squeezing her hand, he got to his feet.

Tanner folded himself through the side window, his foot rooting the wall for a toehold. He found a fragile one on the frame of the lower window. One foot in, one foot out, he muttered, "I can't believe I'm doing this."

Then he made the mistake of glancing up at Eden. The way she looked, her whisper-green eyes glistening, her midnight hair tumbling down her back, her deep red lips swollen from his kisses . . . Tanner sprang back up, unable to resist her, and kissed her hard, catching her sad laugh in his mouth.

She curved her palm against his cheek. Hesitantly she asked, "Will I see you later?"

Tanner studied her eyes. *She expects me to leave her.* "Will I be welcome?"

Before she could give him an answer, gravity tore them apart. Tanner lost his grip and went skidding down the side of the house onto the woodpile, which gave way beneath his weight. Split logs thudded and bounced off his head and shoulders.

"Oh, mercy—Tanner?"

Tanner waved feebly at Eden, who was hanging half-way out the window, to let her know he was all right, then picked himself up along with whatever pride he could gather and limped toward the woods.

The minute the house disappeared from sight, the contrived smile disappeared from his face. Tanner stumbled against a tree and clutched his balled hand to his heart. Could hearts really break? His felt as if it had. He hoped she hadn't seen how badly her refusal hurt.

Above, a sky of rain-washed blue, the color of innocence and new beginnings, mocked him. Annoyed, Tanner pushed away from the tree and hobbled deeper into the woods, his hip smarting from the fall from Eden's window.

She'd been through misery and back for a name. He'd been through misery and back because of his.

Life was funny like that, he reckoned. He had what he never wanted, she wanted what she never had.

God. Tanner shook his head. After last night he thought he'd finally landed upon something that would make Eden believe in heroes again. Make her believe in him. 'Cept the only thing he had that she wanted she wouldn't take.

Heck, could he blame her, though? No sane woman would want his name just then. It wasn't honorable or respected. In fact, it was as near a vulgarity as a true four-letter word. And Eden deserved better than that.

Even that knowledge didn't soothe him much. He still felt battered and bruised, inside more than outside.

At the edge of the creek he stooped to splash his face and water-brush his teeth with his finger. Maybe once he had a name worth offering . . . maybe once he cleared himself of all the scandal . . . she'd take it then.

'Course he still had a long way to go to make it worth—

The thought broke off. The back of his neck prickled. Tanner blanked his mind and listened.

There it went again. A rustle. The snap of a twig. Cautiously, he turned on the balls of his feet and strained to see through the density of trees. Silence now.

Every nerve tightened. Crouching, Tanner drew his gun, checked the chambers even though he knew they were already full. Then, holding the weapon high, he entered the shallow water and stomach-crawled to the opposite bank. A weak whinny. A human voice, low and jumbled. Tanner clutched an exposed root and dragged himself out of the water. Using the pines as shields, he dashed from one trunk to the other, wishing he hadn't stopped to put on his boots when a pinecone crunched beneath his soles.

The voice hushed.

Tanner held himself straight as a maypole when the rustling started up again, sounding hurried. He inched his head away from the sap-sticky tree and peered around. Just more dang trees, many covered in creeping ivy. But the noises weren't coming from that far off.

His gun ready, he sprinted toward another pine, then another. A horse neighed, then suddenly hooves pounded forcefully against earth.

He thrust himself away from any concealments and aimed his Peacemaker at the escaping hind end of a roan—with a white stocking on its left rear leg.

Tanner ran to town, the pain in his bruised hip forgotten. He threw open thc door to the jail, and Tiny sprang from the chair. Without stopping, Tanner headed straight for his cell.

Tiny followed. "Where have you been, Tanner?"

He tossed his carpetbag on the bed and rummaged through it. "I don't have time to chat, Tiny."

"This is serious. Tanner, I realize you are simply trying to be professional, but you must curtail yourself—"

"I saw him."

"Him?"

"The fellow folks keep seeing." He shoved a box of

bullets into his pocket. "I can't swear to it, but he was on a roan—a roan just like the one seen riding away from the scene of Page's shooting."

"Where?"

"In the woods behind—"

"The bank." Tiny completed the sentence with more than his usual austerity. Tanner fixed narrowed eyes on his small friend.

"John spotted someone fitting your description loitering behind the bank before dawn. He came to my apartment, furious when he couldn't find you at the jail. I soothed him as much as he would allow, and determined to locate you—without success, I might add."

"It absolutely wasn't me." He'd been at Eden's all last night, and pleasurably busy at that; no way could he have been spotted anywhere.

"Tanner, John will demand proof. Can you provide an alibi?"

"Yes—" He averted his face to the gear strewn on the cot. "No." Confessing his whereabouts would be the same as announcing to the town that Eden was a loose woman. Nothing could be farther from the truth, but shoot, rumor alone had convinced half the town that he was a crook. "I can but I won't."

Tiny's brows drew severely together. "Unless someone can verify your whereabouts, you are in a tenuous position, and I cannot guarantee that you will escape this predicament unscathed."

Tanner weighed his options. Using her as his alibi would not only destroy the decent reputation she'd built for herself, it would shatter the fragile trust Eden had begun showing toward him.

He closed his eyes. It just wasn't worth it. "Catching this mysterious rider will give everyone—including John— all the evidence they need. When I find the fellow, I'll find out once and for all what he's up to and who's behind his unexplained appearances. Then maybe folks will stop pointing the finger at me and let me do my job in peace."

Tanner slung his bedroll and canteen over his back. "I'm going to round up a posse. Can you find me a horse?"

"Fait accompli."

"Find one for yourself too."

"Me?" Tiny shook his head adamantly. "Tanner, I haven't the experience to track fleeing suspects."

"Then, Tiny, my right-hand man, you're about to learn."

"I lost him up there." Tanner pointed to the rocky crest of Bass Ridge, three miles outside Dogwood Springs. "His prints disappeared on the rocks. There's nowhere to go but down. We'll fan out. Tiny, you, Hollis, Vern, and Pratt circle around that side of the pond. Sullivan, Micaleb, Avery, and I will search this side. Anyone spots hoofprints or tramped ground, holler."

Tension hung like the hazy heat-mist over Bass Ridge Pond as the group divided. No one spoke a word, intent on studying the moist soil for any sign that would tell the direction the rider had headed. The air between Tanner and John Sullivan hummed with mutual strife, but as Tiny had lectured them before the posse set out, they lived and worked in the same town; either they could put aside their differences for the good of the people and follow up on the only tangible lead they had, or they could tear into each other until someone got hurt or property was tampered with.

In any case, each would be sticking to the other like a fly to syrup—so one could not make a move that the other wasn't aware of. Grudgingly, Tanner and Sullivan agreed with the deputy marshal's reasoning.

Tipp Avery broke the stillness with a rebel yell. The band of eight men re-formed. Tanner slid down the side of the mare Tiny had borrowed from Widow Tilly for his use. Hunkering down, he touched a pyre of blackened wood and scanned a stretch of ground where the grass had been flattened the length of a bedroll. "This must've been the base camp," he said grimly. "The fire's been dead awhile, so he must've come back long enough to collect whatever gear he'd left behind after I flushed him out of the woods behind the bank."

"Very convenient that you and your nameless perpetrator were both behind my building at the same time."

Tanner fisted his hands, full up to his eyeballs with Sullivan's sly remarks. "No more convenient than you being in the building before dawn, Sullivan."

Tiny stepped between them in a pitiful effort to keep Tanner from wringing Sullivan's neck. "Let us examine all the facts here, gentlemen. Tanner, start at the beginning."

A long, tense moment passed while Tanner fought to control the frustration building inside him. Focusing on the facts, he repeated them for everyone's ears. "The first holdup matches a swoop-and-hurrah ploy used by the James gang. Rush in, create a disturbance to hold everyone's attention, while down the road, the others loot the express train's safe. Jesse's gang used it at Gad's Hill, then in Muncie, Kansas, in 'seventy-five, and again in Northfield, Minnesota, in 'seventy-six. It came to be known as the Gad's Hill Tactic."

"Sounds like what happened when Page got killed, all right," Micaleb said.

"The band broke up for a while after the Northfield job. A couple of the Younger boys went to the Stillwater penitentiary, a couple of other gang members were killed or died later, and Jesse and Frank escaped. I'd heard that afterward they spent some time in Dallas. So it's possible that they tried the first time and failed, and went back to Missouri to hide out."

"And now they're back."

Tanner's fingers sluiced through his hair. "Jesse got killed. Frank is still on trial, last I heard. The gang broke up. If any of them are responsible for the holdup, why would they be scouting out the town now, almost a year later? All of his men and half the country looked at him as some kind of modern Robin Hood and are loyal to a fault. They wouldn't betray him like this."

"One of his friends did, or he wouldn't be in the grave as we speak," Hollis quipped.

"Even so"—Tanner nudged the dead coals with his toe—"I doubt the James gang has been involved in any of these attacks. It lacks their polish, their flair. My guess is that someone's going around copying Jesse's tactics. That happens a lot with gangs hungry for the glory of seasoned outlaws. Look at how many fellows go around claiming they're John Wesley Hardin or Billy Bonney. And Micaleb will tell you that there has been a band hitting towns just south of here, where they go in and act as if they'll be moving into the area, all the while making note of how the town works."

"Now, isn't that a coincidence," Sullivan sneered. "A similar practice has been occurring in Dogwood Springs over the last few months. Could it be that we've brought the enemy into our very midst?"

With supreme effort, Tanner sidestepped the implication. "Vern, didn't you say you saw someone who looked like me chasing someone else away from the sawmill that night?"

Vern hesitated, then bobbed his blond head yes. "Two of 'em, runnin' into the woods."

"Could it be that you simply scared them off?"

"But what about at the depot?" Hollis asked. "You waved to me, Mac."

"The fellow probably figured it would look less suspicious if he acted as if he knew you than if he fled."

A thickness of sudden unspoken possibilities settled over the townsmen. Sullivan glanced at Micaleb, who silently questioned Hollis. Pratt and Avery exchanged a somewhat chagrined look. They remained silent, and Vern Tilly scratched his head.

"It all ties together, don't you see?" Tanner cried, slashing the air. "Whoever killed Page has come back and plans on finishing the job they started."

Tiny soberly added, "And one of them bears a striking resemblance to you."

Haggard from fatigue after several days of what had become routine patrolling, Tanner returned the horse

Widow Tilly was lending him, then rambled on back to the jail. Soon after their discovery at Hollytree, Tanner had sent half the men back to town to secure their bankrolls and watch the town, while the other half scoured the outlying area for any signs of his look-alike. None had been found. It seemed the fellow had dropped off the face of the earth.

Tanner had no way of knowing when the hit would take place, or who exactly would execute it, but one thing he felt sure in his gut; there would be a hit. The bank was the likeliest target. So at an emergency council meeting, Tiny made up a schedule, marking down which group of men would pull patrol duty, and which would stay behind and pull sentry duty. Dogwood Springs had begun operating like a military fort.

Though duties were being switched back and forth to relieve tedium, and bachelors were called upon more than family heads, the townsmen were getting tired of it, and wanted their lives back to normal. Tanner hardly blamed them. He found himself irritable and restless too, because the longer the mysterious horseman remained at large, the more folks looked at him as though he'd made the whole thing up about sighting the rider to begin with. Just the other day Sullivan had made a remark that still made Tanner bristle: that he had probably realized folks were on to his plan to bleed Dogwood Springs of every dime brought in so he'd purposely led them to the campsite to throw them off track.

And a sick feeling persisted inside Tanner, sharp and burning, warning him of . . . what? What the heck could be so confounded difficult about this case that he couldn't find a single solitary lead to solve the dang thing?

The sign on the jail made him stop short. CITY MARSHAL, it read. Tanner traced the letters. There were times when he just wanted to give up. Quit. Turn in his badge because he felt like he was fighting a lost cause.

Then Eden's face would flash across his mind. *Eden.* Only she kept him going. Her and the hope that he could make her proud enough of him to love him.

Sighing, rubbing his tired, gritty eyes, Tanner left the

door open. Inside, he fired up the stove to heat a pot of coffee, hoping it would help revive him long enough so he could take a bath without falling asleep in the tub and drowning himself. Once cleaned up, he'd head for the big yellow house for a spell.

He needed to see her. Touch her. Bury his face in her hair and his nose in her neck. Feel her comforting arms go around him. Like a fretful kid who needed soothing, he longed to hear her say—

"Tanner, am I disturbing you?"

Wrong. Wrong words, wrong woman.

Tanner peered over his shoulder, where Micaleb's wife stood framed in the doorway. "Come on in, Rosalyn." He held up the pot. "Just fixing myself my morning cup of energy. Would you like some?"

"No, thank you." She pulled nervously at her gloves, finger after finger. "I apologize for barging in on you, but I am here on a little matter that I think you should be aware of. It concerns Eden Page."

"Eden?" he whispered, alarmed.

"Perhaps you should take a look out the window."

With a puzzled frown, Tanner obeyed.

His searching gaze came to rest at the farthest corner of the town square, where the one-room schoolhouse was located. A sycamore tree grew in the middle of the school yard near the road, and beneath its shady branches sat Eden. His forehead rested against the cool glass. He couldn't see her well enough from that distance, but her features were ingrained in his memory. "Beautiful, isn't she?"

Rosalyn gave him a weak smile, then moved beside him. "Tanner, she has been there every single day since school started this week. She walks the children to class, then sits beneath that tree until the dismissal bell is rung. Then, with the exception of Tuesday when she brought them here, she takes them directly home."

"She sits there all day?"

Rosalyn nodded. "As long as she has lived in this town, she has never let them visit other children's houses or attend a social gathering. She will not even attend our

Thursday afternoon Ladies' Literary Society meetings, though I have invited her several times. People have always thought her peculiar. But now they think she might be a little touched in the head. They are calling her 'crazy Widow Page.' "

"She's no more crazy than you or me!"

"I don't believe so, either. I can understand her fear of leaving the children, since she lost her husband. I harbored the same anxiety with Micaleb after my daughter died. However, this pattern I see Eden developing makes me a bit concerned. For her, certainly, but also for how this hovering will affect the children. Other children can be very cruel."

Tanner didn't give a gnat's behind about what anyone else thought, but Eden's strange behavior worried him too. It wasn't healthy.

His coffee and fatigue forgotten, he walked out of the jail without another word to Rosalyn.

Eden didn't give any sign that she'd heard him approach. She hummed quietly to herself, her head bowed over something in her lap. Long black hair that had been spread over his chest in adorable disarray three nights before was wound into its daytime coil atop her head. Pausing for a moment, Tanner let his gaze roam over her. She should wear green more often, he thought, admiring both the way the pale color complimented her dark coloring and the way the simple lines flattered her slender figure. God, she was a sight for sore eyes.

He knelt on a corner of the blanket. "Eden, honey, what are you doing?"

Her timid smile was like a ray of sunshine reaching clear through to his heart.

"You're back."

"Just rode in. I figured you'd be home. I was coming to see you after a trip to the bathhouse. What are you doing out here by your lonesome?"

"I found a big hole in the bottom of your duster." She poked her finger through the ragged puncture in the linen to show him. "I thought to mend it for you."

"I'm obliged, but—"

"Just don't start thinking that I've become your permanent seamstress. I saw it only when I took it off the kitchen peg to shake the dust from it. . . ."

Tanner tipped her face toward his and gave her a gentle, lingering kiss. He backed away, and her closed eyes drifted open. It wasn't nearly the welcome home he hungered for, but it would hold him over. "I missed you."

She averted her pinkening face and licked her lips.

Standing, he held out his hand. "I'm starved. Come have breakfast with me at Hannah's." She needed to get out, get away, do something more than just sit there.

"I can't," Eden refused without hesitation. "I am waiting to eat with the children."

"The noon break is hours away."

"That's all right," she said with strained glee, shoving the needle through his duster. "I am enjoying the sunshine now that the weather has cooled some."

Tanner dropped low and stalled her darting hands with his own. "I haven't seen you in three days. The kids are busy with their schooling. I'm just asking for an hour with you, then I'll walk you home."

Swift as a whiplash, she all but bared her teeth at him and flung off his hands. "I said *no*. Your hour will have to wait because I'm not leaving my children."

They stared at each other for indefinite minutes. Eden's eyes were shiny with tears that didn't spill, and secret pain Tanner tried to—but couldn't—understand. This wasn't the first time she'd turned on him. Struck out at him. In a moment she'd tamp down the burst of temper and go on as if it never happened. He knew, because she'd been doing it for weeks.

Why had he ever told her about the prowler? It hadn't occurred to him to hide it from her, but ever since he'd opened his mouth about the fellow, she'd become so possessive of her kids that it nearly took a crowbar to pry her away from them. She'd been overly protective before, and he, like Rosalyn, had thought it had something to do with her husband dying and a natural fear that she'd lose the kids too.

But this, it went beyond natural fear. It was bordering on frenzy.

"Don't do this to yourself," Tanner whispered in agony, hurting for her, wishing she would trust him enough to share her secrets with him. "Don't do this to them."

"I am *protecting* them."

"You are suffocating them."

Alarm slid like a shadow over the pain in her eyes.

"Bit by bit you are tightening the noose around their necks and choking the spirit right out of them. You don't want that to happen, do you, Eden? See them stop playing and pretending and learning that life has such sweet things to offer, things they'll never taste because they are bound to your side by rules?"

Grief mingled with the pain and alarm; he smelled it in her, on her. A poison eating at her soul, and oh, God . . . he didn't know how to help her.

"I want to be a good mother."

His throat went tight. He could barely swallow. "You are a great mother."

Shaking her head back and forth emphatically, Eden denied the claim. "No, no. A great mother, even a good mother would never have let her baby get stolen."

Tanner stared at her, stunned into silence.

"It happened shortly after Lissa turned a year old." Her tormented gaze shifted to the school. "We were living in a town outside Fort Worth and Seth had arrested a man for killing another. When the man hanged, his son blamed my husband for his father's death and vowed to get even. Seth didn't put any store in the threat and I was gullible enough to believe him when he said that nothing would come of it. Then one day, as I was hanging clothes on the line and Lissa was playing in the front yard, he slipped into the yard and took her. I didn't even hear him. He stole my baby from under my very nose and I didn't even know it."

"Oh, God . . . Eden . . ." Everything made sense. Her irrational fear of taking risks, her fight for perfection, her cries of wanting to be a good mother. . . . "How can you think it was your fault?"

"Because if I had taken the threat seriously, if I had been watching Lissa closer, it wouldn't have happened."

She hugged herself, cradling the pain she'd carried alone for the past six years. "For months we searched for her. Rangers, Pinkertons, county sheriffs, marshals, even bounty hunters. He'd disappeared without a trace. Seth told me I had to accept that Lissa was probably dead. That it was time I got on with my life. How could I go on? Even the knowledge that I was pregnant again did not console me, not when I had a baby out there somewhere, with a man bent on revenge. Was she being fed? Was she cold? Who was rocking her to sleep? Was she even alive?" Fresh waves of torment distorted her features.

He reached for her, gathered her into his arms.

Tucked against him, Eden continued. "Three months and five days . . . every second unbearable. They finally tracked the man down to a seedy hotel room on the wrong side of town. Seth shot him in the head as he held my Lissa in his arms, a gun to her tiny head."

She released a shuddering breath that chased its way across the base of Tanner's throat.

"Seth could have killed her and it wouldn't have mattered to him. As long as he brought in his man. His devotion to his badge was more important than our daughter's life."

Tin man. The word appeared in his mind so clearly, he wondered if he'd spoken it aloud.

"I know what they say about me. That I'm the marshal's crazy widow. Obsessed with my children. But I couldn't survive it happening again."

His arms tightened around her. "You won't have to," he whispered against her temple.

"I want them to be safe. Always."

"We'll keep them safe together."

She pulled back and searched his face as if looking for assurance, security. "Can you promise that if I go eat breakfast with you, nothing bad will happen to them?"

"Nothing bad will happen to them," Tanner vowed. "Trust me, Eden."

The battle of indecision left its mark around her pinched mouth.

Come on, honey.

She set his duster aside. Her hands shook.

That's it. Keep going, Eden.

She went still. "I don't know if—"

"You can. I believe in you."

Closing her eyes, she reached for him, and he took her cold, clammy hand in his own. She went still again. He didn't tug, didn't yank, just let her fight the ghosts that haunted her. And just when he thought she'd lost the inner battle, her fingers clenched so hard they bit into his skin, and she stood.

Breathless, trembling, but she stood.

His eyes misted over with pride. "Take little steps, honey, one at a time. I know it's hard, so if you get too scared, we'll come right back. I promise."

Moments ticked by. An acute stillness settled around them. Not a bird chirped, not a leaf rustled.

Finally, one foot carried over the other.

As Tanner moved with Eden, an emotion so achingly tender, so profound flooded through him. She was sharing this with him, this first step away from her past.

And God, he loved her more than he ever thought possible.

Eden strolled along the boardwalk, her hand tucked into the crook of Tanner's arm. The first time she'd let Tanner lead her away from the school yard, guilt for leaving the children had made breakfast taste like paste and she'd left five minutes into the meal.

But each day it got a little easier. She stayed away a little longer. The tight knitting of fear around her heart unraveled a little more.

At least she'd stopped shaking. Tanner told her she was making progress. It didn't feel like progress.

It felt as if she were walking along a very narrow

ledge, and at any given moment her foot would slip and she'd go tumbling down.

Her hand tightened on his arm. His fingers curled reassuringly over hers. They always did. And the simple touch was like a solid rock against the sliding grains of her courage.

"They'll be fine. Trust me."

She smiled wanly. He always said that. And God—if there really was one—help her, because she was beginning to believe she could trust him. The children were still at school at the end of the day where she'd left them in the morning.

Eden peeked at him, saw his lips move with words she couldn't seem to hear. *So handsome. So gentle.* He filled the lonely void that had been so much a part of her life since childhood. With Tanner there was music. And picnics. And belly-rolling rides on a tree swing. And late at night, when the children were snug in their beds, there was passion, the touching of souls, a completeness she never thought she'd find.

Was it possible? Could she keep her babies safe and still find a glimmer of happiness too?

Eden forced herself not to ponder that dangerous question and concentrated on the conversation Tanner was trying to have with her.

"So Lissa looks at the chicken coop door and points to Myrtle's name then asks me how come Myrtle is spelled with a Y and not a U like turtle." Awe radiated from his features. "She talked to me, Eden. I mean, she came right up to me, looked me in the eye, and talked to me."

There was an earnestness, a frisson of achievement in his voice, his eyes.

And she understood.

Such a little thing, Lissa talking to him, yet it meant so much. He'd been trying for weeks now to form some sort of relationship with Lissa that didn't include searing glares or cutting remarks. He played with them, guided them, entertained them. Just yesterday he'd made a game out of painting the chicken coop while she cleaned the jail. Myrtle now lived in a green-and-white shack behind the jail that looked better than some human homes she'd seen.

The night of the storm had been the beginning of the end, when he'd stayed to help Ruthie through her terror and told Lissa her pa was an angel. Eden saw that now. And she shared in his awe, his wonder, that Lissa's icy air had begun to thaw.

She tried not to grow dependent on Tanner's presence, tried to prepare herself for the day when he wouldn't keep his promise, but she only had to see him sauntering toward her and her will weakened. It didn't matter how late he stayed out, how exhausted he was when he rode in, he was always there for them.

A sensation, soft and vaguely familiar, crept into her heart. The harder she fought to subdue the feeling, the harder it resisted.

"What did you say to her, about the letters?"

His shoulder rolled in a shrug against hers. "Heck, I didn't know what to tell her, so I said that the turtles would get jealous."

She giggled.

"You have the nicest laugh." He grinned down at her, his eyes tender. "Sounds like thick buttermilk sloshing in a jar."

"Buttermilk?" Eden quirked her lip dubiously.

"Believe me, I've churned enough buttermilk to know what it sounds like."

"Do you miss Missouri?"

He looked ahead and squinted into the sun, blindingly bright behind the schoolhouse. "Sometimes. But there's nothing left for me there anymore, hasn't been since my ma died."

"You were very close to her?"

"She was like the land. Tended with love, she provided well. Neglected, she withered and died."

"As most things do," Eden responded.

Tanner tipped his hat at another passerby, who ignored the greeting. He dropped his gaze and bit his lower lip.

She glanced behind her at the man hurrying away be-

fore pursing her mouth and turning her attention straight
ahead, unaware that she'd increased their pace. That was
the fourth person in as many days to stick his nose in the air
at the sight of her on Tanner's arm. Tightly she said, "My
mourning period is over in two days and yet I am getting
snubbed."

"It's not you getting snubbed, it's me."

"Why on earth would anyone snub you? You're the
marshal."

"Let's just say I haven't proven myself to folks yet."

"That's absurd! Who do they think risks his life trying
to prevent their homes and families from being raided?
Blisters his hands quickening his draw so that scum can't
get the bead on him first? Lays awake night after night
beating himself over the head for killing lowlife who'd kill
him without thinking twice?" Her heels clicked over
warped boards while she vented her disgust. "Sorry, un-
grateful damned wretches. They should be *proud* that you'd
wear their pathetic piece of tin."

"Are you proud?"

Taken off guard, Eden stopped short. "Proud?"

"That I'd wear a pathetic piece of tin."

Her eyes lowered to the star on his vest, then rose back
to his face. Surprise shone there. Surprise and something
else.

Hope.

She remembered all the times she'd tried so hard to
please the people in her life, her guardians at the orphanage, the parents she'd so desperately wanted to adopt her,
the man she'd married with such bright hopes for a happy
future. And she remembered all the times they'd kicked her
in the teeth for her efforts, the hurt, the confusion, and later
the numbness. She couldn't do that to this gentle man. Rob
him of his candid emotions, his beautiful smile, his ability
to see good in everyone around him.

"Tanner," she said, her voice raw, "a woman would be
a fool not to be proud of you."

Eden found herself being spun into a narrow alleyway
between Deidrich's and Hannah's. His hand framed her

jaw, tilted her chin. Then Tanner swooped down upon her mouth, cutting off her surprised gasp. At first Eden was too astonished to react. Soon, though, her body responded to the glorious urgency of his lips sliding across hers. Her senses swimming, she groaned her surrender and reached around his neck to draw him close. Her body arched against him, her clothes suddenly restrictive and annoying. Her breasts chafed against the linen dividing his flesh from hers, and she yanked at his hair in a vain attempt to lessen the ache unfolding inside her. The sheer pleasure of being in his arms drew a whimper from her.

She felt Tanner shudder as he drew back and rested his forehead on hers. Warm, moist puffs of air flittered across the tip of her nose, the scent of heat and earth and suspended need clung to both of them.

"My . . ." Eden brought two fingers to her swollen lips. "My . . . what was that for?"

As breathless as she, he said, "For making . . . my wish . . . come true."

Trembling, Eden touched his mustache, then laid her cheek against the warm tin pinned over his heart.

Why did she have to have been born a fool?

"Will I see you later?" she asked, her heart pounding a desperate beat.

He brushed her hair back, smiled against her temple. "Will I be welcome?"

Her hand cupped his sun-roughened cheek. His mustache tickled her palm as he kissed the center, and she felt the hollow of his dimple beneath her fingertips.

He walked away, leaving her alone, and a fog rolled around his feet, swirling up, enveloping his retreating figure.

She watched him disappear, fighting a sense of loss so bleak it numbed her very center. Then she sat beneath the white-barked branches of the sycamore tree and waited for her children.

And waited.

And waited.

Soon her black hair turned iron-gray, her smooth skin wrinkled, the veins in her hands raised prominently. . . . And still she waited, alone, beneath the sycamore tree. . . .

Jolted, Eden's eyes snapped open. She dimly realized that she had been awakened by the peal of the bell signaling the end of the day. Gay chatter of children pouring out of the schoolhouse slowly seeped into her consciousness.

Blinking away the residual effects of the recurring dream, she wasn't surprised to find her lashes wet, and when she swallowed, her throat had to work down an obstruction.

"Mama!" Ruthie called, skipping toward her, the lunch pail swinging at her side, her strapped books clutched to her chest. Behind her, Lissa approached at a more sedate pace, and Little Seth dragged his feet, his face downcast.

Eden rose quickly and enveloped her babies in a collective hug, needing the assurance that she still had them. The empty despair brought on by the dream abated some.

A piece of her soul still wept.

"Miss Thayer said the town's gonna have a mem'ry celebration! Can we go, huh? Can we?"

"It's a memorial, muddle-mouth."

The smile Eden summoned for the children faded. She looked at Lissa. "A memorial?"

"For Pa. For being a hero."

Chapter Seventeen

THE DRONE OF respectful murmuring milled through the September afternoon memorial service.

Every citizen of Dogwood Springs had turned out at Spring Park for the somber occasion, much as Tanner imagined they'd done for Page's funeral. He stood in front of the jail, his hat crumpled in his hand, eyes never leaving Eden.

Tight-lipped and white-knuckled, she looked incredibly dignified yet tragically beautiful in her stark black widow's weeds, with her children around her wearing telling bands on their arms. Folks filed by, pausing to offer a few of their own memories of Seth Page. She would nod woodenly, or grasp a hand now and then, but no more. She was holding herself together by sheer determination, and he could feel how much the effort cost her. She didn't want to be there, had told him so the evening before, and again yesterday, when she came to work.

Rosalyn stepped up to her, looked in Tanner's direction, and said something that Tanner couldn't hear. It brought a brittle smile to Eden's mouth, though.

Hollis, who had taken charge of the whole ceremony, was the last to pay his respects, and only when he left did Tanner feel comfortable in approaching her. There was such resentment in her eyes that he wasn't sure if he was welcome, but when she looked at him, she gave him a tiny smile.

A smile that held such sorrow, it gave him a chill.

"Are you all right?" he asked, keeping a proper distance from her, but rubbing Ruthie's and Little Seth's backs when they curled their arms around his legs.

Eden nodded. "Will you take us home, please?"

Silently, he took Ruthie and Little Seth's hands while Lissa grabbed Eden's. Tanner wished now he would have talked Rosalyn and the rest of the group that had arranged this little fiasco out of giving it. Saying as much to Eden earlier, she'd said, "No, I must keep up appearances," with that stubborn glint in her eye.

Folks would probably wonder why none of Page's kin were showing up at the church where a big spread had been laid out, but in truth, Tanner didn't give a care what they'd think.

"What did Rosalyn say to you?"

"She just reminded me that my mourning period was over."

Tanner felt there was more to it than what she was saying but sensed that he'd get no answers if he pressed her. In fact, Eden looked ready to shatter.

Harshly, and with a hint of tears, she added, "I wish your God would've spared me the misfortune of going to this farce of a memorial."

He didn't know what to say except, "Let's just get you home."

"Marshal Mac! Marshal Mac!"

Tanner stopped, then turned.

Vern Tilly raced up to them, huffing and puffing. "Ya gotta come quick. Billy Joe's done got Bobby Jack laid out on the tracks! The train'll be here in ten minutes!"

With a deep groan, Tanner shut his eyes. Those damn Bentley boys! "Will you be okay until I get back?" he asked Eden.

She looked at him long and hard, then, stiff-shouldered, turned her back on him and walked away.

Tanner got a prickly feeling clear down to his spine.

* * *

"Do marshals gotta go to school, Marshal Mac?"

"You don't like school?"

Seth shook his head.

"How come?"

Seth sighed. " 'Cuz my teacher yells at me when I talk to Patch an' Amos an' Joe. Even when I talk real soft she yells at me. And she won't let me keep my gun neither."

"Did you tell your ma?"

"Yes, sir."

"What did she say?"

"That I should listen to my teacher."

"That'd be a right good idea if you want to be a marshal. Listening is just as important when you're a lawman as letters and numbers. But sometimes the voice you gotta listen to doesn't talk; it's inside you." Tanner pressed his fist to his stomach. "It's called a hunch. And no lawman worth his salt ignores a hunch. He follows what his gut tells him, even if his heart is against it."

And his heart was fighting his gut every step of the way.

"Is your gut talkin' to you?"

Tanner nodded. "It's telling me I have to go away for a while." Eden needed a little space just then. She'd been silent and aloof since he'd returned to the house after untying Bobby Jack Bentley from the railroad tracks, then taking Billy Joe into custody. He figured he might as well use the time away to solve the Page murder case. "I'll be leaving in the morning."

"Can't we go with you?"

"Not this time. It's best if you stayed here. I'm counting on you to be the man of the house. Do you know what that means?"

Seth looked at him questioningly.

"It means you gotta look out for your ma and sisters."

"Are you coming back?"

"I'm gonna do my best, Maverick."

Seth frowned at his sturdy leather boots. "My pa didn't come back. Pas don't never come back."

The last was said in a very old voice. Tanner sighed. How did a body explain death to a five-year-old? "Sometimes, when someone goes away, it's not because they want to. They just don't have a choice." Tanner glanced down at the top of Little Seth's bowed head. "Just like being a lawman means you sometimes don't have a choice. You gotta do what's right."

"Marshal Mac?"

"What, Seth?"

"I love you."

Folding the boy in his arms, a lump of emotion swelled in Tanner's throat, nearly choking him. "I love you too, son," he whispered. "Always remember that."

That night, as he held Eden in his arms, the solace he usually found in her company wasn't there. He'd thought this would be enough, being with her every chance they could steal these intimate moments together. Talking. Laughing. Loving. Sharing everything a man and a woman could share. Except the same name.

Tanner stared at the ceiling, absently clasping and unclasping his fingers with Eden's. Some . . . *thing* had come between them, was threatening the fragile bond beginning to take hold. He felt as if he were losing her, and he wasn't sure he could stop it. "Why won't you marry me, Eden?"

She tensed against him, her free hand stilling on his chest. He'd promised himself he wouldn't pester her about it, but the words slipped out, and he couldn't take them back, even if he wanted to.

"I'd be good to you, Eden. And I'd be good to your kids. I'd never try to take their pa's place, but I'd be a good father to them. Treat them no different than if I'd been the one to sire them."

"It wouldn't be enough, Tanner."

"Not enough?" he cried. "I love you so much that sometimes I think my heart'll plumb explode from my chest 'cause all that love don't fit."

Hurt clawed its way through every fiber of Eden's being because she read the truth in his eyes. He did love her. And she didn't—couldn't—love him back. She just couldn't. Not as long as he wore a badge.

The memorial for Seth had made that wrenchingly clear.

"We are two people with different commitments. I will always belong to my children. You will always belong to your job. It owns you. It gives you life in a way that I never can."

"I'm good enough to make you cry out my name but not good enough for you to take it?" He untangled himself from her arms and sat on the side of the bed for a long time.

Bowed, broken.

"God, woman . . . it's tearing me apart . . . knowing you'll let me touch you everywhere but you won't let me get near your heart."

Eden clutched the sheets to her naked breasts. "My heart couldn't take it, Tanner. I lived with the pain of being married to a lawman for too long. Saw what it did to him, saw what he became. Harsh. Cold. Detached. I couldn't bear it if that happened to you."

"I am not *Seth.*"

Eden scrambled over to him and wrapped her arms tightly around his chest, wanting to hold on to him forever, yet feeling him slip through her fingers. "I know you're not. Can't you see? It's because you're not him that I won't marry you. Because if I married you, if I lived with you every day, slept in your arms every night, I could fall in love with you. And the day would come when my arms would be empty. You'd leave me a widow. With Seth it didn't matter. It would matter with you."

He angled his head. "Are you making me choose, Eden? You or my badge?"

"What would you choose, Tanner?"

She sensed his turmoil.

"I'm an officer of the law. It's what I do."

The hurt expanded so that she felt drenched by it. "No, it's what you *are*. And I'm not strong enough or selfless enough to accept that."

He yanked his trousers from off the floor and slugged

his feet through the legs. "I thought you were proud of me!"

What she'd said was, "*a woman would be a fool not to be proud of you.*" Yet she couldn't make herself admit to him that she was a fool. Instead, she said softly, "Pride has nothing to do with acceptance."

Tanner finished dressing with curt, jerky movements. The last things he donned were his heavy gun belt, the Peacemaker handle kissed by moonlight, and a tin star over his heart.

It shined, glittered, a metal barrier between them.

He stopped at the window, clenching and unclenching his hands. Without turning around, he said. "This'll be the last time I climb out your window, Eden. I'm not gonna let him do this to us. We belong together. You, me, the kids—as a family. No matter what it takes, I'll prove to you that we belong together."

Tanner's fingers dug into his scalp as he reviewed the three columns of facts before him.

Irrational as the thought was, he felt that if he was ever to have a future with Eden, he had to settle this case. Find the man or men who killed her husband. Find the fellow destroying his reputation.

Only then would he be able to make the decision sitting on his shoulders like a load of boulders.

Myrtle picked her way across the floor, pecked at his foot, then gave him a sympathetic cluck.

"This fellow is smart, isn't he, girl?" Tanner commented, stroking the raised red ridge on Myrtle's head. "Smarter than me." He gave the papers a frustrated shove; they fluttered to the floor. Tanner threw himself back in the chair. "Heck, I'm just a marshal, not a detective."

Flapping her wings, Myrtle hopped into Tanner's lap and rubbed her beak against his vest front. Absently, he petted her soft feathers.

"He's fooled half the town into thinking I'm him. He's been spotted near every business in town at times I can't supply a witness to my own whereabouts. He must be watching where I go, then . . ."

At his wit's end, Tanner retrieved the new packet of WANTED posters from the drawer of the desk. There had to be something he was missing, something so bold, so blatant, it had been right under his nose the whole time.

He studied the handbills, some with roughly sketched profiles, some just stating the reward and a brief physical description. Coming across three that he'd already brought in and collected rewards for—Pistol Pete, Johnny River, and Mad Dog Owens—Tanner crumpled their ugly faces and tossed the posters.

The Apache Kid, John Wesley Hardin, an old one of Frank and Jesse James . . .

The robbery Page died preventing had all the odors of a James gang attack. If the blue-eyed bandit was behind Page's death, Tanner knew he might as well close that case right then. Jesse was beyond serving for the crime.

Yet, he couldn't shake the feeling that the two cases— the first robbery and the recent sightings—were related.

Long and hard he stared at Jesse's face.

It meant something, something important.

Swoop and hurrah.

You've acquired an enemy.

He resembles you.

Tanner sucked in.

Swoop and hurrah.

You've acquired an enemy.

He resembles you.

The pain in his stomach erupted, awareness blazing like a match thrown into kerosene. He knew suddenly, without a shred of doubt, who had killed Eden's husband and set up his downfall. Only one question remained.

How could he have been so blind?

Tiny opened his apartment door on the tenth knock. Tanner ignored the fact that the man stood on the threshold clutching a damp towel around his thick midsection. He shoved the paper into his deputy's hands, and, jaw set, paced the narrow landing while Tiny silently read the telegram.

"Where did you get this information?" Tiny finally asked.

"I telegraphed Governor Crittendon of Missouri. They broke out last year." His voice increased in volume and rate. "Tiny, the information was in front of me the whole time and I didn't even see it. My pa rode with the gang long enough to know how they operated. My brother practically worshiped Jesse. If Terron thought that he'd disgraced Jesse by botching the first robbery, he'd try again just to save face."

"Then they were involved in Marshal Page's death?"

"The time frame matches."

"Assuming, then, that they were behind the robbery and returned to correct their bungled failure, what would possess them to remain in town and risk capture?"

"Because they found me."

In the thickening silence, a door slammed. A child wailed. The repeated sound of iron striking anvil sounded like soldiers marching to the hollow tune of Tanner's heartbeat. "That's why he's been spying on the town, making sure that folks see him. Terron and Pa *want* folks to think it's me. What better way to get even with me for not joining them than to rob the bank and make it look like I did it?"

"Yes, I can see how that would be accomplished. Testimony from the townspeople could be very damning indeed, should a crime take place."

"Exactly."

"Then from this point forward we must keep you under guard. Never allow you to leave our sight. If any attempt is made on the bank, you would have witnesses enough to acquit you."

"No, Tiny. I 'preciate you trying to protect me, but I'm not running, I'm not gonna be watched over like a baby, and I'm for damn sure not gonna leave this town open to attack."

Tiny accepted the decision without argument. Tanner

even thought he saw a hint of admiration in Tiny's deep blue eyes.

"Allow me to make myself presentable, then we will inform the men."

"I've got to tell Eden about this first. I owe her that."

Chapter Eighteen

"HE WOULDN'T HAVE." Eden shook her head slowly, denying the schoolmistress's claim. "He wouldn't have fetched the children without telling me."

"Mrs. Page, I saw the marshal myself. He was waiting for them by the sycamore tree. First Ruthie ran toward him—"

"And you let her?"

The late Marshal Thayer's mousy daughter, Jenny Thayer, shrank back. "I didn't realize I should have stopped her. He's all the children talk about. Ruthie has told me numerous times that Marshal McCay will be her new father soon, and the way the two of you have been strolling about town, well, I had no reason to doubt her."

"Do you know where they went?"

"I would assume that he took them to your place."

Eden forced herself to breathe evenly as she hurried back to the house. Maybe he'd wanted only to save her a trip to town to collect the children from school. Yes. That's what he'd done.

And she was going to kill him for it.

She threw open the front door and raced through the house, yelling their names, one by one, knowing even as she did so that they wouldn't answer. An eerie hush had settled over the house, broken only by the hollow beat of her heels clattering on the wooden floors. She searched every room anyway, knowing that if she stopped, she'd go mad.

Out the back door she flew, and before she realized where she was heading, she found herself running for the hotel.

Rosalyn stood at the front desk, shoving mail into one of the cubbyholes on the wall. The door crashing against the wall made her spin around.

"Rosalyn!" Eden scurried around the counter, grabbing handfuls of expensive fabric and soft flesh.

"Eden, what is it?"

"Rosalyn! Have you seen the marshal?"

"Why, he's probably at the jail."

"I've already checked, he's not there."

"Perhaps the Bentley boys got into another tussle— Eden, tell me what's wrong."

"My babies . . . they're gone." The panic she'd tried so hard to control broke free. "Jenny Thayer said Tanner had fetched them and they know never to talk with a stranger much less go to one because they know the rules so I can only believe she's telling the truth but I can't find him and I can't find my babies—"

"Eden, you have got to calm down. You'll make yourself sick. Here, drink this."

"You don't understand!" Eden cried even as she felt a glass being pressed into her hand. "He knows that I always collect the children from school. Why would he fetch them without telling me? I know he was angry last night because I wouldn't marry him—huh," she gasped, whipping her head around to stare wild-eyed at the controlled woman. "Rosalyn, you don't think he would take my children to make me marry him, do you?"

"Oh, gracious no! He'd never—"

"But he said no matter what it took, he'd make me see that we belonged together." She gave Rosalyn a jarring shake. *"No matter what it took!"*

"Drink."

The liquor set her throat on fire. Coughing and sputtering, Eden pressed the back of her hand to her mouth.

"Tanner is one of the most honest men I know. I can see why you would jump to that conclusion considering what he might have done in the past, but all that is behind him."

Her hand lowered slowly. "What do you mean," she coughed, " 'what he might have done in the past'?"

"The robberies he committed with his family. He was just a child, of course—"

"Tanner . . . stole money?"

"You didn't know? Oh, dear, I'd just assumed you'd heard; it's been all over town for weeks. . . ."

The glass fell from her hand and shattered around her feet, along with her heart. "If he stole money, then what's to stop him from stealing my children?"

"No, Eden, there must be another explanation."

But she was beyond listening. She'd believed in him. He'd taken that belief and betrayed her in the worst possible way. She'd always worried about strangers abducting them. She should have been more concerned about tin men. Doubling over from the crushing blow, Eden let out a keening wail. "How could he have done this to me?"

After having searched at Eden's place, the school, the bridge by the creek, and every store in town, Tanner returned to the jail. It was Thursday, so maybe Eden had finally decided to take up Rosalyn's invitation to join the Ladies' Literary Society. He wish he would've thought to ask someone where or what time the ladies had their meetings.

He turned the doorknob with the hope that one of his messages would get to her—and quick.

"Where are they?" came a voice, deadly calm, from the direction of his desk.

Tanner's hand shot to his hip, the warm iron of his Peacemaker seeping into his palm. He saw her face an instant before he drew his weapon.

"Christ, Eden!" he cried. "I could've shot you!"

She didn't seem aware of how close she'd come to having her face blown away. Tanner sagged against the wall, giddy relief swarming over him, making him dizzy. He dragged his hat off his head. "I've been looking all over town for you. We need to talk."

"Just tell me where they are."

"Where who are?"

"My babies!" She sprang from the chair and shot toward him. "Damn you, what have you done with my babies?" She threw a bruising slap to his shoulder, then another, the force of her blows driving him tight against the wall. "You said nothing would happen to them, and I trusted you." Flailing hands raised welts on his skin. "Damn you, I trusted you."

Fighting to keep his balance, Tanner blocked as many hits as he could while making futile grabs for her. Finally, he caught her wrists. "Stop it, Eden! Tell me what happened."

She writhed for freedom. "You damn thief! Why'd you have to take my babies? Did you think you could use them to blackmail me into taking your name? I'll do it, I'll marry you, does that make you happy? Just give me back the children!"

He shook her once, hard. "Listen to me! I didn't take the kids. How could you think I'd sink so low?"

"They'd never go off with a stranger and you were *seen* taking them from school!"

The blood drained from his face. "Oh, God." He released Eden and stared at her ravaged features. "Oh, God, if I'd had any idea that something like this would happen, I swear, I *swear* I wouldn't have pushed you into giving them space. I thought you all were safe here."

Eden ground her teeth. "What the hell are you talking about, Marshal McCay? Something like *what*?"

Tanner dug into his vest pocket and held out the telegraph from Governor Crittendon. She snatched it from his hand.

Why hadn't he told her about Fain and Terron before? No, he knew why'd he'd kept quiet. He'd hoped she'd never learn about his family and he wouldn't have to face the misery of losing her. Have to withstand her looking at him like . . . like she was looking at him now. With loathing and betrayal.

The discovery that his brother and father were very possibly responsible for her husband's death had left him with no choice but to tell her. Except, he was too late. Someone had clued her in first. *Thief. Blackmail.* They were words flung at him by a woman who'd learned that the man she'd taken as a lover was nothing more than a two-bit crook.

" 'I regret to inform you that Fain McCay and Terron Douglas McCay were two among seven convicts who escaped the Missouri State Penitentiary on September 12, 1881. They must be considered armed and dangerous.' " She flipped the paper back at him. "You must be proud." He felt her derision nick his soul like a rusty razor. "But I fail to see what this has to do with my missing children."

"Fain is my father. Terron is my twin brother." He looked out the window. It threw his reflection back at him. "We aren't identical. My face is leaner, my eyes are green and my hair is light like my ma's. He has dark brown eyes and hair like our pa, and he lost his little finger when a gun backfired." For a moment Tanner lost himself in the memories. Whispered wonderings in the darkness of night between two little boys. Treasure hunts and make-believe friends. Learning to ride the oxen while they plowed crusted fields.

They'd been close once, him and his brother. Once.

Tanner wiped the memories from his mind. "But hair can be dyed and gloves can be worn to hide his hand. And if he's grown a mustache, from a distance we could be mistaken for each other."

"You're telling me that your *brother* concocted this whole scheme to steal my children?"

"No, Terron is none too bright, but he's always done whatever my father said. If my father told him to take the kids, he would without question."

"Fain McCay doesn't even know me!"

"He doesn't need to. The fact that you and the kids are important to me is all the reason he needs." Tanner bowed his head and took off his hat, running the brim around and around in his hands. "He never could understand that I wanted no part of the kind of life he chose. Being hunted like an animal, unable to call anyone friend, destroying people's dreams."

Clenching his hat still, he continued in a bitter voice. "But he was attracted to the danger, the risks, the way people cowed to him. He made it sound like a daring adventure that would make us all rich, and Terron believed his twisted reasoning. I reckon deep down he felt that as long as me and my brother worked with him, we'd never be able to testify against him."

Tanner chanced a look at Eden. Pale and shaken, her worst nightmare coming to life, she hung on his every word. "He was wrong, Eden. I turned state's evidence after they killed a woman over a wedding ring she wouldn't part with during a stage holdup. He vowed that someday I would regret betraying him. Shortly after Pa and Terron went to prison, my mother died. I left Missouri and never looked back.

"I can't prove it, but I'd stake my badge on it that Fain was one of the gang that tried robbing the train last September."

Her face went even paler as the implication sank in. "Your father killed my husband?"

"It's possible." Tanner swallowed a thick bulb of shame.

And once he'd found out that his traitorous son was the law in town, Fain would have waited, an iron trap concealed in the grass, holding its jaws open for just the right bait to lure his quarry.

Eden's kids.

"I asked Tiny to post guards around town and tell the rest of the men to be ready to ride at sunrise. We'll find the kids, Eden. We're gonna search from here to hell and back if we have to, but we'll find the kids and see that my father and brother pay." The look he gave her was filled with deadly promise. "And this time, they'll hang."

With his gear rolled in his bedding, the strap slung over his shoulder, Tanner led the borrowed mare toward the yellow house outside of town.

Eden walked beside him, feeling terribly old and forlorn, her emptiness like a black cloud surrounding them. "Why?" she asked.

"Why what?"

"Why did you have to become a lawman?"

The pungent smell of pine needles sharpened the thick air. Hooves hit the road with muted clops. The screeching sound of gears could be dimly heard from Hollis Clark's sawmill.

Tanner pushed against the mare's neck, guiding her around several spilled crates that lay in the middle of the road. A few escaped chickens scurried around the broken boards, while others dodged between the skirts of women strolling down the boardwalks.

Finally, he pushed the brim of his hat up with his thumb and answered, "To be as different from my father as I could be. My choices were preacher and lawman. I didn't think I had any right to stand in judgment of another's sins, so I chose policing. I trained for it. I lusted for it. It's all I know how to do." He paused and squinted at the treetops. "I'm good at it, Eden. You probably don't believe that, but I am."

She saw him again as he'd been the day she'd treated Old Man Washburn. Leaning against the wall, his low-tipped hat brim shadowing his face, his arms folded across each other, the barrel of his Peacemaker resting across his left biceps, his five-pointed badge reflecting inner power.

She'd felt so safe having him standing behind her.

Dangerous, deadly. Hard and cautious.

Heaven help her, she did believe him. Not only was he good, he was the best.

A conviction grew that if anyone could get her children back, it was Tanner. She pounced on that secure thought, seized it with every fiber of her being; it was all she had left.

"Where could he have taken them?" Eden wrung her hands together.

"Pa used to hide out back at the farm, but the law's been watching the place since he escaped, so I don't expect he'll go back to Missouri." Tanner opened the gate for Eden to pass through first. "I reckon he's sticking close by. He'll let us know what he wants—"

Eden's gasp cut him off.

Tanner followed the direction of her gaze and felt the bottom of his heart fall out. On the top porch step lay a familiar bundle of feathers, too still, too silent.

"No . . ." Tanner dropped his gear and raced down the stones, stumbling, tripping. He fell against the steps. His hand hovered above the twisted, lifeless body. "No . . . Myrtle . . ." Moisture sprang to his eyes as he tenderly brought his friend to his chest.

Friends is all we'll ever be.

She left a gift for each of you on the porch.

Myrtle, it's your turn to play the outlaw.

He felt Eden lower herself down beside him, felt the consolation of her hand curve around his shoulder. "Tanner, I'm so, so sorry."

She was embarrassingly blurry.

Tanner lovingly smoothed the feathers behind the sagging neck, and he tried not to look into those glassy eyes that had once held a glimmer of flirtation, or at the beak that had painlessly pecked corn from his hand. Running his palm down her wing, his thumb slid across a sharp object, drawing blood. "What the—"

Lifting the downy fringe, Tanner found a slip of paper hidden between the folds. The handwriting was chillingly familiar, the message cryptic.

Ye have until midnight to bring $25,000 from the bank vault to the third empty boxcar east of the depot. Betray me again, lad, and the bairns will wind up like yer feathered friend.

Tanner laughed bitterly. "He killed my goddamn chicken to make his point. The son of a bitch killed my goddamn hen."

It wasn't so much Myrtle as it was the evidence of what Fain was capable of to satisfy his greed that left Tanner raw and aching. Now he knew for certain that his father had been watching his every move, else Fain wouldn't have known about Myrtle, about Eden, about the kids—Fain knew all his weaknesses, and that scared him to death.

He turned his eyes to the horizon and shook his fist in the air. "You touch those kids, McCay, and I won't stop at seeing you hanged!"

Eden whined against his neck, grief and fear mingling to create a pit of desolation, a barrenness of hope. The monster who'd wrung Tanner's pet's neck had her children.

Lost in drenching agony, she did not immediately recognize a noise tugging at the fringe of her consciousness. It came again, though, and she lifted her head from Tanner's shoulder, listening, straining to identify it.

"Tanner?" she whispered.

The alarm in her voice seemed to puncture Tanner's grief. He tilted his head.

"Tanner, can you hear that?"

Tanner set Myrtle down. Crouching, drawing his gun, he cocked the hammer and slinked to the bottom step. He put his index finger to his lips, motioning Eden to silence. No trace of vulnerability remained on his hardened features.

The man was gone; the marshal was back.

Eden sat still as a stone, afraid to move, afraid to breathe. Her heart slammed against her ribs, too loud.

Tanner sidled along the outside frame of the staircase, at the juncture of the porch and the foundation of the house he stopped, then dropped to his knees.

She heard him laugh. "Eden, he got the wrong chicken."

"What?"

"It's Myrtle. She's alive. I bet he mistook her for one of those that fell off the farmer's wagon."

He rose, and over the edge of the third step, Eden

spotted Myrtle squirming in his arms, pecking at his cheek, seeming very much like she was kissing him. Then without warning, she fought for her freedom, and leapt from his arms. Once again, Tanner fell to a crouch.

His next words hit her with the force of a lightning bolt.

"Come on out, Maverick. Your ma's here."

Eden screamed as she flew off the porch, screamed as she skidded down the steps. Tanner had her son by the arm, barely out from beneath the house when she reached him.

Crying wildly, she wrenched the boy to her breasts, flung him back and forth. "Seth! Oh, Seth, my boy . . ."

The raggedness of her sobbing tore Tanner to pieces.

"Maverick, where are your sisters?" He could barely speak above the blood roaring in his ears. "Where are Lissa and Ruthie?"

Seth peered around, and the fear in his eyes hit Tanner like shards of flying glass. He never knew how valuable a child's trust was until Seth looked at him like that. As if he were the legendary bogeyman come to life.

"Are you all right?" Eden dragged the boy's thick auburn hair away from his face with her free hand. "Did he hurt you?"

Seth's wary gaze didn't leave Tanner. "You were standin' in the woods."

"Not me, Seth. A different man, one who looks like me." *Believe me, Maverick. I know I don't deserve it, but please . . .* "Can you tell . . ." *Us.* The word lodged in his throat. There was no us. Just him, and Eden. And Seth trusted only one of them now. "Can you tell your ma what happened?"

"When I got outta school?"

Tanner nodded.

"You were standin' by the tree. Ruthie ran, and Lissa ran after her, but I fell. And then you grabbed Ruthie by the arm and Lissa told me to run and hide." Little Seth turned to his mother. "So I ran and I ran so fast. I left my gun in my fort 'cause Miss Thayer says I can't take it to school and I was gonna get it to save Ruthie and Lissa and I found

Myrtle in my fort. Then a bad man came so we hid and he went onto the porch with Myrtle's friend"—tears welled in his stormy brown eyes—"and he broke her."

Tanner had no doubt the bad man was his father. Oh, God, why'd the boy have to see Fain's brutality?

Seth sniffled into Eden's shoulder. "I tried to shoot him, but I was scared, Mama."

"I know you were, sweetheart. You did the right thing, my brave, sweet boy. You did the right thing, and I'm so very proud of you."

"But I wasn't a good marshal. Me and Myrtle hid in my fort with Patch and Amos and Joe. And the man broke Myrtle's friend . . . and we didn't do nothing—" His voice caught on a hiccough. "Is Marshal Mac gonna let 'im break Ruthie and Lissa?"

Beneath the stark terror in Eden's eyes, he thought he saw something very much like accusation.

Is Marshal Mac gonna let 'im break Ruthie and Lissa?
Seth's words rang over and over in her head.

A whooshing summer wind fluttered the faded, flowery curtains in the girls' bedroom, carrying with it the scents of humid heat and pine trees.

I swear I thought you all were safe here.

Eden reluctantly slid her arms out from beneath her son's sleeping body. His mouth was slack, his lids frail and red-rimmed. The ordeal of seeing his sisters stolen had taken its toll. She'd put him down for his nap, trying to keep up the pretense of normalcy.

But nothing was normal. Nothing would ever be normal again.

Her heart beat a shallow rhythm in her chest as she descended the stairs. Her girls were gone. How many times would she have to live through this nightmare?

The front door clicked, then whined open. Tanner's shadow darkened the splash of sunlight saturating the dim hallway.

His face, once so wholesome and animated, was creased in lines of guilt-laden torment that rocked her with its intensity. "Tiny's getting the men together. He'll be here in about an hour so we can figure out what to do." His voice was sandpaper-rough.

Is Marshal Mac gonna let 'im break Ruthie and Lissa? I swear, I thought you all were safe here.

She believed him.

Tanner might have come from bad seed, but his parentage hadn't made him rotten fruit. And she realized then just how much strength the man truly had, to walk away from the environment he'd been born into, to make his own mark in the world.

Drawn to him by need, unable to endure this pain alone, Eden rushed into his arms. He enfolded her in his warm embrace, and the odds didn't seem as bleak. He sighed from deep in his lungs, as if needing her as badly.

"I'm sorry. I'm so damn sorry."

"You had nothing to do with this."

"I brought trouble straight to your doorstep. I promised I wouldn't fail you, and I did."

Eden pulled back just enough to look into his anguished eyes, their bodies still touching from knee to chest. "How could you have known? They were in prison."

"I shouldn't have taken that for granted. I should have been checking on them. I was just so damned ashamed that they were my kin, I guess I just wanted to forget they existed at all."

"We have no control over who our kin is, Tanner. We can only do our best to not make the same mistakes and hope that will somehow make a difference." She rubbed the frayed collar of his shirt between her fingertips, her other hand resting lightly at the nape of his neck. "I've been thinking, if we go to John Sullivan and explain the circumstances, maybe he will lend us the money your father is demanding."

"That bastard isn't getting a single dime."

Searching his eyes, she saw only the steel finality of his decision. Horrified incredulity seeped into her very core. "You can't mean that!" she gasped.

The flesh at his temple throbbed, a blue vein pulsed

just below the tanned skin. "He's tried to manipulate me into doing his bidding for the last time, Eden. I'm sworn to uphold the law, not break it—"

Weak with disbelief, she shook her head in denial. "I can't believe you're saying this. You saw what he did to that chicken—you'd let him kill my girls? All for the sake of your *honor*?" Cold and dead inside, Eden sank back out of his arms, the touch she'd found so comforting seconds ago suddenly vile. "Is that piece of tin you wear so damn important that you'd *sacrifice my children*?"

"Giving him the money won't guarantee the girls' safety. Eden, this is the same man that shot your husband down in cold blood! The same man who killed a woman because she wouldn't give him a worthless wedding ring! That's not even counting how many others he's killed. He wants to ruin me—my reputation, my morals, my future. And he doesn't care who he has to destroy to do it."

She backed away from him until the wall blocked further retreat. Nausea churned in her stomach. He could rationalize his decision till he was gray and feeble, but the truth fell around her like bitter ash. He'd remain loyal to his badge no matter what the cost.

She raked him with a glare of pure loathing. "To hell with you, Tanner McCay! I'll get the money myself!"

"Eden, it won't do any good! Listen to me—"

Trembling from anger, an anger greater than she'd ever known before, Eden whirled toward the stairs to collect her son. "Those are my girls out there, *my* life's blood! Giving him the money might not be enough, but at least I'm willing to try. I'll be damned if I'll stand by and do nothing while you fill that glory-hungry ego of yours at their expense!"

He seized her by the shoulders. Her head snapped back.

"Ego! Damn you! You're so busy wallowing in self-pity and hoarding emotions, you can't even allow the thought that other people have feelings themselves! Haven't you realized by now that those kids are more important to me than my own life? That I couldn't love them more if they came from my own loins?"

Eden forbade herself from letting the wealth of suffering in his eyes, the self-recrimination, affect her. She'd been fooled one too many times, all because she wanted so desperately to believe in him.

Starting up the steps, Eden paused on the first one. "Did I tell you that I used to tie ropes to Lissa's, and later Ruthie's, wrists so they could not stray from my side? That I would not allow them to go anywhere without me, even to bed? It took me years to let the children go outside and play by themselves and only then because I'd drilled the rules into their heads until they could recite them in their sleep. Don't leave my sight. Don't speak with strangers. Don't associate with tin men.

"I broke those rules, every one of them and more. And now my girls are alone out there, somewhere, in danger." Suddenly it was all too much to bear. She sagged against the banister, dropping her face in her hands. "Oh, mercy . . ." She choked on a sob. "What have I done?"

"Eden?" His hands fell on her shoulders; he turned her to him and they sank onto the step. "You didn't do anything wrong."

She rocked back and forth, holding her stomach, too weakened to fight him, too distraught to cast blame. "Will they hurt my girls, Tanner?"

Closing his eyes, Tanner again saw the chicken's neck twisted, again heard Eden say how they'd brought Seth Page back to her house gut-shot, remembered every killing he'd read in the newspaper articles . . . It wasn't the father he had known. "I know you don't have any reason to trust me anymore, but I'll—we'll get them back. Somehow we'll get them back."

"How?" she wailed. "You won't comply with his demands!"

After a long hesitation, he said, "I can't promise it will make a difference, but we'll try to get the money, all right?"

*   *   *

"Please, Mr. Sullivan. You are the only one around here with that kind of money—" Eden dropped to her knees, her voice broken, clogged with unshed tears and open anguish. "I'm begging you. I'll pay you back every cent—I'll scrub floors for the rest of my life—"

Sullivan looked down his nose at Eden. "Mrs. Page, get off the floor."

It took every ounce of control Tanner had not to slug him. "Eden, honey, come on. This is a waste of time." Glaring at John, Tanner and Little Seth helped Eden to her feet.

"I have just returned from making a deposit," Sullivan lamely excused. "I simply do not have the money readily available. Even if I telegraph them ahead of time, and they have it waiting, it will still take two days to get to Shreveport and back."

Ignoring the banker, Tanner led Eden out of Sullivan's office. He'd known it was a mistake to give in to Eden's plea, but he'd been willing to do anything to ease her suffering. John's refusal of help had only made it worse. She held tight to Little Seth's hand, shaking so badly she could barely walk. Outside the door, he helped her ease onto a bench.

"What am I going to do?" she whispered, her despair wringing his heart. "John Sullivan was my only hope and now . . . where am I supposed to come up with twenty-five thousand dollars in five hours?"

People milled about inside the austere building, giving her looks of pity from a distance.

"If I can find a way to stall my pa, I know where I can get five thousand. They robbed a bank once and dumped the money with Ma. She refused to use any of it and hid it somewhere on the farm."

"But even if you can stall him, that still leaves us short twenty thousand dollars!"

He doubted she even realized she'd said "us."

"I'll check into selling the place. I don't know if I can, because my pa is still alive and holds the deed, but he's a convict. There's a chance—"

"Mama?"

Eden slid out of Tanner's loose embrace to gaze at her son. Her son, her baby boy, her only.

"I got my penny. Is it enough to buy Ruthie and Lissa?"

"Oh, Seth . . ." In his hand lay the shiny fresh-from-the-mint treasure given to him all those months ago. And he was giving it up for his sisters. Choked, she gathered Seth in her arms. "You are my life, Seth Daniel. The very best part of it." She could talk no more for the tears swimming in her throat.

"Eden?"

She glanced up and saw Rosalyn and Micaleb standing in front of them.

Rosalyn held out a bulging reticule. "There is $823.67 here. I wish we had more. I want you to take it."

A tear fell over Eden's lashes and caught on her trembling lower lip.

"If there is anything else we can do . . ."

"Rosalyn? There is one thing. Stay with me. Please." Only another mother that had suffered the anguish of having a child taken by means beyond her control could understand her barrenness.

Hannah blew over like a gusty wind. "Mrs. Page, word's out all over town about your young'uns. I got close to four hundred dollars here and I want you to take it to help get your children back."

Shame washed through her for all the times she'd felt bitter jealousy toward this woman.

Soon, townsfolk were lined up from Sullivan's office to the front door.

"We came as soon as we heard . . ."

"I done blew the dust off this dollar . . ."

"Here's all my egg money . . ."

By the time the last citizen pushed money into her slack arms, Eden was weeping openly. She'd never done anything to deserve their kindness. Had only distanced herself from them, mistrusted them, even scorned them, and still they'd rallied around her as if she were one of their own.

The door behind them clicked, then swung on well-oiled hinges. Sullivan stood in the opening, his straight lips pulled down in a frown. He reached inside his coat and opened a leather billfold. "It's one thousand dollars. I will release another ten thousand and have it for you in fifteen minutes. It's all I've got."

Eden gaped at the stern man for several minutes before dropping her gaze. "Mr. Sullivan, I don't know what to say—"

"No need for words, Mrs. Page. I have a daughter too."

"John," Tanner said, grasping the man's hand in gratitude, "if you could do just one more thing . . ."

Chapter Nineteen

SCREAMS FROM THOSE inside the bank echoed in Eden's head as she and Tanner burst from the building. The sharp odor of gunpowder seemed to have woven itself into her clothes.

"Wait!"

"No time, Eden, keep running." Tanner towed her behind him into the woods.

Eden stumbled. Righting her balance, she clutched Seth tighter on her hip. His little arms wound around her neck in a choking grip. It was getting harder and harder to breathe. Her lungs burned. Branches scraped her face and left stinging marks. Trees whizzed by as Tanner kept a brutal pace.

Finally, at a bend in the creek far from the sight of town, he came to a stop. Eden let Little Seth slide to the ground. Her breath came out in harsh gasps, her legs were weak and shaky.

Tanner was folded at the waist, his palms braced on his thighs. His chest swelled and sank with labored pants for air.

"What . . . the . . . heck . . . was all that about," Eden managed to say.

"I had to make it look like the bank was being robbed. Sullivan should be organizing a posse right about now."

"Why?"

"To buy time in case my brother was watching."

Eden threw her hands in the air and rolled her eyes heavenward. "Now, that makes perfect sense."

"It does because I know my father. We're still short. He's not gonna just let me walk up and say, 'Here, Pa, here's half your money. See ya,' then let the girls go. Eden, I helped send the man to prison. That's not something an escaped convict takes lightly."

"What else are we supposed to do?"

"Well, the first thing we gotta do is stuff that bag a little more. We'll wait till it gets dark, then sneak on to your place."

"Tanner, we've about bled this town dry. If you have any idea where we can raise another ten thousand dollars in the next few hours, I'd sure like to hear it."

"We'll *make* it."

"The gunpowder must have affected your brain. In case you haven't noticed, my house does not come equipped with a printing press."

"We'll water down some of that green paint Ruthie used on Myrtle's coop and rinse paper in it. That'll give it the look of money, and we'll bundle the real money over it. Hopefully Fain's greed will override his caution and he'll take the bag and run. By the time he figures out he's been swindled, the girls will be out of his reach."

Eden considered the plan carefully and decided that it just might work. Then her head jerked up. "You said *we*."

"Of course I did."

"You're not fixing to fight me on going with you?"

"This is our problem and we'll handle it together."

Tiny sparks of wonder shot through every fiber of her body. "But I am a woman. Don't you think it's a little . . ."

"Adventurous?"

"Yes," she breathed.

"Reckless?"

"Very." Her blood flow quickened.

"Selfish?"

Her voice dropped. "Extremely."

"Those are the things I love the most about you, Eden." His declaration was hoarse with emotion. "The people who left you behind, and the people who turned you away, just couldn't appreciate your spirit."

She swallowed, too worried about the girls to sort through her confusing emotions for Tanner.

"Besides," he added, "I know you. The only way I'd be able to get you to stay behind is if I locked you in a cell, and I've spent too many months working on getting you to come out of your prison to stick you in another."

"What about Little Seth? I don't want him in danger."

"He'll be safer if we take him back to town and leave him with Rosalyn."

Eden shut her eyes briefly, then nodded.

"But there's a little matter that we need to take care of first." Tanner knelt before the boy and took his hand. "Maverick?"

Seth cringed. Tanner held fast. "Son, let's get something straight. There are good men and bad men. Sometimes it's hard to tell the difference. But remember when I told you that a good marshal listens to that voice in his gut?"

No answer. Just wide, wary eyes peeking from under a shank of mussed raven hair.

"Listen hard. Is your gut talking to you?"

Brown brows with a hint of copper formed a V. Seth remained quiet for a time, looking uncertainly at his stomach.

He raised his head, searched Tanner's eyes, then his lips parted in surprise. "Yes, sir," he breathed.

"And what's it saying?"

"It's askin' how come that man stole your face."

Closing his arms around Seth, Tanner buried his nose in the soft hair, inhaling the little-boy scents of mud pies and make-believe and growing up. He'd never take those things for granted again.

"Sun's going down. Let's get to work."

"Don't light that lamp, Eden."

"But I can't see what I'm doing."

"Use the moonlight shining through the window. They'll be able to see our silhouettes in the lamplight."

Their hushed voices centered over Eden's dining room table, where four bowls of green paint had been placed on top of newsprint. Dyed rectangles of paper hung like thin strips of jerky from the clothesline they'd tied from one end of the room to the other. Neat stacks of the finished product had already been banded, and were stored in the burlap sack Tanner had "robbed" from the bank.

"Tiny, did you tell the men where to position themselves?"

"They have received their instructions. Several of the men are still 'searching' for you. Misters Clark and Brandenburger will be stationed on the hotel roof, Misters Avery and Pratt and Vern Tilly have agreed to conceal themselves in the woods. Since Mrs. Brandenburger has already settled young Seth in for the night, Miss Hannah will be at the depot in the company of Mr. Brandenburger, making it appear as if they are awaiting the one A.M. train."

"Good." Tanner let out a tense breath. "Good. I don't cotton to women setting themselves in the line of fire, but we gotta make everything look as normal as possible."

"My hands will never look normal," Eden complained, knowing that if she let herself think of her daughters alone in the abandoned railcar with two dangerous felons, she'd go mad. "They'll be green till Seth graduates from school."

Tanner picked up one of her hands, studied the tapered fingers, the oval nails, then gave the backs of her knuckles a moist, lingering kiss. "Didn't I ever tell you that green has always been my favorite color?"

The smile he gave her held a wealth of sadness that Eden didn't understand. Studying him, she narrowed her eyes. *What are you hiding from me?* "Tanner?"

"How much more do you estimate we should manufacture?" Tiny asked, interrupting any response he might have given.

Tanner glanced around and sized up the fake currency. "I reckon this should about do it."

Tiny removed the glove he'd had the common sense to

wear for the task, then flipped open the cover of his pocket watch. "We must hurry and bundle the remains, or Tanner will be late."

"I'm beginning to think that's my middle name, Tanner 'You're Late' McCay." Under his breath he muttered loud enough for Eden to hear, "I just hope this time I'm not too late."

The fragile shell of courage that had kept her going this long began to crumble.

It was hard to see. Darkness cloaked the land with a netting of black. Misty fingers of moonlight plunged through the trees, casting an eerie glow on the two sets of iron lines stretching east and west. One hundred yards down waited a line of boxcars.

The third held her girls.

Eden lay on her stomach beside Tanner in a gully running parallel to the tracks. On the other side of Tanner she barely made out the miniature man-form of Tiny, who was scanning their surroundings through a pair of field glasses.

Her heart drummed painfully in her chest, every nerve coiled, when Tanner drew his Peacemaker and checked the chambers. Next he checked the bullets in the pistol he'd gotten for her, then shoved the gun back into her numb hands.

"Now, remember what I said. If I don't come out in a half hour, give the signal to Hollis, and sneak in. Don't rush. Sneak."

Eden let her breath escape slowly, then nodded at Tanner. She hadn't argued with him when he suggested she wait with Tiny. Though she wanted with every fiber of her being to confront Fain McCay, she was distinctly aware that Tanner would know better how to deal with his kin than she. It was enough that she was there, had been given a purpose instead of pacing the house, waiting for news.

Rising to a crouch, Tanner gripped the money sack tight and started to leave.

"Wait!" Eden grabbed his sleeve. "Tanner . . ."

He dropped back and looked at her, waiting.

"Tanner . . . no matter . . ." His face became a fuzzy mass as frightened tears burned her eyes. She cleared her throat. "No matter what happens, I will always be grateful to you for trying."

He was quiet for a moment. "I don't want your gratitude Eden. I just want the girls free."

Then he was gone, sprinting low across the tangle of weeds and wooden railroad ties. Reaching the first boxcar, he pressed his back against it, seeming to gather his bearings.

No, Eden silently amended, her heartbeat speeding up, her breath catching, he was taking off his badge.

And in that instant she understood why he's been so adamant about not giving his father the money; why she'd felt as if he were hiding something; why his eyes had been so sad.

He'd never planned on sacrificing her children; all along he'd been planning on sacrificing himself.

Not for her, or his own gain, but for them. Lissa, Ruthie, Little Seth . . . they meant as much to him as they did to her.

Oh, Tanner.

Could he ever forgive her for losing faith in him?

Ever give her the chance to show him how necessary he was to her, to the children? How much she . . . how desperately she loved him. Eden gulped, the truth filling her with a mixture of pain and joy. Pain for accepting it so late. Joy for accepting it after everything that had gone before.

She did. She loved him. Why had she spent all these months fighting what she'd known, deep down, all along?

Pocketing the star within his vest, he pushed away, walked straight and tall directly to the third sliding door, and rapped his fist against it three times. The door opened.

Eden's senses teetered on the brink of swooning.

She was losing the only man she'd ever loved.

"Well, well, m'son the traitor has come a-callin'." Fain McCay greeted Tanner in a blend of Scottish brogue and pioneer twang. His voice was rougher, chillier than Tanner remembered.

Tanner vaulted into the empty container.

"Tan, you ca—!"

"Shush, Ruthie!"

Immediately his eyes searched the darkened car for Lissa and Ruthie. Relief swamped him when he spied them huddled together in the farthest corner, scared but unharmed as far as he could tell.

Resisting the urge to go to them, he faced his father.

Prison hadn't changed the man much, except to add more gray to his already silver-streaked brown hair and a cutting-edge meanness to his slitted bark-brown eyes. "Pa. It's been a long time."

"Too long. Ye don't ken how I been lookin' forward to this day, lad."

No, not mean. Ruthless.

The familiar figure of his twin rose from the shadows. "If it ain't my lily-livered broth—oops, I best not piss off the big, bad lawman, huh, Pa?" Terron snickered.

"Anyone ken ye're here?"

"No, Pa," Tanner answered, ignoring his brother. "No one but the girls' mother knows where I am. I left a false trail for the posse—"

"Did ya bring the money?" Terron rudely cut in.

Tanner tossed the bulging burlap bag to the floor. "Couldn't dirty your hands with this job, huh, Terron?"

"It was loads more fun watchin' you do it." His brother grinned wickedly, plunging a greedy hand into the sack.

God, what had Fain done to him?

"What did ya do with the lady?"

Raw agony sliced through Tanner at the thought of Eden. "She left me. Didn't want anything to do with me after I robbed the bank."

"Look at Tanner, Pa!" Terron slapped his thigh in glee. "He *did* take a shine to that lawman's widder!"

"Why do ye ken I told ye ta take her bairns, knot-head!"

Terron lost his grin and slunk back at Fain's disapproving tone.

"Guess you're satisfied now, Pa," Tanner said. "You've been after me to join you and Terron on your raids long as I can remember. Now I don't have a choice."

"Kenned someday ye'd amount to somethin'. Ye been wastin' your talents workin' for t'other side."

"My mistake," Tanner said flatly. Jerking his thumb toward the girls, he said, "Their mother is waiting for them at the hotel. Might as well let them go to her so we can move out."

Narrowing his eyes, Fain gave Tanner the once-over. "Ye cocky bastard! What makes ye ken I want ye with me, nae?"

Stiffening, Tanner darted his gaze toward his brother, then back to his pa. "I'm a felon now, Pa. You leave me here, I'll go to prison. You take me with you, me and Terron can play the same ruse farther west. We'll scout the towns, him from the outside, me from the inside, and we'll take the banks for every dime before folks know what hit."

"So ye can betray me again, lad?"

"No, Pa," Tanner denied. "I know it'll be a long time before you trust me again, but if you'll give me this chance to earn your trust back, you won't be disappointed."

Fain's thick lips twisted into a snarl.

"Remember that bank in Davis, Pa? Remember how me and Terron held all those people off while you talked them into clearing out their drawers? We almost got caught that time, and you took a bullet in the shoulder. Staging the robberies will be a whole lot less risky than raiding and running. We'll be rich, just like you always wanted."

If any of Fain's teachings had stuck in Tanner's head, it was how to romance an unwilling body into a life of crime. Though he was taking the biggest gamble of his life, his ace in the hole was Fain McCay's greed. Tanner reckoned if he could play on that, the odds of outwitting his father were better than slim. Right now slim was better than none.

"Aye . . ." Fain nodded, his whole stance leery. "Aye,

I ha' nae likin' for runnin' any longer. 'Tis gettin' hard on m'bones."

No, the years had not been kind to him. Fain was sliding past sixty, and wild living and too much drink had done its damage to his body.

"What about them, Pa?" Terron asked, pausing long enough from fanning bundles of money to wave toward Lissa and Ruthie.

Fain's gaze rested on them.

Lowering his voice, trying not to plead, Tanner hedged. "What do we need them for now, Pa? They'll only slow us down."

"Ooo-weee!" Terron cheered, distracting their father. "We got us enough here to live high on the hog for a month o' Sundays, Pa!"

Tanner stepped back.

Fain pinned him with a warning look. His arms hung loose and ready at his sides, his feet were braced apart. Thin to the point of gaunt, he still had the quickest reflexes of anyone Tanner had ever known. Any moment, his mood could shift again.

Take it slow, Tanner cautioned himself. When his pa relaxed once more, and snatched the bag from Terron, Tanner shuffled back again, never taking his attention from the two men.

He felt more than saw that Lissa and Ruthie were right behind him. Kneeling sideways in front of the girls, he told Lissa, "When I lower you to the ground, take Ruthie and run to the gully by the tracks. Your ma is waiting for you there."

"I knew he wasn't you, Marshal McCay. He didn't call Ruthie 'sweet potato,'" Lissa whispered.

"Tan, I wanna go with you."

"No, Ruthie. Be a good girl and just do what I tell you. Lissa, honey, take this." He took his badge out of his vest pocket and placed it in her hand. "Give this to your ma. Tell her that she's worth it. Tell her I love her. No matter what, I'll always love her."

"Why do you have to go?"

"Because I love you. You, your ma, your brother and sister, all of you mean more to me than anything."

Her big golden-brown eyes filled with tears. "If you loved us, you'd stay."

Tanner worked down the tightness in his throat. "I can't, Lissa honey. I want to, but I can't. I'll take you with me, though, all of you. Everywhere I go, you'll be with me in my heart."

Tanner unfurled from his stooped position and pivoted on the balls of his feet.

A gun cocked.

Sweat popped out on Tanner's brow. He went deathly still as Fain stepped into the stretch of moonlight through the open compartment door.

"I warned ye not to betray me, lad."

His face was set in fierce lines. Terron was swiping his palms down his natty pant legs. *Oh, God, they've discovered the painted money.*

Opening and closing his hands, inching his right one closer to his armed hip, Tanner tried stalling his father. "It's not what you think, Pa."

"Ye never were fit to carry the McCay name," Fain spat out.

"It's all I could come up with on such short notice," he explained unsteadily. "Look, I'll get the rest. There's a little on the farm—Ma told me where she hid it before she died," he lied, praying to God that Fain couldn't see his face in the darkness. "I'll get it for you. Then we'll head west. Me and Terron, we can make a killing in some of those towns."

"Why wait? I kin make me a killin' here and now."

Horrified, Tanner watched the gun swing downward.

"What time is it, Tiny?"

He glanced at the pocket watch he'd been holding open in his hand since Tanner had entered the boxcar.

"Nine minutes left to go."

Eden's knuckles ached and she'd nearly worn blisters on the insides of her fingers from wringing them together. "I can't wait any longer."

"Neither can I."

Before the deputy finished the sentence, Eden had the pistol tight in her grip. She lunged to her feet and scurried out of the gulch. She kept low and to the shadows just as Tanner had done all the way to the tracks.

Just as she reached the first iron rail, a shot roared into the night.

Her back arched as if she had been the one hit; her knees buckled. Shoulders hunched, fists bunched, her lungs exploded with an anguished "Nooo!"

"Nooo!" Lissa howled, pushing Ruthie out of the bullet's path and falling on top of her.

A split second later, Tanner dove to the floor, covering their small bodies with his. The bead ricocheted off one wall with a loud *ping,* then landed somewhere behind him. Beneath him, Ruthie's terrified screams cut through his soul like razor blades.

"Shhh, Ruthie . . . sweet potato . . . shhh. . . ."

Her screams came one right after the other. Lissa's frightened moans joined in.

Floorboards creaked, sounding closer. "I warned ye what would happen, Tanner." Fain's voice came from directly above. "Did ye ken to play me for a fool?"

Tanner rocked to one side and drew his Peacemaker. The hammer of his father's gun clicked into firing position. Lord, either way he rolled to shoot, he'd leave the girls open. Sweat streamed into his eyes, stinging them.

A swift clattering, like wheels on steel.

"Throw your weapon down, McCay!"

Tiny!

"Buster, move one inch and I'll blow your brains out."

Eden.

Blinking rapidly to clear his vision, faces matching the voices slowly came into focus. To one side of the car stood his deputy with Hollis and Micaleb, guns trained on Fain; in the other doorway stood Eden, John Sullivan, and Hannah, all aiming at Terron.

Both McCays had to have been taken by surprise, for

Terron was reaching for the sky, and his pa looked as though he'd been in the midst of swinging around toward the noise.

"Ha!" Grinning broadly, Tanner let the short gust of relieved laughter burst into full-fledged chuckles. He arced his arm over Ruthie's and Lissa's heads and stretched his Peacemaker at Fain, who still held his weapon. "Drop it, Pa."

Never had Tanner seen such hatred blaze from a body's eyes as he did when his father looked at him.

Tanner pulled the hammer back. "Don't make me kill you, Pa."

Long, tension-filled seconds crawled by as McCay stared at McCay. Finally, Fain lowered his arm; the pistol slid across the floor of the boxcar.

Suddenly the small confines were filled to bursting with people. Tiny quickly twisted Fain's arms behind his back and cuffed him while John Sullivan did the same to Terron.

Eden raced toward Tanner. He had barely pulled himself off the girls when their mother roughly gathered them into her arms, crushed them to her breasts, sobbing their names over and over again.

Tanner sat back on his haunches, watching the tender reunion. His vision grew distorted, emotion rose high in his throat.

Peering over Eden's shoulder, Ruthie gazed at him, then said, "Hey, Tan, your eyes are leaking. Want me to stop 'em for you?"

He chuckled. She reached for him, and he enfolded her in his arms. Astonishment shot through him when Lissa threw herself at him next. Tanner caught her, tucking his face in the valley their heads created.

He sniffled, then levered himself to his feet, and carried the girls out of the boxcar. Outside, the girls slid to the ground and once again sought comfort from their mother. Eden pulled them close to her thighs.

"Thank you," she told him, her voice watery, tears

streaming down her cheeks. Releasing the girls, she held
her arms out to him, then wrapped him in her embrace.

Uncertain, he slowly raised his arms, folding them
tight across her slender back, inhaling deeply of morning
glories and paradise as they swayed back and forth.

"Tanner, he's getting away!"

Jerking around, he caught sight of Tiny aiming at his
father. His hands manacled, Fain stumbled over the ribbed
ties between the rails.

"Hold your fire!" Tanner tore himself from Eden's
arms and broke into a run down the tracks after his father,
who was now disappearing around the bend. He pumped
faster, closing the distance. Fifty feet . . . The rails began to
quake. Forty feet . . .

Fain came into view, but instead of running away, he
ran toward Tanner, his rawboned features twisted in terror.

Behind him hurtled a monstrous black soot-spitting
steam engine.

"Pa!" Tanner cried.

His voice was drowned out by the ear-splitting whistle
of the one o'clock train. Tanner watched in horror as the
front grate stabbed Fain between the legs, picked him up,
and tossed him against the barrel-shaped engine, where he
rolled off and under the clattering wheels.

Long after the screech of train wheels faded, Eden
raised her head and spat out a mouthful of dirt.

"Can we get out of the ditch now?" Ruthie asked.

Eden had no idea how long they'd lain in the gully
after she'd whisked Lissa and Ruthie out of the way of the
oncoming locomotive, but it must have been quite a while.
Her arms were numb from clutching the girls, and her
cheek had the prickly sensation that came from pressing the
side of her face against a grooved surface for some time.

Taking their hands, she climbed out of the gulch. The
tracks were swarming with half the townspeople, come to
lend their aid.

Eden craned her neck, searching for a familiar lanky
form.

He stood alone and motionless at the bend in the tracks, facing the spot where his father lay, covered by someone's coat. Eden didn't think he was even aware that Tiny had taken his brother into custody.

"Mama!"

She glanced down at Lissa, her eyes softening as she realized that fate—and Tanner—had given her a very precious gift—time. And not a second of it should ever be wasted. "What is it, sweetheart?"

"Marshal McCay said I'm supposed to give this to you."

Puzzled, Eden took the shiny object, traced the outer edge of each of the five points. She'd run from her fears for too long. It wouldn't be easy, being married to a lawman again, but her only other choice was enduring the rest of her life without Tanner. And that was too heartbreaking to consider.

She closed her hand around his badge and headed down the tracks.

Aaron Arnold pulled up in his black buggy, and with the help of Hollis and Tipp Avery, loaded Fain McCay's mangled body onto the stretcher. Tanner bowed his head as they passed by him.

"Wait here, girls." Eden glided across the last few feet separating her from the marshal, stopping when she reached his side. "Tanner?"

He tilted his head toward her voice. Then a deep sigh cut through the night. "I could've killed my own father, Eden. What kind of man does that make me?"

"The bravest one I've ever known. You saved my girls' lives, Tanner. Protected them with your own body."

"How are they?"

Eden curled her arm around his and leaned her cheek against his sturdy shoulder. "Confused. Shaken. But they're alive, thanks to you."

"They wouldn't have been taken in the first place if not for me."

"You don't know that, and neither do I. But I do know that you would have given anything to prevent it, and in my eyes that makes you a hero." She opened her hand. "This belongs to you, Marshal McCay."

He took the tin star she held out to him and stared at it for a long time. "You keep it." He handed it back to her. "I don't want it."

"It's a part of you, Tanner. You can't change it."

"Yes, I can. I'm resigning."

"Why?"

"You asked me to make a choice, Eden," he said gruffly. "I made it. I plan on taking up farming or—something. I don't ever want you or the kids to have to suffer again because of what I do."

"Are you asking me to marry you?"

"I want to ask you," he countered after a long pause, "but I'm afraid to."

Eden stared at the star-speckled sky. "You would choose us over your dreams," she stated.

"You're worth it." Lifting his face, he touched her with his gaze alone, tenderly, honestly. "I told you that no matter what it took, I'd prove to you that we belonged together. If what it takes to make myself worthy of you is giving up my badge, then I'll do it."

Drawn in by the impassioned glitter in his forest-green depths, Eden looked further, beyond, into his soul. There she discovered a grief far and apart from the death of a loved one. He was keeping it from her, trying to pretend it didn't exist. But she knew it was there, felt it as surely as she felt his arm beneath her hand.

He was mourning the death of his dream, and that could be just as devastating.

One day, this golden-hearted man would look at her, and a resentment that would build over the years would burst forth like water gushing from a dam. There would be no more smiles, no more music; laughter would become a distant memory.

He, who would give up everything for her, he who made her believe in wishes coming true, would wither and die.

Yes, she'd made the right decision. "The answer is no, Tanner."

The light in his eyes dimmed; he hung his head. Curving her hand against his stubbled jawline, she forced him to look at her. The pain she saw stole her breath away.

"Promise me," she implored, "that you will never give up your badge. Never stop fighting for what is right. Never lose your faith in God and good." He tried to pull away; she tightened her hand along his jaw. "Promise me that you'll never stop laughing or singing and never stop tripping into things, and never"—her voice broke, then fell—"and never stop loving me and the children. Promise me."

No words were spoken. Just a tortured groan, torn from deep inside of him.

Growling, Eden demanded, "Promise me!"

He swallowed thickly and whispered, "I promise."

"Good." She grabbed his ears, dragged his face close to hers and—in front of God and everyone—planted a long, binding kiss to his unresponsive lips. "Good," she repeated unsteadily. "Now—ask me again."

"What?"

"Ask me again."

A tiny spark flickered. She watched the wonder of hope stir, then take hold.

"Eden, will you marry me?"

She smiled at him, a shy smile, a blinding twinkle of new beginnings.

Chapter Twenty

T HEY WERE MARRIED on October first in a quiet ceremony behind a big yellow house just outside the town limits, a house that, according to the deed given them by John
Sullivan, could never be taken away from them.

Once the vows had been exchanged, Tanner took
Eden's hand and led her to a far corner of the backyard.
The handful of guests they had invited to the wedding remained a discreet distance back, but three smartly dressed
children skipped ahead, followed by Myrtle.

Suddenly Lissa, Ruthie, and Little Seth came to a stop,
then formed a shoulder-to-shoulder line.

"Close your eyes, Mama," Lissa said.

A grin playing at her mouth, Eden obeyed. She felt
them moving about, arguing in hushed tones.

"Move, Lissa—"

"Shhh—"

"But you're steppin' on my foot."

"Ruthie, it's fallin'!" That from Little Seth.

Eden's shoulders quaked with silent laughter.

"Okay, open your eyes, Mama."

Snapping her lids open, Eden looked at the crooked
forked stick jutting from the ground.

"It's an oak sapling," Lissa explained with a proud

grin. "It don't look like much now, but it'll grow stronger every year."

"Tan dug the pit, and we planted the tree. He said it's a cimminin of our love."

"A *symbol,* pea-brain."

"Ma-maa, Lissa called me—"

Tanner narrowed his eyes at them and they instantly fell silent.

The ruffled hem of Eden's apple-green gown swished around her ankles as she approached the sapling, touching the slender branches with awe. "You've given me so much already. The house, your name—"

"It's nothing compared to what you've given me."

Feeling her husband's compelling gaze, she glanced behind her and found him staring at her with such unconcealed love and tenderness that it filled her heart to bursting.

"You are staring at me again, Marshal McCay," she said with a soft smile. He looked so dashing in his dove-tailed coat and snowy shirt. A gray bolo tie and black trousers completed the suit that fit his lean form to perfection.

"Can't help myself, Mrs. McCay. You're prettier than bluebonnets on a hill."

Dropping her hand from the sapling, she glided to his waiting arms. "How did I get so lucky?" she whispered.

"I'm the lucky one," he sighed against her temple. "I just hope you don't regret being the wife of a lawman. I'll give up my badge before I'll give you up."

Eden pulled back to gaze into his adoring eyes. "You are the best thing that ever happened to me and these children. If I ever tried to change you, any part of you, I would lose the man I fell in love with. And I waited too long for you to ever let you go." If she had learned anything from all that had happened, it was that there were no guarantees in life; each day was a risk in itself. But she knew that as long as she and Tanner were together, they could weather any storm. "What about you? Will you be happy with a reckless wife tagging along behind you when word of the agency gets out?"

"Starting the agency to search for missing kids is your idea, Eden. I'd never leave you behind. Tiny already said he'd take time away from his law practice to fill in for me until we recruit another deputy."

"And Rosalyn practically begged to keep the children when we're called away," Eden added. "I hope I have the strength to leave them."

He rubbed his nose across hers. "Let's just take things one step at a time."

"Oh, Tanner." She cupped his face in her hands. "I love you so very, very much."

Just as Tanner tilted his head to seal their lips in the kiss she'd been longing for, they heard Seth cry, "Eeew, yuck."

Chuckling low in his chest, Tanner swerved his face to the side.

Ruthie tugged on his coattails. "Tan?"

He bent down and pulled her into the crook of his arm. "What, sweet potato?"

"The preacher married us. Does that mean I can call you Pa now?"

With nothing more than boyish grin and a charming dimple, Tanner sought Eden's permission. Her eyes dampened. "Nobody deserves to be called Pa more."

In a voice gruff with emotion, Tanner vowed, "You'll never be sorry for marrying me, Eden. I promise you that."

"I know I won't." And Eden made a silent promise of her own. She'd never, ever make Tanner regret giving her and the children the greatest gift of all. His love.

Author's Note

DOGWOOD SPRINGS IS a fictional town in East Texas based on the town where I make my home. I was so impressed with the wealth of history I found that I collected facts and rumors and wove them into Tanner and Eden's poignant story. Authentically, the jail was not a building as I have portrayed it, but a pit in the ground open to the weather, nor did the bank exist until several years later. But I have taken literary license with these facts and other minor details for the sake of the story.

Some of the minor fictional characters were inspired by real-life people, both historical and present-day. The plot is purely of my own imagination; however, Eden's experience with her children is an all-too-common occurrence in this nation.

If your child is missing, or for more information regarding a missing child, please contact the National Missing Children's Center, 1-800-832-3773 or 1-800-316-HOPE, and your local authorities.

I would like to take this opportunity to extend my most heartfelt sympathies to all those parents out there who have suffered or are surviving the ordeal of a missing child. My heart goes out to you, and for what it's worth, I offer you my hopes and prayers that out of your tragedy will come a happy ending.

Our Town

...where love is always right around the corner!

__Take Heart_ by Lisa Higdon
0-515-11898-2/$5.99
In Wilder, Wyoming...a penniless socialite learns a lesson in frontier life—and love.

__Harbor Lights_ by Linda Kreisel
0-515-11899-0/$5.99
On Maryland's Silchester Island...the perfect summer holiday sparks a perfect summer fling.

__Humble Pie_ by Deborah Lawrence
0-515-11900-8/$5.99
In Moose Gulch, Montana...a waitress with a secret meets a stranger with a heart.

Payable in U.S. funds. No cash orders accepted. Postage & handling: $1.75 for one book, 75¢ for each additional. Maximum postage $5.50. Prices, postage and handling charges may change without notice. Visa, Amex, MasterCard call 1-800-788-6262, ext. 1, refer to ad # 637b

Or, check above books and send this order form to: The Berkley Publishing Group 390 Murray Hill Pkwy., Dept. B East Rutherford, NJ 07073 Please allow 6 weeks for delivery.	Bill my: ☐ Visa ☐ MasterCard ☐ Amex _____ (expires) Card#_____ ($15 minimum) Signature_____ Or enclosed is my: ☐ check ☐ money order
Name_____	Book Total $_____
Address_____	Postage & Handling $_____
City_____	Applicable Sales Tax $_____ (NY, NJ, PA, CA, GST Can.)
State/ZIP_____	Total Amount Due $_____